DANGEROUS VENTURE

Young Pistolero Series Book 6
by
Robert J. Alvarado

I0557461

OTHER WORKS

Robert J. Alvarado
www.youngpistolero.com

Non Fiction

Elfego Baca Destined to Survive
2013 Sunstone Press, Santa Fe, NM, First Printing
2016 Sierra Press, Albuquerque, NM, Second Printing

Fiction
Award Winning Young Pistolero Series
The saga follows Rafael Ortega de Estrada, a seventeen-year-old Mexican peón on the run, riding a stolen Appaloosa stallion. After shooting the haciendero who raped his younger sister, Rafael heads north and enters the United States in 1866 and finds life on the other side of the border holds new dangers along with the promise of a new life.

This gritty tale is set in the American Southwest as Americans and Mexicans struggle after the Mexican-American War. In this tumultuous era in the late 1800s, Rafael (Rafe) grows into a man who respects both his heritage and embraces life in his new country.

Young Pistolero (Book 1) 2013 Sierra Press
2018 Finalist for Drama TV Series category, by the Latino Books into Movies Awards sponsored by Latino Literacy Now.
#1 Fiction Book for 2015; by The Latino Author, by Corina Martinez Chaudhry

Star of the Young Pistolero (Book 2) 2014 Sierra Press

Death Stalks the Young Pistolero (Book 3) 2015 Sierra Press #1 Fiction Book for 2016; by The Latino Author
Legacy for the Young Pistolero (Book 4) 2017 Sierra Press #3 Fiction Book for 2017; by The Latino Author
A Reckoning for the Young Pistolero (Book 5) 2018 Sierra Press
Dangerous Venture (Book 6) 2019 Sierra Press
Justified Vengeance (Book 7) 2019 Sierra Press
The Black Phantom (Book 8) 2020 Sierra Press
Lost Treasure (Book 9) 2024 Sierra Press

Other Fiction
The Jalapeño Republic 2020 Sierra Press
2021 International Latino Book Award Medalist. Insights from the ILBA judges, "It was an interesting book, quite different from most futuristic novels I have read."

Jake Flores Mystery
Just Vanished –2020 Sierra Press
2021 International Latino Book Award Medalist. Insights from the ILBA judges, "From the moment you start reading it, you imagine an action TV series that keeps you involved."

Zia Westerns
Set in the New Mexico and Arizona territories of the Southwest, these westerns draw from the Southwest's unique flavor. Originally part of New Spain and then Mexico, the Spanish settlers and native Indians forged an informal peace until the years after the Mexican-American War brought them into the Wild West. These stories are set during this chaotic time and attempt to paint a realistic picture of the meaning of the Zia symbol.

The Spanish Sword 2020 Sierra Press
2021 International Latino Book Award Medalist. Insights from the ILBA judges, "This book is carefully crafted and felt thoroughly researched."

Valentina 2022 Sierra Press

Spanish Language Books

   Este libro constituye la traducción de una obra de ficción realizada por su propio autor. La serie original, galardonada y titulada Young Pistolero, fue escrita en inglés estadounidense y posteriormente vertida al español mexicano por el autor con el apoyo de la herramienta de inteligencia artificial ChatGPT. Cualquier error o imprecisión que pudiera encontrarse en la traducción es fortuito y responde únicamente al uso de dicha herramienta.

Publicación en español de Sierra Press:

   Joven Pistolero (Libro 1)
   Estrella del Joven Pistolero (Libro 2)
   Muerte Acecha al Joven Pistolero (Libro 3)
   Legado para el Joven Pistolero (Libro 4)
   Ajuste de Cuentas para el Joven Pistolero (Libro 5)
   Aventura Peligrosa (Libro 6)
   Venganza Justificada (Libro 7)
   El Fantasma Negro (Libro 8)
   Tesoro Perdido (Libro 9)

PRAISES AND AWARDS

Young Pistolero, Young Pistolero Series
2018 Finalist for Drama TV Series category.
The Latino Books into Movies Awards are conducted by Latino Literacy Now, a 501c3 nonprofit co-founded by Edward James Olmos and Kirk Whisler. The judges for these awards are screenwriters, directors, producers, and others from the entertainment industry. They have deemed these books worthy of consideration for future television and movie production.

Young Pistolero, Young Pistolero Series
#1 Fiction Book for 2015; by The Latino Author
Death Stalks the Young Pistolero, Young Pistolero Series
#1 Fiction Book for 2016; by The Latino Author
Legacy for the Young Pistolero, Young Pistolero Series
#3 Fiction Book for 2017; by The Latino Author

Young Pistolero Series is a great fiction story that incorporates both history and a great story plot of a young man whose life spirals after avenging the rape of his younger sister. It has all the muster of a good western including gun fights, murder, and survival. The author does a fantastic job of incorporating the history of the United States and Mexico during a time when the Wild West was in full swing and struggles occurred on both sides of the border. The descriptions of history add much to the story and make the life of Rafael, the protagonist, really interesting.

Mr. Alvarado weaves a plausible plot and his setting descriptions and actions are right on. His graphic scenarios of land and territories make you feel as if you are right there alongside the rider as he heads through some rough terrain. His characters were exactly what you might expect of people living in the 'rough' west trying to survive the elements and mayhem of that time.

The writer incorporates Spanish words, which allows the reader to identify with the characters; however, he brilliantly illustrates the meaning after each and every word so non-Spanish speaking readers don't miss a beat. The book is filled with so much action that you can't put the book down. It has all the earmarks of a great western series. If you are looking for a good book to read, then this is one to put on your list this year. An excellent read! – Corina Martinez Chaudhry

I know this series will earn many more awards. A wonderful contribution to Southwest Hispano history and culture. **- Rudolfo Anaya, acclaimed novelist, poet, playwright, professor emeritus, 2015 National Humanities Medal Award recipient**

I just completed reading *A Reckoning For The Young Pistolero*. Great book. I've read the entire series and I'm looking forward to the next book. Mr. Alvarado is very skilled at utilizing historical knowledge as well his own personal experiences to keep you captivated from beginning to end. Being from New Mexico, I can personally relate to the language and setting so appropriately used in the book. I highly recommend the entire series. You won't be disappointed. **- Sammy Soto, retired high school educator/administrator Albuquerque, NM**

I am impressed by the historical detail and fast-moving plots. I also like the way he incorporates two very different young men and follows their lives. The author does a good job of developing these contrasting characters so that readers can walk in their boots and see how fate has shaped them. My father was a screenwriter for television when I was growing up in California and he wrote many westerns, including Wagon Train and Gunsmoke. Alvarado's novel could be the basis for one of those television westerns because of its engrossing plot and its clear depiction of heroes and villains. **- Dr. Jennie Nelson, PhD in Rhetoric and Writing, Carnegie Mellon University, post-graduate professor of writing, University of Idaho**

Mr. Alvarado vividly illustrates many rugged times after the Civil and Mexican American Wars through the eyes of a 17 year old peon who comes to the U.S. and adapts and grows into a hero. The Young Pistolero is a great new historical western series!
– by Richard Golenda, post Secondary and College History Teacher post Chairman of the Pueblo Economic Development Corporation.

DANGEROUS VENTURE

This book is a work of historical fiction and is not to be construed as real. In all respects, any resemblance to actual persons, living or dead, or descriptions of events or locales is entirely a product of the author's imagination.

The material in this book is for mature audiences only and contains graphic content and language. It is intended for readers aged 18 and older.

A glossary of *italicized* Spanish words is provided at the end of this book, with the exception of words which are equivalent in both languages, such as *importante* = important, *Mamá* = Mama, or words of Latin origin found in the English dictionary. Other words, phrases, and sentences written in Spanish are immediately explained within the text itself.

Printed in the United State of America
ISBN-13: 9780991477760

Published by Sierra Press
Phoenix, Arizona
First Printing, February 2019

Cover design by John Flinn
Graphic art by Lina Luna

DEDICATION

My fictional character Rafael Ortega de Estrada, known as Rafe in this series, meets George Summers, who becomes his mentor, friend, teacher, and adopted father. George, although not from the same town, ethnic background, or social status, gave of himself to help Rafe reach his potential. Almost everyone I know has or needs a George Summers in their life. Someone who profoundly makes a difference. It might be a relative, neighbor, teacher, coach, or minister, or perhaps as with young Rafe, a stranger.

This book is dedicated to Harold Bell, one of my George Summers in my life.

Acknowledgement

First and always, I owe more than thanks to my wife for her unending hours of critique, review, and clarity. She always keeps me honest in my writing and helps me find and keep each character's vision.

Thanks must go to Rich Golenda and his belief in this project. He is a person of the true values which I try to portray in this series – honor, family, love, trust, and friendship.

I would like to acknowledge the wealth of historical information which is weaved into this work to depict the places and events of this saga's time period. As a work of historical fiction, where real-life historical figures or actual locations are used, the situations, incidents, or dialogues concerning those persons or places are entirely fictional and are not intended to depict actual events or to change the entirely fictional nature of the work.

DISCLAIMER

In an effort to accurately describe the social fabric of New Mexico during the timeframe of this book, readers should consider the author's transitions from the use of the terms, Spaniards and Mexicans. After the discovery of South America in 1492, New Spain, considered to encompass Mexico and much of central America, was under the control of Spanish Kings and Queens.

Over the next several hundred years, Spaniards emigrated north into what is now the American Southwest. Legions of settlers traveled to spread the Catholic religion and to seek fortunes in gold and silver. For their efforts, the Spanish royalty bestowed land and titles to the adventurous settlers. In New Mexico, Spaniards founded Santa Fe as the capital of the Kingdom of New Mexico in 1610. Industrious, the Spanish settlers created a robust economy and raised their families for generations. Rather isolated, New Mexico remained an extension of New Spain until the Mexican Revolution began in 1820.

After the Mexican Revolution ended in 1821, the country now known as Mexico emerged from under Spanish control. After the Mexican-American War ended in 1848, the border between Mexico and the American Southwest was in dispute. Finally, the Treaty of Guadalupe Hildalgo created the border as we know it today. In the treaty, Articles VIII and IX ensured the safety of existing property rights of Spaniard/Mexican citizens living in the Southwestern territories. Despite the treaty's assurances to the contrary, land grants owned in New Mexico were often not honored by the United States because of interpretations of the treaty and U.S. legal decisions. Fraud and greed by powerful American lawyers and politicians stripped many descendants of original land grant owners of their land.

Because this book is set after the Treaty of Guadalupe Hildalgo, the terms Spaniards and Mexicans are often intertwined. Even today, the descendants of the original Spanish settlers maintain their heritage as Spaniards. However, Americans who began settling in New Mexico at that time used the term Mexicans for the local population living in the territories.

In today's world, the term Hispanic is often used to describe a diverse population of Spanish-speaking peoples. However, this book attempts to be true to the fundamental use of the terms, Spaniards and Mexicans, as it might have been used by the different characters in the story. In no way does it intend to disparage the people described by the usage of the terms.

CHAPTER 1

Jed Clements sat at a two-chair table at the rear of the Golden Horseshoe Saloon nursing a beer and watching Bonnie Brunel work the room. Wearing a red velvet ruffled dress, which was cut high showing her stocking covered legs, helped to make the cowboys buy the watered-down whiskey. Watching her swing her hips, Jed sure was glad to be back in Texas.

"Yew doin all right Jed," Bonnie purred at him as she walked by his table.

"Shur nuff. Kinda slow tonight," he responded.

"I got a coupla high rollers over at the roulette wheel. They say I'm bringin em luck."

Jed had come back to Round Rock, Texas, and back to Bonnie after the trip last summer to the New Mexico Territory with Luke Payton. Luke forced Jed to go back to New Mexico with him to find and kill the greaser who killed Luke's brother, Butcherknife Bill. Bill had been the foreman at the Sutton Circle B Ranch just south of San Marcial, New Mexico, where Jed worked as a drover.

Jed was at Big Ed's Saloon the day when Bill and another cowboy, Ponyboy George, tried to dry gulch a greaser for some blooded horses they thought John B. Sutton wanted. The greaser should have been an easy mark. None of the Circle B cowboys could believe it when the greaser came back into town with Butcherknife and Ponyboy's bodies draped over their horses. No Texas cowboy would believe a greaser could ever be that fast.

Jed left New Mexico after Butcherknife and Ponyboy were killed and went back to Austin where he should have stayed. For some stupid reason he came to Round Rock and found Bill's brother Luke and told him the bad news about his brother. He thought Luke might be obliging and would maybe help him find a new outfit needing a drover or just give him some money for his trouble. Instead, Luke forced Jed to go with him back to New Mexico, back to the shitheel greaser town of San Marcial.

Jed left San Marcial the second time shortly after Luke was killed by Big Ed Seeley. Big Ed caught Luke trying to rape John B. Sutton's widow. Luke swore she was just a high-priced whore from Austin who used to call herself, Cinnamon Baker. Luke told Jed he knew Cinnamon when she worked at the Crystal Palace before she got married. Jed thought Luke should have stuck to the mission of finding and killing the Mex who killed his brother instead of going after some whore. Now both Luke and his brother Bill were buried in that shitheel town in the New Mexico Territory and not in Texas.

By the time Jed got himself back to Round Rock, droving season was over and he was spending the winter doing odd jobs and living with Bonnie Brunel. She was the only good thing that came out of the whole mess with Luke Payton. Though a whore by trade, Bonnie was the first woman who ever made Jed feel good about himself. He used to wonder why John B. Sutton ever married a whore, but he found himself having the same ideas about Bonnie.

Bonnie helped him find the only jobs he could get here in Round Rock, tending bar or cleaning up saloons after closing. After a few months, Jed wanted no part of either one of those lousy jobs, but he also did not feel good about living off Bonnie's meager earnings. Most of all he hated seeing Bonnie in the arms of other men. She hustled cowboys so she could pay the rent and buy food.

The long winter months allowed Jed to do some reflecting. He was tired of working as a cowboy. Living on the hot prairie chasing stinking cows was getting old real fast. It was a life for drifters and ex-outlaws and he knew plenty of the hardened men who made their beds on the hard ground. Jed wanted more from life, a soft bed and a warm woman next to him. An idea had been percolating in his brain since he left San Marcial. It was an idea which could make him rich. It was also an idea which could get him hanged.

Jed took Luke's money after paying the undertaker in San Marcial and used it to get back to Round Rock to find

Bonnie. He still had a sizable amount, about a thousand dollars, which he stashed in a safe place. It bothered him some he never told Bonnie about the money and felt some guilt living off of her, yet convinced himself if his idea worked, he could take her away from all of this and make her an honest woman.

Several weeks later, Pete Carter and Jake McNab rode into Round Rock after being fired from the Bar S Ranch in Fort Worth. Jake suggested passing through Round Rock on the way back to Austin. The town of Round Rock, where the Chisholm Trail crossed Brushy Creek, had a wild reputation and a town where the law looked the other way. After their foolishness on the way out of Fort Worth, Jake thought Round Rock might be a safe place to hide until spring. Once the cattle drives started gearing up, they hoped to get hired by one of the large outfits and get out of Texas for a while.

Riding in from the north, they pulled up to the rail in front of the Golden Horseshoe Saloon. It was about sundown and they were cold, dirty, and plenty thirsty. Traveling in Texas during the winter was no easy time. Walking into the Golden Horseshoe, they were surprised the saloon was quiet and there were lots of open spots at the tables and along the bar. It was not the rowdy place they expected.

Jake placed a dime on the bar and ordered two beers. It was Pete who spotted Jed Clements sitting in the back of the saloon and they yelled out to him.

"What the hell r yew two doin here?" Jed asked after they shook hands. Pete and Jake had worked with Jed at the Circle B in New Mexico and had been part of a group of cowboys who left after John B. Sutton was killed. Sutton's widow took over and hired local Mexican cowboys to work on the ranch. Over half of the Texas cowboys left and came home to Texas not wanting to work alongside greasers. Jake and Pete had gone to Fort Worth.

"We're headed back ta Austin ta see my folks," Jake told him.

"I thought yew was in Fort Worth at the Bar S?" Jed

asked.

"Yeah we was. Got fired by the butthole ramrod cause we didn't like how he was runnin things. We was tired of takin his crap," Pete grumbled.

"Yeah, that jasper had no clue how ta run leatherbacks," Jake added.

"What the hell yew doin here in Round Rock?" Pete asked.

"Well, yew ain't gonna believe what I bin through since we got back ta Texas. When yew boys left fer Fort Worth, I came to Round Rock to find Butcherknife's brother, Luke Payton. I wanted to tell im bout Bill being kilt by that curlywolf greaser over ta the New Mexico Territory. Luke made me go back with im ta that shitheel town to kill the Mex. Only in the end Luke got hisself kilt. I came back here ta be with my gal, Bonnie. That's her over thar," Jed said and pointed over to where Bonnie was hustling a young cowboy.

"Shur is mighty purdy," Jake said.

"So, did the Mex kill Luke?" Pete asked. Pete remembered the young Mexican *pistolero* who gunned Butcherknife and Ponyboy and shot John B. Sutton in Big Ed's saloon. Sutton drew first, but the greaser was lighting fast. Shot Sutton in the chest and killed him dead with one shot.

"Naw, yew member Big Ed? He kilt im," Jed said.

"What? He seemed like a good ole boy, why would Big Ed do that?" Pete asked.

"Well, I tell yew. Yew member the whore John B. Sutton married and took ta the New Mexico Territory? Luke knew her as a high-priced whore from the Crystal Palace in Austin. Luke went over ta the ranch house and tried ta rape her and Big Ed caught im and kilt im."

"I'll be damned," Jake said.

Jed signaled Bonnie to bring three more beers. It sure was good to see Pete and Jake. Jed did not have many friends here in Round Rock, except Bonnie. When Bonnie brought the beers, Jed introduced her.

"Just let me know if yew need another. A friend of

Jed is a friend of the house," she said as she walked off. Pete watched Bonnie walk away and thought Jed was pretty lucky.

"Say Jed, we'r in a bit of a bind. Yew see, Jake and I ruffed up that ramrod at the Bar S and took the money he owed us. Then we had ta light outta Fort Worth on the run and we'd be worried the Bar S will spread the word and git us blackballed," Pete admitted.

"Yew boys ain't crooks, why the hell did yew do a fool thing like that?" Jed asked.

"We was desperate fer the money, cause he was tryin to stiff us. We only wanted what we was owed. I'm sorry we did the dang fool thing and now we probly won't git hired by another outfit. We thought maybe we could hole up here in Round Rock fer a little while. We heard they don't like law dogs much here," Jake added.

Jed pondered Pete and Jake's dilemma. He was not too keen on getting himself tangled up with more trouble, but wondered if it would help him with the idea he was pondering since he left San Marcial.

"Yew boys just make yerselves comfortable," Jed told them. He walked to the bar and ordered a bottle of good whiskey and three glasses. When he returned to the table and poured the shots, Pete and Jake tossed them back quickly.

"Boy, that shur is good stuff," Pete said. He pushed out his glass for another shot.

"I shur am glad yer here. I got me an idea that will make us all rich. Cain't say it's legal and cain't say it ain't dangerous," Jed told them after finishing his first shot.

"What yew talkin bout, Jed? We already in trouble here in Texas and we gotta git outta here, maybe go down ta Mexico fer a while," Jake spoke out.

"Let im have his say," Pete said.

"Yew member the cattle ranch we hepped Sutton start in New Mexico. Well, when I was there with Luke, his widder's runnin it with a bunch of greasers. A few of the boys stayed on, but not many. Well, I been thinkin someone cud go up thar and rustle mostta the herd and take it up to Wyomin and sell it to the Army. It be easy pickins," Jed revealed his plan.

"We git caught fer that and we be hanged fer shur," Jake said.

"What makes yew think it be easy pickins?" Pete asked.

"Yew member there ain't no law there and those greasers, well, they be no match fer us."

Jed poured another round of whiskey. He knew it was a bit dangerous to let Pete and Jake in on his plan, but he also needed help to pull it off. He knew a few hardened cowpokes here in Round Rock who might be willing, but he trusted Pete and Jake.

"What do yew say? Yew boys want in on this?" Jed asked.

"I ain't so shur bout yer plan. I wanna go see my folks in Austin," Jake whined.

"Hell, it would git us outta Texas. They don't have no law in that shitheel town. Just a mayor," Pete replied remembering how Ponyboy George made the mayor dance to the bullets from his six shooter. "I think Jed's rat. Rustling em cows be easy pickins."

"Yew know, I bet sum of the boys who stayed thar at Sutton's ranch, like Rip and Jimmy, would jump in and hep us. They probly tired of workin with greasers anyways," Jake replied.

CHAPTER 2

"I'm sorry for pushing you boys," George Summers told Rafe and Carlos. "Especially you, Carlos. You should be home with Bibiana."

"Bibiana moved back home with her parents. Her mother is helping her in these last few weeks, more than I can. Besides, working helps relieve my mind from worrying. They know where to find me if anything happens."

Carlos and Bibiana's first child was expected within the month. Bibiana was in good health and the doctor said all was well, however her nervous parents coaxed her into moving back to the de Soto hacienda where they could tend to her every need.

George needed the boys to help work on a large gun and rifle order for the Texas Rangers. He received the rush order last week at a time when his Santa Fe foundry was already quite busy. Rafe immediately stepped up and also enlisted Carlos to help. The three had worked well into the night for the past week. George was feeling his age, tired to the core, but hoped if they met the Ranger's order date, there would be more orders in the future. If the business continued, George thought 1873 was going to be a good year.

"I sure wish Billy was here," Rafe quipped. "We could use his help with the furnace."

"Yes, you're right," George agreed.

"Speaking of Billy, have you had a letter from your mother recently?" Carlos asked Rafe.

"Yes, I got a letter from her earlier this week. María's baby is healthy and apparently has hefty lungs when he is hungry. Mother and Billy are doing well. They want me to come to Torreón to be there when they get married in July. The date will be set when I write to tell them when Ana Teresa and I can come."

"Is she excited to go?"

"Yes, very much. She says it will complete a gap in her understanding of my life. I'm afraid she is in for a big shock when she sees how I grew up."

"I wish I could go with you. You may need protection. You have thwarted death on both of your last trips to Mexico," Carlos said with a chuckle.

"No es cierto," Rafe responded it was not true, though it was.

George smiled listening to the boys, as he called them, bantering like brothers. Rafe was younger than Carlos by six years, both of them in their twenties. Neither were his sons by blood, but he considered Rafe his adopted son and Carlos, well Rafe considered Carlos his brother. George wanted Rafe to take over the foundry someday and thought Carlos a perfect partner. Of course, it was some years off before George thought he would retire.

"I wish you could go with us," Rafe admitted. Returning to Mexico, where he was born a *peón,* always gave him pause. Life was so different there. In Santa Fe he was an American, a businessman, and protected by American laws. In Mexico he was a *mestizo,* a *peón,* a person of mixed heritage and considered of lower class. Carlos was right when he said Rafe barely escaped with his life on the last two trips to his homeland.

"The baby will be born before you leave and I will discuss the trip with Bibiana. I think she is planning on staying with her parents for the first couple of months after the baby comes," Carlos said.

"Trust me Carlos, you will not want to leave your newborn son or daughter and Bibiana will need your attention," George interjected.

"Still, I would like to go with Rafe and will talk to Bibiana about it," Carlos responded.

Several hours later Rafe could tell George was exhausted. Carlos left about an hour before to make the ride back to the de Soto hacienda.

"I will finish this last gun and clean up," he said.

"No, I'll help you," George replied.

Rafe extended his hand and caught George by the

elbow. "No *don* Jorge, go to bed," he insisted, using his personal name for the man he considered his father. Fifty-four on his last birthday, George walked with a slight limp from the bullet he took in Elizabethtown two years ago. The bullet nicked a vein in his leg and without the expertise of Doctor Carson Lowe, it might have taken his life.

Although working hard every day, George had developed a hefty belly and enjoyed a cigar and brandy nightly. Deep wrinkles were set in George's forehead, his hair showed more gray than brown, and a puffiness under his eyes worried Rafe about his adopted father's health. George needed to slow down a bit, but neither Rafe nor Josefina could convince him to cut his orders or hire additional help.

George put down the gun part and nodded his head. "You are right, I'm tired. Just finish this piece, then you too need sleep."

Rafe finished, put away the tools, and sat down at George Summers' desk. He made notes on the completion of the work they had done that night. By his calculations, they were half finished with the order and maybe a day ahead of schedule, thanks to Carlos' help.

Yawning, he slowly closed the ledger book. The quiet of the foundry was strange, as it was usually noisy and busy during the daytime hours. George Summers designed and forged all types of weapons, guns, rifles, and even small artillery. His design of double-action mechanisms had become popular over the last several years. A double-action gun did not require the user to thumb the hammer for each shot. Each pull on the trigger fired a bullet.

Sitting in the quiet of the office, he reflected on his upcoming trip to Mexico, his homeland. He was born Rafael Ortega de Estrada on *don* Bernardo Reyes' hacienda near Torreón, Coahuila, Mexico. He was born a poor peasant, a *peón*, not much better than a slave to the *don*. The man he thought was his father was killed by the French at Puebla when Rafe was fourteen, leaving him, his mother, and sister María completely defenseless in the servitude of *don* Bernardo.

When Rafe was seventeen, *don* Bernardo raped María. Feeling forced to avenge her, Rafe grabbed his father's flintlock pistol. He shot the *don* and fled north on Rayo, the *don's* prized Appaloosa. It seemed like yesterday and a lifetime ago. It was about a year ago he learned the truth. *Don* Bernardo was his real father, having raped Rafe's mother when she was sixteen. All the shock and anger was gone now. *Don* Bernardo died of a heart attack and Rafe inherited both the hacienda in Torreón and his name. He was now Rafael Reyes de Estrada.

His sister, María, was now married to his boyhood friend Rodolfo Guerrero. They lived at the hacienda in Torreón and were making good progress bringing it back to life. Most important to Rafe, his mother and María's children were reunited again and living in peace. Rodolfo and María's baby was born in early April. They named him Rafael.

Rafe needed to write his mother and give her a date for the trip. She wanted them to be at her wedding to Billy. Rafe still could not believe Billy Swanson, the man he first knew as Desperate Billy, was going to marry his mother. They fell in love while Rafe was in jail and the Santa Fe Spanish aristocrats wanted to see him hang for Diego de la Torres' death. Everyone was so wrapped up in the trial, they completely overlooked the subtle signs of their romance.

The first time Rafe met Billy Swanson was at a stage stop some thirty miles east of Fort Yuma last year. Billy burst through the door at the stage stop – dusty, dirty, hungry and thirsty, calling himself Desperate Billy. At the point of a broken gun he ordered a steak, a bottle of Red Eye whiskey, and then grabbed Ana Teresa wanting to kidnap her and ride away on Rayo. It now made Rafe smile, though at the time he should have shot Billy.

Billy was on the run after a scuffle with a young First Lieutenant, which landed him in the Army stockade. He escaped and made his way across the desert until arriving at the stage stop and accosting Ana Teresa and the passengers. A blacksmith by trade Rafe brought Billy to

Santa Fe to work in the foundry. Now, Billy was marrying Rafe's mother. It was an amusing story Rafe hoped he would tell his grandchildren someday.

Closing the ledger and standing up, he stretched his weary six-foot frame. He locked the large foundry door and headed across the open expansive courtyard to the Summers' main house. Ana Teresa was asleep in the upstairs bedroom. Their house being built on the far hill overlooking his horse barn was not yet finished. Hopefully, it would be finished by the time they returned from Mexico.

A few minutes later, he quietly removed his boots and slipped from his clothes. As he slid into the bed next to his wife, Ana Teresa reached out her hand and touched him.

"What time is it?" she murmured.

"Late. Go back to sleep," he replied. She snuggled beside him and he immediately fell asleep, exhausted.

CHAPTER 3

Gunfire erupted outside of the Golden Horseshoe. Jed heard whoops and yelling as another group of cowboys came into the town of Round Rock. A bullet thwacked the roof outside. It was mid May and the cattle herds were beginning to get organized and on the move. Treeing a town, shooting up in the air and generally wreaking havoc, was the cowboys expression of having fun. Sometimes people or animals got hurt or killed causing the law to get alarmed, but not in Round Rock where cowboys knew the town was a haven for rowdiness.

The gunfire calmed and five rangy cowboys came into the Golden Horseshoe laughing and slapping each other on the back. Spurs jangled on their mud-caked boots and they wore leather chaps. A large bandana wrapped around each man's neck, tied in the back and covering much of their chest. The bandanas and their well-worn hats with a large Texas style brim helped to protect their faces when the wind or rain howled across the Texas plains.

"We want us some beers and women," one cowboy yelled to the bartender.

Jed Clements sat by himself at his usual table at the rear of the Golden Horseshoe Saloon nursing a beer. He glanced over to where Bonnie Brunel was standing near a poker table. She was a whore, but she was his girl. He grimaced thinking she would probably have to take at least one of this sorry lot upstairs for a roll.

The five cowpunchers laughing at the bar were typical of the hardened men who drove the smelly beasts across the Texas plains. Many Texas cowboys were otherwise homeless, knowing only the hard ground for a bed. Some died young from a bullet, from a stampede, or from exposure to the harsh elements.

Jed had been back in Round Rock since last November. Over the winter months, he pondered a plan to turn rustler and he knew an easy mark. Then his friends,

Jake and Pete, showed up and he convinced them how they could rustle the herd from John B. Sutton's widow. He knew from his previous trip with Luke Payton to the shitheel town of San Marcial, New Mexico, it was a big herd probably over four thousand head.

Jed figured it would be an easy task to steal the herd and take it up to Wyoming. The New Mexico Territory was wild and mostly open land. Only an occasional small hamlet run by Mexicans, like San Marcial, would be in their way to Wyoming. Moreover, he doubted anyone could be mustered to give chase. After all, New Mexico did not have hardened lawmen, such as the Texas Rangers, who patrolled outlaws.

Cows on the hoof were bringing thirty dollars per head in good condition. It was one hell of a lot of money. His part of the split would give him enough to buy a small ranch just north of Austin and get it started. Now in his thirties, Jed was tired of working for rich cattle barons. His body showed all of the twenty years of sun, heat, dirt, sweat, and a few scars which were his payment. He was ready to settle down with his woman, Bonnie Brunel.

He thought it ironic Bonnie was a whore, just like Cinnamon Baker who became John B. Sutton's wife. Cinnamon now called herself Cynthia Sutton. After John's death she probably became the wealthiest woman in New Mexico.

Jed's plan to return there and rustle the Sutton herd was gathering steam. Pete and Jake were in Austin waiting for him to gather up more men. Jed had given careful thought over the last several months to find partners for this dangerous venture. Round Rock was a better place than any to find hardened cowboys, like himself. It was also a safe place for outlaws, as Round Rock took a special dislike to lawmen.

He settled on five men he knew here in Round Rock for his scheme. Two of the five he chose already ran on the wrong side of the law, while the others brought specific talents Jed thought they might need. When Jed approached each one, it did not take much persuading to talk them into signing up to rustle cattle from an unprotected ranch in the New Mexico Territory.

First was James Ketchum. James stood tall and lanky though somewhat bowlegged and was about Jed's age, around thirty-five. He kept his face shaved and only sported a long mustache and a small beard under his lower lip. He was Texan, true and true, and he liked to say he was related to the infamous Texas outlaw, Blackjack Ketchum. James was a good rider and experienced drover who might have been a ramrod on any spread except for his slow and deliberate way of talking. He liked to be called Jimbo and was fast with his six-shooter.

Jed met Viper here at the Golden Horseshoe Saloon playing poker. The gambler told no one of his past. Some said he came from Tennessee, others said he came out of Georgia because he had a Southern drawl. He was lightning fast to the draw and everyone guessed it was why he called himself Viper. Jed heard plenty of talk about the man, but no one knew his real name and Jed was scared to ask.

Jed asked Viper to join the group because he was a killer. He killed for a price, no questions asked. Jed thought they might need a ruthless killer if anything went awry. The only thing Viper told Jed was he was tired of Texas and wanted more adventure. When Jed told him of the plan, Viper only nodded as a response with his cold blue eyes.

Jack the Breed claimed he was the great-grandson of the warrior Comanche Chief Iron Jacket. Jack's father kidnapped an Irish woman from a wagon train headed to California making Breed half Irish and half Comanche. He was a big man, quiet and reserved when sober and meaner than an injured wildcat when drunk. He claimed he was good with both a rifle or a bow and arrow from the saddle of his horse. Some said he was deadly with a knife, however Jed never saw him in action. Jed selected Breed to be the tracker. He told Jed he knew where all the waterholes were located on the Goodnight-Loving Trail up to Wyoming. Jed was not exactly excited about including Breed. However, he convinced himself it might be good to have the half-breed along should they encounter Indian trouble along the way.

Pappy Wakefield was the oldest in his late forties. A survivor of many cattle drives, Pappy was deemed too old for most outfits. It riled Pappy who said he could still drove with the best of them. Jed selected Pappy to do the cooking for the outfit and trusted Pappy's experience would be useful in many ways. Pappy also wanted to pull one last big job so as he could retire. He talked incessantly about the beaches of Acapulco, Mexico.

"Mexico's full of greasers. Why yew wanna go there?" Jed asked him.

"I seen me a picture book and ain't no place prettier in the whole world," he replied. Pappy told Jed to only get a packhorse for the first part of the trip, so they could make better speed across Texas. They could pick up a chuckwagon and team when they reached El Paso.

The last man Jed selected was Courtlyn Lange, who hated his first name and went by Corky. He was much younger than the rest and more innocent. Jed thought of him as a wildcard, guessing he might not be twenty yet. What Corky brought to the group was an understanding of Spanish, as well as his youth and enthusiasm. He grew up in a Mexican neighborhood in San Antonio and told Jed he was fluent in Spanish.

Jed knew from his time in the New Mexico Territory, the greasers spoke Spanish and Jed did not understand them. He thought Corky ideal to translate, even though he was not a gun hand or a drover. Instead, Corky would be the wrangler, caring for the horses. When Jed asked Corky to join the group as the wrangler for the remuda, Corky smiled. "Remuda comes from the Spanish word *remonta,* which means remount," Corky told him.

"Each man will have at least one extra hoss and after we buy a wagon, we'll have extra team hosses fer yew to manage," Jed told him. As added incentive, Jed promised to teach Corky to shoot better. "We'll practice every day we can," he promised the kid.

Jed was satisfied with the men he selected. He paid them each thirty dollars to commit to the scheme and to keep quiet about it. He paid Viper fifty. Parting with the cash was difficult, but otherwise the men would not have waited for this venture to begin.

Jed was organizing the final arrangements and buying horses for the remuda. Pete and Jake were waiting in Austin. Viper, Jimbo, and Breed took off to San Antonio, while the rest stayed here in Round Rock. By Jed's estimation, they would leave Round Rock the last week of May and arrive in San Marcial about a month later. The cows should be nice and fat on the spring grasses by then.

"How long will you be gone?" Bonnie asked Jed later that week as he started packing. Jed only told her he picked up a job as he did not quite trust her to keep quiet if he told her the truth. She was quick to assume he meant a job as a drover.

It was after midnight and they were in the bedroom of her small house. Taking off her skimpy dress, she hung it in the closet. She washed the night's saloon grime off her face, arms, legs, and was now tenderly washing her privates. May brought cowboys back to Round Rock as the herds started to move. Tonight she serviced five. The money was good, but Bonnie was tired of being on her feet or her back starting at noon and ending at midnight. Jed was a bright spot in her life and now he was telling her he was going back to the New Mexico Territory.

Jed sat on the bed pulling off his boots while admiring Bonnie's nakedness, especially when she bent over to wash her legs and feet. Jed thought Bonnie was beautiful, light eyes and tendrils of light brown hair fell around her pale face. He was sure glad he came back to Round Rock to be with her. She supported them by whoring at the Golden Horseshoe and he did not like it. Tonight she came home dog tired and he knew he should not try to make love to her and let her sleep.

"Yew sure are purdy, honey," he said.

"Yew are a sweet talker, Jed." Bonnie finished washing and walked over to where Jed sat on the bed. "I'm gonna miss yew mightily when yer gone to New Mexico."

Bonnie's touch raised his pecker into a stiff post. She

reached down and wrapped her hand around him. "When yew leavin? I have tomorrow off," she said as she played with him.

Jed groaned with pleasure. "Next Tuesday mornin," he croaked as she squeezed him harder. "Are yew sure yew want to leave me?"

"Yew know I dun wanna, honey, but I gotta get us a grub stake and this job is easy as pie."

"I don't like it, Jed. I just got yew back and I'm afraid something will happen to yew, just like Luke Payton gettin hisself kilt down thar," she said. Leaning over she kissed his cheek and then his mouth.

"Dun yew worry none honey. I ain't loco like that galoot. He went down thar lookin fer trouble. I'm goin down thar to work and make us a bucket full o money. Yew know I hate ta see yew work so hard fer what little yew git from that saloon. When I get back we'r gonna go ta Austin and buy that little ranch I tol yew bout. Thar ain't gonna be no more hustling drinks from cowpokes fer yew honey," Jed promised. He wrapped his arms around her and pulled her into the bed.

Bonnie rolled on top of Jed. She was tired, however making love to Jed was not a chore. His leaving scared her. Perhaps he would not or could not come back. She watched him go last year with Luke Payton, but had only known him a short time. Now she was in love with him. Tightening her hug, she kissed his neck. His stiff penis pushed against her belly.

Well if he was really leaving again, Bonnie was determined to give him a royal sendoff. There was no way Bonnie wanted Jed to forget to come home.

"Yew the biggest Jed," she purred. "The biggest and the best." Jed lost himself as Bonnie slid his stiffness between her legs as she straddled him.

CHAPTER 4

Rafe found George sitting on the veranda enjoying the warm sun and reading the newspaper. It was George's routine as he ate breakfast before heading to the foundry.

"Good morning," Rafe greeted him as he walked up and sat down across the table.

"Relax and have breakfast before we start work today." George smiled at Rafe folding the newspaper.

"I updated the ledger last night and believe we are half finished with the order for the Rangers."

"Thanks to Carlos help," George acknowledged.

"Anything interesting in the newspaper?" Rafe asked.

"Yes. Trouble up north on the Baca land grant. More easterners have arrived claiming ownership of parcels of land based upon fraudulent deeds they purchased."

"Fraudulent deeds? What do you mean?"

"The squatters are being sold official-looking documents for land on Royal Spanish Land Grants. They come west unaware they have been cheated and the deeds are worthless. It is particularly rampant on the Luis Maria Cabeza de Baca land grant."

"Isn't that north of Las Vegas?" Rafe asked. The town of Las Vegas was only a half day's ride from Santa Fe.

"It is one of the largest land grants ever allotted at over 500,000 acres. Because it is so huge, the Bacas have no way to patrol the claim. Some of the squatters have already built houses and tilled fields before the Bacas locate them. When they try to force them to leave, the squatters threaten bloodshed."

"But I remember learning the land grants were protected after the United States and Mexico signed the Treaty of Guadalupe Hidalgo. The people already living here were given citizenship, if they accepted the laws of the constitution," Rafe recited some of the education he learned when he came here to Santa Fe.

"Yes, after the treaty Mexicans in the annexed areas

had the choice of relocating to within Mexico's new boundaries or staying and receiving American citizenship with full civil rights, including their land ownership rights."

"So what has changed?" Rafe asked.

"People are pouring into Texas and Oklahoma by the thousands from the eastern states looking for land to call their own. Oklahoma was mostly open range or Indian land, so people easily took squatter's rights. It was supported by the government under the Homestead Act, but New Mexico is different. Vast parts of our territory are owned by Spaniards who received their land grant as payment for colonizing the area, even as far back as when *don* Juan de Oñate claimed New Mexico for the King of Spain in 1598. It was known as the Kingdom of New Mexico then." George stopped and took a sip of his coffee.

"So why isn't the government putting a stop to it?"

George shook his head. He agreed it sounded simple for the government to simply outlaw any sale of land already owned as Spanish land grants, to arrest unscrupulous land sellers, and to stop the migration west. However, he knew nothing was simple when it came to power, greed, and politics. The fact that most of the current population spoke Spanish and New Mexico's history as the northern frontier of New Spain, only helped to create confusion. The muddled heritage of these Spanish land grants translated into thousands of profitable acres for grazing and mining rights. As such, New Mexico held enormous opportunity to those willing to bend the law or to incite turmoil for profit.

"The Daily New Mexican has been running articles and editorials recently to educate the public to the crisis. Here, read this editorial in the newspaper today," George said and passed the newspaper across the table. Rafe picked up the paper while he finished his breakfast and read:

"These newly-arriving Americans do not understand or seem to care about our complex New Mexican history. When this vast and wild territory was under Spanish rule, the King or Queen expressed appreciation to loyal subjects with gifts of land and title. Beginning in

the 1600s, even before the Pilgrims landed in Massachusetts, New Mexico was settled using a 'cross and sword' method, combining religious conversion with military might to claim the territory. Large parcels of land were granted to brave conquistadors, caballeros, landed gentry, and the hard-working families who settled this treacherous country. Many perished from Indian attacks, famine, illness, or the simple lack of basic necessities.

Along with the land, the King bestowed a designation of nobility with the right to use the title of Don [de origen noble], in front of one's family name. In return, the grantees had to give the king a fifth of any treasure, specifically gold they acquired or profit from enterprise. It was called the King's Fifth.

These Spanish Dons earned the right to their land with their family's blood. They tamed this land, raised their children, and buried their dead in New Mexico. When the Treaty of Guadalupe, which officially ended the Mexican-American War in 1848, was signed it acknowledged these Spanish and Mexican land grants and recognized the owner's property rights. How then can these land grants now be deemed illegal?

All over New Mexico squatters are demanding ill-gotten ownership. Fraudulent deeds are sold on land belonging to our proud New Mexican families. A dangerous group of lawyers and politicians, known as the Santa Fe Ring, are at the root of the problem. Using the English-based American law, they are intimidating the Spanish-speaking landowners.

Will New Mexico fall to the same type of land swindlers who orchestrated the California Land Claims Act of 1851? Supposedly a means of adjudicating claims, the Act imposed a darker cloud on California property ownership. According to this observer, the federal government passed this Act to settle private land claims, but really to unsettle them, keep them unsettled, and squash the vanquished Spanish claims altogether.

The Spaniards of Santa Fe and all of New Mexico must learn how to fight for their rights in the American courts and rebuke the Santa Fe Ring."

Rafe read the editorial and agreed. Both his best friend Carlos Zuniga's family, and Ana Teresa's family were denied their rightful ownership by force. Ana Teresa's father was run off his estate in Rancho Simi, while Carlos' father was shot on the steps of their family home in Los Lunas. The evidence of pending trouble was already evident here in New Mexico.

Putting the newspaper down Rafe said, "I hope the *dons* here in Santa Fe read this article and understand what is happening."

"You are right, but most do not speak or read English. I'm afraid the editor of the newspaper is not reaching the audience he expects."

"What about the local Santa Fe government? Many politicians are Spaniards. Why are they not fighting for their friends?"

"The Santa Fe Ring is usurping power from the government. It is said they are lawyers, businessmen, judges, politicians, and local ranchers. They operate in secret, protecting the identities of each other, so no one can be charged with any crimes. I am afraid they are experts at using the American law against the people here," George explained.

"So the *dons* should unite against the Santa Fe Ring. The *dons* still have a lot of influence."

"I've heard rumors some *dons* are sympathetic or even aligned with the Santa Fe Ring. They see profit from the unsettling of the Spanish land grants and want to protect themselves at the same time. I'm afraid there is no simple solution to the problem. Santa Fe and all of New Mexico is particularly susceptible because of the language barriers."

Rafe stood up having finished his breakfast. "Father, save the newspapers for me. I will start reading them as you do. Santa Fe is my home and I need to pay more attention to politics here, but right now we need to get the Ranger's gun order finished."

George nodded in agreement. "I'll be along to the foundry shortly."

CHAPTER 5

May in Santa Fe brought warm temperatures to the high altitude town and its residents were out for Sunday strolls around the central plaza. Rafe, Ana Teresa, and Lolo were enjoying a cool drink at an outside restaurant facing the plaza. Children chased each other while mothers sat on benches keeping a casual eye on them. Several Indian artisans sat on blankets along the sidewalk selling silver and turquoise jewelry. Rafe watched the activity around the plaza reading the local newspaper while his wife Ana Teresa and Lolo, the Summers' eldest daughter, engaged in conversation.

"I am so excited to see Boston. Father has told us so much about where he grew up and all the history. Of course it is not like Santa Fe. My uncle is making arrangements for us to meet several prominent families and we are going to a gala." Lolo was bursting with anticipation of the family's upcoming trip to New England to meet relatives.

"I hope someday Rafael and I will go there. Perhaps if you marry a gentleman from Boston and live there, we can visit you," Ana Teresa said excitedly. She remembered going to Spain when she was eight and then Mexico City when she was ten years old with her parents. She remembered the marvels of the large cities with masses of people moving about in all directions. As a little girl it both excited her and scared her as she held tightly onto her mother's hand.

Los Angeles was larger than Santa Fe, much larger. Still it was a western town with mostly adobe houses and dirt streets. Rancho Simi where she grew up had open rolling hills and large Spanish haciendas. Her father's land grew grapes, vegetables, citrus trees, and pastured a few horses. From Lolo's descriptions, Ana Teresa imagined the eastern cities of the United States would be more like Madrid, Spain, with towering cathedrals and huge palaces.

Rafe only half listened to his wife and Lolo as they chatted about Boston. Instead, he was soaking in the warm weather and thinking how nice it was to sit with the girls on the plaza without any harassment. Only several months ago, he was in jail and the Santa Fe aristocrats wanted him hanged for Diego de la Torre's death. Several Spanish dandies came to the jail wanting to lynch him, disbelieving his innocence.

Now his life was peaceful and the town and some of the aristocratic Spaniards had changed, like Ana Teresa's uncle *don* Pedro. After the trial, *don* Pedro invited them to dinner. It was the night a robber killed Alvaro Gutierrez and Vicente Vargas outside of the Palacio Cantina. Oscar Peralta identified the robber as an Anglo, but the man was never caught.

Don Pedro changed last spring, accepting Rafe and Ana Teresa's marriage and he welcomed them at his home. The *don* also acknowledged Rafe's superior blooded horses. He purchased one foal and Rafe was training the young colt. The *don* came to visit Rafe's horse barns three times to see the progress. Rafe hoped the colt would be completely broken before he headed to Mexico in July.

As he sat soaking up the sun, Rafe spotted a caravan of six well-worn covered wagons clanking through town on the south side of the plaza's *paseo*. A burly, grizzly man in a slouchy black hat and buckskin coat barked orders to keep the caravan moving. Four other armed men rode two on either side of the caravan. Three of the wagons were pulled by bone-skinny horses and the others were pulled by tired mules.

The wagons were full of personal belongings. Farm implements, chairs, and other assorted items were lashed to the wagon sides. From his vantage point, Rafe thought the people driving the wagons looked down and out. Several ragtag children skipped or walked alongside the towering wagons and one had two cows in tow that looked ready to die. Rafe watched the caravan turn and head north on the trail to Las Vegas, New Mexico.

He wondered if the weary wagon train was another

set of settlers with fraudulent deeds. Several days ago, he and George discussed the situation concerning the land grants and the unscrupulous Santa Fe Ring. According to George, shysters were selling official-looking deeds to poor farmers in the East and Midwest. The people paid dearly for the deeds, thinking they were getting good parcels of farmland, but instead found the land was part of a Spanish land grant.

Most of the farmers were probably good people, hearty stock, and anxious to begin a new life. Also, most of them had no idea about the New Mexico Territory and the history of the Spanish land grants. When the Spanish owners attempted to evict the squatters, it caused chaos and even armed conflict.

"Rafael, we are ready to go and you haven't finished your drink," Ana Teresa spoke and shook Rafe out of his thoughts.

"What is the matter Rafe?" Lolo asked giving Ana Teresa a quizzical look.

"Oh, nothing. Just enjoying the sun and watching people go by. I'll finish the drink and we can go," Rafe responded and gulped the drink.

After dropping the girls at the Summers' house, Rafe drove the carriage to the horse barn. Reymundo, his stableman, came out of a stall and grabbed the reins. Rafe jumped down from the seat.

"Reymundo, how is the new foal doing?"

"Jefe, the young one can run like the wind. His color is beginning to look like Rayo," he said. The young foal was birthed almost two months ago, an Appaloosa like his sire, Rayo.

"Let him run in the pasture for a while today with Rayo, but bring them back to the barn later. The foal is still too young to be in the pasture alone," Rafe told him. "Do you have a name for him yet?"

"I think you should name him *Cuate,* you know it means twin," Reymundo suggested.

"It is a good name. I will think on it," Rafe told him as he walked from the barn. He would never forget the day

Rayo was born as a tremendous thunderbolt struck the large tree just outside the barn. The crack of the thunderbolt frightened the mare into pushing the foal out. It was why Rafe named the colt Rayo, meaning thunderbolt. This colt offspring looked surprisingly like Rayo, brown with a white splotched rump. The young one had rear white ankles. Watching the young colt run brought Rafe joy as he remembered Rayo at that age.

Rafe's brand of blooded horses was growing. The young colt was his ninth foal born and his reputation for fine quality horses was growing in and around Santa Fe. He could ask top dollar for his blooded horses. *Don* Pedro told several other Spanish *dons* of Rafe's stock and they made inquires. Benjamin Pacheco's father, *don* Ramon, already paid for a yearling. In March after the trial, Mayor Billy Thornton bought a black mare sired by Carlos' black stallion, Santiago. Rafe thought the mayor was embarrassed about his accusations against him before the acquittal and it compelled him to buy the mare. Regardless, the mare brought a good price.

When Carlos came to visit or work at the foundry, they let Santiago and Rayo run in the pasture with all the mares and young ones. The sleek black stallion and the Appaloosa were friends. The two studs ran and played together on the hillside and never fought over the mares. It was somewhat unusual for two studs. Nevertheless, Rafe thought he needed to add another permanent stud and at least two more mares to support his growing business.

CHAPTER 6

The gun order for the Texas Rangers was completed a day earlier than planned. George was preparing to take the shipment personally. Rafe grumbled at him, but George insisted he did not need any help with the delivery. "I can't take you away from your new wife every time I need to deliver an order," George told him.

"This is not a small delivery," Rafe retorted.

"I already asked Harry Phillips. He's heading out with a caravan on Wednesday morning. I'll join up with him."

Wednesday morning George was leaving with the shipment packed in the wagon for El Paso. Rafe helped him with the last minute details and pressed him one more time.

"You should not go alone, *don* Jorge," he cautioned his adopted father.

"I will be fine. You watch over the girls and the other orders at the foundry for me. I'll be back before next Friday."

Rafe watched as George drove the team down the lane and out of sight. He headed for his horse barn. It had been several weeks since he rode Rayo and the spirited horse needed frequent exercise. Thankfully, Reymundo rode him several times while Rafe and Carlos worked late at the foundry. Reymundo made glowing comments about Rayo. According to Reymundo, Rayo was a special horse, like none he had ever ridden.

Rayo was in the back of the barn when Rafe strode in and whistled. The large Appaloosa's ears perked and he pushed a few mares aside to reach Rafe. The horse nuzzled Rafe's hand.

"Hola amigo," Rafe said as he stroked Rayo. "Are you ready for a run or would you prefer to annoy the mares?"

Rafe always talked to the horse. Having raised him from a foal, the big Appaloosa and Rafe bonded more like friends than horse and master. Rayo pushed hard into

Rafe's hand, then snorted throwing his head up and down as if to say, "Well, let's get on with it."

Saddling Rayo, Rafe hopped aboard. He trotted out of the barn and turned away from the main house. Up the hill behind his barn was a long fenced pasture. Several mares and colts ran free on the green slope. Once clear of the barn, Rafe kicked the horse twice gently. Rayo burst into a gallop.

Shortly after Rafe and Rayo rode off, there was a clatter of hooves in the courtyard. Benjamin Peralta stopped and waited as Reymundo strode to meet him.

"Buenos días señor," Reymundo greeted him.

"Buenos días. Is Rafael here?" Benjamin asked.

"He went on a ride *señor.* He took the Appaloosa."

Benjamin seemed to ponder the information for a few moments. "Which way did he go?"

"He went east on the trail out from behind the barn."

"Gracias," Benjamin thanked him and kicked the flanks of his horse. Once past the horse barn, Benjamin found the east road and followed the fresh tracks.

Rayo galloped with abandon. The feeling of power and speed on the magnificent animal never ceased to bring a smile to Rafe. It was always as if he and the horse were one. Finally, Rayo slowed as they reached the foothills of the Sangre de Cristo Mountains. The large horse was breathing hard, though Rafe knew he would go on if urged.

"You're right Rayo. Let's take a break."

Hopping down, Rafe dropped Rayo's reins. The horse would not stray. The view from the foothills was splendid. The rooftops of the large buildings of the town of Santa Fe were visible in the distance. Spring had turned the valley green with new life, and yet the top of the tallest mountains still sported a cap of white. Overhead a teal blue sky was dotted with puffy white clouds.

The last several months since the trial, had renewed Rafe's spirit. A year ago he was a captive slave on an agave and opium farm in Jalisco, Mexico. Many times over the past year his life hung by a fragile thread, but God intervened. He was now married to Ana Teresa, his new ranchhouse was almost complete, María's baby was healthy, and his mother and Billy were to be wed soon. When he rode in the town of Santa Fe, he rode without fear or shame. After the trial, the Spaniards relented and although he was not an aristocrat, most accepted him as a businessman. Even the silver bars, stolen by Rodolfo in Mexico, were sold by George's miner friend, Bill Moore. Bill sold the silver for $1.30 per ounce at auction and it brought in just over $19,000. Everyone got a cut of the proceeds. Rafe wired Rodolfo's share to the bank in Torreón instructing the banker, Gregorio Zamora, to make the funds available.

Rafe was glad to be rid of the ill-gotten silver. It was more than a thorn in his side and almost resulted in Ana Teresa's death, though now it seemed a distance memory. Some of the proceeds were spent getting his house finished and the rest helped to shore up his local funds for his horse business.

As Rafe rested, he heard Rayo snort lightly. Rafe knew every move of the horse and this meant he smelled or heard something or someone. It was probably a bird or small rodent. Rafe opened his eyes and stood up. Scanning the trails, he picked up a small dust trail coming his way. Rayo's ears perked forward. Picking up Rayo's reins, Rafe stepped up beside him. He was unafraid. His double-action pistols were in the gunbelt wrapped around his waist.

In a few minutes, Benjamin Peralta rode up to him and jumped down.

"*Hola* Rafael, I've been looking for you," Benjamin said.

"How did you find me?"

"Your man told me you took Rayo for a run."

"What's the matter?" Rafe asked him. Though he and Benjamin were now friends, it was surprising Benjamin would seek him out in this manner.

"I need your help," Benjamin said. "Yesterday all the local *dons* were served a summons. We all have to produce our land grants to the land office in Santa Fe before the end of the month.

"That's preposterous," Rafe replied. "Why?"

"The summons states it is for our benefit and protection. With the problems on the Baca land grant north of Las Vegas, all the *dons* must prove the legitimacy of their grants. The letter cites the Governor's proclamation to all Spanish land grant holders. He hopes to prevent the same problems which are happening on the Baca land grant from happening in other communities."

"So, present your document and be done with it. It is only a precaution," Rafe said.

"Not all the *dons* can produce a legal document. You know how many of the land grants were made by proclamation of the King or Queen of Spain. Some were written, not all. My father is not sure he has a legal document to our land, even though it has been in our family since the late 1600s," Benjamin admitted.

The boundaries of Spanish land grants were marked by stone markers, placed on the corners of the land. In the past, fences were not necessary. Spaniards recognized ownership and respected it regardless of documents and papers.

Benjamin's dilemma touched Rafe in his heart. Carlos' family lost their land in Los Lunas and Ana Teresa's parents theirs in California. They were only two of many Spaniards who had been dispossessed of what was rightfully theirs by new settlers and the new American laws.

"So why are you seeking me. What can I do?"

"You know what is happening in Las Vegas. The *dons* are afraid an all out war is brewing. We need weapons. We need double-action pistols and rifles, like the one you gave me. The *dons* are willing to fight for their land, but this will not be a fight with swords."

Chapter 7

Tuesday morning May 27, 1873, three men left Round Rock, Texas. Jed, Corky, and Pappy left with a remuda of fifteen horses and one packhorse. Jed bought the small herd, the packhorse, and supplies with Luke Payton's money. Pappy helped him decide on the supplies stowed on the packhorse for this part of the trip. Pappy argued they needed to make speed getting out of Texas and could pick up a chuckwagon and team when they got to El Paso.

Last night Jed made love to Bonnie four times until they were both exhausted. He promised her when he got back they would marry and get the small ranch. Bonnie clung to him this morning and cried when he left.

They headed southwest toward Austin where they would hook up with Jake and Pete. The rest of the crew he recruited in Round Rock were to meet them just west of San Antonio on Friday. After Jed explained how the shitheel town of San Marcial had no whores, Breed, Viper, and Jimbo took off to San Antonio several weeks ago to have some fun before the long trip to the New Mexico Territory.

On the way to Austin, Jed helped Corky with the remuda until the youngster learned how to handle the herd of horses. Corky seemed a quick learner and Jed trusted Corky would be able to get the horses to New Mexico without much help. On Wednesday afternoon they found Jake and Pete at the Devil Dog Saloon.

"Who's the old codger and the kid?" Jake whined. "I thought it were just us three."

"Use yer noggen Jake. Yew think the three of us can rustle that herd?" Jed retorted. "I got me three more waitin fer us in San Antone and hope a few frum the Circle B will join up with us, too."

"That's a lot of splitting," Jake grumbled, but Jed ignored his comment.

"Boys, this here is Corky. He'll handle the horses and speaks good Spanish. Pappy will be our cook. These two are Jake and Pete. They used to work with me on the Circle B," Jed introduced the men to each other.

"Yew boys ready ta go?"

"Yeah. Let's git goin. I'm tired of juss waitin round," Pete replied and drained the beer sitting on the bar top in front of him.

Jimbo, Viper, and Breed left Round Rock more than three weeks ago to have some fun. All of them agreed to join in Jed's venture to rustle a herd in New Mexico and take it to Wyoming, but the waiting around started to get boring. They came to San Antonio because Viper wanted to gamble before heading to New Mexico. Several saloons in San Antonio ran high stakes poker games and Jimbo and Breed only saw Viper occasionally over the last several weeks.

Tonight Viper joined Jimbo and Breed to visit the Spanish side of town. Jimbo was familiar with this neighborhood of San Antonio. It was a *Tejano* barrio, a place where the original Spaniards settled and now a place where only Spanish was spoken. When Jimbo worked for the Spur brand, San Antonio was the closest large town. He and his friends spent many nights frequenting the local saloons in both the American and Mexican side of town. Jimbo hated to admit he found the Mexican girls more appealing. No self-respecting Texas cowboys could admit such a thing without scorn from his friends.

"Yew better be right about the good-lookin whores here," Viper growled.

"Prettiest in all of San Antonio," Jimbo bragged.

"They still greasers," Viper grumbled.

Jimbo led them across Salinas Street until they crossed a creek, then turned south on Laredo Street. The strumming of a guitar and the voice of a woman singing a lively Spanish song greeted them when they arrived at a cluster of small adobe buildings. At a dimly lit cantina on the edge of San Pedro Creek, Jimbo signaled to dismount.

"Remember, they don't like gringos much here," Jimbo reminded them as they tied their horses to the rail.

"Well I ain't no gringo," Breed muttered.

Inside the cantina, a graying man played a guitar sitting on a short stool behind the singer. Raven black hair flowed down past the singer's shoulders. Her breasts bulged from a low cut embroidered blouse and a red and black skirt swirled as she swayed to the song. Several *vaqueros* sat near the woman who stood singing a Spanish love song. Several others leaned against the bar. They turned and looked at the strangers, but made no obvious move to deny their entrance.

Jimbo led the others to a table across the room from the singer. He frequented the Spanish side of San Antonio, drawn to the music, the tequila, and mostly the raven-haired women. A young girl with long black hair came to wait on them.

"Tequila por favor," Jimbo requested the popular Mexican liquor.

The girl returned with a bottle and clay cups. One cup was filled with slices of lime. Jimbo pulled a fifty cent coin from his pocket and handed it to her. *"Gracias señorita."*

It was not long before Viper was staring as if mesmerized at the raven-haired singer. Her voice was silky and smooth as velvet. Despite the fact he did not understand the words, hearing them roll off her tongue was soothing.

More than an hour later, horses neighed and nickered as they came to a halt in front of the cantina. Each horse carried a bright Mexican blanket under a tall saddle. Long lariats wound from a strap near the tall saddlehorn. Four *vaqueros* jumped off their horses and tied them to the rail in front of the cantina.

"Eh Nacho, I get Conchita first tonight!" one of the *vaqueros* named Pepe spoke out.

"Chingate, I get her first, then you can have her after I loosen her up," Nacho bellowed with a chuckle.

As they walked into the cantina, their silver spurs sang as they strode across to the bar. All eyes in the cantina assessed their arrival and the woman stopped singing.

From his vantage point, Jimbo noticed the *vaqueros* were heeled and wore crisscrossed bandoliers across their chests stuffed with bullets. He knew this type of men, tough range-hardened Mexican cowboys who ran cattle from Mexico into Texas or rustled herds south across the border. They obviously were well known and others gave them wide berth, moving down the bar away from them.

"*¡Tequila!*" Nacho yelled out loud enough for the entire cantina to hear. All four removed their dusty sombreros, dusted them on the side of their legs, and sat them on the bar. Nacho's sombrero was more ornate with gold embroidery around the edges of the large brim. A tassel hung from the top of the peak.

"*¡Música!*" he shouted. The guitar player restarted the song and the woman began to sing. The bartender placed several bottles of tequila on the bar with a dish full of limes. Jimbo watched as the other customers relaxed and the *vaqueros* took swigs from the tequila bottle and sucked on the limes. The leader tapped his foot enjoying the woman's song. When she finished a second song, she walked off and disappeared into a back room.

Later in the evening, the bottle in front of Viper was almost empty. Jimbo could tell Breed was showing the tequila's effects more than Viper and decided they should finish the bottle and leave. The four *vaqueros* at the bar were finishing a second bottle and they made Jimbo nervous.

From the second floor, a sultry voice turned everyone's attention. The guitar started and a young woman began to sing as she descended the stairs. She was stunning. The young Spanish singer was dressed in a satin gown of red and gold. Her raven black hair cascaded down her shoulders topped with a red veil and held by a silver *peineta*. The tops of her tan breasts mounded above the low neckline of the bodice of her dress. Jimbo recognized the woman they called Conchita. Her voice was magical, haunting.

Conchita swayed her hips to the music. Her voice rose in crescendo and then turned soft in other parts of the song. The *vaqueros,* especially Nacho, watched captivated by her.

During Conchita's third song, Breed rose up and gave a screeching yell. He began to dance as he moved in circles near their table.

"Breed stop it, sit down," Jimbo hissed at him. Instead, Breed picked up the almost empty bottle of tequila and continued to dance and yell.

Nacho, followed by his *compañeros,* quickly moved toward Breed.

"Cállate pendejo," Nacho told Breed to shut up and called him an asshole. He pushed Breed back into a chair.

Breed, drunk and out of control, came up with a knife so fast Jimbo saw it only as a blur and had no time to react. The knife sliced Nacho across the arm. Breed screeched a war cry and raised the bloody knife.

Conchita stopped her song and screamed. Everyone was stunned including the *vaqueros.* They stood motionless unable to react to what was taking place before their eyes. Before the *vaqueros* recovered from the shock, Jimbo grabbed Breed and pulled him toward the door. Viper jumped up following behind them. Shots erupted as they ran for the door. Viper pulled his pistol, turned and returned fire, making the *vaqueros* take cover. Jimbo and Breed crashed through the door and ran for their horses. Running toward the door, Viper pulled out a second pistol and fanned four shots at the *vaqueros* coming behind him.

Jimbo pushed Breed atop his horse and slapped it hard on the rump. He jumped onto his, kicked it hard, and hightailed it north to Laredo Street.

Behind them Viper reached his horse. Four shots sounded from the door, two hit their mark and Viper slumped trying to keep a hold of the stirrup strap. "That crazy fuckin Breed. I didn't even git a chance to git my tallywacker wet," Viper groused at no one as he fell to the ground.

CHAPTER 8

Jed Clements and the others wound their way out of Austin heading west. Jed knew there was no way out of Austin that did not take them across the Colorado River. It was deep and wide in spots with rough areas and rapids where it narrowed. In the spring it turned muddy red-brown, which is why the Spanish named it Colorado, meaning red. At Cross Creek, a ferry took them across and then they headed southwest to San Antonio.

Keeping to the old stagecoach road, they put miles behind them. The first night they camped north of the Blanco River. It was more like a creek, but a good place to water the horses. Any Texas cowboy worth his salt knew never to pass up a watering hole.

Pappy Wakefield served up a stew of carrots, potatoes, and beef from the rations. Jed helped Corky secure the horses making sure the kid tied the tethers correctly. Pappy made a pot of coffee and they sat around the campfire while Pappy cleaned the dishes.

"How many days to El Paso?" Corky asked full of his youthful exuberance.

"Quit askin so many fuckin questions," Jake groused at Corky.

"Ah, leave the kid alone. He's just curious, like yew was at his age. I member when the old cowboys laughed at us when we asked stupid questions. About two weeks kid," Pete spoke out and answered Corky's question.

"I never asked no stupid questions," Jake grumbled. "The kid is just pure dumb."

"Hell, yew didn't know the difference tween a cow and a bull, till yew went an tried to milk one like that ol cowboy tol yew to. That bull kicked yew when yew tried to milk its pecker," Pete said followed by good-natured laughter.

Jake kicked at the dusty ground in front of him. "Well, I think we just dun need no greenhorn on this trip."

"Give it a rest Jake," Jed butted in. "Git some shuteye."

The following afternoon Jed and the gang arrived in San Antonio. Every Texan held a special place in their heart for the Alamo Mission and the battle fought there. Many Texans spilled their blood fighting the Mexican Army led by Santa Anna, leaving a lasting scar on the town and Texans. Jed pushed past the downtown area and finally found the meeting place, the Lady Gay Saloon, on the far southwest side of town. They found Jimbo and Breed nursing beers at a table.

"Where's Viper?" Jed asked looking around at all the poker tables.

"Dun rightly know. I ain't his keeper," Jimbo lied. He had not seen Viper since the gunfight at the Mexican cantina. Jimbo suspected Viper was dead.

Breed only shrugged at Jed's question. Jimbo told Breed what happened at the greaser bar, but Breed had no memory. It was like that when he drank too much. They agreed not to tell Jed.

"I thought yew three was here together?" Jed replied.

"Yew ever tried to rassle a rattlesnake?" Jimbo said with a shrug. Jed knew he meant Viper was not a man you could control and let it drop.

"Well we cain't wait too long fer im round here. We gotta be movin along. I guess we'll wait til mornin and if he ain't here, we'll go," Jed said trying to muster as much authority as he could over the group.

The following morning they moved on and arrived at Johnson's Ferry where they could cross the San Antonio River. The recent spring rains made the river muddy and it flowed swiftly. The ferry was mid-river taking three riders across. As Jed watched, the small ferry barge tossed about in the current. The three men and their horses were struggling to stay on their feet.

Jed had taken the ferry numerous times. Usually it was a calm trip across the river. Later in the summer, when the river was even lower, horses and cattle could swim across.

"Cain't take the remuda," Breed said.

"We've gotta git em across," Jed replied.

"They git scart, they bolt and drown," he warned.

Finally, the ferry arrived safely on the other side and started the slow pull back. Jed watched the ferry and regretted buying the remuda in Round Rock. He could have waited and bought the herd in El Paso, but worried they would be more expensive or not available.

After watching the ferry, Pappy walked over to Jed and suggested, "Take the hosses in sets of threes. Those three younger hosses kin go last."

Jed thought it a good plan. It would take longer and cost more for each ferry ride, but reduced the risk of losing the remuda. "Yew, me, and Corky will go first. We'll leave Corky on the far side to hold the hosses as we bring em across."

It took six trips to get the group and the horses over the San Antonio River. By the time they were finally assembled on the other side, Pappy said it was as good of a place to camp as any for the night. He built a small fire and grilled a mess of fresh catfish he caught. The fish were small and Pappy called them fiddlers. He crusted them in corn flour and fried them in grease. He served flaky biscuits and jam with the fish.

"This here is purdy good grub, Pappy," Pete complimented him.

"Much obliged. We ain't gonna starve on this trip, not with me as cook we ain't," Pappy replied with pride.

CHAPTER 9

Rafe and Benjamin rode back to the Summers' ranch from the foothills. As they rode, they talked of many things, both the past and the future. Last spring Benjamin was instrumental in clearing Rafe of murder charges. The local *dons* were out for Rafe's neck because of Diego de la Torres' unfortunate death. Diego was killed when his horse fell on him the day he and Rafe fought on horseback in the plaza. That was the past and now Benjamin sought Rafe's help.

"The *dons* do not understand the American law. They have lived on their haciendas for generations and will fight for their land," Benjamin restated the problem.

"They need to understand New Mexico is changing now that it is a territory. I think the *dons* should make sure their land grant documents are in order at the land office in Santa Fe and also hire a lawyer. I recommend Ron Iverson. He is the lawyer who helped me during my trial. Tell the *dons* to retain his services," Rafe continued.

"That's a good idea, but unfortunately some of the *dons* do not speak English."

"You must encourage your friends to help. The Spaniards must work together." Rafe knew many of the younger generations of Spanish families, such as Benjamin, were fluent in both English and Spanish.

"Yes, I will talk to my friends. Also, I heard my father say the *dons* are planning a meeting to discuss the proclamation. I will tell them we must help each other to support our claims."

"Tell them to find old letters, documents, even newspaper articles where their ownership is discussed. Obviously however, the original Spanish land grant document would be best. Ana Teresa's parents went to Spain to try to obtain proof of their land grant in California."

"Did they find any records there?" Benjamin asked.

"I don't know. She has not heard from them for some time."

"I'm very worried, Rafael. *Mi Papá* is very upset and his heart is not good. I'm afraid the stress will kill him. *Mi Mamá* is taking pictures off the walls and hiding them. I am more worried for them than myself."

"I hope all this will pass, but New Mexico is changing. Help your parents to understand there needs to be a place here for both the Spaniards and the newcomers."

"You know they will not give up easily. Their ancestors fought for this land and they believe in the Spanish traditions. Spaniards are very stubborn and determined," Benjamin said.

Rafe knew the history about the Spaniards fight against the Moors for hundreds of years and their conquest of the New World. Not only were Spaniards determined, they were brave and unyielding.

"I'll sell the *dons* the pistols and rifles, but also tell them they need to fight this in the American courts. Killing a squatter will only land them in jail and probably get them hanged."

As they reached Rafe's horse barn, Benjamin turned to him and said, *"Gracias amigo.* I am glad we are friends." Benjamin then reached out his hand and Rafe took it.

"Adios amigo. I will get more guns and rifles made quickly. Tell the other *dons,* but remember what I said. You must fight this by the American law."

Rafe left Rayo with Reymundo after the ride for a good brushing and a hearty helping of oats. He strode from the barn to the main house. Benjamin's news was foremost in his mind and after a quick lunch he would review the current guns orders and decide how to increase production to sell to the *dons* and present it to George when he returned from El Paso.

Josefina and Juanita were in the kitchen when he stepped inside.

"Did you wipe your boots?" Juanita pointed to his riding boots splashed with mud.

"No, lo siento," he said he was sorry and stopped

before stepping further into the room. "Perhaps you can fix me a plate for lunch and bring it to the foundry?" he asked.

"Humppf," Juanita grumbled at him.

"I'll bring it Rafael. You go on about your work," Josefina told him.

"Can you tell Ana Teresa I will be busy in the foundry for the rest of the day?"

"*Sí,* she is upstairs with Lolo helping to pick dresses to take to Boston. Lolo keeps changing her mind and then they start over again," Josefina said with a smile.

Rafe turned and headed back into the courtyard between the house and the foundry. He was almost across the yard when a man on horseback rode up.

"*Buenas tardes señor. Una carta para Ana Teresa,*" the man said he had a letter for Ana Teresa and handed it to Rafe.

"*Gracias,*" Rafe thanked the man. As he watched the man ride off, he remembered him as one of the barn workers at *don* Pedro's hacienda. Rafe looked at the letter and it was postmarked from Madrid, Spain, addressed to Ana Teresa in care of *don* Pedro de Soto, Santa Fe, New Mexico. He thought about taking it immediately to her, then put it in his pocket.

Later that evening Rafe came to the main house for supper. Stopping to take off his boots, Rafe walked to the dining room in his socks. Ana Teresa was setting the table for the family meal. She wore a blue polka dot dress with bows on the sleeves. Her long brown hair fell in waves down her back. Rafe snuck up behind her wrapping her in a hug. He laughed when she squirmed in his embrace.

"Stop it Rafael. You're going to make me drop these plates," she protested. Releasing her, Ana Teresa put the heavy plates on the table and turned to him.

He kissed her cheek and pulled the letter from his pocket. "This was delivered for you today."

Ana Teresa took the letter reading the envelope. "Oh Rafael, it is a letter from my father." Hurriedly, she went to the window where the late afternoon sunlight shone brighter into the room. She unfolded the letter and read:

I apologize for the long interim between my letters. Your mother and I are leaving Madrid for Seville tomorrow. There we will board a ship to return to Mexico. Regardless of my efforts, I have been unable to locate documents for our land in Rancho Simi. However, I have found a claim to de Soto land in Southern New Mexico.

I trust this letter will find you are well, living with uncle Pedro's family. Your mother and I will arrive in Santa Fe sometime this summer. We look forward to regaining our status and reuniting with you.

Father

"So, he does not know we are married?" Rafe asked.

"You know we decided not to write."

"So when they arrive, we will tell them. We are married now. There is nothing they can do," Rafe said.

Ana Teresa slumped into an overstuffed chair still holding the letter from her father. Tears ran down her cheeks. Looking down at the floor, she did not respond.

"What is the matter?" Rafe asked looking at his despondent wife.

"If my father could not get the documents to verify he is the rightful owner of his property in Rancho Simi, then all is lost for him. I know my parents would hate the land in Southern New Mexico. Uncle Pedro told me it was land awarded to the de Soto family during the Pueblo revolt against New Spain in the 1600s. It is not fertile land for grapes or horses," Ana Teresa said as the tears flowed.

"I am sorry, *querida*. It is happening to many Spaniards. The good thing is they will be here in New Mexico. They will be near us and someday our children, if we have any," Rafe said taking her hand.

Ana Teresa burst into sobs. "He will disown me when he finds out I married a *mestizo*. I am sure of it," she sobbed.

Her parents, aristocratic *Californios,* were raised in a world when Spaniards controlled the California government. Her father was a powerful *don* and her mother gave elaborate parties at their *rancho*. She loved them both, but believed they would never accept Rafael as her husband because of his mixed blood ancestry. She and Rafe had discussed the issue many times. They married without her father's approval and it was unacceptable for a Spanish *señorita* to marry beneath her station. Her father would be offended by both, but more by Rafael's lowly heritage.

Rafe was a bit surprised she was so upset, but realized facing her father was different than talking about it. "He will be angry, yes. Your uncle has come to accept me, so will your father and mother. We will make them understand," Rafe tried to assure her.

"He will have you shot," Ana Teresa wailed.

"We knew this day would come. You need not worry. Your father cannot undo what is done. They will live in southern New Mexico and we will live here. If he disowns you, that is his problem. We will continue our life here in Santa Fe."

"Yes that is true, but they will hate the land near Las Cruces. My father will have to start over and I am not sure he has the funds to do so. I don't even think there is a house on the land," she said.

"Perhaps *don* Pedro will help them get started," Rafe suggested.

"I'm sure Uncle Pedro will do all he can to help, but he is limited on funds. Bibiana told me the harsh winter hurt his business and he has debts to pay."

Rafe's thoughts swirled to his discussion with Benjamin earlier that morning. Ana Teresa's uncle, *don* Pedro, was a Spanish landowner who also needed to prove his land grant. He could lose his hacienda if he could not produce the original document.

"Do not fret. Your father and mother can come and live with us. Our new house is big enough for all of us. My horse business is doing well and working at the foundry has given us plenty. Remember, I got money from the sale of the silver. Do not worry, we will help your parents in any way we can."

"You would do that?" she asked looking into his eyes.

Rafe lifted her from the chair into his arms and held her tight.

"Yes of course. All I can tell you is we will welcome them here and will help them as much as we are able."

CHAPTER 10

Just after sunset two days later, Jed Clements and his small band of would be cattle rustlers rode into the small town of Uvalde. "Corky, find a place where yew can git em hosses corralled fer the night. We'r gonna git rselves a proper meal and a soft bed afor we head across the Comanche territory. Meet us at the restaurant over thar when yer done," Jed ordered.

Dismounting, they grabbed their saddles and put the tired horses with Corky's remuda. Corky led the horses to the south side of town and found a livery, which had a corral large enough to hold the horses. The liveryman promised to feed, water, and keep them safe overnight.

Corky walked back to the restaurant where the gang surrounded a table with beers sitting in front of them. Jed ordered beef stew with mashed potatoes, biscuits, and pie for everyone and ordered another round of beers. As they sat drinking before the meal was served, Jed asked. "Anybody know anythin bout this here town?"

"I know it is a long way from El Paso," Pete said with a laugh.

"We shudda taken the Military Road. At least they be forts along the way fer pretection," Jimbo grumbled. Several well used trails crossed east and west through Texas. The Military Road, also called the San Antonio to El Paso road, was farther north and was the road most stage coaches and caravans took. It was protected from Indians by a series of forts built approximately a day's ride apart.

"I tol yew. It's better we dun git spotted as a gang," Jed retorted.

When the waiter put the meals on the table, he sat a large clay jar in the middle.

"Best honey yew'll ever taste. The Mescans call it *guajillo,*" the waiter said. He opened the clay jar to show a light-colored honey.

Corky dunked his finger into the sticky honey and

licked it off. "Mmmm. That shur is good."

He grabbed two biscuits and smothered them with the honey. The others followed Corky's initiative and dug into their suppers. It took little time for them to clean the stew bowls and devour the biscuits and most of the honey.

"Jed, tell us again how yew got this deal worked out and tell us bout the Mescan town. Arc ycw shut they dun have no law thar?" Jimbo asked. He was a slow and deliberate talker and thought out his questions before he asked.

Jed looked around the small restaurant wanting to see if anyone was looking or listening to what they were saying. Satisfied only a Mexican family ate dinner across the room from them, he relaxed.

"Like I tol yew back at Round Rock, John B. Sutton moved his cattle bidness to a range just south of a greaser town name of San Marcial. Ain't no law thar, just a mayor. The closest law is in a larger town called Socorro, bout sixty miles north. It will be easy pickins fer us. The ranch has some Texas cowboy friends of ours and I know we can talk em into heppin us take the herd. Thars gonna be some greaser cowboys thar, but we'll just kill em. Ain't no big deal. We round up the main herd and drive em north to Wyomin," Jed told them again.

"Jed's tellin it like it is. Me an Pete hepped drive the herd to New Mexico. It's damn good cattle country. We jess didn't like that shitheel town. The only saloon thar didn't have no whores and we didn't like the town being run by stinkin greasers. Soon as ole man Sutton got hisself kilt by a greaser gunman, me and a bunch of us headed back to Texas," Jake spoke up.

"Once we git the herd, we drive em northeast on the Goodnight-Loving Trail and head em north thru Raton Pass and through Colorady on up to Wyomin. By that time we will be just another cattle drive on the trail and no one will ask any questions. By the time the mayor of San Marcial alerts the law we will be long gone," Jed explained.

Truthfully, Jed had not planned further than rustling the herd without getting caught. He had not even contemplated the brand or other details of this venture. He was blinded by the thought of getting a small ranch just north of Austin and Bonnie's sweet pussy.

"What if sumone comes after us? What brand do they carry?" Jimbo asked.

"The Circle B," Jed said and drew the brand as a large B with a circle around it with his finger on the table.

"Ain't good to have that brand git rekonized," Jimbo said.

"How big is that herd?" Breed asked.

"We took four thousand head down thar. I would guess we gonna find bout three thousand, nuff to make us rich," Jed told him.

"That'd be a lotta cattle fer us six to handle," Jimbo said.

"Like I tol yew, we'r gonna git some of the Texas boys thar to hep us. Jake an Pete r gonna ride in ahead of us an work it out with those boys before we sweep in an take the herd," Jed added.

Breed sat back listening to Jed. He had ridden the Goodnight-Loving Trail many times and it was a rough trail, especially through Indian country in Northern New Mexico. Apaches and Navajos often attacked traveling herds early in the morning, driving off what they could before the camp woke up. He said nothing. He thought the Indians deserved to take what they could as payment for passing through their territory.

"Let's go ta the saloon and get us sum whiskey and sum women," Pete spoke out. The others agreed and followed him next door to the Lone Star Saloon. Mostly, the place was quiet with only several cowboys standing at the bar nursing beers. Inside was not smoky, the piano was standing alone, and there were no girls about. Pete led the way to a table near the entrance. He signaled the bartender and ordered a bottle of whiskey.

"Quiet place," Pappy spoke out.

The bartender brought the bottle and glasses and placed them on the table. Jed paid him and the man asked, "Anythin else fer yew'll?"

"Hey, where are the painted ladies?" Pete asked.

"Too early boys, stick around," the bartender replied.

Jed poured drinks for everyone, Pappy relaxed, and Jimbo was watchful. Corky took a second shot before the others and was feeling the fluid warm his body. He downed the second shot and was about to fill the third, but Jimbo stopped him. "Take er easy boy. We'll be carrying yew to bed iffin yew don't."

"Aw hell, I kin handle it," Corky replied giving him a wild-eyed look.

"Jimbo is rat, that stuff will grab yew by the ass and quickly," Pappy said and laughed after he threw down his second shot of whiskey.

They were halfway through the bottle when the sound of jangling spurs was heard before the batwing doors slapped open. Five cowboys, each wearing wide dusty chaps from their hips down just above their boots, followed a tall man with a heavy handlebar mustache to the bar. The man looked Mexican, dressed in a traditional Spanish *caballero* jacket. His large spurs jangled each time he moved. Quickly, the bartender poured each a beer and set out two bottles of whiskey and shot glasses on the bar.

"How yew been, King?" the bartender nervously asked.

"Been doin just fine, Ralph. All quiet here in town?"

"Yes sir, no problems atall," the bartender answered as he poured the shots.

"Jed, that be King Fisher," Jimbo whispered and pointed with his chin. It was obvious the man and his friends commanded both respect and fear from the bartender and the few cowboys standing at the bar.

"Yew shur? I guessed he be a Mescan," Jed said.

"I seen im in San Antone some years back. He likes to dress like a *caballero,*" Jimbo told him.

"He a bad one?"

"He's a gunslinger."

Once the first round of beer and shots were finished, John King Fisher turned around and scanned the room. He took another shot of whiskey and strode over to the table where Jed and the gang sat. He was wearing an ornamented Mexican sombrero, a black Mexican jacket embroidered with gold, a crimson sash, and silver-toed boots. At his sides hung two silver-plated, ivory-handled revolvers swinging from his gunbelt.

"Yew gents ain't frum round here?" he said as a question.

"No sir, we just passin thru," Jed spoke out.

"Whar yew'll heddin?" King asked looking at each one sitting at the table taking measure.

"We be headed over ta the New Mexico Territory ta hep out a friend in the cattle bidness thar," Jed answered. Everyone else kept quiet, Breed kept his hat low and his head down and let Jed do the talking. Only Corky showed a wide whiskey grin on his face looking up at the man in awe.

"What' wrong with im," King asked looking at Corky.

"Aw, he's a greenhorn and just learning ta drink whiskey. He'll be passed out real soon."

"Em yer hosses in the corral?" he asked then continued, "They'll be a target fer the Comanche. Yew need to be mindful," King said.

"Been much Indian truble lately?" Jimbo spoke up.

"Some, not much. Yew boys shudda taken the Military Road up north."

"Yeh, mebbe we shudda," Jed replied.

"Well I wish yew boys well. Iffin yew need anythin, yew just tell folks the King says yew awrat," he said and spun on his heels and jangled back to the bar.

Corky had two more shots and had to be carried to a hotel room, but not before he emptied his stomach several times. Pappy and Jimbo took charge of getting him cleaned up and put to bed. Jed bunked with Pete and Jake, while Breed headed to the livery. Hotels, even in a nowhere place like Uvalde, did not allow Indians to sleep inside.

CHAPTER 11

Rafe worked diligently for several days increasing production of both pistols and rifles for the Spaniards. Benjamin rode by yesterday and they discussed the situation again. Rafe read the proclamation in yesterday's newspaper and two opposing editorials.

One of the editorials protested a group who called themselves the Santa Fe Ring. Rafe read the editorial by T. Edward Evans:

The government is doing nothing to protect Spaniards who have owned the land for generations. In fact, it seems to me the politicians are doing everything they can to eliminate the Spaniards' control over vast portions of the territory. The powerful and corrupt alliance called the Santa Fe Ring, consists of American lawyers, judges and territorial officials. They manipulate the court system which is alien to Spanish-speaking hacienda owners in a method to drive them out. They are working with speculators from the East. Is it any wonder their bank accounts are bulging?

It is not only the Spaniards who are victims. Their unscrupulous ways are bilking the hopeful settlers who make the treacherous trip from the east to find they have been swindled. Is it any wonder these desperate people turn to violence?"

This morning the Santa Fe newspaper, The Daily New Mexican, reported bloodshed in Las Vegas. Two squatters were found dead. One of the local *dons* was accused because his barn had been burned down several days before. In some way it reminded Rafe of the animosity between himself and the *caballeros* here in Santa Fe. They burned his half-finished house in revenge for Diego's death.

Rafe wished George was back from El Paso, though he believed George would agree to supply the *dons* with the guns. Rafe promised Benjamin three pistols and two rifles.

Behind the foundry, George built a testing range for

new pistols. As was the practice, each new firearm was tested for both feel and accuracy. Rafe used the testing to practice his drawing and shooting skills.

When he had first learned to draw and shoot, he spent hours practicing until his hands and arms ached. Calluses formed on his trigger fingers. His speed and accuracy were probably not equal in Santa Fe, although he did not use it for evil.

Methodically he worked with each new gun. Every part needed to be flawlessly smooth, sanded to perfection. The wooden handles were polished to a shine. Rafe aimed at the target and pulled the trigger six times. The gunshots reverberated around him.

"Nice shooting," a voice said behind him. Rafe had not heard his best friend walk into the practice area.

"Hola Carlos, when did you arrive?"

"Just a few minutes ago. Reymundo said you were back here and then I heard the shots."

"How is Bibiana? The baby, did it come?"

"The doctor says anytime. It's why I've been staying close to home. We moved back into her parent's home so her mother could help her."

Rafe saw worry lines across Carlos' forehead. He knew his friend well, although becoming a father was new.

"Don't worry amigo. I can't believe you are going to be a father. I only hope Ana Teresa and I will be as lucky soon. Someday our grandchildren will be playing together," Rafe said with a smile.

"Of course I'm worried about Bibiana and the baby, but I have come on other business," Carlos replied.

"Business?"

"You've heard the proclamation to the *dons?"*

"Sí. It has all been in the newspaper."

"Don Pedro is frantic. He said his father, *don* Manuel, told him he saw the grant when he was a small boy. Manuel remembered it well because it was drawn on a scroll of paper and had official seals. When *don* Pedro's grandfather died, Manuel could not find the scroll. They have looked for it for years, but never found it. *Don* Pedro told me this

in confidence. He does not want to worry Bibiana in her fragile state."

"Surely the scroll was put in a safe place. It must be in a hidden drawer. You know how the old furniture has hidden compartments. At least you know the scroll was at the hacienda. Surely it can be found," Rafe tried to think of something to calm Carlos. He knew this proclamation hit Carlos in his heart. Carlos' family lost their land grant in Los Lunas at the point of a gun. Americanos killed Carlos' father on the steps of their home.

"Bibiana's family is not the only one. *Don* Pedro said many others are having problems finding the original documents. Some of these grants are hundreds of years old. Many of the haciendas were burned during the Pueblo Revolt and then rebuilt. It is unfair."

"Yes. Benjamin said his father cannot find their documents either. He has asked me for guns to protect his land. I think a war might be brewing."

Carlos nodded his head in agreement. It was not for himself he was concerned. Already stripped of his birthright, he found peace with his new life as a teacher. He did not need to be addressed as *don* Carlos Zuniga to feel complete, but felt empathy for his father-in-law and the others facing harsh consequences.

Rafe took a deep breath. Carlos' revelation affected Ana Teresa also. Her parents had not been able to find their document for the land in Rancho Simi and probably hoped *don* Pedro could help them. Now *don* Pedro's land grant was in question.

"Ana Teresa received a letter from her father. They are returning to Santa Fe. Her father was unable to locate documents for the land grant in California, but apparently there is some de Soto land in southern New Mexico."

"*Don* Pedro also had a letter. It only made him more worried. He said the land in southern New Mexico is poor and barren. The do Soto's lived there during the Pueblo Revolt, then returned here in 1698 and resettled and rebuilt the hacienda here in Santa Fe."

"Carlos, you better get back home. I'm rushing more

gun orders, however I will tell you what I told Benjamin. The Spaniards need to fight this in the American courts. Guns are not the answer."

Later that evening, Rafe joined Josefina and the girls at the main house for supper.

"Rafael, George telegraphed from Albuquerque. He will be home tomorrow night," Josefina said.

"A day early," Rafe responded happy with the news.

"Yes, the caravan made good time to El Paso and he is pushing to get home."

"He needs to get home so we can go to Boston," Lolo interjected. "I'm so excited I can hardly wait. Ana Teresa and I have been packing and repacking my trunks so I have just the right traveling and social clothes."

"All you ever think about is clothes," Lizzy scoffed.

George promised Lolo the trip east to Boston as a graduation present. The entire family would travel to Boston to visit his relatives and see the city. Lolo, the Summers' eldest daughter, was the most excited, saying it would be her chance to meet Eastern gentlemen. She was almost eighteen and craved the excitement of a large city.

"Clothes are very important. I must be acceptable to society there if I want to fit in and find a husband."

"I want to climb up to the steeple where Robert Newman and Captain John Pulling climbed up and held up two lanterns as a signal for Paul Revere that the British were marching to Lexington and Concord by sea across the Charles River and not by land. It started the American Revolutionary War," Lizzy proudly informed the family. She had no interest in Eastern society, but was excited by the trip. She was interested in seeing the historical sites in Massachusetts and the Atlantic Ocean.

"Why do you care about the old history of the United States? New Mexico was part of Spain back then," Josefina asked.

"True, but we are now part of the United States. Someday we will be a state."

"Lizzy's right. California has been admitted and soon so will Arizona and New Mexico," Rafe agreed with Lizzy.

When she was younger, Lizzy was more flighty and fun loving than her older sister. Her emotions always spread on her face – happy, sad, angry. Over the past year, Rafe noticed Lizzy was changing. She read books voraciously and spouted history and science ideas. It was a new side of her developing as she matured.

"Don't you want to see where the Boston Tea Party happened, or Harvard Square, or Constitution Hall?" Lizzy asked.

"You can have those stuffy old places," Lolo dismissed her younger sister.

"Stuffy? Just north of Boston, in a town called Salem, they hanged women because they accused them of witchcraft. Some people say their spirits still haunt the area at night."

"Disgusting. You can have all that creepy old stuff, while I dance at a ball with an educated Eastern gentleman," Lolo said with a haughty tone in her voice.

"And you can have those snobbish men. What are you going to talk about, the weather?" Lizzy retorted.

Rafe and Josefina laughed at the girls. Two years apart in age and with completely different personalities, the banter was typical between them.

The following Thursday morning was chaos in the Summers' household. For several days, the girls were giddy with excitement for the upcoming trip to Boston. Ana Teresa and Rafe laughed about it at night when they were alone.

"They have no idea how cramped the stage will be," Ana Teresa said. "Remember the stage we took to Tucson was so full we almost sat on each other. What will they do with all that luggage?"

"I don't know. Perhaps Reymundo will have to follow the stage until they reach the train depot in Denver."

Rafe and Ana Teresa stood on the front veranda waving goodbye to the Summers' family Thursday morning. Esteban drove the carriage and Reymundo followed driving the small wagon loaded with trunks and satchels. The stagecoach left at ten for Denver where the family would catch the Denver Pacific Railroad east to Boston. Rafe wanted to ride into town, but George told him to stay close to the foundry. George thought they would be gone almost a month, not returning until late June.

"I am leaving the foundry in your hands," George told him. The delivery to the Texas Rangers brought not only great compliments, but an additional order to add to the work already in progress for the local *dons*. After the carriage rolled out of sight, Rafe kissed his wife and headed for the foundry.

Chapter 12

Two days out of Uvalde, the rustlers were making their way west. From a distance just below a rise, Jed was the first to hear gunfire. He raised his right hand to stop the group and listened again. Yes it was gunfire, he was sure of it.

"Jimbo, did yew hear it?" Jed asked. Jimbo rode up beside him after Jed gave the halt signal.

"Ya, I heard it. What yew wanna do?"

"Pete, Jake, git up here," Jed called out. "Pappy, yew and Corky keep em hosses calm and be ready for trouble. Breed yew scout thataway." He pointed to the north.

"Git yer guns ready. Let's go." They drew their pistols and kicked their horses hard into a gallop.

They rode abreast toward the gunfire. When they got to the top of the rise, they saw four Indians circling a covered wagon. "Comanche!" Jimbo yelled, spurred his horse, and got ahead of the group in a fast gallop.

The Indians circled firing at the wagon and someone under the wagon fired back. The gang was still some distance away when they saw one of the Indians fall. Another was on the ground screaming a war cry. Another volley erupted, then they heard a girl's voice screaming.

"No! Get away! Help . . . !"

Jimbo and Jed were closing the distance, while Jake and Pete rode close behind. Two Comanche lay on the ground, but another was pulling a young girl out of the back of the wagon. Throwing her astride, he jumped on behind her and followed the other Indian as they rode away. The Indians were not far off when Jed and the gang arrived at the scene and Jimbo took several shots at the retreating savages.

"Careful, Jimbo. Yew might hit the girl. Pete, stay here and see ta the people. They may still be alive," Jed ordered, then he, Jimbo, and Jake spurred their horses chasing after the two Comanches escaping with the girl.

Pete jumped from his horse. Under the wagon he found a dead man with a rifle still clutched in his hand. On the other side of the wagon was a naked woman. Blood covered her chest and spilled on the ground around her. Pete gagged when he realized her breasts were cut off. Near her an Indian with a bloody knife lay dead of a bullet. At least the man under the wagon was able to kill this murderous savage. "Fucking redskins," Pete cursed.

Several yards away another Indian lay in the dirt. Pete walked toward him thinking he was dead. As he approached the Indian rose up pulling his knife. Instinctively Pete pulled his pistol and shot the Indian in the face. Pieces of bone and blood splattered as he fell back.

Of all the Indian tribes, the Comanche and Apache were the most brutal. They were not content to kill, but like what they did to this woman, they enjoyed mutilating the bodies or made their victims endure a harsh and painful death. Pete knew if Jed and Jimbo could not save the young girl, well he did not want to even think about it.

Pete shrugged away the sour feeling in his stomach as he searched and found a shovel strapped to the side of the wagon. He wanted to bury the people, especially the woman, before Jed and the others came back with the girl.

With the Comanches still in sight, Jed spurred his horse to give him all the speed it could muster. Jimbo did the same, and Jake trailed a little behind. The horse carrying the Comanche and the girl trailed behind the other one with the added weight. Jed and Jimbo were catching up. As they neared, Jed took the right and Jimbo took the left. The young girl bounced erratically as the Indian's horse galloped.

"Gotta take him careful or the girl will git kilt," Jimbo yelled to Jed. Reaching the Indian, Jed and Jimbo approached on both sides.

Black paint covered the Comanche's face from the bridge of his nose to his hairline. Four white lines were striped down below his chin starting just below his eyes. Long stringy hair flowed in the wind. Four eagle fathers tied into a headband flapped as he rode.

Jed and Jimbo pointed their pistols at him and motioned for him to stop. Instead, the Comanche gave out a screeching war cry and drew a long blood-covered knife. He waved it at them and screamed. He brought up the knife and was about to drive it into the girl's back. From the left, Jimbo reached over with his right hand and at close range shot the Indian in the head careful not to miss. It took two bullets to stop the Comanche. Riding on the other side, Jed quickly grabbed the girl's arms and yanked her off the dead Indian's horse. Her body was limp.

"Jimbo, yew and Jake keep going and git the other one before he gits away. His hoss shud be gittin tired by now. Dun take no chances. Kill that sumbitch," Jed hollered.

Jed brought his horse to a halt. Gently he got off his horse while still holding the young girl in his arms. Suddenly, the girl shrieked.

"No! No! Let me go!" She twisted and fought his grasp until she realized he was not the Indian. Jed set her on her feet.

"Thar now, here drink this water," he tried to calm her down handing her the canteen. She looked at him and her panicked screams turned to sobs. Whimpering sob after sob shook her body as she clung to his arm.

Finally she took a swallow of water, then another, between sobs. Her dress was torn off her shoulder almost exposing her young breasts. There was a wild look in her eyes and she shivered and cried.

"Yew be alwrat now Miss. Em Comanches ain't cumin back," Jed tried to assure her. She took another swig from Jed's canteen.

"What's yer name Miss?" Jed asked.

"Gle . . Glen . . Glenda," she mumbled in between sobs.

Jed helped the girl up to his horse and they headed back. When they arrived, Glenda slid from the horse and ran toward the wagon.

"Mama! Papa!" she yelled. She saw Pete off a little

way from the wagon with a shovel in his hand.

"I'm sorry miss, I'm sorry," was all Pete could think to say. Beside where Pete was digging, a mound of freshly dug dirt was piled in a body-sized form. He was thankful the girl never saw what the Comanches did to her mother.

Realizing what he meant, Glenda fell on her knees. Silently she rocked back and forth lost in her thoughts. Finally, Jed went over and helped her to her feet.

"Cum on Glenda," he said.

Glenda sat on a pile of clothes which were thrown from the wagon, stunned and distraught, starring at the scene and the men who saved her. They were cowboys, dressed in well-worn leather chaps and checkered shirts with large bandanas. Jed the man who saved her from the Indian wore a wide brimmed hat and a leather vest.

She and her parents saw few people as they crossed the barren plains of Texas. Then the Indians attacked and these cowboys appeared. Glenda wondered how it was possible they were here. She knew her father would have said, "It was God's plan."

When Pete finished burying the woman, he called to Jed who helped him move the man from under the wagon and they placed him gently in the ground.

Jed looked at Pete, "Take yer hoss and go git the rest of the crew."

While Jed covered her father with dirt, Glenda wept. Her world was shattered.

When Pappy, Breed, and Corky arrived at the wagon, the two dead Indians had been pulled away and Jed told them what happened. Pappy jumped into the back of the wagon. Inside he found pots, pans, clothes, bedding, and tools. The contents were mostly intact. One of the team horses was dead, but the other stood patiently hobbled.

Leaning out of the back of the wagon Pappy yelled to Jed. "This wagon is in good shape. Got a lot of good stuff we're agonna need. What yew say we up hitch the packhorse and take it?"

Jed pondered Pappy's suggestion for a few moments. Taking the wagon would slow them down and they were sitting smack dab in the middle of Comanche country. However, it would save them good money they might need later.

"Corky, go unload the pack hoss and help Pappy hitch em up," Jed ordered.

About an hour later, Jimbo and Jake returned. They returned with a feathered headband and beaded vest from the dead Comanche. Jed did not need to ask whether they were successful.

Pappy continued to straighten the inside of the wagon and Glenda crawled up inside with him.

"Yew be all right," Pappy told her in a soothing voice. "Did them Injuns hurt yew?"

The girl stood beside him, tears rolling down her cheeks. The young girl was slender with light brown hair tied back in a ponytail. Her gingham dress was dirty and torn at the shoulder and along the hem. She was barefoot.

"No," she replied.

"Yew be all right now girlie. Pappy will take care of yew."

Glenda could not stop trembling. Everything in her life was perfect one minute, then the Indians came swooping down upon them. Her father told her to crawl into the wagon and hide. She heard the gunfire and then heard her mother's screams. She wanted to run to her, but was petrified. Then after the gunfire stopped a rough hand grabbed her. The savage flung her onto his horse and Glenda remembered the horse took off in a gallop, then she remembered nothing until the cowboy, named Jed, gave her water.

She could tell the cowboys were getting ready to leave. The horses were hitched to the wagon and Pappy finished organizing the wagon.

"Wait! We need to say a prayer," she told Pappy and jumped from the tailgate.

Everyone gathered near the two fresh graves. One man held two crosses made of sticks and bound with leather. The men took off their hats. When the man holding the crosses took of his hat, Glenda screamed at

Breed as his long Indian hair fell around his shoulders.

"No Miss. It weren't him. He's just people like yew and me," Pappy told her. Glenda seemed to calm at Breed's presence hearing Pappy's words.

Breed handed the crosses to Jed and hung his head. He understood the young girl's fear and took little resentment from it.

"What were yer ma and pa's names?" Pappy asked her.

"Frank and Lydia Bell from Alabama. My pa was a minister and we were going west to start a new church. My pa told me to hide when the Indians started following us and told me not to cry out no matter what. He told me how much he loved me, both him and mama. They didn't deserve to die like this," she wailed.

"I know Missy. It's a terrible thing. Do yew want to say a prayer?"

Glenda nodded and started reciting the Lord's Prayer. Several of the men chimed in.

Jed and Pappy both spoke a few words over the graves of Frank and Lydia Bell asking God to give them space, then Jed stuck the crosses at the head of each mound.

With the horses hitched, Pappy helped Glenda into the back of the wagon. He jumped up to the driver's seat and snapped the reins.

Jed was angry at himself for not taking the Military Road. He thought he was being smart staying away from prying eyes, but now the reality of the Comanche was bearing heavy on him. On top of that, he had the young girl to take care of, at least until they reached El Paso.

He wondered what had happened to Viper? The only reason he asked Viper to join this gang was for his guns. The man's name as well as his nasty demeanor made Jed nervous, but he wished Viper was here now for protection.

"Jimbo, Breed," he called out. "Ride on ahead and keep an eye out fer em stinkin Comanche. We'll take turns ridin shotgun."

West Texas was wild and open country. Not many

towns or forts in this stretch of Texas gave them any protection or respite. Jed pushed the group to make as many miles as possible from the Comanche raiding site, changing horses several times.

Three days later the group rode into Del Rio, Texas. The tiny town sat on a dusty patch of southwest Texas scrubland. The only reason Del Rio clung to existence was a bend in the Rio Grande, which snaked beside it. Water was king in these parts of Texas and the river ensured the town's survival. Across the river, Mexico stretched out to the south.

Jed led the gang to a clearing on the west side of town along the riverbank. Pappy unhitched the team horses and began to clear a spot for a fire.

"Corky, get the hosses watered," Jed barked instructions.

Dust caked the men from head to toe. After they unsaddled the tired horses, they stripped naked and waded into the shallow river. Standing knee deep, they splashed the dirt and grime from their bodies.

"I'm getting me a whore tonight," Pete announced as he bathed. "Whiskey and a woman. That's my goal."

"I want *cerveza* and a *puta*," Jake said trying to make the Spanish words and everyone laughed at him.

"Una cerveza y una puta por favor," Corky corrected his Spanish.

"What did yew say?"

"A beer and a whore please," Corky interpreted.

"Yeah, well I want me two whores," Pete said with a laugh.

"Una cerveza y dos putas por favor," Corky said in Spanish.

Jed listened to the good-natured banter as the men splashed in the shallow Rio Grande. When Corky was finished with the remuda, he walked back to the camp.

"Corky, yew better git cleaned up if yer goin into town with em boys," Jed told him.

"Yew mean I kin go?" A smile spread across his face from ear to ear.

"Yew stay close and translate fer em."

"Yes sir, I will." Jumping out of his clothes, Corky ran into the river. Jed was surprised Corky's body looked even younger naked. With barely any meat on his bones, Corky looked more like fifteen than nineteen. He did not have the body of a grown man.

CHAPTER 13

Glenda heard the men laughing and talking as they splashed in the river. She peeked from the back of the wagon, seeing them washing and playing naked in the water. She heard their banter about whiskey and women. Glenda had seen naked men and knew why they wanted women in town.

It happened last summer, when her family went down to visit her uncle in Biloxi, Mississippi. Glenda and her cousin Katie Sue stayed late at the beach talking to some sailor boys from the nearby port. Katie Sue, several years older than Glenda, took off with one of the sailors down the beach leaving Glenda behind with two others.

The young sailors were friendly enough, bought her ice cream, and walked with her along the beach. She had not noticed, but they walked far enough away from where people mingled near the refreshment stands. Suddenly one of the young sailors grabbed her from behind and carried her to where the sand made a small valley between two large sand dunes. The other one took her by the legs. She tried to scream, but the one behind her put his hand over her mouth. She bit him, but it did not stop him.

They pushed her down and unbuttoned her blouse and pulled up her skirt. One of them covered her mouth with his hand as the other pulled off her underwear and spread her legs with his knees. He then pulled down his trousers. His large penis stuck straight out. He moved in toward her and she felt it pushing between her legs. She tried to scream, but through the other one's hand only a muffled sound came out. Finally he pushed into her and it hurt badly, but all she could do was cry. He only pushed in and out a few times before he groaned and fell on top of her.

"Hey get up, it's my turn," the other one complained.

The sailors switched places, but by now she did not bother to scream. When the second finished with her, they pulled up their trousers and ran away leaving her lying on the sand. She felt violated and ashamed.

Later that night her cousin Katie Sue told her how the young sailor wanted to marry her. She blabbed about how men were so stupid just because they wanted a piece of ass. The sailor bought Katie Sue a huge stuffed bear and won a fake diamond ring at the carnival stands.

"You kin get anything you want," Katie Sue told her. "Just wiggle that little behind and tell them anything."

The men who saved Glenda after the Comanche raid had not yet tried to touch her, except Pappy. He only wrapped a comforting arm around her shoulders, like her father used to do. She knew they had to take her along. She heard them laughing about getting women in town. Thankfully they had not thought of her in that way, yet, but they were men. Glenda pondered her situation. She heard they were headed to El Paso and she figured they would dump her off there. A young woman alone in the world probably meant her only option would be to become a whore. Well, she would not let that happen.

Jimbo, Jake, Pete, and Corky shook the dust from their clothes after the swim in the river and headed into Del Rio. They walked, because the campsite was within sight of the small town. The town consisted of a main street, several dozen houses, a livery, a jail, and three saloons – the Del Rio Cantina, Pedro's Cantina, and the Pecos Saloon. It was typical of a town whose only existence was support of cattle drives across this arid part of Texas.

Cattle pens built of wire, rope, and odd shaped branches of cottonwood stretched behind the buildings along main street. Tonight, only a small herd was corralled in one of the pens. The buildings in the town were made of adobe mud with twisted straw roofs, as wood was scarce in this part of Texas.

Jimbo led the gang toward the Pecos Saloon. Tinny piano music filtered out from the batwing doors. He pushed open the door and the gang followed him to the bar.

"Whatcha got?"

"Nickel a beer, dime fer a shot or a half dollar a bottle," the bartender replied.

Jimbo put two dimes on the bar. "Beers around."

Breed and Jed stayed around the campsite after the others left for town while Pappy fried up some taters.

"Hate these no place cowpoke towns," Breed grumbled as he forked a bite of potato.

"Whadda mean Breed?" Jed asked.

"Take this here town. Only here causa the river. I'll tell you zackly what they'll find down there. A cuppla dirty places that call themselves saloons. The whiskey will be made from cow piss," he explained.

"I hope they don't git into trouble, especially Corky. He's pretty green," Jed said.

"Jimbo will look after him," Pappy replied.

After supper, Breed stood and nodded to Pappy and Jed. He headed toward town. Jed stayed near the fire listening to Pappy tell stories as the darkness enveloped them. Glenda sat off the wagon's tailgate.

Being in charge was new to Jed. He felt he could not go to town with the others leaving the remuda and Glenda unprotected. He could not get drunk or even get a look at the saloon girls. In the past, Jed had always been just one of the cowboys on a cattle drive. When the boys went to town, he was always with them. He was beginning to realize being the head of this would-be outlaw gang was more than he bargained for.

About an hour later a lone dark figure walked up the dusty trail. As the figure approached, Jed recognized Breed's bulky form.

"Done drinkin already Breed?" Pappy joked to him.

"Go fuck yerself," he grumbled. Jed thought Breed's response harsh. Pappy meant no disrespect. Breed took his bedroll and walked somewhat away from the camp where he would be alone.

"What's the matter with him?" Jed asked Pappy.

"Probly the saloon woodn serve him," Pappy whispered.

"Why?"

"Half breed, whole breed, no matter. Black or white is one thing, Injuns is another."

Pappy and Jed stayed up talking for a while, then Pappy said good night. Jed stoked the fire and unrolled his bedroll near the remuda.

In town, Jake bought a bottle of whiskey for everyone to share and found a table. Jimbo joined a poker game at a table with three other men. Wide-eyed Corky was ogling the saloon girls. They purred in his ear and Pete shooed them away. Two of the women were probably twice Corky's age, another one was a Mex with big hips, all hard core whores.

Pete doubted if Corky had ever had a girl. He told them he was nineteen and boasted of two or three whores he bucked, but Pete thought he was lying.

When Corky reached for the bottle, Pete put out a hand. "Slow down thar boy. We got all night to drain that thar bottle."

"Yew ain't my pa," Corky grumbled. "My pa always told me no to everthin. I want to live a little."

"Yer pa was trying to keep yew from gittin yerself kilt," Jake said.

"I dun need yew two tellin me what to do." Corky got up and staggered to the bar. Pete counted only four shots and shook his head at Corky's back.

"Dumb kid," Pete muttered. Pete knew Corky had no money in his pockets, so unless a kindly saloon girl or cowboy bought him another drink, he was done for the night.

Jimbo had a small pile of coins stacked in front of him. The other three poker players were a well-worn cowboy, a local rancher named Ray Jacobson, and a narrow-nosed gambler wearing a black hat. Jimbo studied the man with the hat. Under the heavy mustache and dark eyebrows, Jimbo decided the man was a Mex. He spoke little, but spoke English and when he did Jimbo detected an accent.

Normally playing poker or drinking with a greaser did not bother Jimbo, but the fight with the *vaqueros* back in

San Antonio hung heavy in his mind. He was sure Viper was dead, though he pretended to Jed the gunslinger had just disappeared. It was his fault for taking them to the barrio and he felt guilty about it. Damn *vaqueros* had no right to shoot Viper. Jimbo should have sent Breed on his way and gone back to help, but he was scared for his life and left Viper to his fate.

Jake and Pete traded shots of whiskey. A little while later Corky wandered back to the table and sat down. "I need nother drink," he whined. Pete looked at Jake and shrugged, then poured Corky a shot.

"Take it easy Corky or yer gonna be sick," Jake told him.

Corky was feeling little pain and angry at being treated like a kid. He was nineteen and pulling his share of the work for the gang. He knew they thought he was green. He was, but so what. They were green once too. Corky tossed the shot down his throat in one swig. While it nearly choked him as it burned down his throat, he tried hard not to react.

It happened in the blink of an eye. Jake heard a noise behind him and suddenly the sound of a chair hitting the floor.

"Fucking Mex. Yew tryin to cheat me dealin off the bottom," he heard Jimbo snarl.

"No you are wrong. I not cheat," a voice with a thick accent said.

Pete and Corky were staring at the poker table. Jake turned to see Jimbo holding a gun on the player with the black hat.

"I saw yew cheat and I'm callin yew out greaser," Jimbo growled.

"He's not armed. Cheat or not, he doesn't have a gun," Ray Jacobson hollered at Jimbo.

"Then he should git one."

"It ain't worth it mister. We have some law round here. See that sign over above the bar." The sign read: Pecos Saloon and Courthouse.

"We got us a judge who don't like cowboys causing

trouble round here. He circuits these parts every coupla weeks," Ray Jacobson said.

"Please, I not cheat. You can have my pot. I not cheat," the Mexican player said.

"Damn right I kin take yer pot," Jimbo said standing up and pulling the man's money into his pile and then brushing all of it into his hat.

Jake picked up the almost empty bottle of whiskey and hissed at Pete and Corky, "Cum on. We gotta git."

Jake, Pete, and Corky stepped into the night. It was dark with bright stars twinkling in the otherwise moonless dark sky. Behind them the batwing doors of the Pecos Saloon slapped and Jimbo caught up to them.

"Jimbo, why didya go after that one? Was he really a cheat?" Jake asked.

"Nah, I just had enough stink of that Mex. Figgered he'd back down." Jimbo grabbed the almost empty bottle and finished it. He pulled his pistol and shot three times into the air. "Yeehaa! All yew greasers git outta my way," Jimbo shouted.

He shot two more shots into the street, subconsciously knowing to keep one bullet in the chamber in case someone came after him.

Jed heard the gunshots. They woke him, though he was only dozing. Three shots, then two more. He jumped from his blanket and stared into the darkness toward the town.

"Damn idiots. Hope they didn't git in no trouble," he muttered under his breath.

Jake and Jimbo arrived back to the campsite first. Pete was almost dragging Corky along. He dropped Corky near his unrolled bedroll with a laugh.

"Probably have the shits in the mornin," he said to Jed.

"Was there trouble?"

"Just sum fun. Nobody got kilt."

Chapter 14

Carlos and Bibiana's baby arrived on the sixth of June at ten in the morning. Carlos sent word to the Summers' house to announce the arrival of a healthy baby boy.

"Rafael! Rafael!" Ana Teresa came running into the foundry to find him.

"It is such good news," Rafe hugged his wife.

"We must go tomorrow to see them. I have several gifts I bought in town for the baby and Juanita and I finished a quilt."

"Yes, we will go. Send a reply to let them know to expect us tomorrow afternoon."

Ana Teresa kissed his cheek and skipped off. Her exuberance made him smile. They talked of children, but so far were not blessed.

The following day, Rafe hitched the mare to the buggy and he and Ana Teresa rode to the de Soto hacienda loaded with gifts. As they drove under the archway, he was bombarded with memories, some good and some bad. It was not long ago he was not welcome here.

"Bienvenidos," don Pedro welcomed them after the maid ushered them to the parlor. He was beaming with joy. "Come, Bibiana is upstairs."

Bibiana was in bed surrounded by white pillows. A small bundle in her arms was wrapped in a blanket. Carlos had a smile stretched across his face. Rafe gave him a hearty *abrazo*.

Ana Teresa knelt near Bibiana and peeked at the small baby's face. "Oh, she's beautiful," Ana Teresa said loudly and winked at Bibiana.

"She? He is a fine boy, my son!" Carlos admonished her, puffing out his chest with pride. Ana Teresa and Bibiana giggled at their joke on him.

"Have you decided on a name?" Rafe asked.

"Not yet."

When Bibiana tired of the company, Rafe and Carlos

left Ana Teresa with her and returned to the parlor with *don* Pedro.

"I'm glad you are here Rafael. There is trouble brewing," the *don* said.

"You mean with the land grants?"

"Yes, that and Ana Teresa's parents are coming here. Her father, *don* Bartolo, wrote me to expect their arrival. They are sailing as we speak."

"They also wrote to Ana Teresa," Rafe told him.

"It is a very bad time, with the new baby and all the trouble about the land grants . . . " *don* Pedro sighed and the sentence was left unfinished. Rafe thought he looked worried.

"*Señor*, I told Rafael of your problem finding the actual documents. You may speak freely," Carlos said.

"Oh, well I suppose that is good. It is complicated. You see, *don* Bartolo is my older brother by two years. He should have inherited this property from our father. It was rightfully his by birthright." *Don* Pedro stopped and took a deep breath. "My father's brother, our uncle *don* Silvio, lost his family to the cholera epidemic in California. He owned a large estate in Rancho Simi where he grew grapes. Bartolo and my *tío* Silvio were very close, closer than Bartolo was to our father. *Don* Silvio made Bartolo his heir. That is how he came to own the land grant in Rancho Simi."

Rafe pondered the information, though could not understand why it was now important. *Don* Pedro could see confusion on their faces, so he continued his explanation.

"Carlos must have told you I have been unable to find the original documents. I have no knowledge if the documents were ever formally registered into my name. I doubt it, as I remember my father searching for the scroll many years back. If I don't find it, I have no way to prove my rightful ownership to the land office and if I find it unregistered, Bartolo rightfully owns this property."

Don Pedro's shoulders slumped. Rafe felt sorry for him. He should be rejoicing in the birth of his first grandson not worrying about the ownership of his hacienda.

"Surely your brother knows this property is yours. He chose to accept the inheritance of the land in Rancho Simi," Carlos said.

"You do not know my brother Bartolo. He is used to being rich and powerful. He chose the rancho in California because it was worth much more than this property. He rose to power in Rancho Simi. He often had visitors from Spain, who he entertained lavishly. He considered this hacienda not much better than a poor man's ranch. But now facing poverty, this hacienda is much superior to the de Soto land in Las Cruces. He would think nothing of kicking me off my own land."

The description of Bartolo hit Carlos in his heart. His older brother, Benicío, was cut of the same cloth as Bartolo. The oldest sons of a Spanish family were raised to believe they were superior, both to others and to their siblings. Benicío tolerated little, barely tolerated Carlos. He had turned into a murderous outlaw after losing his birthright to the Zuniga land in Los Lunas.

"I will help you look for the scroll. We will scour this house until we find it. Then you can make sure your claim is legal," Carlos suggested.

"You are right Carlos. I should not be worrying about my brother, when the ownership of the hacienda has not been verified. All of this, all that I own might be lost to the land grabbing going on here in New Mexico."

"We will find the land grant scroll and make sure it is filed properly with the land office," Carlos told his father-in-law.

"Can I help?" Rafe asked *don* Pedro.

"I need guns to protect my land. You have heard what is happening near Las Vegas. Squatters have moved onto the Baca land grant. They will not leave, stating they purchased the land and have a deed and bill of sale. Gun battles have broken out. I need the weapons you make at the foundry."

"I will tell you what I am telling others. I will make guns for you, but you must comply with the government decree. You have to fight this within the legal system of the

United States," Rafe replied.

They heard voices in the hallway coming their direction.

"Shhh, do not tell any of what we discussed to your wives," *don* Pedro cautioned them.

Doña Agustina and Ana Teresa entered the room full of smiles. "Pedro, you have not even offered the boys a drink," she told her husband seeing no glasses in their hands.

"Quite right my dear. We should all drink a toast to the new baby."

After pouring brandy into stemmed glasses, *don* Pedro raised his glass.

"¡Bebe a la salud de mi nieto!" don Pedro toasted to the health of his grandson. They all raised their glasses and sipped the brandy.

Doña Agustina asked Rafe and Ana Teresa to stay for supper, but Rafe declined. He had much work to do at the foundry.

On the way home, Ana Teresa held tightly to his arm. Holding Bibiana's tiny baby made her anxious for one of her own. Though she and Rafe made love frequently, she still was not pregnant.

"Bibiana is so relieved the baby is finally here and healthy," Ana Teresa said.

"Of course, we are all happy. Carlos is a lucky man."

"He is so tiny. When I held him, I thought he could break."

Rafe laughed. "Babies are tougher than you think, but they certainly tell you when they are hungry or unhappy."

"I fear Bibiana is not used to being responsible for something so . . . dependent. She was raised by servants and I fear she expects the same for her child. What is she going to do when she and Carlos go back to their home?"

"She knew what Carlos had to offer when she married him," Rafe responded not understanding what she meant.

"You don't know Bibiana. She is used to getting what she wants. She is not used to doing work or being responsible."

"I think you worry too much. They will figure it out."

Ana Teresa paused before answering. She too had been a pampered Spanish *señorita*. She had been raised to be the indulged wife of a wealthy California *caballero*. Yet, here she was married to a Santa Fe businessman. Perhaps Rafe had a point. She changed. She learned how to be an independent woman after her father lost his land in California. She loved her husband and loved her new life.

"You are right. She will learn." Ana Teresa leaned onto Rafe's shoulder as he drove the buggy the rest of the way back to the ranch.

CHAPTER 15

Rafe spent his days working long hours in the foundry. Ana Teresa split her time between running the Summers' household and visiting Bibiana and the baby. Each evening after visiting Bibiana, Ana Teresa told Rafe how the baby was beginning to change.

"He looked at me and cooed," she said at the evening's supper. They were in the kitchen, not in the large dining room, because the Summers family was gone. "I think his eyes are blue."

"All babies have the same color eyes," Juanita interjected into the conversation.

"His are not so dark, but his hair is very dark. We think his mouth looks like Carlos," Ana Teresa continued.

"Is that what you do all day? Try to imagine what he will look like," Rafe asked.

"No, of course not. Bibiana is learning to nurse. I'm really proud of her. She's not complaining unless he cries and she does not know what to do. The doctor wants her to stay in bed, so I have been walking and cuddling the baby until he falls asleep."

Juanita sat with them at the large kitchen table, along with Reymundo, Esteban, and Juan. In the Summers' household each person was treated with respect. The workers who lived on the property were always fed and housed. Usually day workers, like Juan, returned home each evening. Tonight Juan joined them for supper, because he helped Rafe with the foundry orders late into the night.

"*Mi esposa* wraps our babies tightly, like a burrito. She says it makes them calm," Juan said.

"How many *niños* do you have?" Rafe asked. Although he had worked with Juan for years, he realized he knew very little about his family.

"Five, but two have died and are with God," Juan said.

"I'm so sorry Juan," Ana Teresa said.

"It happens. My baby girl died of influenza and my son died from a fall," Juan said in a matter of fact voice. *"Mi esposa,* she is pregnant again."

The conversation drifted from babies to horses and the work at the foundry. Ana Teresa however, found herself still thinking about babies and children. Juan did not show grief for the loss of his children, rather accepting it as part of life. Ana Teresa wondered if she could ever do the same if she and Rafael lost a child. What if Bibiana's baby died?

Rafe returned to the foundry and worked late into the evening. Juan left around ten after Rafe told him he would shutdown the big furnace and cleanup. Juan protested, but Rafe told him to go home.

When Rafe returned to the house, the lights were dim. It was June and no fires were needed in Santa Fe. The weather was almost perfect. Warm days and cool, but not cold, nights. Rafe lit the candle by the kitchen door and walked down the hallway and up the stairs to his room.

Tiptoeing into their bedroom Rafe tried not to wake Ana Teresa assuming she was asleep. After removing his shirt, pants, and boots, gently he pulled back the sheet and eased into bed. Ana Teresa turned and wrapped her arm around his neck pulling him to her. Her mouth found his in the dark. The kiss started lightly, testing, teasing, and then she pushed her body into his.

Rafe felt her breasts on his chest, though they were covered in her light nightdress. Her hands felt for his hips and lightly brushed near his manhood. A groan escaped from his lips. Often during sex they talked and teased with one another. Enjoying the time and not hurrying. Tonight he sensed an urgency in her, a need for him.

Reaching his hand down her leg, he found the hem of her dress and pulled at it. Ana Teresa quickly pulled the lightweight nightdress over her head. Tonight in the absolute dark, his hands wandered her nakedness. Quickly he wiggled out of his undergarments pressing his stiffness against her hips.

Her hands grabbed at him, pulling him into her. Her

tongue searched for his and sucked on it. Her urgency and fervor surprised him. She was a passionate woman, full of love and an openness to lovemaking. Tonight however, her lust ripped at both his body and soul. He cupped her breast in his hand and pulled his lips from hers to take her nipple into his mouth. As he sucked, she groaned in pleasure. Her hips ground into his.

She nibbled on his ear, driving him mad. He could no longer wait to be inside her. In a long thrust he entered and her hips met his thrust. Her hands clawed at his back, grasping and pulling at him. As her fingernails clawed across his back, the more sensitive scars reacted with a gripping sensation.

Ana Teresa craved Rafe's body. She needed his closeness and his love. She needed the sexual release of making love to him. He made slow and long thrusts into her. It drove her crazy until she lost herself in the feeling. All time and space ceased to exist, except for their bodies. Her groans became cries, like a wounded animal.

Rafe could hold no longer and burst inside her, joining his wife in the cries of the passion. He did not want it to end. He did not care if he died, he only wanted to stay inside her forever.

Their bodies were dripping in sweat and their lungs panted. The moment had passed, yet something new had happened between them. They clung to each other, their skin tingling with nervous sensation. Finally, Ana Teresa snuggled against his side and within minutes they were both asleep, still clinging naked to each other.

Rafe woke early before the sun lightened the window. He lay on his back staring into darkness. He could hear Ana Teresa's rhythmic breathing beside him. The magic of their lust and passion last night still enveloped him. His love for the woman sleeping beside him transcended anything he could imagine. He would not be able to live without her, would not want to.

His thoughts wandered to the night he and Billy desperately searched the Chihuahua Trail. Jerry Carr and Bo Preston stole the rickety wagon full of silver ingots in

San Marcial. All they wanted was the silver, but Ana Teresa was inside organizing the supplies. She could have easily been killed that night. When he and Billy finally found the wagon stopped along the river, Bo was trying to rape Ana Teresa in the back of the wagon. The thought of her close brush with death still made him shudder, even more this morning.

By chance, Ana Teresa found Billy's old pistol under a blanket as Bo assaulted her. She shot him dead. She did not feel guilty for taking the kidnapper's life, however sometimes she woke from nightmares and Rafe would find her sitting up against the headboard shaking and soaked in perspiration.

Now, he needed to go to Torreón for his mother's wedding to Billy. He tried to convince Ana Teresa it could be a dangerous venture and she should stay here in Santa Fe. Danger always lurked on the Chihuahua Trail. Highwaymen frequently stopped coaches and wagons, stealing, looting and often killing for no good reason. Even if no harm befell them, the trip would be long and arduous.

He wrote his mother saying he planned on getting to Torreón by mid July. George and the family should be arriving home here in Santa Fe any day. As soon as the Summers arrived home, Rafe could leave for Mexico.

Ana Teresa was insisting on going with him. "I'm not afraid. If I survived the kidnappers, I can survive anything with you by my side," she had told him.

"We were lucky that day. It could have turned out badly."

He had allowed Ana Teresa to be put in danger once and vowed it would never happen again. But could he actually promise to keep her safe? Life was fragile. A stray bullet, an illness, childbirth, even a skittered horse could snap a life in a moment. In reality, life could only be lived.

As his brain wandered through his thoughts, his own anxiety in returning to Torreón nagged him. Life in Mexico was extremely different than life here in New Mexico. President Benito Juárez had changed many laws in Mexico to help the lower classes. His death allowed for turmoil in

Rafe's home country. The limited news printed in the Santa Fe newspaper wrote articles about the new President, Tejada, and how he was struggling to retain power. Porfirio Díaz, a military general and aristocrat, was attempting to thwart Tejada's presidency. Díaz believed in repressing the common people and restoring glory to the wealthy.

It made Rafe wonder if his sister and Rodolfo could retain the rights to the hacienda in Torreón. Inherited under Juárez' newly created Mexican laws, Rafe signed the deed over to them and they were struggling, but making headway in restoring the hacienda to productivity. The hacienda had belonged to *don* Bernardo Reyes, the man Rafe learned last year was his real father.

Ana Teresa knew little of his early childhood life at *don* Bernardo's hacienda. She knew he was *mestizo,* a peón, a person of mixed bloodlines. It was the reason the aristocrats here in Santa Fe did not accept him. It was the reason her father would probably disown her when he returned from Spain and found they were married. Pure blood Spaniards were not allowed to marry *mestizos* under the old caste system.

Ana Teresa stirred, then settled. He put out his hand and laid it gently on her naked back. Feeling her steady breathing he was sure she was still asleep. Carefully he slipped from bed, dressed, and headed to the foundry to start the fire in the huge furnace.

CHAPTER 16

A telegram arrived on June twenty-third from Ana Teresa's parents. Their ship arrived in Veracruz from Spain. They were well, although the ship encountered a vicious storm. They expected the rest of their trip would take several weeks, first by train to Mexico City and then stagecoach to Santa Fe.

"Rafael, what should we do?" Ana Teresa asked him as they ate breakfast in the kitchen.

"Perhaps it will be better if we are not here when they arrive. We will be in Mexico at my mother's wedding," Rafe suggested.

"Better? Not only will they learn I am married to a *mestizo,* I'm off to Mexico with him. They would be devastated."

Secretly Rafe was relieved. He was not anxious for Ana Teresa to make the trip to Mexico with him. "Yes, you are right. You must stay here in Santa Fe and greet them when they come. I will go on to Torreón alone."

"When will you leave? Carlos and Bibiana are to baptize the baby as soon as Bibiana is able and you know Carlos wants to name us *padrino y padrina,"* she told him. Rafe and Ana Teresa agreed to become the baby's godparents.

"As soon as I can, but I am worried about your parent's arrival. My mother is expecting me to be there, so how can I not go?"

"Yes you must go. My parents will arrive here in Santa Fe and go to Uncle Pedro's ranch. They will expect to find me there."

"Then that's where they should find you, at least until the truth can be explained."

"Oh Rafael, I'm afraid."

"I will speak to your uncle. *Don* Pedro has accepted me and we have become friends. Hopefully, he will vouch for us and convince your father I am a good man and the marriage is a good marriage."

As they were speaking, Reymundo came running from the barn.

"Rafe, the foal is coming!" he shouted.

They ran from the kitchen to the horse barn. In the third stall, two newborn foals were lying on the straw. "Twins!" Rafe shouted.

Twin foals were rare. The two were almost as large as a normal foal, but one seemed much weaker. The other was already trying to stand on wobbly legs.

"Rafael, they're beautiful. Look at their delicate legs."

"Yes, but twins are not common and a mother horse usually can only sustain one foal at a time."

When Rafe was a boy he often helped *don* Pablo in the horse barns in Mexico. In return, *don* Pablo, a horse master, taught Rafe about the care and tending of horses. Several sets of twins were birthed and *don* Pablo tried his best to keep both alive. Usually the weaker of the two died in the natural order of life. Only once was *don* Pablo able to save both.

Ana Teresa was shocked. It was not possible to think one of these beautiful foals might die. She grabbed Rafe's arm.

"You must do something Rafael. You can't let . . . " she could not finish the sentence.

"Reymundo, go bring the mare from the field. The one with the recently weaned colt. Here take this blanket with you and rub it all over the colt before you bring the mare back."

"Why?"

"The mare still has milk. We will use the colt's smell to try and trick the mare into accepting this foal as her own."

While Reymundo ran with a halter and blanket to the back pasture, Rafe searched for rags and a bucket. Quickly he ran to the pump for water. When he returned, he gathered the stronger of the two twins in his arms and carried it to another stall.

"Ana Teresa, bring that bucket and the rags."

"What are you doing?"

"We need to wash off his afterbirth and remove his scent. Hopefully the other mare will nurse him. It is probably its only chance to survive."

"Why this one? Why not the weaker one?"

"The weaker one needs the mother. If she tends to it properly, it may make it. She has foaled before and was a good mother."

Quickly, but gently, Rafe and Ana Teresa cleaned the stronger foal. It was healthy, but fell to its knees several times on the spindly legs. Reymundo brought the blanket and was trailing the mare.

"Keep her quiet until we finish with the foal," Rafe instructed.

He rubbed the clean foal with the blanket to dry him, trying to transfer the colt's smell. He placed the blanket near the foal and motioned to Reymundo to bring the mare. Rafe took her halter as she entered the stall.

The stronger twin was standing quietly. The mare bent her head and sniffed. Rafe picked up the blanket and rubbed it on her nose. She nudged the foal several times and made no threatening moves. Rafe rubbed the mare and spoke to her quietly, keeping her calm.

Finally the foal sniffed the mare's underbelly. It smelled her milk. Slowly Rafe backed from the stall and closed the gate. From here it was in God's hand.

Reymundo was working in the other stall. The weaker foal was not yet able to stand. A foal needed to stand to be able to nurse. The mare dipped her head hearing the small foal's cries. Carefully she nudged it. Falling several times, finally the small newborn stood. It moved its right front leg and fell again. The mother mare encouraged it with nudges and snorts.

"Reymundo, come. We have done all we can. Nature will take its due course," Rafe said.

Ana Teresa was overcome with emotion. First holding Bibiana's baby and now watching the miracle of this birth made her weep. She clung to Rafe's arm. Her husband's strength and knowledge never ceased to amaze her.

"Do you think they'll make it?"

"If the mare accepts the new foal as her own, yes I think we have a good chance they will both live."

The following day, both foals were nursing and doing well. Rafe readied the buggy and he and Ana Teresa headed to *don* Pedro's ranch late in the afternoon. When they arrived, *don* Pedro greeted them in the courtyard.

"Hola, I am glad you have come. We have much to discuss."

"Uncle, twin foals were born yesterday," Ana Teresa was bursting with the news.

"Twins? Isn't that unusual?"

"Yes. They are both doing well. I was able to get another mare to act as a wet nurse," Rafe explained.

"Seems as if babies are popping out all over. *Don* Daniel's granddaughter had a boy yesterday. It is *don* Daniel's first great-grandchild. He sent the good news to all the *dons*. Come Carlos and Bibiana are upstairs. The doctor will not let Bibiana get out of bed yet. She is still weak, but the baby is strong," *don* Pedro said.

When they climbed the stairs, the baby began to cry loudly. Apparently nothing was wrong with the baby's lungs.

"Hola, I'm delighted you have come," Carlos hugged them both. Ana Teresa ran to Bibiana's side and hugged her cousin. The maid was holding the baby trying to calm him.

"Ana Teresa, Benicío has missed you. Go see if you can calm him," Bibiana said.

"Benicío? You've decided on a name then? Benicío. Baby Benicío," Ana Teresa repeated the name several times.

Rafe took a glance at Carlos. Benicío was Carlos' murderous brother's name. Benicío killed Chiwiwi before Carlos killed him. Rafe could not believe Carlos named the baby in honor of his brother. There was no way Rafe could be the godfather to the baby named after that miserable murderer.

As the women fussed over baby Benicío, Rafe silently fumed. Finally, they left the women to fuss over the baby and returned to the parlor. *Don* Pedro poured brandies.

"Salud," he toasted.

"Did Carlos tell you we have found the land grant scroll? You were right when you said it was in a secret drawer," *don* Pedro said.

"No, I guess there are several things Carlos has not told me." Rafe's reply was surly.

"However, it is as I feared and I am not named as the successor, nor is Bartolo. He is the oldest heir apparent. I will present it to the land office before my brother returns and hopefully he will not know anything about it." *Don* Pedro let out a long sigh.

"Speaking of Ana Teresa's parents, she received word they landed in Veracruz and hope to be here in several weeks. This presents a problem for us."

"A problem?"

"Yes, I need to go to Mexico to attend my mother's wedding and also check on the hacienda in Torreón. I must leave as soon as the Summers return from their trip. This will mean I will not be in Santa Fe when Ana Teresa's parents arrive. They will expect her to be living here with you. I am hoping you might allow her to live here to greet her parents and help her break the news of our marriage to them gently, or pretend nothing has happened until I return."

"I see," *don* Pedro nodded in agreement.

"So you plan to go to Mexico alone then?" Carlos asked.

"Yes."

"Father, with Ana Teresa here to help with the baby, I want to go with Rafael to Mexico. It will be a short trip and Bibiana agrees we can have Benicío's baptism this Sunday after Mass."

"I do not need you to go." Rafe's response was brusque after hearing the baby's name again.

"You need protection," Carlos insisted.

"Protection? Who saved your life the day your murderous brother left you for dead?" Carlos heard the anger in Rafe's voice. He knew making Rafe understand why he needed to name the baby after his murderous brother would take some explaining.

"Trouble seems to follow you, no matter where you go. This time I will be there to protect you," Carlos replied.

Rafe drank the brandy from the glass and set it down. "I need some fresh air," he grumbled. Carlos set his drink down and followed Rafe outdoors catching up to the man he considered like his brother.

"Rafe, I know you are mad, but you don't understand."

"What do I not understand? You named your baby son after your murderous brother. He killed Chiwiwi! For years he haunted me in my nightmares." The hurt in Rafe's voice escalated as he spoke. "How can you expect me to think of that every time I hear someone call to your son? How can you expect me to be his *padrino?*"

"*Cálmate,* Rafe. You know killing my brother was against everything I hold dear in my faith. Even though he was a murderous outlaw and an evil man, he was my brother. It was a sin against man and God," Carlos said.

Rafe knew of Carlos' upbringing and his years studying at the seminary in Madrid. He would be a priest if his father's land and money were not lost. Carlos was devout and held his faith in God close to his heart.

"Since that day I have struggled to atone for what I did, struggled to believe I am not doomed to hell for my action. Nothing can change the events of that day, not for you, Chiwiwi, nor me. After the baby was born, I prayed. I thanked God for a healthy son. I thanked God for everything, especially my life – the life you saved when you took me to the Isleta pueblo. It was through God you saved me that day. I thought about naming him Rafael after you. Your name means 'God the Healer,' in Hebrew. Benicío means 'blessed.' By naming him Benicío my soul believes good will be put back into the name. We can never forget what happened, but we do not need to curse the name forever. It has finally given me peace," Carlos finished his explanation.

Rafe did not respond for a long minute. He pondered Carlos' words. He loved Chiwiwi and Benicío murdered her. Carlos was right in saying nothing could change the events of that day. Their lives moved on. Carlos was married with a newborn son and Rafe was married to the most wonderful woman in the world. It would probably be hard for a while, but Rafe understood. He grabbed Carlos in a hearty *abrazo*.

"So do you think Bibiana would let you come to Mexico with me if Ana Teresa is here to help her?" Rafe asked.

"Yes, she told me I should go. Actually, I am looking forward to this trip. Someone has to keep you out of trouble and you know it," Carlos said and laughed.

"How did you know I would ask?"

"*Don* Pedro also received a telegram from his brother. I guessed you might decide to do exactly what you asked *don* Pedro to do. I know you well brother. I know you are worried about Ana Teresa's father and how he will react to your marriage."

"Yes, you know how *don* Pedro first reacted when he found out I was *mestizo*. I'm sure her father will be even more incensed."

"I will speak more to *don* Pedro about this before we leave. Right now he is concerned about the land grants. He and the other *dons* are having meetings on how to deal with the situation. He has asked me about buying more GSW guns. They think it might come to a fight and the *dons* need to have the firepower to deal with it."

"I have been working to capacity as it is. When George gets home I believe he will continue the orders while we go to Mexico. You need to impress on *don* Pedro, this is not a fight with swords or guns. It is a fight in the courts, with lawyers and words."

CHAPTER 17

The trip from Del Rio across west Texas was hot, long, and tiring, but at least they steered free of any more Comanche trouble. One of their horses went lame and had to be shot. The trip took a bit longer than Jed estimated and he was thankful to finally reach El Paso.

Viper never showed up. Jed surmised he lost the fifty dollars in up-front money at a poker game and decided to do something else. It was of concern, but not as much as Glenda Bell. At first Glenda was quiet and watchful. When she cleaned herself up, she was quite pretty. She helped Pappy with chores and did the men's laundry when they had water. Surprisingly she turned out to be a fair shot with a gun. Several times she killed a rabbit for dinner and once a small deer.

They enjoyed having her around. At night sitting around the fire, she would sing and the men would join in. Jimbo had a fairly melodic voice, too. Any of them would have gladly bedded her, but Pappy made sure none of them got any lusty ideas. Jed noticed she took a shine to Corky and he to her. Sometimes she would walk or ride with him trailing the remuda. It was not surprising as they were both still teenagers.

When they found Glenda, Jed assumed he would leave her in El Paso. After all she was not his responsibility. He felt good enough about saving her, burying her parents, and bringing her this far. However, in the back of his mind he knew what it meant. Glenda, alone and penniless, would simply become another whore at one of the saloons in town.

At times he pondered letting her stay with the gang. She was nice to have around and helped Pappy. Jed decided to push the decision about her fate to the day they left El Paso. Perhaps she would figure out something or find a job in the meantime.

"We'll be here several days while I buy a better team

of hosses for the wagon and yew men have sum fun," Jed told the gang.

"Whoopee," Corky howled.

"Yew better keep that kid frum gittin into trouble," Jimbo told Jed. "I ain't babysittin him this time."

Jed shrugged at Jimbo's comment. Corky was the least of his problems. When he imagined this venture, Jed had not factored how difficult it was to manage a group of men. Unlike a cattle boss, these men owed him no loyalty nor was he paying them a wage for their time. Any money he paid them upfront was spent long ago. He talked them into joining this venture for a split of the profit. That profit was a long way off and they wanted whiskey and women now. Jed gave Jimbo five dollars to pay for drinks before they rode to town.

"Corky, git those hosses watered and brushed before yew go to town," Jed ordered the young wrangler. Corky grinned and jumped up to make short work of tending to the remuda.

Jimbo, Pete, and Jake rode off after unloading their gear. El Paso was a large town. The most western town of Texas, it sat along the Rio Grande, spitting distance from Old Mexico. Breed made no move to get mounted. Jed noticed he had been more quiet than normal.

Corky finished tending the horses and walked up to Jed.

"I'm all done. Glenda and I r goin to town."

"Not by yerself, yer not," Jed replied then added, "Pappy, I'm a taking Corky and Glenda to town. Yew'll git yer chance tomorrow."

"I ain't never been to El Paso," Corky told Jed as they rode toward town. He and Glenda were riding double.

"Yew ain't never been nowhere," Jed remarked. Corky was about as green as they came. Though Corky tried to act older, Jed thought he must be only a teenager. It was not uncommon for young boys of his age to start working the range. Jed was only fifteen when he started.

Some of El Paso was considered Mexican Town. It was the portion of the city built when the Southwest was part of New Spain. The buildings were made of adobe and the people brown-skinned. The newer side of El Paso reminded Jed of Austin. The clapboard buildings sat in a row along a wood sidewalk. The hotel and bank were made of stone, quarried from the riverbed.

Jed remembered Lilli Jean's Saloon when Luke Payton forced him to tag along to New Mexico. It was a nice place and Lilli Jean welcomed him and Luke Payton, providing a free drink. In fact Luke told Jed, Lilli Jean took him for a roll upstairs.

Jed led the way into the American part of El Paso. Loaded wagons and horses lined the streets. Several women in bright dresses strolled along the boardwalk carrying packages wrapped in brown paper. They passed the bank, a cafe, and the Hotel Stratton. Jed recognized Jimbo's horse tied to the rail in front of the Gem Saloon. Further down the street, Lilli Jean's pumped out music into the street.

Jed stopped in front of the mercantile. "Corky, yew and Glenda can do sum walkin." He flipped Corky a fifty-cent piece. "Buy yerselves a soda or sumthin."

Jed walked his horse down the street to Lilli Jean's. He thought El Paso would be a good breather for the gang before they headed north into the New Mexico Territory. They had been on the trail for more than three weeks and the next part of the trip would only get harder.

The next morning, Jed gave everyone chores. Corky was up early filling Pappy's ear about El Paso.

"It were the biggest store yew ever did see," Corky told Pappy about the mercantile store. "Why they had shirts in six colors and boots of black, brown, tan, and snakeskin."

"That right?" Pappy responded with a smile.

About an hour later, the bacon sizzling on the campfire wakened the others. The men seemed in good spirits after a night in town.

"Jimbo, can yew go with me to town to see about a team fer Pappy's wagon?" Jed asked.

"Sure, I'll git saddled up."

Riding down the main street of El Paso, Jed looked for the livery stable. The town was quiet. Jed thought it odd until he remembered it was Sunday morning. The saloons' doors were closed, the windows on the mercantile covered, but the cafe had several horses tied in front. Jed knew frontier towns gave God his due on Sunday morning, but after noon the town would open again. Cattle drives had no calendar and cowboys worked seven days a week.

Jed pulled up in front of Hasting's Livery. He remembered the place from his trip with Luke. As he and Jimbo walked in the large front doors, a big black man greeted them.

"Mornin boys. How's kin I be a hep?" Charlie Hastings asked.

"Yew the boss man round here?" Jed asked.

"Chahlee, Chahlee Hastings. That be me," he responded with a smile and a wink.

"I'm looking for a team of hosses to pull a chuckwagon. Yew got anything like that?" Jed asked.

"Yew herdin cows or hosses?" Charlie asked.

"Does it matter?" Jed thought it an odd question.

"I's just curious. Yew boys dun got neither. Heerd yews all was camped up by the river, east of town."

Shocked the liveryman knew of their situation, Jed stammered, "Well . . . "

"We be meetin up with the herd north of here, up Albuquerque way," Jimbo finished the sentence.

Charlie shrugged. "I got me a coupla oder nags wuld work. Iffin yew want a younger team, I need a coupla days to round sumthin like that up. Cum on, I shows yew what I got."

Jimbo thought the older set of team horses might be good as a backup, but told Jed they needed to look for a set of mules or a younger team. Charlie said he would see what he could find and gave Jed a price. He would send word to the camp when he found a suitable team.

Jed left the livery feeling a bit dejected. Everything seemed more difficult than he expected. He was paying for this venture with Luke Payton's money, a little over a thousand to start and Jed had spent over half already. Shrugging he thought they were lucky to have found Glenda and the Bell's wagon in the desert. It saved him a bucket of money.

Chapter 18

The gang seemed calmer this morning, laughing and talking around the camp after a night in town. Jimbo and Pete played a little poker. Jake took a nice long swim with a bar of soap in the river. Corky and Glenda were sitting by the Rio Grande talking. They sat on a log watching the shallow water flow by.

Last night she and Corky walked all over El Paso. They got sodas at the mercantile and later stick candy. Corky bought her a new pair of socks. He was a bit tongue-tied at first. By the end of the evening, she was holding his hand and he kissed her goodnight on her cheek before she climbed into the wagon.

Sitting with Corky beside the river today she asked, "What are you going to do in New Mexico, Corky?"

"Jed, he has some bidness at a cattle ranch thar and he needs hep movin a herd up to Wyomin. I never seen so much country and it shur be an adventure fer me," Corky told her.

"After Wyoming, then where are you going?"

"Well I dun rightly know. I thought about goin to Californee. I'll have lots of money by then," Corky said.

"Lots of money? How would you get lots of money?"

"Well, yew see this here job up New Mexico way will make us all rich. We'll be rolling in dough," Corky puffed his chest a bit as he bragged.

Glenda heard things over the last several weeks riding with Pappy. Jed's business in New Mexico was a plan to rustle a herd. She knew it would make all of these men rich and she wanted in. Rustling was a hanging offense, but Glenda figured she had little to lose. She could stay here in El Paso and become a whore or try to finagle a way to stay with the gang.

"I sure would like to go with you to California, Corky. I sure do like you. Why don't you kiss me again?"

"I . . .ah . . . I . . . yew shur yew want me ta kiss yew?"

"I surely do." Glenda puckered her lips and closed her eyes pushing her chin and lips toward Corky.

She sure was pretty with the afternoon sunlight hitting her brown hair through the trees. Corky leaned over and pecked her lips with his.

"That ain't no kiss. Is that how you would kiss a girl if you really liked her?" she asked. Grabbing his head she planted a wet kiss on his lips until he responded in kind. "Now that was better," she said.

"Whardcha learn to kiss like that, Glenda?" Corky asked. Barely nineteen, his pecker pushed hard against his denim pants ready to explode from just her kiss.

"The boys back home were always chasing me. One of the older boys caught me by myself one day and taught me things bout kissing and other things. I can teach you, Corky," she said. "Let's go over by that big cottonwood and I'll show you." Glenda did not wait for an answer before she stood and grabbed at Corky's hand. He followed her to a grove of cottonwood trees down the river a little way.

Late in the afternoon, a large dust cloud appeared in the distance. It was not uncommon for the wind to kick up dust in this parched part of Texas, but Jed knew it was cattle. A herd was coming. Their camp was well off the trail, safe from harm, but Jed kept a sharp eye on the incoming herd.

A scout and hardcase cowboy rode ahead of the herd. The hardcase carried his rifle in his hand. Behind, the cows could be heard snorting and bellowing to each other. Cattle expressed themselves vocally. Any cowboy knew the noises and their meaning. The cows alerted each other or complained with grunts and bleats. When upset, a cow bellowed.

When making a drive, the most aggressive were forced into the middle of the pack. This helped to stop stampedes. When surrounded by the pack, the more aggressive cows were overwhelmed by the chorus of vocalizations and their bellows lost in the din. Younger calves were kept to the edges so they were not hurt by the larger animals.

As the herd moved past their campsite, Jed watched carefully. He estimated the herd at over a thousand. They were managed by the scout, ten or twelve cowboys, two supply wagons, and followed by a wrangler and a remuda of about ten horses. Estimating the herd and cowboys made him rethink his plan.

They were seven, really five after excluding Corky and Pappy. He hoped three or four of the men still working the Circle B in New Mexico would join them. He also hoped to rustle a large portion of the herd, maybe three thousand head. Perhaps he was overestimating how many cows eight or ten cowboys could keep in line. He was also worried about how many of John B. Sutton's herd were branded.

He designed an easy fix to the Circle B brand whereby adding a long bar that cut the circle on the flat side of the B would change it to the Circle Bar 3. He thought it an easy fix, but catching and rebranding the cows would take precious time.

Finally the passing herd was well beyond their camp and the dust settled. As it was late in the afternoon, Jed was sure the herd would be corralled in El Paso for the night.

After supper the men wanted to go to town. Corky wanted to stay in camp. "Ok kid, the rest of us will go," Jed said. "You can come too Pappy. Corky'll watch over our gear and Glenda," Jed called over to where Pappy sat near the campfire.

Corky and Glenda watched the men ride off to town. This afternoon in a thicket near the river, Glenda let Corky take her twice. She was sure he was a virgin. He was shy at first, not wanting to hurt her and blew his wad in her hand. After getting the hang of it, he kissed her passionately and stroked her tenderly, not rough or grabbing. She let him explore her body. Later when he was ready again she took him willingly.

"Why don't you get some more wood for that fire Corky. I'll just be in the wagon brushing my hair," she said and ran her hands through her hair fluffing it. "When you're done with the fire, maybe you can come in the wagon and help me with some things."

While Glenda waited for Corky to build up the fire, she unbuttoned her blouse and took off her skirt. Tucked in her belongings, she had a tiny bottle of perfume. She dabbed a tiny amount behind each ear.

Corky was not the leader of this gang, Jed was. She pondered if she should not be siding up with Jed instead, but Corky was young. Jed and the others were more an age of her father. Thinking about bedding them, made her cringe.

When Corky jumped up on the tailgate, Glenda was waiting for him. "Come here Corky. I got something for you," Glenda offered.

Jimbo was in the lead on the way to town. He stopped and dismounted in front of the first saloon they saw. Tinny music was drifting through the open door.

"Cum on. First round is on me," he called back to the group.

Breed was the last to dismount. He pulled at his long dark hair and wound it on his head and pulled his hat down low over his face. The bandana he wore around his neck, he pulled up a bit to cover his neck and chin.

The Horseshoe Saloon was busy, and the saloon girls young and pretty. A piano player plinked out tunes. A game of Faro was taking up a large table near the back. At two other tables, poker was the game. A large roulette wheel was spinning. Jimbo bought everyone a beer.

"Yew with the herd that just came in?" the bartender asked as he put the beers on the bar.

"Nah, we just passin thru," Jimbo replied.

Jake and Pete downed the beer in a few gulps and wanted more. Jed bought another round. A pretty young woman sang several songs with the piano man playing the tune. Breed kept his hat low over his face only lifting the bandana a bit to take sips.

"I'm goin to the livery and check on those team

hosses," Pappy said after two shots. "Yew boys have fun tonight." Pappy used to be able to drink more, but lately it gave him a gnawing bellyache after two or three shots.

When three cowboys left a table open, Jed bought a bottle and they sat at the table near the stage. The whiskey sure tasted good. The singer sang a set of songs The piano man played solo for a while, then the singer returned and sang again.

Several hours later, during one of her songs, a group of cowboys walked in. They looked trail weary and dusty. Jed recognized the hardcase cowboy as one of the men in the group.

"Hot damn!" one of the cowboys yelled and another let out a whistle at the singer. They had obviously already been drinking. Walking up to the bar the hardcase groused at the barkeep, "Yew better git those glasses filled quick."

Jed was used to cowboys. Most were more bluster than not. He judged this one was trying to act tough in front of the others. When the woman ended her song, the cowboys hooted and yelled for another.

Jimbo glanced up at the cowboys by the bar. He had seen plenty of their kind over the years. Men as wild as the land. Often they were outlaws or had spent time in jail. Dogging cattle was a hard job and it took hard men. They cared little for life or property. After the problems in San Antonio, Jimbo did not want any trouble. He wanted to tell Jed they should leave, but it seemed foolish. This was El Paso and these cowboys were Texans, not Mexican *vaqueros.*

Several of the cowboys wandered to the Faro table. A couple others got a bottle and sat down at a table. The young woman sang several songs and then said she would return later. The saloon quieted.

It was a typical night in a Texas saloon. Locals tended to shy away from saloons at night, especially when cowboys were in town. For cowboys, most days were spent on the back of a horse punching the nasty critters. Any day or night off was pure joy, especially if the cowboys were in a town.

A little while later, the singer came to stand beside the piano player and sang four more songs. Everyone cheered and yelled for more. Smiling she said, "Later boys, drink up."

CHAPTER 19

By the end of the singer's next set of songs, one of the Texas cowboys standing at the bar was beginning to sway. "Nother shot," he called to the barkeep.

"Maybe yew should sit down," the bartender told him.

"N maybe yew shud shut yer trap. I dun need no piss ass barkeep tellin me what to do," the cowboy hissed in return. One of his friends put out a hand and tried to get him away from the bar to a table, enraging the cowboy even more.

The cowboy staggered away from the bar without another drink. "This here shitheel saloon dun want ta give me a drink!" he yelled at the top of his lungs. People in the bar looked at the drunk cowboy, but no one made any move to stop him, not even his friends.

Kicking an empty chair the cowboy staggered left and right as he continued to yell. Jimbo saw the bartender speak to one of the girls, who darted out the front door. Jimbo knew she was sent to get the sheriff.

The cowboy fell against a table almost knocking it over and then yelled, "Git that woman back out here ta sing. I wanna hear more singin!"

He was moving closer to the tables near the stage as he stumbled. Finally, he worked around an empty table and reached the table where Jed and the gang sat. A bottle sat on the table, about two-thirds drained. The cowboy reached out and grabbed it.

"Yew'll dun mind givin a cowpoke a drink," the drunk cowboy slobbered.

Tipping the bottle he took a long slug. Jed saw a look in Jimbo's eyes and shook his head slightly back and forth. He did not want any trouble and a bottle of whiskey was a cheap price to pay.

The cowboy took another long drink off the bottle before Breed growled, "Git yer own fuckin bottle."

Breed rose up to his full height and grabbed for the bottle. Swinging his long arm, he barely missed Jed's head. The cowboy let out a laugh and took another swig.

"Now that ain't neighborly," he admonished Breed waving the bottle in the air.

Jed got up quickly between Breed and the cowboy. Breed was drunk and angry. Jed hissed to him to sit down, but Breed held his ground. The cowboy was unsteady on his feet. He stank of too many days without a bath.

"Take the bottle with yew," Jed offered the cowboy hoping he would take the bottle and leave.

"Fuck yew Jed. That's our bottle." Again Breed reached for the bottle in the cowboy's left hand. As the man tried to evade Breed's reach, his right arm swung wildly knocking Breed's hat off. Breed's straight black hair fell to his shoulders.

"Yer a fuckin Injun. We dun let no fuckin Injuns in here ta drink our whiskey."

The cowboy reached for his pistol. Instinctively, Jed pulled his gun and pushed the cowboy back. In the blink of an eye it was over. The cowboy raised his pistol, swaying off balance, his gun barked as he staggered. Jed's bullet hit the mark. The cowboy fell to the floor.

Jed stared at the bleeding cowboy on the floor. The gun drooped in his hand. He was not a killer by nature, not like Viper. The man drew first. It was instinct to protect Breed. He would have done it to protect any of the men.

Jimbo whistled.

"Fuck, that cowboy nearly shot my arm off," Pete grumbled feeling a sting on his arm.

The gunfire quieted the saloon, stopping all conversations in midsentence. The bartender grabbed for his shotgun, which he kept under the bar and a few patrons sought the corners of the room for protection. Suddenly Jed felt a rough hand grab his shoulder.

"Set the gun down," the voice of the hand ordered. Jed obeyed and set the pistol on the table. By now a crowd gathered around the scene.

"He drew first Sheriff," Jake said seeing a badge on

the skinny man's chest. "He was drunk and was gonna shoot Breed here." Jake pointed to the dead cowboy on the floor.

The sheriff looked at Breed. Cowboys hated Indians more than Mexicans. The difference however, no one ever got convicted for killing an Indian, even a half-breed.

"Breed's not packin Sheriff," Jimbo told him.

"We don't serve Indians here. What's he doin in here."

"He's with us. Ain't no sign saying he cain't come in here."

"He can come in. Don't mean they have ta serve him."

"We weren't doin nuttin, Sheriff, just sittin here mindin our own bidness," Jake spoke up.

"I've been winged!" Pete yelled out. Blood stained the sleeve of his shirt and the palm of his hand.

Three of the cowboy's friends were now watching the sheriff closely. Their friend was a hothead. It didn't surprise them he got himself shot, but getting shot over an Indian riled them.

"He was a good man," one of his friends spoke up. "He didn't mean no harm. He was just funnin, if he pulled his gun."

"Just funnin? His gun went off first," Jimbo reported.

"I coudda been kilt," Pete whined.

"Well are yew kilt?" the sheriff asked.

"Damn near close."

Sheriff Nathan Peters put Jed's gun behind his belt. Taking Jed by the arm he said, "Yer comin with me til I sort this out."

Turning to the dead cowboy's friends he ordered, "Yew better git im back to yer camp or to the undertaker, whichever yew want."

"It were murder Sheriff," one of the cowboys tried to get in the last word.

"Maybe it is and maybe it ain't," Sheriff Peters replied. "Go on now and git im outta here and everyone go back to yer bidness," he hollered to the crowd. Turning, he then said directly to Jimbo, "Git that breed outta here and see he don't come back."

Jed gave the sheriff no resistance. It was self-defense pure and simple, even if it was in defense of Breed. Bucking the sheriff now would only cause more trouble, so Jed calmly walked beside him. Once outside Jed said, "Yew dun hafta yank me Sheriff. I'm cumin peaceably."

The sheriff dropped his tight hold on Jed's arm and they walked to the jail. Sheriff Peters pushed in the door. An older somewhat disheveled deputy lounging behind the big desk bolted to attention.

"Jackson, get this prisoner back to cell four."

"Yes sir," the deputy replied. Jackson grabbed Jed's arm and led him to the back. Opening the far cell, he pushed Jed inside and clanged the door shut.

"Was it a shootout?" Jackson asked returning to the front office area.

"He kilt some drunkin cowhand down at the Horseshoe Saloon."

Jed sat on the small cot in the cell. Whiskey still blurred the events of the evening. The jasper was drunk. The gang was just drinking and watching the show, paying the other cowboys no mind. Jed even told the cowboy to take the bottle of whiskey.

Holding his head in his hands, he slumped. It was all about Breed. When Jed looked at Breed he just saw a man, not an Indian. The others treated him well and no one complained. Breed knew about the prejudice against Indians and accepted it, not usually creating any problems. Tonight he should have left well enough alone and maybe he was a bad choice for this trip. Jed settled back on the cot with his hands linked behind his head. Letting the whiskey relax him, he fell asleep.

The next morning Pappy was up first cooking breakfast. He remembered hearing the men ride into camp late last night even though they tried to be quiet. As he stoked up the fire he noticed Jed's bedroll was flat. Last evening he made a list of supplies to stock the chuckwagon.

He had all day today to get the supplies in town and to get the wagon organized in the way he liked. Slicing the last two potatoes into a cast iron skillet heating on the fire, they began to sizzle. The coffee pot was perking on the side of the fire. Jimbo was the first to wake.

"Mornin Pappy," Jimbo said yawning. Stretching his large frame and jerking on his boots, Jimbo walked off toward the river.

Later Corky rolled out from his bedroll with a silly grin on his face remembering last night with Glenda in the back of the wagon. She let him explore her body and they made love three times. Corky never had a gal before. Glenda's skin was soft and her breasts firm. She smelled like a morning rose damp with dew. The scent and the silky spot between her legs drove him wild.

Jake finally rolled over and sat on his bedroll. "Where's Jed?" Pappy asked him.

"In jail."

"Jail? What fer?"

"Kilt a drunk."

"That dun sound like Jed. He's not a hothead," Pappy replied.

"The drunk threatened Breed and shot Pete in the arm."

Corky whistled under his breath.

"The sheriff arrested Jed. Dun know what will happen. It was self-defense," Jake explained.

Pappy made another pot of coffee as the rest of the gang woke up. They talked quietly over breakfast. Breed said nothing.

"Whadda we do now?" Corky asked.

"We wait. The sheriff has to release him after he knows the facts. We need to just sit tight," Jimbo said. "And we don't need no more trouble. Keep low and keep away from those other cowboys til they leave town," Jimbo added.

Jed woke up in jail with a throbbing headache and a bad taste in his mouth. The events of the previous evening swirled in his mind. He was defending Breed. No doubt the drunk cowboy was prepared to shoot. He winged Pete.

"Hey," he yelled toward the front room.

Jackson strode toward the cells. "Yew want coffee?"

"No I want outta here. Yew ain't got no rat to hold me fer self defense."

"It's up to the sheriff," Jackson responded. "Yew want that coffee or not?"

Jed slumped. "Yea. Coffee would be good."

The deputy returned from the other room with a metal cup. He handed it through a slot in the cell bars. "I'll bring yew sum breakfast later. There's a piss pot in the corner."

CHAPTER 20

It was Jed's third day in jail and the sheriff seemed in no hurry to release him. It was self defense, not for his life, but for Breed's. For two days the sheriff told him it was more for his protection. The cowboys from the ruckus at the saloon were still in town and swearing rumors of revenge.

Jimbo came shortly after the sun was up.

"Hey Jed."

"Hey."

"Wanted to git here afor those cowboys got up. We've been keeping close to camp til those jaspers leave town," Jimbo told him.

"Thanks for keeping the gang together. We'll be on the move north soon as I git outta here."

After Jimbo left, Jed sat in the cell pondering the events of the last several days. It was not fair he was in such trouble. Murder was a hanging offense. Pondering his fate made Jed think about the rustling idea. It too could mean death or hanging if they were caught. The grim prospect made the hair at the back of his neck prickle. Deputy Jackson disturbed his thoughts bringing coffee for Jed and the two men in the other cell.

"Mornin."

"Where's the sheriff? When is he gonna let me go?"

"Sheriff Peters will be in later. Yew want sum breakfast?" Jackson asked.

"Later, I guess," Jed said dejected.

The sheriff arrived at the jail after ten in the morning and long after Jed finished breakfast. Jed was pacing in the cell. When he heard the sheriff's voice in the front room he yelled, "Sheriff, let me outta here. Yew got no right ta hold me!"

Sheriff Peters walked back to the cell. His skinny frame made him look even younger than he was, though Jed guessed he was only in his mid twenties. "Yew calm yerself now. Yew shot a man in cold blood. I gotta wait until Judge Van Wagner gits ta yer case so we kin have a trial. Yew ain't his only case."

Jed ignored the sheriff's comment about the judge's case load. "It weren't cold blood. That cowpuncher drew first. It was self defense, plain and simple."

"Weren't yew he was gonna kill. It was a half-breed. That changes everything."

"Don't see how it matters. He drew his gun. He winged one of my men," Jed whined.

"Ain't my fault. There just ain't no black and white law on sumthin like this. I gotta wait fer the judge ta git to yer case."

"An when will that happen?"

"Don't know. Judge Van Wagner's a busy man and got lots of cases ahead of yers. Could be a coupla weeks."

"A couple weeks. I cain't wait that long." Jed fumed and grabbed onto the bars of the cell.

"Well I don't see if yew have much choice. An if yer thinkin yer friends can break yew out, yew just better think again," the sheriff warned him placing a hand on his pistol, then walked back to the front office area.

In Sheriff Nathan Peter's holster, he carried a GSW pistol given to him by the last sheriff, Danny Watkins. Danny retired after he was shot by Roy Reynolds. Nathan was his deputy at the time. The pistol was a gift from Rafael Ortega to the sheriff after the ruckus with the Reynolds several years ago. Rafe had used a similar double-action pistol to kill Roy and Eldon after Roy shot the sheriff and threatened Rafe's uncle.

Danny showed Nathan how the pistol was a huge edge over the single-action pistols most cowboys carried. "It'll save yer life," Danny had told him. Nathan practiced with it frequently and had become a right good shot, but not as good as Rafe. The young Mexican *pistolero* was the fastest draw Nathan ever saw.

The sheriff closed the door to the front office area leaving Jed alone in the cell. Jed slumped back on the cot. Nothing about this plan was going right. Viper never showed up, they lost days bringing the wagon and burying Glenda's parents, and now Jed was stuck in the jail for no good reason.

His men were camped by the river waiting for him to get out. It was his plan to go rustle the herd in San Marcial, but Pete and Jake knew the layout of the Circle B ranch and knew men working there. Nothing might stop them from going on without him. Although it was his idea, Jed doubted the gang would be loyal to him.

The following day Jimbo visited Jed in the afternoon. After checking in his gun, Sheriff Peters let Jimbo into the cell and brought a checkerboard and set of checkers.

"That herd moved out yesterday afternoon, so I let the boys come to town last night."

"At least nuttin else happened." Jed was thankful the cowboys had not retaliated. Perhaps it was better he had been in jail out of their reach.

"King me," Jimbo said as he jumped two of Jed's checkers and reached the king row.

The diversion to the otherwise boredom in the cell was a welcome change. Jed told Jimbo what the sheriff said about the judge.

"Got yew this game," Jimbo said as he jumped Jed's last piece. "Setter up again."

After a while when Jimbo thought the deputy was out of earshot and the two men in the other cell were not listening, he spoke quietly. "The men are restless. They may not wait til the judge hears yer trial."

"Don't blame em. Dumbass sheriff says it's causa Breed. That cowpuncher was gonna shoot Breed and it's legal to kill an Indian. So he's not sure iffin it is self defense. I'd do it again. Dumbass, drunk cowpoke shudda kept to his own friends and left us alone. We weren't hurtin nobody."

"Breed's mighty thankful. He told the others, not many a man would defend him. He'll stick around and so will Pappy and Corky."

"How about yew?"

"I'm here ain't I?"

"Yeah, thanks."

"Been thinkin. Maybe I shud send Pete and Jake up to that thar cattle ranch to scout it out. Yew said they know where it is. They could find out how many head and how many men are protectin the herd, stuff like that," Jimbo suggested. "Maybe there ain't no herd and we all wastin our time sittin around."

"That's a purdy good idea. They could see what men from the Circle B are still there and how many greasers the widder hired."

"By the time they git back, yew should be outta here."

When Jimbo left and Jed had some time to think, he thought the plan a good one. Pete and Jake were not smart enough to pull off this rustle without help. His only worry was them shooting off their big mouths when they were in San Marcial and ruining everything.

CHAPTER 21

On the last Friday in June, Santa Fe was washed clean from a heavy persistent rain over the previous two days. The heavens poured leaving the air clean, the roads muddy, and delaying Rafe and Carlos' departure. Rafe and Ana Teresa were in the barn stowing gear on the packhorse. Ana Teresa was helping Rafe finish final preparations for the trip to Torreón, Mexico. He and Carlos were leaving this morning as soon as Carlos arrived.

"I should be going with you," Ana Teresa complained.

"My mother will be disappointed, but you must be here when your mother and father arrive," Rafe told her.

"I know. Carlos promised me to keep you safe," she repeated what they had talked about several times. Her parents would be arriving soon and expecting her here in Santa Fe.

"I saved his life more than once. No doubt I will have to keep him safe," Rafe responded and laughed trying to keep the mood light. "Reymundo will take you to your uncle's house later this morning. I hope the baby will not keep you up all night. Carlos told me the baby is more fussy lately," Rafe warned her.

"Yes, Bibiana told me. She is dripping cold chamomile tea in his mouth and says it seems to calm him down. I will remember it when we have our children," she said reaching out and putting her palm on his face. For the last several nights, Ana Teresa clung to Rafe in the dark. Their lovemaking, although somewhat curtailed since the Summers family returned home, had grown in passion and desire.

"Follow me," he took her hand.

"Where are you taking me *señor?*" she asked and resisted slightly.

"Come, do not be afraid of me *señorita,*" he teased her when he felt her resist.

"You are mistaken *señor.* I am no longer a *señorita.* I am a married woman," she protested with a smile, but allowed herself to be pulled into an empty horse stall.

"Yes you are, and I am the luckiest man in Santa Fe to have the most beautiful woman for my wife. Come with me, you will not be disappointed. I promise," he enticed her. Pulling her to the back of the dark stall, his hands found her breasts as his mouth found hers. He sought her response as his kisses devoured her neck working their way to the tops of her breasts.

Teasingly she pushed away from him. "You are a devil *señor.* I think you just want your way with me."

"Yes, now and forever," he responded and pulled her to him.

An orange, pink, and gray sunrise hung above the Sangre de Cristo mountain range as Carlos shook hands with *don* Pedro in the courtyard. The rain stopped last night, leaving the courtyard muddy.

"I will take care of Bibiana and my grandson," *don* Pedro assured him. Carlos already said his goodbyes to his wife and cuddled Benicío. Torn between staying and leaving, his heart was heavy.

"I promise I will be home as soon as possible. Ana Teresa will be here later this morning," Carlos said.

Don Pedro nodded. "I will do as we decided. *Don* Bartolo will believe Ana Teresa is still a *señorita,* but Rafael must return immediately to face him and tell him the truth."

Carlos nodded and stepped up onto Santiago's back. Rafe told him to only bring his personal gear. Everything they needed would be provided on a packhorse.

As Carlos rode into the Summers' courtyard, Rafe was bringing the packhorse from barn.

"Hola, I'm ready to go," Rafe called to him.

Reymundo held eight-year-old Rayo's reins. The Appaloosa pranced side to side and whinnied and snorted with excitement. Santiago, Carlos' black stallion stood quietly. Both horses were bred in Mexico on *don* Bernardo's hacienda. Santiago was four years younger than Rayo and almost as tall.

"Glad the rain stopped," Carlos commented.

"I am glad it did too. Everything is ready."

Ana Teresa ran out of the barn looking a bit disheveled. When she reached Rafael, they clung to each other for one last kiss, before he untangled her arms and jumped up on Rayo's back.

"Let's go," Rafe said.

Rafe waved to Ana Teresa. Josefina had joined her on the veranda and they both waved goodbye. This was not Rafe and Carlos' first trip to Mexico together. Each trip, though carefully planned had brought surprises. Rafe hoped this trip would be quick and without trouble.

Carlos was looking forward to whatever adventure awaited them. He loved his wife and new baby and enjoyed his teaching position at the Catholic school, but it was summer and he looked forward to the trip. The newborn baby was the adored focus of everyone's attention in the de Soto household. Carlos thought Bibiana was accepting all the help she could get and not trying to regain her strength. Perhaps by the time he got home, she would be ready to return to their house and renew their personal life.

The man riding next to him was as close as a true brother. They were bound by both honor and friendship, not blood. Now that Carlos felt released from his real brother Benicío's ghost, his soul was freed. He finally felt forgiven for killing Benicío and looked forward to a long and happy life with Bibiana and more children.

Throughout the day they rode at various speeds, sometimes galloping and other times allowing the horses to walk. They talked and laughed recalling other adventures to pass the time.

"Rafe, I need to stop in San Marcial to see my cousin Tomás. He sent me a package containing the Armijo land grant documents and a letter asking me to present the documents to the land office for verification. I need to take the documents back to him."

"Is it all in order?"

"Yes. He was worried about the Governor's proclamation. He said a few squatters showed up in the area not long ago," Carlos said as they rode toward Albuquerque.

"There's trouble coming. People from the east are finding out about land here in the territories and are taking big risks coming here to get their share. It was lawyers who took your father's hacienda, now it is people buying illegally sold land."

"Yes, I fear for all the Spaniards, whether they can produce their land grants or not. The squatters will not look on Spanish land grants as valid. They don't care about what happened so many years ago and will not believe in Spain's sovereignty over the land. It is America now."

"I agree with you Carlos. Change is coming and coming fast," Rafe said with a sigh.

Chapter 22

A blazing red horizon over the San Mateo Mountain range to the west greeted Rafe and Carlos as they rode down the main street of San Marcial after three long days on the trail south from Santa Fe. The village was quiet and no people were out in the streets, as it was nearly supper time. They rode straight to the mayor's house, Carlos' cousin. The stableman greeted them and took the horses. They dusted their clothes, before they knocked on Tomás' door.

"*¡Bienvenidos!*" Tomás Armijo exclaimed surprised to see his cousin and Rafe. "Why did you not write you were coming?"

"There was no time, *primo*. I hope our visit finds you well," Carlos said to his cousin.

"*Bienvenidos,*" Tomás' wife Teresa greeted them. "Come, supper will be on the table shortly. I will have the cook fix two more plates."

"*Gracias, Teresa,*" Carlos said and gave her an *abrazo*. Rafe did likewise, before they were escorted to the dining room.

"What brings you this way?" Tomás asked as he handed them each a brandy.

"Rafael asked me to go with him to Torreón for his mother's wedding," Carlos replied.

"Your mother? I thought your mother was living with you in Santa Fe."

The weather was warm and Tomás led them out to the covered veranda. The Armijo hacienda ran on both sides of the wide Rio Grande, the house stood on a knoll on the west side of the river. The river was shallow near his hacienda, especially in the dry summer months, but had been known to flood.

"It is a long story, an unbelievable one in fact. I found someone to love and now so has she. One day, I will tell you about how she met Billy," Rafe told him not wanting to go into great detail.

"Congratulations are in order for you and Ana Teresa."

"Have you not heard? Carlos is a proud new *papá,*" Rafe asked.

"What! We had not heard the news." Tomás grabbed Carlos in an *abrazo* and slapped him on his back. "Now we must make a special toast to your health and the health of the baby."

When Teresa came to the door, Tomás told her the news. Squealing in joy she quickly grabbed Carlos in a hug. "How could you leave the little one and Bibiana?" she asked.

"Bibiana has more help than she needs and Ana Teresa will stay with her, but I miss them both already. By the way Tomás, I took the land grant documents to the land office and everything is in order. Are you having trouble here in San Marcial?" Carlos asked.

"No not yet, but it will happen. I was told there was trouble with land being sold illegally down near Monticello. There has been bloodshed on both sides. I am told the people who bought the land will not give it up and are well armed. I guess, I cannot blame them, if they think they bought the land legally. Some of the land grants are not well defined and some of the original documents are lost or misplaced. Unscrupulous land sellers know this and are taking advantage of the document problems," Tomás told them.

"It is the same in Las Vegas and the *dons* in Santa Fe are worried. We see a bad time ahead for the territory. Many people may die because of land disputes," Rafe responded.

"I have studied my grant and have found the markers. Just to be sure I have my men fixing them and making sure they are properly marked as Armijo. Still I worry. Who knows what the government will do about the grants. American land officials are scrutinizing the land documents and not saying what they will do," Tomás told them.

"There is a powerful and corrupt alliance of lawyers, judges, and territorial officials the people are calling the Santa Fe Ring. They manipulate the legal system knowing it is foreign to Spanish-speaking landowners. If the original land grant cannot be produced, they sell the land to the highest bidder. Even if a Spaniard can produce the grant, they are complicating the process and saying the grants are invalid," Carlos divulged what he knew.

"Yes Carlos is right. The newcomers could care less about land granted long ago from the King of Spain or the government of Mexico. This is a United States territory and land can be bought or taken. In the newspaper I read where in Oklahoma they just grabbed any land they could. Mostly there it was Indian territory or open range. The Indians fought back, but the government stood behind the squatters and sent in troops," Rafe explained.

"I heard some local sheriffs and U.S. Marshals are trying to maintain order. Individual landowners cannot patrol their own land. The plots are too large and remote in some cases. Sometimes squatters have already built a house and barn before the rightful landowner knows they are there. I'm lucky my grant is much smaller and my men are keeping a watchful eye," Tomás said.

"Some Spaniards are beginning to organize hoping to take care of the problem themselves. *Don* Pedro has joined with many other *dons* in Santa Fe to help each other after they heard a *don* and his *vaqueros* tried to run off squatters north of San Gabriel and a gun battle erupted. The *don* was killed, as well as two of his *vaqueros*. Several squatters were also killed, including a woman and a child. All the surrounding squatters are banding together for protection. It seems an all out war is inevitable, the newcomers against the original families who settled and received land grants generations ago," Carlos added.

Ever since General Stephen W. Kearny and his troops entered Santa Fe claiming the New Mexico Territory for the United States in 1846, Spaniards and Americans lived in peace. The New Mexico Territory was only a stop on the way to California. It was not destination for

Americans. Even Arizona was growing faster than New Mexico. However, the Santa Fe Ring was trying to change that fact. They knew the Spanish had little faith in the American legal system or did not understand it. When it came to land disputes, the *dons* mostly lost. The Santa Fe Ring of lawyers and politicians deliberately extended the duration of litigation, at times taking years before a decision was rendered for or against the Spaniards. In the meantime they protected squatter's rights.

They talked long into the evening about the political problems. Tomás was not only worried for himself and his family. He was the mayor of San Marcial and the only form of law. The people in the village looked to him for guidance.

The next morning, Rafe and Carlos left San Marcial just before sunup wanting to get to Las Cruces by the evening and through El Paso the following day. From there it should take them four or five days to get to Torreón.

Jake and Pete rode north on the trail and were many miles north of El Paso on their way to the Circle B ranch south of San Marcial. Jimbo asked them to ride north and look over the situation at the ranch while Jed was stuck in jail.

As they rode, two men came into view standing near their horses. One man was unloading a packhorse while the other was inspecting one of the horse's hoofs.

"Yew need hep mister?" Pete asked as they rode up.

The two men were dressed in suits and one wore a black Stetson. As the men looked up, Pete was surprised to see they were Mexicans.

"I think the packhorse is going lame," Rafe responded.

"That's a bad break. El Paso ain't so far. Anythin we kin do?" Jake asked.

"No, much obliged."

"Hope you make it to El Paso." Pete smiled showing a missing tooth and held out his hand.

As the two cowboys rode north, Pete was perplexed.

The well-dressed Mexican in the Stetson looked familiar. The one with the long scar down his cheek was a stranger for sure. He would have remembered that face. The other with the lean handsome face and straight white teeth conjured up some memory.

"Hey Jake, yew ever seen that Mex in the black Stetson afore?"

"Nah."

"Yew shur?"

"Them Mexes all look alike ta me," Jake replied.

Later in the early evening, Rafe and Carlos rode into Hastings Livery. Jumping down Rafe called out, "Charlie, Charlie Hastings!"

"Well I's be if it ain't Mista Rafe. How yew be?" Charlie Hastings came out of a stall and headed toward Rafe. He took Rafe's hand in his big bear paw and squeezed it hard.

"Hello Charlie. I need some help. This packhorse is going lame. Do you have one I can buy?" Rafe asked.

"Sur, I gotta good one. Where's yew goin?"

"Mexico. Billy and my mother are getting married," Rafe told him. Last winter Billy worked several weeks for Charlie while Rafe and Ana Teresa were in El Paso.

"Billy and yo momma?" Charlie asked laughing. "Why I's be."

"Yes it is hard to believe, but they fell in love in Santa Fe. Billy drove her back to Mexico to help my sister with her new baby. They plan to live there."

"I's get the packhorse ready to go fer yew in the mornin. That ok?"

"Thanks Charlie. Have our belongings taken to the hotel. We'll be back early to get started. We are already behind our schedule."

Rafe led the way out of the livery, leaving Rayo and Santiago in Charlie's care. As they walked past Lillie Jean's Saloon, familiar tinny piano music floated out, along with the stale aroma of smoke. Nothing changes, Rafe thought, except for Roy and Eldon Reynolds were no longer on this earth. The memory of those two scoundrels tickled the nape of his neck. Walking to the end of the sidewalk, Rafe continued to the tented part of El Paso, called Chinatown.

"Two baths," Rafe told the small old Chinese man who greeted them at the tent opening.

"U want smokee?" the old man asked, if they wanted to smoke opium.

"No, just a bath," Rafe told him handing the man several coins.

"Farrow me prease," he said, turned, and led them through the silks hiding the back of the tent. The pungent smell of opium filled the air. Opening the flap to a larger tent, an older woman bowed to them. The old man spoke to her in Chinese, then she clapped her hands twice loudly and waved for Rafe and Carlos to follow.

Large wooden vat-shaped tubs stood in a row. Four young Chinese girls entered carrying buckets of steaming water. The girls were dressed in silk pajamas. The pale silks were embroidered in flowers and birds. After three trips with the steaming buckets, the older woman motioned for Rafe and Carlos to strip.

The girls led Rafe and Carlos to separate tubs then left. The steam smelled of hibiscus flowers.

"Ahh, this feels wonderful," Carlos said half groaning and half sighing as the hot water soaked his body.

"Have you never enjoyed a Chinese bath?" Rafe asked.

"No."

"George introduced me to this simple pleasure on our first trip through El Paso."

After they soaked a little while, the four girls returned. Each carried a bar of soap and a sponge. Kneeling on either side of the tubs, they reached in with a sponge and began soaping and scrubbing Rafe and Carlos.

"Hey," Carlos blurted out as one of the girls grabbed and scrubbed his privates. The other girls giggled. Rafe closed his eyes and enjoyed the four hands wandering over his body.

Refreshed after the bath, Rafe and Carlos laughed as

they made their way to the hotel.

"You should have told me about the bath girls," Carlos chided Rafe.

"Were you embarrassed? Or perhaps you liked it too much," Rafe bantered back.

They were still bantering when they passed by Lilli Jean's Saloon. Engrossed in their conversation, the batwing doors pushed open in their path and a cowboy strode out bumping into Carlos, almost knocking him down.

"Watch whar the fuck yer walkin Mex," the drunken cowboy yelled out and pushed Carlos with both hands hitting his chest and pushing him backwards.

"Hey, back off," Carlos warned and held his ground.

"Dun yew sass me yew fuckin greaser. Yew better go fer yer gun," the cowboy challenged him and stepped back and placed his right hand near his holster.

"I do not need a gun to best the likes of you," Carlos replied defiantly.

The drunk cowboy hesitated when he saw Carlos was not armed and quickly looked at Rafe's guns and demanded, "Yew, yew give im yer gun!"

"I suggest you be on your way. My friend does not like guns, but if you have a sword he'll take you on, or drop your gun and he'll take you on with his fists," Rafe told him. "But if you still insist on guns, I'll be your huckleberry." The challenge came out of a lingering old rage Rafe carried with him, a rage now hidden deep in his soul from his *peón* upbringing. Though not a killer by nature, Rafe would not stand down.

The cowboy was confused by the whiskey, looked from Carlos to Rafe and back to Carlos. Rafe calmly and purposely took two side steps to face the cowboy and dropped his hands by his guns.

"Ah rat greaser, time yew learnt sum manners, Texas style," the cowboy hissed. How dare this greaser talk down to him. The cowboy squared up toward Rafe and put his hand on the butt of his pistol when a loud voice interrupted the scene.

"Vern Miller, what the fuck yew doin?" Sheriff

Nathan Peters asked sternly.

The sheriff pushed his way between Rafe and Carlos and stood in front of them with his fists on his hips staring at the cowboy. "One of those greasers pushed me sheriff and the other called me out. Go away Nathan, I kin take care of these Mescans myself."

Rafe had not recognized Nathan Peters. He was still skinny, but probably twenty pounds heavier and his voice had an air of authority. The cowboy called him sheriff.

"Yer gonna git yerself kilt, Vern. This man is a *pistolero* from Santa Fe and be the same man who gunned down the Reynolds boys."

"I ain't skirt of this fuckin greaser and those Reynolds were nuttin but trash. Move aside Sheriff!" The redeye whiskey in Vern's brain kept him from listening. Side stepping the sheriff, Vern tried to get his eyes back on the greaser.

Nathan pulled out his pistol lighting fast and pointed it at Vern. "Come with me Vern, yer under arrest. Rafe yew and yer friend go about yer bidness."

"What the fuck yew doin Nathan?" Vern whined.

"I'm savin yer life Vern," the sheriff explained to the drunk cowboy.

Nathan Peters tipped his hat. "Nice to see yew again Rafe. Yew stayin fer a while?"

"No, we're headed to Mexico in the morning."

"Well yew say hello the next time yew cum through town." Nathan pulled Vern by the arm toward the jail leaving Rafe and Carlos staring at his back.

"You know him?" Carlos asked.

"He used to be the deputy. He helped save my life when I had trouble here in El Paso. He sure has grown up and now he's the sheriff. Good for him."

CHAPTER 23

From a distance Rafe and Carlos spotted smoke rising from the town of Chihuahua, Mexico. Tired from riding long hours, they looked forward to a good meal and a soft bed.

"There is a hotel near the city center I have stayed at on several trips to Mexico City," Carlos said.

"Well, let's go there. Do they have baths and a livery?" Rafe asked worried about the horses. Rayo and Santiago were blooded horses and could easily be the target of thieves. They would bring a high price.

"Yes and a good restaurant too."

Long shadows stretched across the town by the time they reached the hotel.

"Buenas tardes señores," a man standing on the front steps greeted them.

"Buenas tardes," Carlos replied. "We need the horses tended and secured."

"Si señor. I will make sure they are well cared for." Carlos jumped down from Santiago and handed the man a *peso.* He pulled his saddlebags from the black horse while Rafe dismounted. Rafe untied both his saddlebags and took his rifle with him, then they walked up the steps and into the hotel.

The cool lobby was tastefully decorated with Spanish colonial art and overstuffed chairs and a couch. Several business men sat around a table shuffling papers. Their talk was animated, as they discussed the papers, perhaps a business deal. Two other men sat in the overstuffed chairs smoking cigars and reading newspapers.

An elderly man greeted them at the front desk looking at them over wire rim spectacles, *"Bienvenidos. ¿Norte Americanos?"* He welcomed them and asked if they were North Americans.

"Yes. A room and a bath for each of us," Carlos ordered and signed the registry.

"Si Señor Zuniga," the desk clerk acknowledged the name from the ledger book.

"Tell me which is the best restaurant in town?" Carlos asked.

"There is trouble in the city *señores.* If I were you I would not stray far from the hotel," the desk clerk warned them.

"Are our horses safe in the livery?" Rafe spoke up.

"Si señor, but the streets are not safe, especially for two well-dressed *Norte Americanos,"* he replied.

It was late evening by the time they cleaned up. Heeding the desk clerk's warning, they stayed to eat at the hotel's restaurant. There were only a few tables occupied by what looked like businessmen.

"Why is it not busy here?" Carlos asked the waiter.

"Mexico is not a safe place right now *señor.* There is much unrest and *bandidos* are taking advantage of travelers," the waiter said and took their order.

"Why?" Rafe asked.

"Ever since *Presidente* Benito Juárez died last year, General Porfirio Díaz has been stirring up rebellions across the country. The general never accepted losing the presidency to a *Indio.* He always disrespected President Juárez calling him an ugly Indian. Now he is going after our new president, Sebastián Lerdo de Tejada. Tejada will not last long as *presidente*, if General Díaz prevails," the waiter informed them.

"Were you aware of all this unrest?" Rafe asked Carlos.

"My uncle David has been writing to me. There have been riots in Mexico City. It is troubling. Tejada is continuing the reforms started by Juárez. General Díaz is supported by the aristocracy. He is a traditionalist and he and his supporters want to return to the caste system and control the *peóns,"* Carlos explained.

Rafe nodded thinking how he benefited from President Juárez' reforms. Because of changes to the laws, *mestizos* such as himself, could inherit land. He inherited the Reyes hacienda.

"I don't like it Carlos. If Díaz is starting a revolution, it could mean trouble for Rodolfo and María. What about the hacienda? Do you think the government could reverse my claim?" Rafe asked.

"I don't know."

"My poor mother and Billy. Billy could be killed just because he is a gringo. You know that could happen or they could rescind my deed to the property," Rafe said.

"Yes, I know. In Santa Fe the *dons* think Díaz will be the next president of Mexico. When Juárez became president Díaz resigned his military command and went home to Oaxaca. He led a rebellion against Juárez' second election, but failed. Then, Tejada assumed the presidency after Juárez died last year and offered amnesty to the rebels. Díaz again retired to his *hacienda* in Veracruz, though he still has many supporters," Carlos repeated what he his uncle had written to him.

"I see trouble coming for my family, Carlos. Mexico is a volatile place, always has been, but Rodolfo, María, and my mother love Mexico and would never leave," Rafe expressed his fears.

All was quiet in the city the following morning when Rafe and Carlos rode south toward Torreón after a good night's sleep. Rafe calculated it would take four or five days to reach the hacienda. He was excited about returning to his birthplace. He could ride into Torreón on Rayo with his head held high and without fear. *Don* Bernardo was dead and Rafe's family now owned all that was left of the Reyes' wealth. Unfortunately, the hacienda had been ransacked and needed plenty of money and work to get it up and running properly.

"Carlos, we must stay alert."

"I agree. If the waiter is right about trouble, we better be careful and ready if anyone approaches us," Carlos added.

Most nights on the trip they stayed in stage stops or small inns. However, on the first day south of Chihuahua, Rafe noticed the horses seemed tired. He was not prepared to put either horse in danger by pushing too far. They found a small creek lined with cottonwood trees for their evening campsite. Rafe hobbled the horses at a nearby grassy spot, while Carlos prepared a meal for them. They sat drinking a hot chocolate before Rafe took the first watch.

"Wake me up to take the next watch." Carlos curled near the fire wrapped in a blanket.

Rafe walked along the creek, first south, then north. All was quiet except for the disharmony of the nocturnal insects sounding their presence. A coyote howled and yipped only to be answered by a mate or partner from a distance. He walked to check on the horses. Rayo did not like being hobbled and snorted several times complaining to Rafe. Stroking the horse's neck and face, Rafe spoke quietly and it seemed to calm him. He added another log to the fire and sat leaning against a cottonwood and listened to the night.

Rafe woke Carlos when the moon was high in the sky, then curled under his blanket. Carlos woke him as the eastern sky was just beginning to lighten.

"You should have wakened me sooner," Rafe said.

"I was awake and meditating. It is good for you to sleep," Carlos responded.

Rafe was familiar with Carlos' ways. Schooled at a Catholic seminary in Spain, Carlos remained devout, though not a man of the cloth. He meditated every morning thanking God for the day and asking for guidance.

After a cup of coffee and a quick breakfast, they continued south. To fill the time they talked of many things.

"Carlos, there is something you need to know before we arrive in Torreón," Rafe started to tell Carlos something which he had kept secret.

"I thought we had no secrets? What have you never told me?" Carlos retorted with a jovial laugh. He and Rafe shared many adventures and Carlos thought he knew everything about Rafe's life.

"I want to tell you how Ana Teresa and I met Billy."

"Billy?" Carlos replied surprised the secret concerned

Billy Swanson.

"You know how the vigilantes ran us out of Los Angeles and the northern roads were closed because of snow and we headed for El Paso last Christmas. The stagecoach stopped at a waystation some thirty miles east of Fort Yuma. At the waystation, Billy burst in yielding a broken pistol, demanding a steak and a bottle of redeye, and spouting he was horny as hell. He called himself Desperate Billy."

Carlos laughed at the name. "Desperate Billy? Why would he call himself that?"

"Billy had broken out of the Fort Yuma stockade and trekked across the Arizona desert for days and was hungry and thirsty when he got to the stage stop," Rafe continued.

"He was in the Army? Why was he in the stockade?" Carlos asked. No one ever mentioned Billy's past, except he was a blacksmith.

"He punched a young hothead officer. Billy's friends broke him out and he found his way to the waystation. He was quite desperate at the time for food and water and to get away from the fort. It seems comical to me now, but as the cook responded to his demands, Billy looked around for a woman."

"Of course he spotted Ana Teresa," Carlos said nodding his head.

"Yes, he grabbed her and put her between me and him. I would have shot him on the spot, but could not take a chance and hit Ana Teresa. When the cook placed the steak and whiskey bottle in a sack, Billy told Ana Teresa to take it. Well, she took it and slammed it at Billy with all her might. I came up with both my pistols pointed at him," Rafe said, paused, and laughed.

"And you did not shoot him?" Carlos asked shocked and wondering why Rafe was laughing.

"Ana Teresa told me not to. Later she told me she thought he was not a bad man, just scared. The manager of the waystation locked him up in the barn behind the station, but he escaped and jumped on the stagecoach down the trail. He told us his story and Ana Teresa felt sorry for him. I guess we both did. I paid for his ticket to El Paso."

"Hard to believe. He sure did seem likable," Carlos responded.

"He told me he was a blacksmith and we needed help at the foundry. It was Ana Teresa's idea for him to ride shotgun on the wagon with the stolen silver," Rafe finished.

"Wait! I know you brought a wagon with silver to Santa Fe. You stole it?"

"Not me, Rodolfo stole it."

Carlos put his head down and shook it. "I guess there are several things you have kept secret from me."

Rafe filled the long empty hours telling Carlos about Rodolfo, the stolen silver, and how Jerry Carr and Bo Preston tried to steal it.

CHAPTER 24

Jimbo bellied up at the bar. He started coming to Lilli Jean's Saloon instead of the Horseshoe after the incident where Jed killed the cowboy, despite the fact the event which landed Jed in jail had long been forgotten. In El Paso, like most western cow towns, killings happened frequently and forgotten quickly.

He was drinking alone. Jake and Pete rode north to San Marcial five days ago to scout the Sutton ranch, Pappy seldom came to town except for supplies, Breed steered clear of town, and Corky was smitten with Glenda. A shot of whiskey and beer sat on the bar in front of him.

Jimbo worried about the ragtag would-be rustlers. It was never much of a gang anyway. Viper was supposed to be the lead gunhand and was no doubt dead. Pappy was old, Corky was green behind the ears, and Breed might be more of a hindrance than a help. Secretly he was beginning to hope Jake and Pete returned from the greaser town with news the herd had been already sold.

Every day he went to the jail to visit Jed. It was tiresome. Jimbo felt it was his responsibility to keep the gang organized. He signaled the bartender for another shot while subconsciously hearing the batwing doors slap the side walls as they were hit by a brute of a man who strode in with spurs jangling.

The man wore a tall tan Stetson hat with a silver band around it. Long blond hair curled out from under it. A big round ruddy face went along with the brute of a body. A large red bandana hung around his neck with the triangle tip pointing down to his chest, covering most of his blue shirt. The large man strode to the bar and thumped a deformed right hand on the bar top.

"Whiskey barkeep," he said.

"Cumin rat up." The bartender quickly poured a shot in a small glass. As he went to move the bottle, the man's deformed claw hand stopped him. "Leave it."

The brute looked over at the men standing along the bar, then took a second look before he hollered out, "Jimbo, what the hell r yew doin so far away frum Round Rock?"

Startled hearing his name, Jimbo looked up to see a man he only ever heard called Crabclaw standing down the bar. He never heard how Crabclaw came to get his deformed right hand, which looked a bit like the claw of a crab. The rumors about the deformed man ranged from gunslinger or rustler to an evil killer. Jimbo thought most of the rumors were based upon his appearance. He frequently came through Round Rock on his travels and to Jimbo's knowledge he was not on any wanted poster.

"Hey Crabclaw. How yew been?" Jimbo answered and walked over. Crabclaw stuck out his left hand and Jimbo shook it.

"Yew want sum of this?" he asked grabbing the bottle's neck with his right thumb and his deformed fingers. It looked like the fingers were fused together, but he had no trouble lifting the bottle and pouring a perfect shot.

"Not rat now, I got sum," Jimbo downed his shot and lifted his beer chaser. "Why yew in El Paso?" he asked Crabclaw.

"Well, I was makin easy money rustling a few head from both sides of the border down around the bend," Crabclaw lowered his voice and made sure the barkeep was down the bar. "The man I was workin with had a buyer fer rustled cattle fer a good price. The buyer was shippin em down river to sumplace on the Guf of Mexico. From there I ain't shur where they went. Anyways, the Rangers caught up to us south of the village of Marfa moving a stolen herd. I managed ta git away, but sum of the other fellers got caught."

The barkeep walked near them and they busied themselves sipping the liquor.

"Why yew here?" Crabclaw asked.

"We been on a long haul from Round Rock, but one of our gang is in jail. We bidin our time til he gits out,"

Jimbo told him.

"Then whar the hell yew goin?" Crabclaw asked. Jimbo was a bit surprised Crabclaw's demeanor was open and friendly and he did not seem as intimidating as his appearance suggested.

"We'r on our way up ta New Mexico."

"What'r yew aimin ta do up there?"

"We gonna hep a widder woman with a herd of cattle and move em to Wyomin." Jimbo made it sound more like a job. "Yew goin back ta Round Rock?" Jimbo asked.

"I dun know rat now. Been here a couple days. Guess I'll stay round here whar I kin slip on across the border iffin the Rangers cum lookin fer me."

Jimbo and Crabclaw drank and talked for several hours. Finally Jimbo headed back to the camp, but had an idea percolating in his brain.

The following morning Jimbo ate breakfast at the camp and headed to town to see Jed. It had been a week since Jimbo sent Jake and Pete to the greaser town to see about the herd. Jed was still in jail, fuming, but unable to get the sheriff to change his mind. The judge was too busy. Sheriff Peters asked for a quick ruling, but the judge said he had never heard such a case and needed time to research it.

Each day Jimbo rode to the jail and helped Jed pass the time playing checkers or just talking. He kept him updated on the men. This morning he came with an idea he needed to talk over with Jed.

"Good mornin Jimbo," the older deputy greeted him by name.

"Good mornin Jackson. I brung Jed some of Pappy's cookin," Jimbo told him as he walked toward the back cell area.

"Hey, gotta have yer gun. Yew know the rules."

Jimbo dropped his gunbelt on the desk and Jackson let him into Jed's cell.

"Thanks," Jed said uncovering a plate of biscuits, bacon, and fried potatoes.

"I see Vern's back in. What did he do this time?"

Jimbo asked seeing Vern Miller snoring on the cot in the first cell. Over Jed's time in the jail, several others had come and gone. Vern Miller had spent a night last week after provoking two Mexicans for a draw.

"Heard the deputy scold him fer eggin fer a fight again. Seems like he gits mean when he's drunk," Jed replied.

"Did Jake and Pete git back yet?" Jed asked changing the subject.

"Not yet. Spect them soon. Just how far north is that thar town?"

"I dun know. Maybe couple hunderd miles. Any other problums?"

"Nah, just Corky and Glenda. They'r a sparkin."

Jed had all but forgotten about Glenda Bell. She was mighty pretty and Corky was only a couple years older than her.

"When did that start?"

"Dun ratly know. Maybe they was doin it in private, but now everybody knows it. She's teaching Corky to shoot."

"She's teaching him?" Jed asked surprised.

"Yeah, she's a fair good shot. Says her pappy learnt her."

Jimbo won the third game of checkers in a row. "Come on Jed. Yew better'n that."

"I'm sick of this cell and I'm sick of checkers," he stood and beat a fist against the cell door making it clang. "Do yew hear me! I'm sick of waitin fer that stinkin judge. It ain't fair!"

Quietly he whispered to Jimbo, "Yew gotta git me outta here."

"Yew loco? We'd both end up dangling on a rope," Jimbo replied.

"I do have an idea. Yew member a feller named Crabclaw?"

"Shur. He's got a bum hand with fingers looks like a claw."

"Well I ran into him last night over ta Lilli Jean's. He

told me he was rustling a herd to Mexico, but the Rangers got wind of it and now he's just kickin around," Jimbo said quietly lowering his voice to a whisper so the deputy would not hear.

"So?"

"Whatcha think we ask him to join up. We could use a gunhand to replace Viper and Crabclaw, he's trustworthy," Jimbo suggested.

Jed vaguely knew Crabclaw, knew more of him from rumors. He was supposed to be tough and Jed heard talk he was a rustler. His deformed claw hand did not stop him from hard work nor using a pistol with his left hand.

"We could use another man. Dun say nuttin yet. We gotta wait fer Jake and Pete ta git back and fer the fuckin judge to hear my case so I kin git outta here," Jed told Jimbo.

Deputy Jackson walked back toward the cells. "Yew fellers want sum coffee? I just perked a new pot."

CHAPTER 25

Two days later, Rafe and Carlos arrived at the village of Jiménez, in the state of Chihuahua. The sun was losing its brilliance and the oppressive July heat was dissipating. By night the desert would cool down drastically.

To the west over the Sierra Madre mountains, a fiery red glow silhouetted the highest peak and spread across their path into town. Rafe and Carlos welcomed the sight of Jiménez, hoping they would find lodging where they could cool down and a soft bed to sleep.

They had traveled near Jiménez on their trip south to kidnap Rafe's mother and sister from *don* Bernardo's hacienda several years ago, however on that trip Rafe and Carlos were traveling incognito and slept in the wagon outside of town.

"Carlos, do you know this town?" Rafe asked.

"No, I mostly traveled by stagecoach and it never stopped here. It looks big enough to find food and a place to sleep."

They rode in on a dusty road to the center of the town towing the packhorse, where they found a small hotel above a restaurant. When they pulled up in front of the hitching rail, a man dressed in white cotton *camisa* and *pantalones* ran out to take the horses. Rafe pulled a *peso* from his pocket and handed it to the man.

"Gracias señor," he said with a broad smile showing several teeth missing.

Pulling their saddlebags and weapons they walked up the steps and into the lobby.

"Buenas tardes señores. ¿Cómo puedo ayudarte?" a young man wearing a white shirt with a thin black bowtie greeted them from behind the counter and asked how he could help them.

"Habitación para la noche," Carlos told the clerk they wanted rooms for the night. He then asked about where to wash up and about the restaurant.

"You can go out back to wash up and the restaurant has good food," the clerk assured them.

"What about our horses?" Rafe asked.

"Do not worry *señor,* Manuel will take good care of them."

"Have them ready to go at sunup tomorrow. We plan to leave early," Carlos told him.

Later they were seated at a table by the front window of the restaurant. The waiter informed them what was on the menu for the evening. "Beef steaks or *cabrito al pastor* made of roasted goat or *burritas,*" which he explained were wheat-flour tortillas wrapped around a filling of *machaca,* dried beef with peppers.

They both ordered a beef steak and a beer while they waited. Before long they were served the steak with tortillas and rice along with whole pinto beans. After the meal the waiter served them sopaipillas, pieces of dough deep fried to create a small pillow. The desserts were smothered with brown sugar and molasses.

"The clerk was right about the food. It is delicious," Rafe said wiping a drip of molasses from his lips.

As they were savoring the delicious dessert, a commotion erupted outside. Rafe looked through the unwashed window and saw several *Federales,* Mexican Federal Police, pushing and yelling at a small group of ragged *peóns* to move forward. The police were armed with rifles and used the butt ends to push them along. Rafe asked the waiter where the police were taking them.

"Those men will be shot in the morning to send a message to the *peóns.* They are innocent. Ever since President Juárez died, the *desgraciado* Díaz has been causing trouble for our new president. Everyone knows he hires men to dress up like *peóns.* They raid haciendas, act as *bandidos,* and rob the silver mines in Zacatecas, then the government blames innocent *peóns.* The *Federales* round up suspected people and executes them publically to intimidate the peasants. Díaz wants to convince the aristocrats they need to return to the *casta* system," the waiter said sadly looking out of the window and shaking his head. "One of those men is a good friend of mine and another is my wife's sister's man."

"Why don't you do something?" Rafe asked the waiter.

"Do what *señor?* We are just lowly people, *peóns.* We do not have guns to fight the *Federales.*"

Rage burned in Rafe's heart. Just when it seemed the peasants could make a better life in Mexico, Porfirio Díaz was inventing ways to squelch any reforms. Raised a *peón* himself, Rafe knew only too well about the poverty of the Mexican peasants. Most *peóns* were *mestizos* like himself, people of mixed Indian and Spanish blood, born here in Mexico for generations. The wealthy Spanish landowners used the *peóns* for slave-like labor allowing them only meager food and living conditions. To be born a *peón* meant a life of dismal poverty and an early death with an empty stomach.

Rafe woke Carlos in the very early hours of the following morning. He had slept little and was already dressed. "Meet me in an hour on the road south. You will find Santiago saddled and the packhorse ready behind the stables. Take them and go south," Rafe told him. Before Carlos could ask why, Rafe slipped from the room and was gone.

The darkness of the early morning suited Rafe as he quickly saddled the horses behind the stable. Luckily, Manuel the stableman snored loudly in the loft and took no notice of Rafe's work. Last night as he and Carlos walked on the plaza, he spotted the small jail where the *peóns* were locked up. On the side wall of the jail, dark stains ran down the wall where others had been summarily lined up and shot.

After saddling Rayo, he placed several *pesos* on a haystack for the stableman and walked out into the dirt street. Walking Rayo quietly to the jail, Rafe tethered him in the side alley. His plan was foolish, but the rage in his heart burned hot.

Testing the front door of the jail, he found it

unlocked and quietly pushed the lever down and pushed the door in. One of his GSW pistols was in his right hand. It was dark and only soft snoring of several men broke the silence. Standing just inside the door, he waited for his eyes to adjust to the total darkness.

No one sat or slept in the front room. Walking softly, he made his way to the back where the cells were located. In one of the empty cells, a fully clothed policeman was stretched out on a bunk bed. Next to him on a small table was a single candle almost burned to the bottom. A rifle leaned against a nearby wall. Rafe walked over, blew out the candle, and nudged the policeman.

"Huh, huh . . . ," the sleepy man muttered before he became fully aware of a man standing before him with a pistol pointed at him. The man with his face covered by a bandana and a hat, nudged him again with the pistol.

"Levántate," Rafe told him to get up.

"¿Qué quieres aquí?" What do you want here the policeman grumbled.

"Quédate quieto y abre la puerta de la celda," Rafe told him to be quiet and open the cell door. Rafe nudged the policeman with his pistol to make sure the man obeyed. He was a local policeman and not a *Federale*.

"No me mates," the man begged Rafe not to kill him.

The policeman opened the cell where the *peóns* were held. One of the *peóns* wakened to the voices and woke the others. Rafe told them to light a candle and look for rope.

Rafe left the *peóns* tying and gagging the policeman. Outside, Rafe quickly walked in the shadows to where he left Rayo tethered. Jumping to Rayo's back, he kicked the big horse to a gallop. He had done what he could to help the *peóns* and hoped they could escape. He knew his actions could get him arrested and the sentence would be death, but he did not care. The rage in his heart pumped any fear from him.

Daylight broke in orange, pink, and gray over the eastern horizon as Rafe rode a far distance down the trail from Jiménez. Rayo's keen sense of smell led him to a creek near the trail. Rafe let the horse drink while he waited for Carlos.

"Why did you leave so early?" Carlos asked when he rode up a short time later.

"I freed the *peóns,*" Rafe replied without further explanation.

It took Carlos a few moments for Rafe's words to sink in. Rafe's actions were reckless. He had no right to put them in danger over internal squabbling of the Mexican government.

"What were you thinking? This was not your problem. You had no right to bring trouble down on us like this. The *Federales* will come after us," Carlos groused with anger in his tone. Normally Rafe was more measured in his actions.

"I did not let the policeman see me. It was dark and I kept my face covered. I only opened the cell and left. It is up to the *peóns* now. How could I let the *Federales* kill those innocent *peóns?*" Rafe asked him.

"I understand your feelings, but you cannot go on trying to save the world. I came on this trip to protect you from danger, but I did not expect you to bring danger down upon us!" Angry, Carlos wondered if this trip with Rafe was foolhardy. Carlos was a father now. He should be at home with his wife and baby, not traipsing around Mexico trying to keep Rafe from harm, especially when Rafe encouraged it.

"I cannot help it Carlos. Something takes over in me, something I cannot control. The Aztec healer Xihuitl, who saved my life, believed the star amulet which stopped the bullet and left a star shape scar on my chest was a sign from the Goddess Coatlicue, the Goddess of life and death as taught by the ancient Aztec legends. He told me the Goddess would guide me and protect me. I'm sorry, but I could not ignore the urge to help those poor people."

Carlos listened and pondered Rafe's explanation. He could only relate the Aztec legend with some of the Catholic Saints who were believed to have similar powers. Regardless, Rafe's actions bothered him greatly. Without answering he snapped Santiago's reins and kicked the horse's flanks. *"Vámonos."* Carlos prayed as they rode asking God to protect them. He loved Rafe like a brother and usually respected him. Today however he was annoyed. Rafe had no reason to put them in unnecessary danger.

Several hours later they stopped to rest the horses. Carlos built a small fire making coffee and frying strips of bacon. They ate the bacon wrapped in a tortilla. Neither spoke more about Rafe's foolhardiness in Jiménez and in fact barely spoke at all.

After the short break they returned to the trail heading south to Torreón. Carlos noticed Rafe checked their back trail often, riding Rayo back and forth. They pushed south with as much speed as possible, seeing only wagon caravans on the Chihuahua trail heading north and passing several heading south. Carlos insisted they stay away from any towns along the way, fearful the *Federales* were looking for Rafe.

Three days later, they rode into Torreón late at night, dog tired, and filthy from sleeping on the trail.

"Carlos, we'll stay here tonight and go to the hacienda in the morning," Rafe told him. Exhausted, Carlos only nodded a response as they walked up the steps into the Hotel Bilbao.

Chapter 26

The following morning, Rafe and Carlos rode to the hacienda. Rafe led the way under the archway leading to the main house. Women and children came out of the *jacals* to have a look at the two strangers, one riding a big black horse and the other a magnificent Appaloosa. Children ran behind the horses giggling and daring each other to touch the tails of the stallions prancing ahead of them.

The *jacals* along the main road to the courtyard were in various states of repair, some better than others. The old *jacal* where he grew up was whitewashed and the bushes around it trimmed. He noticed the guest *casita* near the main house was newly painted and the broken windows replaced. A garden was flourishing with vegetables, just like he remembered seeing growing up.

The last time he came to the hacienda was over three years ago. He came to kill *don* Bernardo Reyes, the man he later learned was his real father. Riding toward the main house bombarded him with painful memories.

Don Bernardo had shot him and left him for dead in the canyons of the southern part of the hacienda. Several months later after recovering from his wounds, Rafe confronted the old *don* in his bedroom on the second floor of the main house intending to kill him. *Don* Bernardo must have thought he saw a ghost and died of a heart attack, cheating Rafe from taking revenge. Only later did Rafe learn *don* Bernardo Reyes was his true father. It did not change Rafe's feelings toward the *desgraciado*, but it did change his life. Now Rafe, a bastard and oldest son of *don* Bernardo, owned the hacienda because of a new law in Mexico allowing *mestizo* bastards to inherit property. It was a godsend to his family here in Mexico.

When they reached the main house, Pablo came out and grabbed the reins welcoming them, *"Bienvenido Rafael, bienvenido Carlos."*

"Good to see you Pablo," Rafe jumped down and

gave his old friend a hearty *abrazo*.

"We have been expecting you. Go in the house, your mother is there with María and the baby," Pablo told them and took the horses. Carlos followed Pablo and the horses toward the barn, allowing Rafe time to greet his family.

With much anticipation and some anguish, Rafe walked up the front steps and into the main house. He did not call out for his mother, but instead simply walked around looking for her. The main house of the hacienda, as it had been when he was a boy, was etched in his mind. Now it seemed very different and he saw it through new eyes.

In the main living room crude wooden benches sat in rows. Rafe remembered his sister telling him she taught school at the house. The huge carved dining room table was polished much as he remembered. The stairs to the second floor were also polished to a shine, but no paintings hung on the walls. Finding no one in the main rooms, he wandered to the kitchen. Looking out the window, he saw two young women sitting on a bench in the yard. One woman he recognized as his sister.

"María, we're here. Where is mother?" he called out as he went out the kitchen door.

The other woman turned toward him and said, *"Mijo, ¿no reconoces a tu propia madre?"* Celiá asked if he did not recognize his own mother.

"¡Mamá!" he exclaimed. The vision of a beautiful and young woman walking toward him stunned him. She was dressed in one of the Spanish dresses he bought for her in Santa Fe, but never wore. Her hair was pulled up and held with a silver *peineta*, a decorative comb.

It had only been four months since his mother left Santa Fe, but Rafe could not help thinking her face looked ten years younger. Rafe hurried down the steps and grabbed her in a tight *abrazo*.

"Mijo, gracias a Dios," she thanked God. Celiá's tears sprinkled her son's shoulder. María stood nearby watching her mother and brother in a tender moment.

"Mamá, you . . . . you look so beautiful. You never

wanted to wear those clothes in Santa Fe," was all Rafe could say.

"I know *mijo,* but now I have a reason to look my best for Billy. He has brought love and joy back into my life. I love you and María, of course, but this is a love I thought I would never have. I am so happy, *mijo."* Celiá looked into her son's eyes for a reaction.

"I . . . . I . . . I'm so glad for you. Where is Billy?" was all Rafe could stammer out trying to believe the transformation of his mother standing before him.

"He and Rodolfo are out looking for stray horses. So far they have found ten strays in the canyons south of here. *Don* Pablo says they are horses *don* Bernardo let run in the canyons to evade *doña* Carmela's demands," María spoke out.

She stepped beside her brother. "Welcome home Rafael," María said and gave him a heartfelt embrace. "Come, I will introduce you to your namesake, Rafael Guerrero," she told him and a smile spread across her face. "You have given us a new life and we owe you so much. It was Rodolfo's idea to name him after you, but of course I agreed."

The afternoon passed quickly while Rafe and Carlos told María and Celiá all the news from Santa Fe. They were delighted to hear about Carlos' son, Benicío. "Seems as if babies are popping out all over," María said as she bounced baby Rafael in her arms. "Four have been born just since *Mamá* and Billy arrived."

It was nearly dark when Rodolfo and Billy arrived back at the hacienda. Welcomes and congratulations were exchanged among them. It was obvious to Rafe and Carlos, everyone here at the hacienda was content. Rafe's mother and sister left the men to talk and headed for the kitchen. Carlos followed Rodolfo to the barn to see the most recent young strays.

Billy stayed with Rafe, but an awkwardness came between them. Billy looked at Rafe, then spoke, "Look Rafe, first I want to apologize for running off from Santa Fe without asking your permission. Celiá thought it best to leave without telling you, against my wishes. She was afraid what you would think. We were so in love and she wanted to return to Mexico to be with María before she gave birth. She also wanted to bring María's children back." Billy seemed to run out of apologies.

Rafe had thought about this conversation many times. Sometimes he was angry and wanted to give Billy a piece of his mind, but after seeing the joy in his mother, Rafe felt differently.

"Billy, I was shocked at first and then angry. I thought you stole my mother after what you pulled on me at the stagecoach waystation. I might have killed you that day, but Ana Teresa convinced me you were a good man and I came to know it for myself. All I want is for my mother to be happy and in fact she looks beautiful."

"Celiá and I are more in love now than when we left Santa Fe. Just look at her, she looks like a different woman. She is energetic and full of life. María's baby is healthy and the children are glad to be with their mother. Your mother wants the best for you and Ana Teresa. She told me she is hoping for many grandchildren from you," Billy paused for a moment. "Also, coming here was the best for me. The Army can't touch me here, although I may never be able to return to the States. I don't care. My home is here now and I will help to make this hacienda and the people prosper."

CHAPTER 27

Gunfire rippled across the plateau near Raton, New Mexico. Near the northern border of the Baca land grant, stockmen for the Baca family returned fire against a group of squatters near Chicorica Creek. It was not the first confrontation with the squatters on the Baca land grant, but the first to escalate to gunfire.

The Baca family land was now managed by Jose Ramon Baca and his brother Tomás Baca, the eldest of Luis' seventeen children, after *don* Luis was murdered. Luis was accused of harboring contraband in the form of beaver pelts for a known hunter and trapper. The New Mexican governor sent soldiers to seize the pelts as payment for taxes. When Luis refused the soldiers entry to his home, they killed him. *Don* Ramon cited the story often telling his family and workers, "My father's blood is on this land." Like his father, *don* Ramon carried a grudge against the New Mexican Territorial government.

A huge tract of land, the Baca land grant covered many acres of northern New Mexico Territory. It was high desert, east of the foothills of the Sangre de Cristo Mountains and extended north into southern Colorado Territory and east to the eastern fork of Chicorica Creek. Less than fifty years ago this part of New Mexico was mostly deserted, except for Navajos, and no one cared about the Baca land grant, until American expansion brought people west.

In 1830, the governor of the New Mexico Territory issued a grant to the town of Las Vegas adjacent to the Gallinas River overlapping the Baca property. Luis Maria Cabeza de Baca's heirs contested. The government used legal maneuvers to extend and delay the proceedings until the town of Las Vegas was formally established.

The government cited the lack of planted acreage and formidable dwellings by the Bacas as reason to vacate the original grant. They claimed the small village of Las Vegas now had the rights to the land along the Gallinas River. Later it became known the railroad had plans to service the town. The outcome of the contestation formally created the Town of Las Vegas, New Mexico Territory, and the Baca land boundaries were redrawn.

The Bacas continued life and ranching operations on the mostly empty arid high-desert land, ranching sheep estimated at over 5000 head. The Baca *pastors* or sheepherders moved the herds regularly to high ground in the warmer summer months and the lower foothills in the winter.

Several weeks ago, two Baca *pastors* noticed squatters while chasing strays on a ridge and reported the sighting upon their return. *Don* Ramon asked Henry Arango to investigate and to mediate because Henry, a half Irish and half Basque man, spoke English.

A week ago, Henry Arango rode into the squatter camp and politely insisted they move. Some families lived in covered wagons, while several others had hastily built sod and wood shacks, others lived in tents. Henry knew the people probably could not survive a winter in the flimsy structures. Further down the creek, the tops of a few similar shacks and wagons dotted the landscape. Patches of land were already cleared and planted.

A rabble of poorly dressed children ran and played near the water. Their laughter filled the air. Three women were doing laundry in the creek. It was a peaceful scene, nothing about the people was threatening. However, this land was Baca land. The land grant was clearly marked with stone pillars and documented in the land office, however Henry had to admit these people had no idea about land grants nor stone markers. The almost 500,000 acres of the Baca land grant stretched for miles in all directions, most of which was vacant.

When Henry explained the situation, one of the squatters presented a deed to twenty acres. It was an official looking piece of paper with a United States government seal on top. Henry explained the deed was fraudulent. He was sorry, but they needed to move on.

Today Henry and a group of Baca workers returned to enforce Baca's sovereignty. He was greeted by a man pointing a rifle and threatening to shoot. Henry jumped from his horse walking up to the man, but did not pull his pistol.

"Tell your boss man we are not moving," the man said as Henry approached.

"You do not own this land. Why can you not understand?" Henry asked him. "You should go to Las Vegas. The town is growing and you and your families will be safe there."

Other men began to shout. Several were armed. "We are farmers. We will grow corn and wheat in this valley," the man responded. The squatters were not city dwellers. They made the treacherous journey to the New Mexico Territory for one reason – land.

"We do not want violence," Henry told them raising his empty hands, still restraining from pulling his pistol. "*Señor* Baca will grant you another week to gather your things and leave."

"Ain't no sign saying that Baca feller owns this here land, while this here piece of paper says I own it," the man retorted.

"*Señor* Baca's family has lived here for many years. His father, Luis Maria Cabeza de Baca, was granted this land from the Viceroy of Mexico," Henry tried to explain.

"Where is his home, where are his fields, his cattle or horses?" the man asked. "Seems like he has more land than any one man needs. We ain't seen nuttin for miles and miles and ain't seen no fences."

"Still, he owns the land. You need to leave."

"Tell your boss we will never leave. We bought this land with our hard earned money and we intend to stay."

Henry shook his head. He hoped the people would listen to reason. He turned to leave, returning to his horse. Five hardened *Baca* men sat on their mounts. Henry stepped up into his saddle and called back to the squatters standing near the camp.

"You must leave. The next time I return will be with

154 Robert J. Alvarado

more men," Henry threatened. He should have seen it coming. One of the squatters raised a pistol and aimed toward Henry. Seeing the action, one of the Baca men shot first. The squatter screamed.

Henry kicked his horse hard and jumped to a gallop. Gunfire erupted behind him as the sheepherders rode to take cover. They crouched on a nearby ridge overlooking the squatters campsite as gunfire peppered them.

"Hijos de putas," one of the *pastors* cursed calling them sons of bitches and fired off a shot.

Both the squatters and the *pastors* were out of range, so the gunfire was more symbolic than threatening. Finally Henry signaled for the Baca men to mount up and leave. Today was not the day to confront these squatters as they were outnumbered. Henry decided instead to report conditions to *don* Ramon and *don* Tomás.

Riding back Henry pondered the situation. He was sensitive to the squatter's plight. His mother was the daughter of Irish squatters living closer to Las Vegas. His Basque father, a part-time trapper in Colorado and part-time sheepherder in the summer months, was born near Cimarron, New Mexico. The territory was changing. Mexico no longer owned the territory after the Mexican-American War. Henry could hardly fault the squatters believing they had rights to the unused land. He knew they were just people looking for a life, just like his mother's parents.

He wondered if he could persuade *don* Ramon to allow the squatters to stay. Although not generally a hard man, *don* Ramon was rigid about the land. "The family has already paid for this land with their blood," he reiterated many times. However, the land along this portion of Chicorica Creek was remote. The Baca sheep seldom ventured this far north. He could see little harm in a few families trying to eek out an existence. Besides, after their first bitter winter they would probably leave on their own accord.

CHAPTER 28

Judge Albert Van Wagner finished with the outstanding cases on his docket on Wednesday. It was the sixteenth of July 1873. He was always busier in the summer months because Texas cowboys were a sorry lot and did not believe laws applied to them. Trigger-happy and often whiskey-mean, cowboys used little judgment other than their guns.

Sheriff Peters had Jed Clements sitting in jail over a killing in a saloon several weeks ago. It was an odd case where Jed killed another cowboy in defense of a half-breed Indian. The judge had never heard of such a case. Killing an Indian was never considered a crime, no matter what the circumstances. It was not self defense, because the cowboy drew first against the Indian. Judge Bert Van Wagner reached for his books on law and spent the afternoon reading. Later, having found nothing to help him, he walked to the telegraph office and sent a wire to a colleague in Chicago, then headed to Lilli Jean's Saloon.

Shortly after the judge sat down, the madame of the saloon, Lilli Jean, came to the table carrying a bottle and a glass. Dramatically, she clinked the glass down in front of him expertly pouring a shot of whiskey.

"Hello Bert honey," she drawled in her southern way of talking. "Betty Lou and Cindy have been complaining yew ain't been round lately." The judge was a regular customer of Lilli Jean's brothel. The girls liked the judge because he was a generous tipper and treated them respectfully. Lilli knew he preferred blondes and she always tried to have one of her two light-haired whores available when the judge came in.

"Now Lilli, yew know I've been busy with cases fer the past coupla weeks."

"Yew here now Bert. How bout I have Betty Lou ready fer yew upstairs in about an hour?"

Bert Van Wagner smiled and gave Lilli a wink. "Yew

shur know how to make a man happy, Lilli."

A ruckus from the far side of the room diverted their attention.

"I tole yew to quit pawing her," a gruff voice yelled.

"Yew dun own her, so back off," Vern Miller shouted back. Vern shoved the cowboy and grabbed Callie Sue around the waist. Callie's dress was cut low and her ample breasts showed plenty of cleavage. Vern dragged Callie Sue toward an open area between several tables and pretended to dance. He nuzzled his face into Callie's tits making her squirm trying to make him release his grip.

The cowboy grabbed Vern by the collar and yanked him. "I tole yew to quit pawing her. She was sittin havin a drink with me."

Callie Sue had sat at the cowboy's table a little while ago making small talk. He hoped they would go upstairs a little later and then this drunk grabbed her away and started to paw at her breasts.

"Get outta here Vern, before I hafta call the sheriff again," Lilli Jean shouted as she walked up. Vern was a habitual bad drunk and Lilli knew his traits well. More often than not, he roughed up her girls, especially Callie Sue and Cindy. He even tried to grab Lilli's large breasts on a couple of occasions after finishing a bottle of rye.

"Go on Lilli. I ain't doin nuttin, but tryin to dance." Vern's voice slurred as he spoke.

"Yew know the rules Vern. Callie, go back ta what yew was doin with that nice young cowboy. Yew git on Vern, before I call Sheriff Peters," Lilli scolding him.

A message from the judge about Jed's case reached Sheriff Peters late Friday afternoon. That evening he found the judge drinking a whiskey in Lilli Jean's Saloon.

"Evenin Judge." Nathan eased into a chair at the table.

"Evenin Nathan," he replied and took another sip of whiskey.

Nathan, like his predecessor, respected Judge Van Wagner and attempted to keep on the judge's good side.

The previous sheriff told Nathan the judge carried grudges if crossed, but otherwise applied the law fairly.

Lilli poured shots from the bottle into the small glasses for Bert and Nathan. "Evenin sheriff," she purred and walked off.

The judge picked up his glass and downed the whiskey in a single gulp watching Lilli Jean's ample form sway back and forth as she walked from their table. Just as Nathan was about to ask about the case, a waiter brought the judge a plate with a steak and potatoes piled high.

"Do yew mind, Nathan. I've had a long coupla weeks and anything yew have to say can wait until Monday. Come see me then bout that case."

Nathan stood, drained the glass of whiskey, and tipped his hat as he walked off.

The next morning when Nathan walked into the jail Jed called out, "Sheriff, when am I gonna git my hearin?" Jed asked for the umpteenth time.

"Keep yer britches on. It's Saturdee and the judge won't hear any cases til next week. He tol me yer case is on top of the list fer Monday," Nathan responded.

Jed was surprised. It was not the typical, I don't know response, he had been getting.

"Monday? Yew mean I'm finally gonna git my trial?"

"Seems that way. The judge is weighin on it," the sheriff replied.

"Yew know it were self defense. Yew make shur to tell him that," Jed said. Knowing there was nothing more he could do, Jed quieted. He tried not to dwell on the alternative the judge might find him guilty. Murder was a hanging offense and he had plenty of long hours sitting in this cell to think about it.

Pushing the morbid thoughts out of his mind, Jed sat back down on the cot and focused on the rustling job. Time was running short for his scheme. While sitting idle in the jail, Jed reviewed the plan over and over. He knew if they did not get to San Marcial by the end of July and get the stolen herd started up to Wyoming, his plan was finished before it started. They had to make Cheyenne before the end of October or they could get snowed in and never make it. Every day's delay ticked like a clock in his head.

Yesterday Jimbo told him Jake returned from San Marcial. Pete was hired at the ranch and they surmised it was a way Pete could really scout the herd. By the time Jed and the gang arrived, Pete could have more men lined up to join them.

It seemed a logical plan to Jed. From what Jake reported, the herd was growing fat on the green grasses of the river. The cowboys at the Circle B told Jake they probably had over 4,000 head. Of course, Jed knew most cowboys had no idea how to estimate a herd and most could not count to one hundred. Regardless, Jed took the news as their plan was still in play. All he needed to do was get out of this stinking jail.

Jimbo found Crabclaw at Lilli Jean's Saloon. He had been keeping an eye on him, sharing a few bottles of whiskey, but had said nothing about the rustling job. Jed was counting on getting sprung soon and they decided it was time for Jimbo to approach Crabclaw about joining the gang.

"Hey, save sum of that redeye fer me," Jimbo walked up beside Crabclaw standing at the bar.

"Hey Jimbo. We kin always git more," Crabclaw said with a smile showing several yellow-brown teeth. The bartender placed a second glass on the bar top and Crabclaw filled it to the top. Several shots later, Jimbo suggested they should find a table and paid for another bottle.

"Yew ever met a feller named Luke Payton?" Jimbo asked.

"Ol Luke, shur. I gambled with him many a time back in Round Rock. How is ol Luke?"

"He's dead. Got hisself kilt in New Mexico messin with a whore," Jimbo replied.

"Dead! Damn that's too bad. Always thought ol Luke would git it over a game of poker not over sum whore."

"Well, that whore ain't no whore no more. She's one

of the richest women in New Mexico after a Texas cattleman married her and they moved the ranch to a place called San Marcial."

Crabclaw whistled at the news, then Jimbo continued, "Her husband got hisseff killed by a curlywolf greaser and now she's a widder, a damn rich widder."

"Now that's one lucky damn whore. How is it yew know all this?" Crabclaw responded.

Jimbo lowered his voice to a whisper. "I'm workin with a feller and we got an idea on how to relieve that widder woman of sum of them fat cows." Jimbo watched Crabclaw's eyes and saw a flicker of interest in his blue eyes and a slight jerk of his head.

"After her husband was kilt, this here widder hired a bunch of greaser cowboys. Sum of the Circle B Texas boys stayed too, but we got us a plan to take a bunch of her cows to Wyomin and turn a big profit." Jimbo tried to describe the basics of the plan without saying too much.

"Circle B, I heerd of that outfit. Used to be a big spread outside of Austin." Crabclaw knew the spread had been owned by John B. Sutton and knew some men who used to work for the hard cattleman, but did not let on to Jimbo. Being a sharp gambler, Crabclaw knew never to tip your hand.

"Yew want in on sumthin like that?" Jimbo asked.

"Sounds interestin. Yew runnin this show?"

"No. Jed Clements is runnin it. He's been sittin in jail, but the judge is finally gonna hear his case and he thinks he'll git out. Then we'r ready ta go."

"Why's he runnin this gang and not yew?"

"Jed worked fer the Circle B and knows the layout and knows men up there. We figger on gittin most of the Texans still workin the spread to join us and killin any greasers who git in our way."

Crabclaw never heard of anyone named Jed Clements, but the idea sounded interesting. If Jed was just a no name cowboy with a plan, Crabclaw knew he could put a target on his back. Rustling was not a job for an amateur.

"Find me when this Jed feller gits out of jail. I wanna

talk to im.”

Jimbo was surprised when a woman’s silky voice came from behind them. “Craig Moss, yew sly devil. Yew sneaked away from me while I was sleepin last night. We got sum unfinished bidness?” Lilli Jean, the owner and madam of the saloon, gave Crabclaw a coy smile. Lilli was an older woman, maybe in her forties, with ample hips and huge breasts spilling over the top of the bodice of her blue gown. Jimbo only ever knew the man sitting with him as Crabclaw and was surprised when Lilli Jean called him by a given name of Craig Moss.

“Why, Miss Lilli. I tole yew I had a game over at the Gem and yew wooden let me leave. I made me a fine hat full of money,” he told her.

Lilli walked over to Craig and pressed her bosoms on his arm and whispered in his ear, “Ya know I like what yew do ta me with that claw of yers.”

Craig laughed and grabbed her around the waist not able to fully reach to the front and pulled her to him and snuggled his face on her neck. “Guess what honey. I’m here now and would like nuttin better than spendin tonight with yew.” She gave a small squeal, when he grabbed one of her breasts and gave it a gentle squeeze.

“Miss Lilli, I’d like yew ta meet my friend Jimbo.”

“Howdy Jimbo. Yew a friend of this here feller, yer a friend of mine. I’ll have one of my whores take care of yew, on the house. Craig, yer cumin with me.” After signaling to one of her girls, Lilli pulled Craig Moss by his arm and led him upstairs.

CHAPTER 29

A bright hot sun on a July afternoon at the Santa Fe plaza urged people to seek every bit of available shade. *Don* Pedro de Soto sat under a honeysuckle pergola sipping a cool tea as he waited for the stagecoach to arrive from Chihuahua, Mexico. According to the last telegram, his brother Bartolo de Soto and his wife Marcella, Ana Teresa's parents, were arriving today. Ana Teresa stayed at the de Soto hacienda with Bibiana caring for Bibiana's baby. Pedro knew Ana Teresa was dreading her parent's arrival and Pedro was feeling about the same.

"*Buenas tardes don Pedro,*" *don* Ramon greeted him.

"Ah, *don* Ramon come sit, get out of the heat."

Don Ramon Pacheco took off his flat crowned hat and wiped his brow with a handkerchief. His tie was undone and his shirt was soaked with perspiration. He ordered a cool tea as he sat down across from *don* Pedro. "What brings you to town on this the hottest day of summer?"

"My brother and his wife are on the next stagecoach from Mexico. They are coming from Madrid, Spain, where he was unsuccessful in securing a verification of his Royal Land Grant in California. His land was taken because American lawyers found what they claimed was a discrepancy in the documents. My brother had to prove it was granted to our family from the King of Spain."

"Ah yes, *Californios* have been suffering since it became a state. I suppose it was only a matter of time before it started happening here in New Mexico. Did you hear about the squatters up on the Baca grant trying to claim parcels along Chicorica Creek? The newspaper said the squatters shot at Baca's *pastors,*" *don* Ramon stated.

"Yes, Carlos read the article to me. I heard two more caravans stopped last week at the mercantile and bought supplies. Now the governor is demanding proof of our land grant documents, while he does nothing to stop the violence," *don* Pedro groused.

"I heard the Santa Fe Ring is pushing the governor. *Desgraciados.* They are the ones demanding verification of each grant. They manipulate the American legal system knowing it is unfamiliar to many of us Spanish-speaking hacienda owners. The land is then sold to speculators from the East. I have my original documents, but I still hired the lawyer Ron Iverson, the same one who defended Rafael Reyes. He says he will verify my land grant is legal and protect my rights," *don* Ramon said.

"I am doing same, but it is unfair. The squatters are buying land from unscrupulous land sellers in the East and they think they have legal rights to the stolen land. The United States government should do something about the land sellers. We are a territory, yet they do nothing," *don* Pedro expressed his concerns.

"The government in Washington does not care about New Mexico. I read Stephen Elkins, our representative in Washington, has been pushing statehood, but the gringos in Washington keep denying us. They think we are ignorant because we do not speak English," *don* Ramon groused.

"My father told me something before he died. I have to laugh about it now. Like your father, he witnessed General Kearny march into Santa Fe and conquer New Mexico without firing a single shot. He told me, "Son, we took this land from the Indians and now it is being taken away from us. Such is the way of history. Those who are the strongest dominate those who are weaker," *don* Pedro said and sighed.

"We must work together. *Don* Leonardo and *don* Daniel came to my hacienda three days ago. They are trying to get the *dons* to have a meeting and form a resistance. *Don* Leonardo argued we must stand together to fight this problem," *don* Ramon explained.

"I agree. We must fight against the squatters and our own government if we have to. This is our land and no one is going to take my land from me without a fight," *don* Pedro warned.

"By the way *amigo,* have you bought those special

rifles and guns from *Señor* Summers? Benjamin has a pistol and we ordered more rifles. Have you received any?"

"*Señor* Summers is busy making many orders. I have not received my order yet, though expect it at any time."

"*Gracias,* I must leave you now. I see my son Benjamin coming down the street. He was at the saddle shop buying a new saddle for the colt he bought from Rafael. The young horse has grown and is ready to be ridden. *Adios amigo.*"

An hour later the stagecoach arrived late. It stopped at the hotel across the plaza. Pedro hurried to meet his brother and wife. There was trepidation in his heart about his elder brother's return. The eldest son in a Spanish family had all the birthright authority over other siblings. Both Pedro and Ana Teresa had ample reason to be concerned with Bartolo's arrival.

By birthright, Bartolo was the heir to the de Soto hacienda here in Santa Fe. Instead he inherited a more profitable property in Rancho Simi, California, until that land grant was invalidated by lawyers. Bartolo was not able to locate the original documents and now Pedro could only hope his older brother would not try to exert his birthright over the hacienda in Santa Fe.

It was also worrisome that his brother was both homeless and no doubt short on funds. Last years' profits were reduced by a drought here in Santa Fe, so Pedro doubted he could be of much financial help to his brother at this time. The only thing he could do was graciously ask Bartolo and Marcella to stay at the hacienda until a solution could be worked out.

"Bartolo!" Pedro called out when he saw his brother. Bartolo wore a gray Spanish *caballero* traveling suit with a white ruffled shirt. A thin red bow tie was tied at the neck and a red sash wrapped around his waist. His flat crowned hat had a plain silver band about a half inch in height. He looked every inch the aristocratic gentleman. As he stepped from the stagecoach, Bartolo held his head up displaying his proud Spanish heritage. He reached his hand into the stagecoach door to help his wife disembark.

Looking at Marcella, Pedro could see an older Ana Teresa. No one could mistake where Ana Teresa got her beauty. Marcella was dressed as if going to a ball instead of riding in a dusty stagecoach, no doubt the latest style worn in Spain. A thin silk veil starting from the brim of her hat covered her face and draped her shoulders.

Bartolo turned and accepted an *abrazo* from his younger brother, returning the hug with an aloof stiffness. Pedro likewise hugged Marcella. *"Bienvenidos a Santa Fe,"* he welcomed them.

"Gracias hermanito, ¿dónde está Ana Teresa?" Bartolo thanked his brother and asked for his daughter. His demeanor was cold and haughty. Marcella stood nearby smoothing her dress and complaining to the stagecoach driver about the bumpy ride.

"Ana Teresa is at the hacienda helping Bibiana with the new baby. She is anxious to see you. Come, I have a carriage waiting. Manuel will gather your belongings. How was your trip?"

Bartolo gruffed as if mildly annoyed at Pedro's response. His daughter should be here to greet them. "It was a long trip from Spain. We stayed in Veracruz for a few days to rest from the seasickness. Marcella had a bad case and I did not escape it either. The storms at sea were vicious. I hope never to be on another ship as long as I live. The long dusty trip by stagecoach was deplorable."

Pedro ignored his brother's grumblings. "Agustina is looking forward to having you at our home. She is having a special New Mexican meal prepared in your honor. I am glad the trip is over. Now it is time to rest. You may plan to stay with us in Santa Fe for a long as you desire," Pedro said. Internally, he hoped for a short visit. Perhaps they would return to California or would accept the land grant near Las Cruces. It was not much, but land was land.

"We are looking forward to spending time with your family and of course with Ana Teresa," Bartolo responded thinking they would stay as long as they pleased.

CHAPTER 30

Ana Teresa sat in her room at the de Soto hacienda in front of the mirror at the dressing table. Uncle Pedro left several hours ago to meet the stagecoach which would bring her parents to Santa Fe. She took extra care with her appearance. The reflection in the mirror was of an older and wiser woman, not the young girl her parents left. Would they notice?

Everyone agreed her parents would not be told of her wedding until after Rafael returned. Ana Teresa worried if they found out too soon, they might try to abduct her back to California or send her to a convent. She did not want them to find out until Rafael came back from Mexico to stand up for her. In the meantime, she would pretend to be a *señorita*.

Her aunt Agustina was busy in the kitchen making sure the servants created a tasteful meal for the evening. Her uncle and aunt were almost as nervous as she about the visit. Her father, *don* Bartolo, was the eldest son. *Don* Pedro his junior by three years. It was typical in Spanish families for the elder son to be given more rights and respect.

Ana Teresa used to think her uncle Pedro a hard man, but he was now kind to her and here at the hacienda treated everyone with respect, even the *vaqueros* and servants. She knew in contrast her father was arrogant and egotistical.

Clipping her long hair into a silver comb, Ana Teresa checked her image in the mirror again. She wore a more subdued gown of blue and green with a modest neckline. The last thing she did was remove her wedding ring. Tenderly she kissed it and hid it in a small pouch and tucked it into the drawer.

Ana Teresa was sitting with Bibiana in the parlor when they heard the horse and carriage outside in the courtyard. Suddenly butterflies filled her stomach. Handing the baby to Bibiana, Ana Teresa stood and walked to the front door.

"Mija," she heard her mother's voice. Ana Teresa ran down the veranda steps into her mother's arms. Releasing the hug, her mother looked at her. "You look tired, *mija,"* her mother said. Ana Teresa was not surprised by her mother's comment. It was typical for her mother to find fault with everything, including her.

"You look well *Mamá.* Perhaps Spain agreed with you."

Don Bartolo looked at his only daughter. She looked older, more mature, with a certain grace about her. She was nineteen years old and unmarried. It annoyed him his younger brother had not taken care of that problem. He should have found her a suitable husband here in Santa Fe. Now she was practically an old maid. The last thing he wanted was to have to provide for her the rest of his life.

"Mija, it is good to see you," *don* Bartolo said and kissed her on the cheek.

"Gracias Papá," she dipped in a slight curtsy.

Thankfully, Bibiana brought the baby to present to her aunt and uncle. Marcella cooed over the sweet baby boy, taking him in her arms. It was a tenderness which surprised Ana Teresa. Her mother was not tender to her growing up. Ana Teresa was raised by her *mestizo* nanny. Her childhood nanny treated her lovingly, while her mother spent most of her time fussing over dresses, parties, and furnishings in the house. The nanny tended her when she was sick, brushed her hair for hours, and held her when she was sad.

"He's so precious Bibiana. Where is your husband?"

It was a question that made Ana Teresa's stomach sour. Carlos was with Rafael in Mexico. Ana Teresa had been so nervous about Rafael, she forgot completely about Carlos. Her parents would think it was odd Bibiana's husband was not at home tending to his wife and baby.

"Carlos is on a business trip, aunt. He will be home in several weeks," Bibiana lied smoothly.

"Well, men are no good with babies anyway,"

Marcella said and laughed.

Agustina took Marcella's arm and said, "Come, I will show you to your rooms."

Later in the evening, the family sat around the large dining table. The candelabras had been polished to a shine and new candles were used. The servants brought heaping platters of meats and vegetables and served *don* Bartolo and *doña* Marcella first. The aroma of the spices filled the room.

"You have done well here in Santa Fe brother," Bartolo said after taking several bites of food. "It is nothing compared to my hacienda in California, but the old house looks well tended." Pedro refrained from reminding Bartolo he no longer had a hacienda in California.

"Agustina takes great pride in the house. Her cooks are some of the best in Santa Fe."

"I noticed the barn has some rotten timbers. You need to get your *peóns* to work fixing it."

"We do not have *peóns* here. This is New Mexico, not Mexico. Here we hire our labor and pay them."

"*Americanos* made a huge mistake in giving freedom to all people. *Peóns* are ignorant and slovenly. They can never amount to anything much better than dogs," Bartolo blustered.

"Surely your vineyard in California was worked by hired labor. California has been a state for many years and *peónage* is not allowed by the United States."

"Perhaps laws say you cannot keep a worker indentured in your debt, but in California my workers only made a wage on paper. Nothing changed after the American laws came into favor. If you are not doing the same here in New Mexico, you are more a fool than I thought Pedro."

Her father's pompous views made her stomach churn. Ana Teresa saw her uncle's eyes flicker in hate.

"You will find many things are different here in New Mexico. Perhaps you will not like living here and will return to California or Spain," Pedro responded.

"We would have stayed in Spain, but our funds would not allow it. I suppose I will have to get used to your

New Mexico way of life here in Santa Fe."

"You are staying in Santa Fe? I believed you would retire to the de Soto lands in Las Cruces," Pedro said. "Your letters indicated you found the land grant for our family's lands there."

"That property is only for slovenly pigs. A poor excuse where our ancestors lived in squalor during the Pueblo Revolt. You could not have expected us to live there. This is our family home, my home," Bartolo responded.

Pedro tried hard not to react to his brother's words. He hoped any discussion about the properties would be handled later. To his disgust, his older brother was already planning to take over his hacienda.

Agustina rang the bell for the servants as a distraction. Additional quantities of food were served and more wine poured. The servants' presence temporarily stopped the conversation. Bartolo took another sip of wine and grimaced.

"The wine is distasteful. Bring me brandy," he roughly commanded one of the servants.

Finally after dessert, the men retired to the parlor and the women took their leave to the kitchen. Bibiana returned upstairs to her bedroom. She was still quite weak since the birth. Ana Teresa thought she did not try hard enough to regain her strength and preferred for someone else to manage the child.

Pedro offered his brother a cigar and more brandy. "You are probably tired after your long trip. We will finish this brandy and perhaps you should retire. Tomorrow I will take you into Santa Fe," Pedro offered.

"Do not think I do not know what you are thinking," Bartolo hissed. "You will do as I command little brother. Only if I choose to go to town, you will take me."

Leaving the kitchen to her aunt and mother, Ana Teresa tiptoed up the staircase toward the bedrooms. Half-way up she heard her father's angry voice and she stopped to listen.

"Why is my daughter not married. Is she not

beautiful?" he groused.

"Yes, she is beautiful. I had a suitor ready to marry her, but he was killed in a fight. He was a man from a good family. Then she returned to California for several months to recover from the distress," Pedro told him. Regardless most of the statement was a lie, it sounded good. She knew her uncle's reference to a suitor was the scoundrel who violated her, Diego de la Torre.

"So why have you not found another. *Caballeros* should be lining up at your door for her hand."

"Remember Bartolo, she does not come with a dowry. It is not as easy as you think without money."

"Because of your negligence she may need to be put in a convent. You know my Marcella was unable to bear more children and I do not have a son. It would be a shame if Ana Teresa bore me no grandchildren."

She felt her face flush at her father's comments. It took all her resolve not to walk down the steps and tell her arrogant father of her marriage to Rafael.

"She is young. She is beautiful. Perhaps if you can spare a small dowry, the problem will resolve itself." Pedro continued to lie. He had promised not to tell Bartolo about Rafael until he returned to tell him face to face.

"That will take time as I get this hacienda into shape. She will only get older. You have failed me brother."

Pedro felt himself shaking. Everything he anticipated about the arrival of his older brother was coming true and even worse than he hoped.

Ana Teresa walked back down the stairs and floated into the parlor. "Uncle, Bibiana is asking for you to come kiss your grandson goodnight." She stared hard at her uncle hoping he understood her request was meant to distract the conversation.

"Ah . . . ah, yes. Please excuse me. Enjoy more brandy if you please. I must see to my grandson," Pedro stumbled a bit on his words. Ana Teresa took her uncle's arm and they walked up the staircase together.

Chapter 31

Billy and Celiá's wedding was greatly anticipated at the hacienda in Torreón, Mexico. Despite the fact Billy was an Anglo, the people accepted him as one of their own appreciating his skills. Even with rudimentary tools, Billy constructed metal door hinges, fixed several wagons, created a lightning rod for the house, and made various pieces of furniture. He was also becoming quite proficient in Spanish.

The people at the hacienda were free *peóns*. María and Rodolfo owned the land and the people enjoyed the fruits of their labor equally. María taught school each morning, teaching the children how to read, write, and count. She asked Billy to teach them words and phrases in English. Although he did not quite understand, he was told the Spanish caste system kept peasants poor and uneducated. The peasants, called *peóns*, with no other options worked as indentured slaves to the large landowners. To him it seemed just another type of slavery.

For Billy, life here in Mexico was a blessing. No longer afraid of the Army finding him and shooting him for desertion, Billy enjoyed the pleasant weather and the people. He found they were hard working, gracious, and full of joy. Most of all he was madly in love with Celiá and never happier in his life.

Leaving the women cooking for the wedding feast the following day, Rafe, Carlos, and Billy hitched up a wagon and team and headed for Torreón. Billy drove the wagon with Rafe sitting beside him, while Carlos chose to ride Santiago. In town, they left the wagon behind the mercantile. Rafe spoke with the clerk and left a list of supplies to be loaded.

"The money you sent to the bank account has been a godsend. Rodolfo spends it sparingly," Billy said.

"You have done well," Rafe responded. Over the past several days, Rafe and Carlos inspected the hacienda.

Pablo proudly showed off new corrals behind the barn. Over a dozen young horses were in various stages of being trained. Four large fields were planted with grain, corn, and vegetables. The fields stretched out green against the brown hills. Almost all the *jacals* had smaller gardens growing vegetables and fruit trees. Billy had helped the men create a series of watering canals and a water capture system to store rainwater.

"It is not me. It is the people. They work hard, tirelessly," Billy replied as they walked down the plaza stopping at the saddle shop.

"Buenos dias señores," Encarnacion the owner greeted them. It tickled Rafe to be so greeted by a man who in the past would not have even acknowledged him. "How may I be of service?" he asked.

Billy picked up several harnesses and ordered a saddle.

"¿Ustedes son norteamericanos?" Encarnacion asked Rafe and Carlos if they were North Americans.

"Sí, we are from Santa Fe, Nuevo Mexico," Rafe replied.

Encarnacion lowered his voice. "You be careful here in town. The *Federales* are watching everything, especially strangers and *peóns.* The memory of the *Federales* arresting the *peóns* in Jiménez was still fresh in Rafe's mind.

Billy nodded his head in agreement with the saddle shop owner. Because he was not a *peón,* Billy often made the trip to town from the hacienda to pick up supplies. On several recent trips, he saw *Federales* in their uniforms carrying guns. He watched *peóns* in town cower and hide when the *Federales* were about. He overheard discussions in the mercantile about some man named General Díaz who wanted to be president and wanted to return to the glorious days of Mexico. The wealthy landowners supported him. One thing was clear to Billy – unrest against *peóns* was increasing.

As they left the shop they talked quietly. "When Celiá and I were in town last week, we heard *peóns* were put up against a wall and shot. It is said the *peóns* were innocent,"

Billy stated.

"We saw the same on our way here, but Rafael broke them out of jail before they were executed. It happened in the town of Jiménez," Carlos replied.

A surprised look flashed on Billy's face, then he chuckled. Billy knew Rafe would not allow such an injustice if he could do anything about it.

"The *Federales* are hassling *peóns* everywhere. I have been buying the people simple work clothes, so they do not dress as *peóns*. Each man, woman, and child has shoes and socks. Celiá is worried about the people coming to town for the wedding tomorrow," Billy said.

"It is a good idea. Come, we need to buy more clothes from the mercantile before we go," Rafe said.

Rafe let Billy pick anything from the racks and piles of clothing, while he and Carlos picked hats and bandanas. Soon the counter was piled high with woven or plaid collared shirts, brown pants, and women's dresses. For the children, Billy picked out tan pants in various sizes.

"Put it on the Reyes account," Rafe told the clerk.

"*¿Quién eres tú?*" Who are you the clerk asked him.

"Rafael Reyes de Estrada."

"*Perdóname señor,*" the clerk asked Rafe to pardon his question upon hearing the name.

On the way home, Billy drove the wagon and discussed the situation with Rafe.

"I am afraid we will not be able to defend ourselves if the *Federales* decide to attack the hacienda," Billy warned. "We have guns, of course, but if we use them the *Federales* will only make it worse for us."

Ever since he rescued the *peóns* from the jail in Jiménez, the idea of the *Federales* coming after his family at the hacienda nagged at Rafe. He knew there was no way to fight the Mexican government. They could come and take what they wanted by force. His family might not survive.

"It is a fine line between defending your rights at the hacienda and confronting the *Federales*. You must be careful and keep Rodolfo and the other *peóns* from causing any trouble."

"I know what you mean. There is a definite Spanish upper class here, in the same way it was in Santa Fe. Rodolfo hates it and I have to calm him down and keep him focused on the ranch. He must set an example to the people who follow him and not cause trouble. They are good people and will do anything he asks of them," Billy told him.

"Yes the aristocratic Spaniards have had control over the *peóns* for centuries. They will not give up their power easily. You saw how they treated me in Santa Fe because I am a *mestizo,* a mixed blood peasant," Rafe reminded him.

Billy needed no reminding. He remembered the Spaniards who wanted to hang Rafe. Alvaro Gutierrez was the ringleader, but several others followed his commands. Billy owed Rafe his life and he repaid that debt by eliminating two of the Spanish scoundrels outside of the Palacio Cantina. It was the night he and Celiá left Santa Fe for Mexico and they vowed to take that secret to their graves.

"Rafe, what happened in Santa Fe after the trial. Are those dandies still after you?" Billy asked, pretending to be ignorant of the situation.

"No, Santa Fe is changing. *Don* Pedro has accepted me and blessed my marriage with Ana Teresa. He has purchased several horses. Benjamin Pacheco is now a good friend. Alvaro Gutierrez and Vicente Vargas were robbed and killed outside the Palacio Cantina. As a matter of fact it was the same night you and my mother left for Mexico," Rafe told him. The coincidence nagged at him. "You didn't have anything to do with it, did you?" he asked Billy.

"Me? No, shit! I mean I didn't like them fellows for what they wanted to do to you, but I ain't no killer. You know that," Billy answered with the best surprised look he could muster.

"I'm glad to hear that. The killer was never caught, though Oscar Peralta described the killer as a large gringo."

Arriving home, Carlos, Rafe, and Billy walked up to the main house letting Pablo and several men unload the wagon. Sitting on roughly made chairs in the living room,

Rafe continued questioning Billy about the situation here at the hacienda.

"Billy, have the *Federales* hassled anyone here?" Rafe asked.

"No, not yet. They have left us alone, but I fear it is only matter of time. I will tell all the people to burn their *peón* clothes."

"Is there anything else you can do to protect the people?" Carlos asked.

"The *Federales* are accusing innocent *peóns* of theft and vandalism, then shoot a few just to intimidate others. Rodolfo and I have talked with the mayor and the padre. We assured them our people are not stealing from other haciendas. We have to try everything we can at this point, but if they come we have weapons and ammunition," Billy stated.

"I don't see how you can fight the *Federales* with guns. There are too many of them and using weapons will only make the situation worse," Rafe responded. "The men here are farmers, not soldiers. Yes they will fight, but what about the women and children?"

"Rafe is right," Carlos agreed. "If the *Federales* come, you will only get people killed if you resist with the guns you have."

"We are hoping the *desgraciado,* General Díaz, tires of the sham he is leading or is elected president so he will end this. All of Mexico's people should be free. All they want to do is care for themselves and give their children a better life," Rodolfo added walking into the room and hearing the conversation.

"You are living a dream, Rodolfo. The Spaniards here, the ones with the power and money will back Díaz. The aristocrats want to keep *peóns* working for them like slaves. If Díaz wins the presidency, I'm afraid they will come and take the hacienda."

They talked and argued politics until Celiá walked into the room.

"You men need to forget about this for now. We have a wedding tomorrow. Everything is ready for three o'clock in the afternoon. I will not let anything interfere with my wedding," Celiá spoke out, her voice stern, but everyone laughed. She broke out with a grin taking Billy's arm.

"You are right *Mamá*. Come, let's go see the new ponies Rodolfo found in the canyon yesterday," Rafe said.

Rodolfo led them to the corral next to the horse barn and pointed out the two new colts. "Pablo separated the mature stallions from the mares. He asked if Rayo and Santiago could be used as studs while you are here. Two mares are in heat," Rodolfo said.

"Good idea. Tell Pablo to let the horses run with the mares. I'm sure the studs will gladly perform their duty and I know the mating will give quality foals," Rafe agreed.

"I have picked one blooded mare for Rayo and hope we get an Appaloosa. Santiago will have the run at the others." Pablo walked from the barn hearing them talk.

"I have no doubt you have a plan, Pablo," Rafe teased him. Pablo was the horse master here when Rafe was a boy. He taught Rafe everything about horses.

"Come I will show you the mares," Pablo said and led them into the barn.

"Those are fine looking mares," Rafe commented. "They will give you some good offspring, Pablo, especially with Rayo or Santiago as the stud."

"It is part of our plan to make money, along with the corn and alfalfa we are growing. Pablo says he knows most of the *haciendaros* who bought horses from *don* Bernardo. When the young ones are trained, we will approach them," Rodolfo added.

"The *haciendaros* know it was Pablo who bred the best blooded horses in the state of Coahuila, some even came from south of Chihuahua to buy from *don* Bernardo," Rafe said remembering his youthful days helping the horse master he used to call *don* Pablo.

Chapter 32

Celiá descended the stairs in a beige dress. She looked radiant. Rafe took her arm and led her outside to the carriage Pablo borrowed from the livery in town. Billy and Carlos rode to town earlier to make sure everything was ready at the church.

About ten men and women and three little girls loaded into a wagon driven by Pablo and rode behind the carriage. The men wore pants and collared shirts with *vaquero* hats. The women wore cotton dresses in gingham and flowered cotton prints. The rest of the people at the hacienda stayed to watch the children and prepare the feast, which was planned for later in the evening.

At three o'clock, Monday July 21, 1873, Celiá Estrada and William Swanson married at the *Catedral de Nuestra Señora de Carmen,* located on the south side of the plaza in downtown Torreón. A silver *peineta* holding a embroidered veil of the same color as her dress covered Celiá's face. Two little girls held up the veil as Rafe walked her up the aisle. In front of her another little girl threw rose petals as they walked to where Billy stood waiting.

At the altar Billy Swanson waited with a wide grin. Next to him stood Rodolfo Guerrero, acting as his best man. Billy chose to dress in a Spanish *traje,* a navy blue waist length suit, a white ruffled shirt, a thin black bowtie, and his trousers had silver stars down the side to where the trousers met his boots. Rodolfo was dressed likewise, except Billy towered over him. Rafe looked up and saw Billy waiting and his heart skipped a beat. It seemed unbelievable his mother was marrying Desperate Billy, and yet Rafe was thrilled. As they reached Billy, Rafe took his mother's hand and put it on Billy's arm.

Rafe sat next to Carlos and María. Happy tears ran down her cheeks, dripping onto her baby's blanket. Behind them, the normally busy church was essentially empty. Only people from the hacienda were sitting in the pews.

Rafe thought it sad any people his mother used to know when living on *don* Bernardo's hacienda were either dead or gone, except for Pablo who sat nearby with a smile stretched across his face.

Rafe suddenly wished Ana Teresa was here with him instead of in Santa Fe. The quietness of the church reminded him of their wedding at the mission in El Paso. At least there, the brothers filled the pews. Rafe looked toward the altar and caught a look exchanged between his mother and Billy. It brought moisture to Rafe's eyes, then the priest began the ceremony.

Several hours later, the entire hacienda was gathered around a large bonfire in the courtyard of the main house. The children were playing tag while their parents ate their fill. Everyone celebrated the event. Men slapped Billy on his back and then took turns drinking from a bottle of tequila.

The bonfire licked high into the sky with tiny embers floating and catching the setting sun. Maxorro sang several songs in his rich deep voice and Ernesto plucked on a guitar.

Suddenly the clattering sound of horses broke the air. Three *Federales* rode into the courtyard. The lead officer jumped off his horse. His blue uniform was a bit shabby. A sword in a sheath hung from his dirty white belt, but the blade at the end of his rifle glinted in the firelight. His tall plumed hat was tightly strapped under his chin.

"Bienvenido," Rafe welcomed the head officer and asked how could he be of help to him. As Rafe spoke, Carlos walked up to Rafe's side.

The officer looked at Carlos who was definitely Spanish and walked with an air of authority. "You and your men should leave now," Carlos said. "You have no right to be here."

Both men standing in front of him stared defiantly. Addressing his question to Carlos he asked, *"¿Eres el haciendero de este rancho?"* The officer asked if he was the owner of the ranch.

"I am. My name is Rafael Reyes de Estrada. What do

you want here?" Rafe stepped forward a step as he responded. While his rage at the *Federales* churned, he kept his exterior demeanor calm.

"I was told this *hacienda* was owned by *don* Bernardo Reyes," the officer said in Spanish.

"Yes, he was my father, but has passed away. My family owns this hacienda now."

"Do you have papers proving you are the owner?"

"Pablo, get the legal papers," Rafe commanded. While Pablo ran to get the documents, the people who had been celebrating shrank away behind the bonfire. Billy stood with his arm around Celiá. He could feel her shaking slightly. Several of the women crossed themselves praying to God for help. A few men quietly picked up pieces of wood or long sticks to use as weapons. *Peóns* were used to harassment, had lived with it their entire life. However, the rumors of firing squads of *Federales* killing innocent *peóns* had reached all parts of Mexico.

Pablo returned with the documents and handed them to Rafe. "Here is your proof. I inherited the hacienda from my father and deeded it to my sister and her husband. They own the land now."

María and Rodolfo waited nervously for the man to take the papers. He leafed through the documents until satisfied the documents were official, then turned to Rafe, "I have a complaint, saying *peóns* from this hacienda are stealing stock from the Santos hacienda. Have all your people here immediately so that I can see them. I have descriptions of the thieves. Call them now," he ordered.

Rafe saw the look in the officer's eyes and knew the man was lying.

"You are mistaken. The Santos are our neighbors and friends. We are land owners. No one here would steal any livestock from anyone," Rafe retorted. "We are celebrating a wedding and everyone is here."

Rage burned in Rafe's stomach. Images of the *peóns* he freed from jail flashed in his mind, and he fought hard to keep it at bay. Thoughts of killing these *Federales* swirled in his brain. Although he knew it was stupid, he wished he was wearing his pistols. Luckily his pistols were upstairs in the house lying on the bed.

The officer looked at the people surrounding the bonfire. One woman wore a lovely beige dress with a long veil. Several men wore dark suits. One man wearing a suit was an Anglo. Other men wore pants with woven shirts and the women wore simple dresses. None of the people wore the traditional white cotton *camisa* and *pantalones* with straw hats worn by peasants.

"Where are the *peóns?*" the officer gruffed.

"We have no *peóns* here *señor*. The people you see here are free to work here or somewhere else, if they so choose," María spoke out. Rodolfo put a hand on María's arm hoping to keep his headstrong wife from saying more.

The officer expected *peóns*. No hacienda flourished without *peóns*. He was ordered here by his *capitán* after the wedding was noticed in town. "Take several of the *peóns*, put them up against a wall, and shoot them. Word will circulate around the local haciendas as we have been commanded by General Díaz to create fear in the *peóns*. Accuse them of causing trouble," his captain ordered.

Seeing he could not pretend to identify any *peóns*, the officer mounted up. However before he and his men rode out he warned Rafe. "If you are hiding trouble-making *peóns,* there will be trouble for you *señor*. My men will be keeping a watch on this hacienda and if they see any *peóns,* I will personally come back and arrest you along with the trouble makers," he warned Rafe before he spun his horse around and rode off with his men trailing behind him.

After the *Federales* rode off, the people cheered and shouted with their victory. They felt powerful and vindicated. Several large logs were added to the bonfire and the flames licked higher into the darkening sky. Later Carlos, Rafe, and Rodolfo talked at length. Rodolfo knew the *Federales* would return. When that time came Rafe would not be here to defend the people.

CHAPTER 33

Monday morning Jed paced in the cell anticipating getting his freedom. The hours of waiting dragged by more slowly than the three weeks he had been in jail. While he waited he drank four cups of coffee and did a lot of worrying.

When Sheriff Nathan Peters went to the judge's office on Monday morning, Judge Van Wagner dropped the charges with little animation. A colleague from Chicago wired him case law which applied.

Nathan thought the judge could have found his answer sooner, but decided not to complain. He arrived at the jail shortly after eleven o'clock.

"Well, the judge says yer free ta go Jed," Nathan said as he walked to the back of the jail and opened the door to the cell.

"Well, it's about damn time, Nathan. Yew know yew didn't have no call to keep me locked up," Jed grumbled.

"Dun git sullen with me Jed. Dun want us to part as enemies," Nathan replied. Over the last several weeks, the two started calling each other by their given names.

Nathan handed Jed his pistol and holster. "Go have a whiskey and yew'll feel a lot better."

"It'll take a whole bottle ta do that."

Jed headed for Lilli Jean's Saloon. Jimbo told him it was where Crabclaw had been hanging around drinking and taking Miss Lilli upstairs. When Jed walked in, Jimbo was standing at the bar.

"Jed!" Jimbo called out as Jed walked up beside him.

"Give me a hit of that redeye, barkeep," Jed ordered.

The bartender poured two shots and Jimbo put two dimes on the counter. "Come on."

Crabclaw was sitting near the door drinking alone. Jimbo and Jed walked over. Jed heard of the deformed outlaw, but had never actually met him. When Craig saw them walking up, he picked up his whiskey bottle with his deformed hand. "Yew wanna nother shot?" He poured the whiskey, not giving Jed a chance to answer.

Jimbo sat down and threw the shot down his throat in one swallow.

"This here must be Jed, I'm guessin?" Crabclaw asked. Jed pushed the glass across the table for another shot. His belly warmed up quickly with the whiskey as the days in jail faded away from his psyche.

"So, tell me bout this here cattle ranch over ta the New Mexico Territory? Who's this rich widder who owns it?"

"Well, several years ago me an a bunch of cowboys hepped John B. Sutton move his herd to a range just north of Fort Craig and south of a shitheel town named San Marcial. Sutton and my friend Butcherknife Bill were both kilt by a curlywolf greaser. He was faster than lightnin. The widder was left with all of Sutton's wealth and all his cows. That widder hired a bunch of no good Mex's to hep on the ranch. Me and sum others left and came back to Texas."

"That curlywolf greaser still there?" Crabclaw asked.

"Nah, he was just there visitin when it all happened. Sum relative of the mayor. Em cows are all fattened up and just waitin to git on the move. I figger we be the ones to take em on up ta Wyomin," Jed told him.

"Jimbo says yer needin sum good men."

"Sure could use some more good men. We plan on taking several thousand head and Jimbo says yew got sum sperience with that sorta thang."

"Yer gonna need at least ten men for each thousand head. Yew got that many?"

"Well not yet. A bunch of the Texans who stayed on at the ranch will join up," Jed responded.

Craig Moss poured another round for each of them. Jed found himself staring at the man's deformed hand. He was feeling no pain after the shots of whiskey and asked, "Kin yew handle a gun?"

Craig whipped out his pistol with his left hand, twirled it several times, pointed it at Jed, then expertly twirled it back into its holster in a single move. All the while he had a grin showing his yellowed teeth and looking Jed straight into his eyes.

"I kin handle a pistol and ain't afraid to kill."

"We're splitting the take equal. That okay with you?"

"Sounds fair."

"Be ready to go at sunup. Me and the boys are camped just east of town," Jed told him.

For his part, Craig knew he needed a way to get out of Texas and make some money doing it. Only problem for him, he did not know any of the players, except for Jimbo. This Jed fellow might be a good drover, but Craig was sure he was a novice when it came to rustling. He would be ready at sunup to go with Jed and the gang. He would see how it all worked out or he would find a way to run this group of would-be cattle rustlers and take most of the money for himself.

When Jed first arrived back at the campsite, only Breed and Pappy were hanging around. He saw relief in their faces. Breed smiled and welcomed him back. Hearing of Jed's release earlier that day, Pappy made a trip to town and stocked the wagon with grub for the trip. The men were tired of waiting and ready to get going north.

"I got the chuckwagon all ready ta go," Pappy said proudly.

"Thanks Pappy. It sure feels good to git sprung. Where is everybody?"

"Well, Pete, yew know he didn't cum back frum up north. Jake and Jimbo are in town and so are Corky and Glenda."

Jed stayed around the campsite until night crept up on El Paso. Pappy cooked a stewed chicken and biscuits. Jed ate two helpings.

"I'm goin to town and find Jimbo and Jake. Yew tell everyone we'r a leavin in the mornin. I need a bath, a woman, and a soft bed afore we git on the trail tomorrow."

Saddling his horse, Jed rode directly to the Chinese end of town and paid a quarter for a bath. The two young girls giggled as they bathed him and his privates. "Yoo wantie?" one of the girls asked holding his penis. Jed knew she would off him for another quarter, but he wanted a real woman. He shook his head no. Bathed and dressed, he headed to town.

He was surprised when he did not see Jake and Jimbo's horses tied in front of Lilli Jean's. Riding further down the street, he spotted them in front of the Horseshoe Saloon. "Damn," he muttered to himself not wanting to revisit the place where he had so much trouble. He thought about turning back to Lilli Jean's, but after almost three weeks in jail, he sought the companionship of his friends. Of course Crabclaw might be at Lilli Jean's, but something about the strange deformed man gave Jed a shiver.

"Hey Jimbo, hey Jake." They were standing at the bar with a bottle between them. The singer was standing near the piano player and singing a sad song.

"Howdy Jed," they responded. "Barkeep, we need another glass."

The redeye burned as it slid down Jed's throat, but it sure did taste good. After three shots, he was tapping his foot to the music.

When the bottle was close to empty, Jed asked the barkeep, "Who's the madam round here?"

The barkeep made no verbal response, instead signaling with his hand. In a few moments a young blonde woman moved beside Jed. He had seen her on the floor and thought she was just a saloon whore because she looked so young.

"Yew be needin a poke tonight hansum," she purred.

"Yeah three of yer gals. One fer each of these jaspers and yer best fer me and a bed fer the night," Jed responded and pulled a handful of money from his pocket.

Sallie Jeffries sized up the three cowboys. Two of them had been frequent visitors over the past several weeks and the other looked a bit familiar. The new man was obviously freshly bathed.

"What's yer preference? I got lots of variety."

"I like blondes, like yew," Jake spouted quickly.

"Not me, they all fake anyways," Jimbo laughed. "I like me a bit darker meat." Jimbo was both surprised and pleased Jed was paying for a whore for each of them. The bulk of his money ran out weeks ago.

"How bout yew stranger?"

"I like em young and I'll pay fer the whole night. I need me a soft bed," Jed replied.

Jed Clements woke up with a start in total darkness. Hooting and hollering came from somewhere, but it was a gunshot which woke him. Disoriented, his brain thought he was still in jail. Instead he was naked in a soft bed. Jed rolled over to get up and reached for his gun. Beside him a naked woman stirred. The fog in his brain cleared and he remembered the whore Sallie gave him last night. Her name was Lisa.

"Whatcha doin Jed? Yer crushing me," a soft voice spoke.

"Uh, I didn't know where I was. I heard gunshots," Jed sputtered.

"It's probly some drunken cowpokes downstairs. Cum on honey, give me sum more of that thing tween yer legs. Yew paid fer the whole night." Lisa took his pecker in her hand and squeezed it bringing it to life.

Jed did not resist. Lisa was a pretty gal and had the firmest breasts he ever felt, even firmer than Bonnie Brunel's. The thought of Bonnie back in Round Rock nagged him a might. He had done a lot of dreaming about her while he spent the many long and boring hours in jail.

He was pretty sure he loved Bonnie Brunel. Sitting in jail and worrying he might get hanged for killing the cowboy made him ponder the scheme about rustling cattle. The awful thought of a noose around his neck made him sweat. Now away from that cell, he did not want to have it happen again. Rustling was a hanging offence if they got caught or they could be shot by a posse and never make it to the gallows. A part of him just wanted to go back to Round Rock and forget all this nonsense about rustling the widow Sutton's cows.

CHAPTER 34

In the morning, Jed rolled Lisa one more time before he dressed. The morning sun was peeking over the mountains and he sure hoped everyone was ready to get on the trail. Even though it was only the twenty-third of July, Jed knew they would need all the days they could get to take that herd to Wyoming before the snow started flying in earnest.

Reaching the camp, Jed found Pappy cooking breakfast.

"Smells good Pappy," Jed said as the smell of bacon frying greeted his nose.

"Be dun in a few minutes. Iffin yew want coffee, hep yerself."

Breed already had his bedroll tied to his horse. Jimbo was behind a bush. Jake was fixing the saddle straps on his horse. Jed looked around the campsite. The remuda was tied properly and standing quietly, but Corky was not visible anywhere.

"Pappy, where's Corky?"

"Ah, he and Glenda sleep by themselves, tight like," Pappy replied.

Jed had all but forgotten about Glenda Bell. He did not like the idea, but he planned on leaving her here in El Paso to fend for herself. A cattle rustle and drive was no place for a young girl. He wondered if Corky was so smitten he would quit this venture leaving Jed without a wrangler to manage the remuda.

Craig Moss rode the east road from El Paso just before sunrise. He was totally relaxed after a long satisfying night with the insatiable Lilli Jean's ample body. He did not want Jed's proposition, but Craig was basically broke. Lilli had not charged him the past several nights and gave him free whiskey. Finally he saw Jimbo standing near a fire a little way off the main road.

Craig rode up assessing the small scene. An older

man stood over the cooking pot, Jed was eating from a metal plate, Jimbo stood near the fire. Another man was just crawling out of his blanket and a young kid and girl were folding blankets near the remuda. He was not impressed.

As he rode in Jed called out, "This here is a famous cattle rustler, goes by the name of Crabclaw. He's joinin up with us," Jed announced to the group.

Everyone looked at the man getting off his horse and knew immediately why Jed called him Crabclaw. Jed began to introduce the gang. Corky and Glenda came walking from the remuda toward the campfire.

Just as Corky and Glenda reached the group, two rangy cowboys rode up as if they belonged. The group looked at them suspiciously.

"Hey Craig. I guess we'r in the rat place," one of the cowboys said.

"We was hoping yew'd git here first. Worried Lilli Jean'd wear yer ass out last night," the other cowboy said and laughed.

"Jed, this here's Tom and Rick. They be joinin up," Craig announced.

Jed was stunned. He had not given Crabclaw any notion to invite more hands to join up. Sure they needed more men, but Jed wanted to be the one who picked them.

Jed took a good hard look at the two. Both had sparse whiskers and wide-eyed looks on young faces. They did not look much older than Corky and Jed could not believe these two boys were experienced cattle rustlers.

"What the hell, we cain't take these here pups on the big job in New Mexico," Jed complained.

"Dun let thar age fool yew, Jed. These boys are good rustlers. They ran with me and the John Kinney Gang down in Dona Ana County in the New Mexico Territory. They know the territory like the back of thar hands. They can shoot, ride and know cattle. Rick here speaks some Spanish," Craig said in an even tone. "Besides, by the look of this sorry group, yew need all the experienced hands yew can git."

Jed took another look at them, still not believing the two boys were part of anything, let alone part of a cattle rustling gang. He was about to ask them what they did with the gang when Rick spoke up, "Craig's rat mister, we can shoot and ride. As far as cattle goes, we know how to handle em nasty critters. Every time we rustled a herd, it was me n Tom's job ta keep the strays in line. We know how ta handle stampedes too."

Jed did not like it, but Crabclaw was right when he said they needed more men. Reluctantly he introduced everyone.

Craig assessed the young couple standing near Jed. The girl was young and pretty. Her light brown hair hung around her face and shoulders. She had an air of refinement not often found out here on the prairie. Craig thought the whole operation had just brightened up a bit.

"These two here are Corky and Glenda. They will take care of the remuda and Glenda will help Pappy cook. Everybody git saddled up, we need to git ridin," Jed said trying to sound in charge of the ragtag group. How dare Crabclaw, or Craig or whatever his name was, bring two more cowboys in on this rustle without his permission. Grumbling, Jed quickly busied himself tying his saddlebags and bedroll trying to subdue his anger.

Orange, pink and gray graced the eastern sky and rain clouds moved north over El Paso when Jed and the would-be cattle rustlers rode north on the road to Las Cruces. They passed several caravans slowly winding their way north. With the horses fresh, Jed set a steady pace wanting to push as many miles as they could on the first day into the New Mexico Territory.

As Jed led the group, he thought about the mix of characters following him to San Marcial. He found himself unsettled about this morning's events. If trouble came within this group, he wondered who would side with him. He trusted Jake and Pete, Pappy would back him, and he hoped Corky would be there for him. The two newcomers, friends of Crabclaw, would follow the deformed gunslinger for sure. Jimbo was a wildcard. Jimbo knew Crabclaw and might think him a better bet. Breed, well Breed owed Jed big time.

Trailing the group, Corky and Glenda kept the remuda in line and were far enough back to where the men on horseback were only a small dust cloud ahead. They passed two wagon caravans, one carrying large clay pots, the other had their wares on the wagons covered up. Both Corky and Glenda used bandanas to cover their noses to keep the dust away.

Glenda's thoughts kept thinking about Crabclaw. She noticed the way he looked at her when Jed introduced her and Corky. His look was lecherous, the look of a nasty, deformed, older man. She wanted to tell Corky she was worried, but the dumb kid might confront Crabclaw and get himself killed. Corky was sweet, kind, and sort of dumb. He could not read or write. He wanted to marry her after the rustling job and settle down somewhere. Glenda worried he might not be her best option in life.

When she asked Corky about where they were going to rustle cattle, he said he had never been to the New Mexico Territory. Jed told him they were taking the herd north to Wyoming. All he knew was his job to care for the remuda.

Glenda did her best to make friends with Jake and Jimbo while Jed was in jail, asking them questions from time to time. Neither gave her any helpful information. Jake talked to her once about some widow who owned the herd they were going to rustle. Nothing more.

Jed told Pappy to find a good campsite just north of Las Cruces. When they pulled up, the men jumped off their horses and started to make camp. While Jed was untying his bedroll, Jake walked up beside him.

"Kin we trust em?" Jake whispered. Jed knew he meant Crabclaw and his two friends.

"We dun know em, but they kin shoot and dun rustling before," Jed replied. "Dun see I had a choice."

Craig, Rick, and Tom did not strip their horses or help at the campsite. "We'r goin over ta the Mexican side of town. Iffin yew wanna come, let's go now," Craig announced.

"Awrat, git goin, but we leave early in the morning," Jed agreed. Jake needed no urging and jumped to his mount and joined them.

When they arrived at Panchos Cantina, guitar and trumpet music blasted out along with the powerful voice of a woman singing some love song. Craig pushed the door open and they walked in.

"Four beers and shots," he ordered the bartender to bring it to a table. They sat at an open table near the door.

"Drinks are on me boys," Craig said. The Mexican singer moved around the room flirting with several *vaqueros,* before stopping at their table. When she stopped, she visibly retracted seeing Craig's deformed hand. He was so used to it, her reaction did not bother him.

When the singer moved on, Craig asked Jake, "Tell me again bout that ranch. Tell me bout that widder."

"Jed and Pete and me know that ranch from top ta bottom. We hepped git that ranch a goin fer Mister Sutton and em cowboys at the Circle B are Texans. They r friends and r gonna be a big hep gittin the herd outta that shitheel town. Pete'll have everythang lined up by the time we git thar, yew'll see," Jake assured him.

"Jed said there were greasers. Said a greaser kilt Sutton," Crabclaw continued to pry for information.

"The widder hired some local greasers to hep after old man Sutton got hisself kilt. They don't worry me none. Only that curlywolf greaser who kilt Sutton is a threat, but he dun live there. Lives up Santa Fe way," Jake explained.

Craig took the information about the setup with only an outward reserved interest. He knew there was little allegiance within any outlaw gang. His two recruits, Rick and Tom, would be loyal to him. Only Jimbo worried him a bit. The others would be swayed by the money. Once they arrived at the ranch, he would decide how to deal with Jed before he ruled the gang and took the cattle for himself.

CHAPTER 35

Two days after the wedding, Rafe, Carlos, Billy, and Rodolfo headed to Torreón. They headed directly to Nicolás Jiménez' office. Jiménez was the lawyer who helped Rafe inherit the hacienda and also worked to transfer the deed to Maria and Rodolfo.

"Buenos dias señores," Nicolás greeted them graciously. "How may I be of service to you?"

"Señor, the *Federales* came to the hacienda after my mother's wedding. You know all the people living there are free *peóns.* Carlos and I must return to Santa Fe. I am worried the *Federales* will make another excuse to return after we are gone," Rafe told him.

"I see. Yes, it is a problem. The *capitán* is acting on General Díaz' orders. Many of the local *haciend"os* support Díaz, wanting to have authority over *peóns."*

"My sister and Rodolfo legally own the hacienda. How can we protect them?"

Nicolás pondered a few moments. He knew what Rafe said would probably come true. The *Federales* had executed several *peóns* at local haciendas. No *peón* was safe here in Torreón or anywhere in Mexico.

"I cannot make you a promise, but I can discuss the matter with the *alcalde.* He is aware your hacienda is peaceful and run by free *peóns.* The *alcalde* and I have spoken about it."

"Is that all? Can you not file an injunction?" Carlos asked. More schooled about legal matters, Carlos felt the lawyer's solution a joke, thinking the *alcalde* was probably in cahoots with the *Federales.*

"It is impossible to file an injunction against the government here in Mexico. They have the supreme authority."

"What about the legal deed. Is everything in order?" Rodolfo asked. Even though the *capitán* accepted the paperwork yesterday, it was well known the government could find fault where none existed.

"The paperwork was all filed legally. There is nothing else I can do," the lawyer responded.

"What about *la mordida?*" Rodolfo finally spoke out.

La mordida, or the bite, was a centuries old way of bribing bureaucrats for doing their duty or looking the other way. Bribing officials was common and in many cases expected. It was a way for officials to supplement their otherwise meager incomes. It was well known many government officials, even local police, bought their positions so as to extract *la mordida.*

Everyone looked at Rodolfo. "It's the way of life here in Mexico. Is that not so, *Señor?*" Rodolfo asked.

"It is so," the lawyer agreed.

"What the fuck Rafe. You mean to tell me we got to bribe our way to stay alive?" Billy asked.

Rafe didn't answer Billy, but asked the lawyer, "Nicolás, what will it take to keep the *Federales* away from the *hacienda?*"

"I do not know, but I will start with the *alcalde.* I will send a message to Rodolfo when I get the number."

Rafe stood and shook Nicolás' hand. He knew him to be direct and honorable, though worried about how much *la mordida* was going to cost.

"Gracias."

"Good luck my friend. May you have a safe journey home. I will do what I can," the lawyer assured them.

They walked from the lawyer's office to the bank. Rafe signed over additional funds to Rodolfo and introduced Billy to the banker. He explained, either man should have access to the account as necessary.

"I don't get this General Díaz feller. Why does he have so much power here? He's not the president," Billy asked as they rode back to the hacienda.

"He became a general during the battle against the French at Puebla in 1862. It was a great victory for Mexico. Later when Maximilian was deposed, Díaz wanted to be president, but Benito Juárez was elected by the people. Juárez was a *Indio,* the first native person to hold power here in Mexico and he led many reforms," Carlos explained the history.

"Like the law that allowed me to inherit the hacienda even though I am a bastard," Rafe added.

"Díaz retired from the Army to his home in Veracruz and eventually sided with Juárez. When President Juárez died last summer, Díaz rebelled against the next president Tejada, no doubt wanting the presidency. Tejada is continuing to make reforms for the *peóns* and the aristocrats of Mexico are angry. They are supporting Díaz' ideas to return power to them and return to the caste system. As we are witnessing here in Torreón, Díaz is using the power of the *Federales* to intimidate the poor," Carlos explained, trying to make a very complex issue simple to understand.

"What I don't get it why the president, this Tejada feller, doesn't stop General Díaz and the *Federales,*" Billy said.

"Mexico is too large. President Tejada is in Mexico City and cannot control what goes on in the rural parts of the country," Rodolfo added. "We can only hope it ends soon."

"I worry about you and my family here. I know you won't leave. Billy can help you and I am glad he is here, but you know as well as I do, only money and guns talk," Rafe said speaking directly to Rodolfo.

"Even if we pay the fucking *Federales* off with this *mordida* shit, how many more officials will want their bite?" Billy expressed his worries.

Rafe shook his head back and forth. He had no idea how many or how much it was going to cost to bribe his family's safety.

"Hell, we'll run out of money in a week. I think bullets are a lot cheaper," Billy groused.

Several days later, Rafe and Carlos packed up their saddle bags and readied to leave. Rafe kissed his mother and sister several times, wondering if he would ever see them again. It felt like he was abandoning them for a second time.

"Te amo, Mamá," he told his mother he loved her and wrapped his arms around her in a tight embrace. Tears fell from her eyes, both happy and sad. Rafe shook Billy's hand hard. "Take care of my mother and sister," he said.

With only a minimum of supplies on the packhorse, Rafe and Carlos made good time headed north. Two days later they were nearing the village of Jiménez.

"We are not stopping in Jiménez and taking a chance on being recognized by the people at the hotel and restaurant. No one in the village is crazy enough to do what you did, putting the guard in a cell and releasing the *peóns.* For all we know the *Federales* may have gathered another group of people and executed them for what you did," Carlos said emphatically.

"I know. I'm sorry I put you in danger," Rafe replied.

"I thought about it afterwards and I know now you were justified in what you did. I was angry with you until the *Federales* came to the hacienda after the wedding. The image of the *Federales* possibly rounding up those people is still lingering with me."

"Knowing those *peóns* would be put up against a wall and shot just to scare the village . . . I could not let that happen when I could try to prevent it," Rafe said.

Rafe could tell the anger he felt lately from Carlos had dissipated. Carlos was his one true friend and he quietly thanked God for turning his heart.

"Now, about Desperate Billy and the stolen silver, I want to know if you have any other secrets hidden away you have not told me?" Carlos asked teasingly.

Rafe had only one more secret. It was how he escaped Longwei's opium plantation in Jalisco. Though it seemed unnecessary now, he decided it was a secret he would keep. Telling Carlos could do nothing for those poor men Rafe left behind at Longwei's plantation.

"No, only the secret about how I am better looking than you," Rafe bantered.

"Ha!" Carlos retorted with a grin.

CHAPTER 36

Jed and the gang arrived south of Fort Craig on the last Sunday in July. Pappy made a nice camp near the river where tall cottonwood trees gave them shade from the hot afternoon sun. Corky let the horses take a long drink in the river and then rubbed them down. Glenda helped him and Jed watched as the two played and splashed in the river. As the afternoon sun dipped over the San Mateo Mountain range, sundown came quickly in the tall thicket of cottonwoods.

The Sutton cattle ranch was about ten miles north. The proximity of Fort Craig worried Jed a bit, as he forgot how close the military fort was located to San Marcial. He remembered soldiers running maneuvers against Apaches and saw a few in town occasionally, though did not think they interfered in private police matters. Specifically, when Butcherknife Bill and Ponyboy George raped and killed the greaser woman, no soldiers helped in the search for the killers. Otherwise the only law nearby was the local mayor. Jed's plan assumed only the mayor and any townspeople could be formed into a posse to chase them after they rustled the cattle. He hoped his assumption was correct.

After Pappy prepared the supper meal, Jed gathered the gang around the campfire to discuss the plan. "We be bout ten miles south of the Sutton ranch. Jake will go thar at first light and find Pete. Jimbo and Tom, yew go north along the ridges and scout for the herd. The rest of us will stay here. No one kin go into town fer nuttin, yew hear me. That town is so small and people will remember, especially Big Ed, iffin he sees us."

A general grumble circulated the group. After five days on the trail, they wanted whiskey.

"We will stay here til Jake and Jimbo git back tomorrow night with what they've learnt," Jed finished with the instructions.

Craig Moss sat leaning against a tree only half

listening to Jed talk. His eyes followed Glenda as she worked on gathering the dishes. She was just a slip of a girl, although her hips swayed nicely under her cotton dress. She was Corky's girl and otherwise Pappy kept a sharp eye on the men's actions toward her.

After supper, Glenda went to the edge of the river to clean up the dishes. The long shadows of evening stretched across the river valley. The water of the Rio Grande flowed gently and Glenda knew it was not deep. A bath would feel good. After setting the dishes on rocks to dry, she looked around and saw no one near. Pulling off her dress, she sat on a good sized rock partly submerged in the river with water slowly flowing over it. She took the bar of soap and began to wash.

The river water was cool, but not cold. She dunked the soap several times in the water and scrubbed her arms, humming a tune. She thought about diving in, but decided to just dunk her head instead, worried about a current or creatures living in the water. Dipping her head several times to rinse the soap, she finished, and rose heading toward the shore. Just as she reached near the river's edge, a dark form rose from a crouch. She screamed.

"Dun be scart little gal, I ain't gonna hurt yew. Yew shur r purdy." Crabclaw had followed Glenda to the river and was enjoying the show. Her lithe naked body glistened from the dripping water. Before Crabclaw finished what he wanted to say, Jed and Pappy came up running toward her scream.

"What the fuck yew doin, Crabclaw!" Jed called out when he got to the river.

"Nuttin, I jess came here ta git cleaned up and I found the gal coming outta the water. Tain't my fault she's naked," Crabclaw said with a huff, turned, and stomped back to camp.

"Turn around," Glenda ordered. She got out of the water and quickly shimmied into her dress. Hearing her scream, Corky came running passing Crabclaw on the path. He found Jed and Pappy standing near Glenda with her soaking wet hair dripping down her back.

"What the hell's goin on Jed?" Corky asked.

"He's not doing anything. I saw a rattlesnake go by and screamed. They came here to see what happened," Glenda lied not wanting Corky to tangle with Crabclaw for he would surely die.

"Yew all rat now Missy?" Pappy asked her.

"Yes."

"Yew best not be alone in the dark again miss," Jed told her.

"Cum on honey, let's git yew back to camp," Corky told her taking her damp hand. Pappy gathered the clean plates and bar of soap and they slowly walked back. Corky was sure Crabclaw scared her, not a rattlesnake. Everything about Crabclaw rubbed Corky wrong. The deformed man was devious and no doubt a ruthless killer. Corky saw him several times watching Glenda and it made Corky's skin crawl.

Crabclaw picked up his bedroll and moved to a spot behind a large cottonwood tree. There was a special prize in this exploit – Glenda. She was young, maybe sixteen or seventeen. He saw her slender body as she waded out of the river. Her small breasts were bigger than they looked under the loose cotton dress.

Glenda was Corky's girl, but the kid was green and stupid. She might not like him now, but when Craig became ramrod of this outfit and Corky was left for the buzzards, she would change her tune.

Over the long days coming up the trail, Craig had quietly watched the players. He already sized up everyone and knew he could take over the outfit on the way to Wyoming. Jed, Pete, and Jake knew the location of the cattle ranch and the surrounding territory. Jed told him Breed knew the Goodnight-Loving Trail and all the watering holes. Jimbo would follow the money, as would Pappy.

He had not given much thought to Corky, until now. It had been a long time since Craig had a sweet young pussy. Nice girls ignored Craig because of his deformed hand. He guessed Glenda was maybe sixteen. She was not beautiful, but one would call her pretty. Pappy told him the story how they saved her from Comanches in the west Texas prairie. Craig decided to keep a close eye on her.

All the next day, the would-be rustlers in camp spent their time wading in the river to cool off from the late July heat. Jimbo was cleaning his rifle and pistols when Corky came up to him, "Hey Jimbo, hep me with my draw. I'm havin trouble thumbing the hammer before I level it at my target. I always shoot low, I cain't git my thumb to not pull too quick."

Yesterday's trouble with Crabclaw worried Corky and he knew the only option he had was to get quicker on the draw.

"Well, let me see you draw, but don't pull the trigger," Jimbo told him and walked to Corky's right side to see the action. Corky, drew the pistol as quick as he could, but did not shoot like Jimbo asked. Corky practiced his draw several times.

"Now, watch me." Jimbo drew the pistol in slow motion. "Take notice how my trigger finger is outside the trigger guard, but ready to slip in it once I git my target. Then I slip my trigger finger in and thumb the hammer at the same time. Now yew try it," Jimbo instructed.

"Like this?" Corky drew the pistol slowly just like Jimbo showed him. He slipped his trigger finger in and thumbed hammer all in a single motion. It felt awkward.

"That's it, now practice slowly at first, then speed it up when yew feel comfortable and squeeze the trigger. Use an empty gun to practice," Jimbo told him and went back to cleaning his weapons keeping an eye on his student.

Corky stood nearby drawing over and over until his fingers hurt. He thought he was making progress. Jimbo sat nearby and watched him between working on cleaning his guns. The kid was a novice and it showed. If he ever had to draw in a fight, he would be a dead man.

"When yew git better with that draw, I'll teach yew how ta fan the hammer for rapid shooting," Jimbo told him.

Crabclaw sat in the shade of a cottonwood and dozed

most of the afternoon. Pappy busied himself getting the evening meal ready. Breed slept most of the afternoon with his hat pulled low over his face. Glenda stayed near camp and did not venture anywhere alone. Even though Crabclaw made no more attempt to come near her, she caught him looking her way several times.

Later in the afternoon, she and Corky took several horses at a time to the river's edge, then to feed. Corky said nothing about the event yesterday at the river. She had lied about the rattlesnake, afraid the deformed man would retaliate if she accused him. The brute scared her and she knew none of the other men could do anything to stop him if he came after her, most of all Corky.

Near sundown Jake rode into camp carrying a hunk of beef given to him by Rusty, the cook at the Sutton ranch. "Here Pappy, how bout cookin this fer us tonight. Beef sure does sound good," Jake said dismounting and handing the sack of beef to Pappy.

"Shur will boy. Beats em rangy rabbits and wild turkeys we been a havin." Pappy took the beef and began cutting steaks and putting more wood on the fire.

An hour later they gathered around the fire after finishing the steaks and a heap of potatoes. Jimbo and Tom had returned earlier in the afternoon. The herd was well contained in one of the grassy basins near the river south of the ranch. Only a few strays dotted the escarpment.

"Whatcha learn at the ranch?" Jed asked Jake.

"Like yew tol us, the herd is gittin fat on the grass near the river. The Texas boys are plannin to take half the herd up to Wyomin in a couple of weeks," Jake responded.

"How many Mescans are workin thar?" Jed asked.

"Only six. Pete says they won't be any trouble. They be heeled, but we kin take care of em quickly iffin we have ta," Jake bragged.

"Whar's Pete? Why didin he cum with yew?"

"He'll cum tomorrow night. I told him where we was camped."

Chapter 37

"Bartolo already thinks he owns this hacienda," Pedro groused to Agustina, his wife, as they readied for bed.

"Shhh, my love. They might hear you," his wife shushed him.

"What does it matter. I have invested years in this home and he thinks he can just come here and start ordering my *vaqueros* around. He almost dismissed Ernesto today for not saddling his horse faster."

"Perhaps he is just blustering. Surely he does not think they can move in here with us. Marcella has been extremely kind and gracious, though she finds fault with everything."

"I don't think they want to move in with us. I think they want us to move out!"

"*Cálmate*. Let us see where this leads," Agustina tried to act calm continuing to brush her long hair. Outwardly she held her reserve, but inside she was scared. Marcella acted kindly to her, although a certain aloof attitude prevailed. Everything was better in Spain or California, according to Marcella. The wine tasted better, the servants bowed lower, the weather was more temperate. To each inferred criticism about Santa Fe, Agustina merely nodded. The only thing Marcella fussed about was baby Benicío. She spent hours in Bibiana's bedchambers rocking the small baby. With no grandchildren of her own, Marcella seemed obsessed with the child.

Agustina promised to take Marcella shopping in town tomorrow. She was sure her sister-in-law would be sorely disappointed. Santa Fe did not have the latest styles nor any large selection. Agustina usually had a local dressmaker design her gowns.

"Perhaps they will realize Santa Fe is only a small town and they will desire to return to California or Spain," Agustina suggested.

"Or hopefully Bartolo will fall off his horse and break his arrogant neck," Pedro added bitterly.

Late the following morning, Agustina called for the carriage. It was a beautiful summer day in Santa Fe with a clear teal sky. She and Marcella arranged their bonnets before the open air carriage drove out of the gates.

"Spain was so elegant," Marcella gushed. "You would not believe the gowns worn by the ladies at court, even the courtesans. I suppose one must understand the importance of style in their social position."

Marcella's haughty tone was almost intolerable. Agustina could care less about the Spanish Court and Pedro told her of the recent unrest in the country. "Marcella, I believe Spain is no longer a monarchy, but a Republic. Is that not true?"

"Bartolo says this blight of power will not last. Alfonso, Queen Isabella's son, will regain power soon and the court will resume in visions of its past glory," Marcella dismissed any notion of Spain's current political turmoil.

"Is that why you returned to the United States? Will you return to Spain when a new King is crowned?"

"I certainly hope so. New Mexico is so primitive. Look at those people, those cowboys and the children are running wild in the plaza." The carriage had reached the Santa Fe Plaza and true to normal conditions, Americans wearing suits and cowboys with chaps and bandanas stood outside of the saloons and mercantile. The women wore cotton frocks in gingham and bright floral patterns. Several children were running in the plaza chasing a ball.

Agustina signaled to Esteban to stop in front of the dressmaker's shop. "We will be several hours, Esteban. You may rest or get a drink."

"How can you dismiss him in such a manner? Our drivers would wait all day and night if necessary until our return. You are too soft Agustina," Marcella faulted her.

Carmelita Santos, the dressmaker, looked up from her sewing when two women walked in. She knew *doña* Agustina de Soto. The second woman wore a gown in green brocade, the likes of which Carmelita had never seen.

"Bienvenidos señoras," Carmelita welcomed them with a bright smile.

"This is my sister-in-law, *doña* Marcella de Soto," Agustina introduced Marcella.

"¿Puedo mostrarte algunos vestidos?" Carmelita bowed slightly to Marcella and asked her if she could show her some dresses. *Doña* Marcella barely gave the dressmaker a glance.

"I've come to take a fitting on the new dress you are making for me and *doña* Marcella is interested in your talents. She may be living here for some time and will be needing gowns."

"Most certainly. Agustina come to the back. I have the dress ready for you to try on," Carmelita said.

Marcella thumbed through several pre-made gowns while Agustina went behind a curtain. She clucked disapproval at all of them. The materials were inferior as was the quality of workmanship. If Bartolo insisted on moving to this godforsaken place, she would have to import her own dressmaker.

Marcella impatiently waited for Agustina to complete the fitting. When the dressmaker asked if Marcella was interested in any of the dresses the answer was a flat impersonal, "No."

As they were about to leave Carmelita said to Agustina, "Tell Ana Teresa her dress is ready. She was so excited for it to be done before her husband returned home."

Agustina choked hoping Marcella did not hear or understand the dressmaker's comment. "Oh yes, thank you for my fitting. We must be on our way home," Agustina said loudly hoping the dressmaker would not say anything else and hustled Marcella from the store.

Leaving the shop, Agustina looked along the *paseo* for the carriage. Taking Marcella by the arm, they walked along the *paseo*. Marcella did not ask about the dressmaker's statement and Agustina made small talk about the lovely weather.

As they walked, a group of *vaqueros* rode toward them

down the main street of Santa Fe. In the lead was a *caballero,*
dressed in his finest silver-studded *traje* and his horse
jangled with silver *conchas.* Behind the rider, a wagon
followed and held two bodies draped in canvas.

"The Americano land grabbers killed my son and one
of my men," the *caballero* shouted for all to hear. "They
were killed on our own land. Come everyone and see that it
is true. See the future for Spaniards in Santa Fe," he yelled.
Agustina shuddered. Violence had come to Santa Fe just as
her husband predicted.

"My son is dead. Next it will be your sons!" the
caballero continued to shout.

Agustina watched the commotion in the plaza as the
sheriff and deputy came to talk to the *caballero.* She knew
Pedro was worried about the escalating violence against
Spaniards over their land. Her husband's land grant was
valid, but perhaps so was the land grant of this unfortunate
caballero.

Marcella watched, but said nothing about the
unpleasant incident. Several minutes later, Esteban brought
the carriage to the curb and helped them up into the seats.
All the while Marcella pondered the dressmaker's comment
about Ana Teresa.

Chapter 38

When Ana Teresa dressed for dinner, she took out her wedding ring from the drawer in the dressing table. As was her ritual each night, she picked it up tenderly and put it on her finger where it belonged. She held up her hand looking at it, then put the hand on her heart and said a prayer.

It was almost the end of July and Rafael was due to get home soon. The thought thrilled and terrified her. Uncle Pedro, Aunt Agustina, and Bibiana were carefully keeping their part of the lie that Ana Teresa was still a *señorita*. They all agreed to keep the ruse until Rafael returned to Santa Fe to address her father directly.

Ana Teresa finished her toiletries and carefully put the ring back into the drawer. Satisfied, she headed to Bibiana's room. For the past week, her cousin felt strong enough to partake meals with the family in the large dining room downstairs.

"Bibiana, are you ready?" Ana Teresa tapped lightly on the door.

"Yes I'm ready, come take Benicío," Bibiana answered.

Ana Teresa gathered the tiny baby up in her arms, pulling a light blanket around him. He looked at her and cooed with his big eyes melting Ana Teresa's heart.

"Look, I can fit into my red gown," Bibiana said and twirled around.

"You look lovely. Won't Carlos be surprised when he gets home and you are up and healthy again."

They walked to the top of the stairs and Ana Teresa carefully held the baby in one arm and pulled at her skirt with the other so as not to trip on the hem. Below she could hear her father's voice, loud and angry, almost yelling.

"You are a fool Pedro. How could you let this happen?"

Pedro responded, but the girls could not understand the words.

"I trusted you and this is how you repay me?" *don* Bartolo's voice reached a crescendo.

When they walked into the dining room, *don* Bartolo turned to Ana Teresa and screamed at her, "*¡Puta!* You did not have my permission to marry!" he growled at her.

Ana Teresa looked from her father to her uncle in disbelief. Her uncle dropped his eyes toward the floor. Her father's face was red with anger. Her mother and aunt were standing on the other side of the room. Her aunt looked ashen and her mother looked stern.

"Father, there was not time. Letters would take too long to reach you and we did not know when you would return. I fell in love with Rafael. Besides I had no dowry and you know how my betrothed in California rejected me when he found out I had none. The *caballeros* here in Santa Fe treated me badly when they found out I had no money. Rafael loves me for me and did not care I had no dowry to offer."

"Well, humph, humph," her father blustered. Everything she said was true. Domingo, her fiancé in California rejected her after the loss of the de Soto estate in Rancho Simi. Domingo married a less pretty girl whose father owned a large vineyard and offered a large dowry.

"I am your father and you needed my permission to marry. Who is this Rafael? What credentials does he have? Who are his parents and ancestors. Where in Spain do they come from?" her father blustered trying to keep his tone of authority.

"Father perhaps we should sit for supper. The servants are ready to serve," Ana Teresa hoped to soften the tone. She handed the baby to the maid and went to her chair waiting to be seated.

"Yes, let us eat. Raoul, please pour the wine, or would you like brandy *don* Bartolo?" Agustina asked.

Marcella had said nothing to Agustina about the dressmaker's comments on the way home, however she must have told *don* Bartolo. He came down to supper with vengeance in his heart. Agustina noticed Marcella seemed more aloof toward her, cold and dismissive.

After the meal was served, *don* Bartolo asked Ana Teresa again about Rafael's credentials.

"His name is Rafael Reyes de Estrada. His father is from Cordoba." Rafe told her *don* Bernardo's ancestors came from Cordoba, Spain. "He is a horse breeder here in Santa Fe and breeds the finest horses. Doesn't he *tío?*"

"Yes, that is true. He rides the finest Appaloosa you will ever see. He is training a yearling for me now and I expect it will be the envy of all the other *dons,*" her uncle replied.

"Why is he not here?" Her father's demeanor softened a bit as he heard about Rafael. The man sounded at least somewhat a decent match for his only daughter. She was right in saying most *caballeros* would not want to marry her without a dowry, even though she was beautiful.

"He is in Mexico checking on his hacienda there. His mother is remarrying and he and Carlos went to the wedding."

"He has a hacienda in Mexico? I thought you said he is a horse breeder here in Santa Fe?"

"When he inherited the hacienda, he gave it to his sister and her husband. They live and run the hacienda now," Ana Teresa replied.

At first *don* Bartolo felt relieved. The man she married had a hacienda, even if it was in Mexico. He must be a man of some power and wealth. Bartolo sat eating the New Mexican meal of spicy pork served with tortillas and potatoes roasted with chilis. It was simple fare and tasty. His mind tried to process the news about his daughter while he ate.

Something did not make sense. Bartolo was well aware of inheritance laws, although not specifically in Mexico. If Rafael's mother, the *doña* of the hacienda remarried, the new *don* would own the property. Bartolo pondered the issue in his brain as he sipped at his brandy.

Finally he asked, "And what of his mother? As *doña* of the estate, she would relinquish her rights to the new *don.*

Does he not own the hacienda now and not your husband?"

Ana Teresa swallowed hard. Her father's eyes bore into hers. She knew this was the moment of truth. How could she ever make her father understand? Steeped in the Spanish traditions of the caste system, he could never accept her marriage to Rafael.

"His mother is not a *doña*. She is part Indian and worked on the hacienda. Rafael is *mestizo*," she came out and told the truth which her father and mother would detest. Their daughter married a lower class mixed-blood *mestizo*. Her father would be shamed as well as angry.

Her mother gasped. Her father at first looked stunned, then turned to Pedro and growled, "You . . . you let this happen!"

Turning he screamed at Ana Teresa, "How dare you taint the de Soto bloodline? *¡Puta!*" he repeated calling her a whore. "For all the generations de Soto blood has been pure Spanish blood, now you ruin everything by marrying a *desgraciado mestizo.*"

Her father's words made her ashamed and sad. She knew her marriage choice opposed his traditional Spanish beliefs. Ana Teresa sat for a moment quietly looking at her hands in her lap.

Bartolo turned his vehemence toward his brother Pedro. "You sniveling *desgraciado.* You let my only daughter marry a *mestizo* and did nothing? You should have killed them both when you learned the truth, but you lied to me. You will pay for that."

"It is not uncle Pedro's fault. He refused to let us marry and sent me back to California. I married Rafael in El Paso. You don't understand, I love him *Papá.*"

"Then go to him. You are no longer my daughter, you *puta.* Leave my sight and never return," her father growled at her.

Tears stung in her eyes wanting to spill down her checks. She looked at her mother, but her mother's eyes were looking at her hands in her lap. She knew her mother would never cross her father. Her mother was weak and subservient, a typical *doña* married for her dowry and her beauty. She embodied everything Ana Teresa did not want in life. Rafael loved her, trusted her, and wanted her not for money or beauty, but for her, all of her.

Taking her napkin, Ana Teresa dabbed her cheeks and stood up, then looked at her father.

"You are a pathetic, pompous fool living in the past. You have nothing, no money, no land. Yes Rafael is *mestizo*. He owns land in Mexico and owns a profitable business here in Santa Fe. He is a good man, an honorable man. He is not like the arrogant *caballeros* you would prefer for me. He loves me, not for money or the power a marriage might bring. He told me before he left to tell you, you are welcome to live with us. We have a house large enough for all of us and our future children, your grandchildren, when we have them. What a pity you will never know them. I may now be a *puta* in your eyes, but I do not care what you think," Ana Teresa looked at her father with fire in her eyes, not tears. Pushing away from her chair, she left the room.

Chapter 39

Two days after *don* Eduardo Martinez brought his murdered son and *vaquero* into Santa Fe, the local *dons* called a meeting at the Palacio Cantina in the older part of the city. The Palacio was one of the few places in Santa Fe used exclusively by the Spanish aristocrats, excluding Americanos. It was a place the Spanish *dons* felt safe to discuss the assaults against them.

Twelve of the most prominent landowners were seated at the tables. Their ancestors before them had been the law and political clout here in Santa Fe before the Americans took over. Each one owned a family land grant for many generations, obtained from the Spanish Crown or Mexico. Their ancestors settled New Mexico, taming it into a hospitable place to live.

After the *dons* were served a brandy or tequila, *don* Leonardo called the meeting to order. Out of respect, he let *don* Eduardo speak first.

"My son Javier was murdered in cold blood. Two wagons of Americanos came onto my land and are building houses. They stole some of the cattle grazing on my range and built a corral. I went to the deputy in Tesuque. He promised to look into it. The *desgraciado* did nothing. Two weeks later my son and several *vaqueros* were rounding up my cows. They were moving them to higher ground, further away from the squatters. One of the Americanos called my son a thief and shot him. He was still alive when they brought him home, but he died in my arms that night."

Don Eduardo sighed deeply. The men gathered in this room knew Javier was Eduardo's only son and heir to his legacy. Eduardo raised cattle and prize bulls on his large hacienda north of Santa Fe. His dairy cows supplied much of the butter and cream for many locals.

A general grumbling circled the room, however they gave *don* Eduardo time to speak without interrupting.

"When I brought Javier's body here to the sheriff, I expected him to arrest the squatter and hang him. Is that not the American law? One of my *vaqueros* is able to identify him, but the sheriff has done nothing."

The room erupted with angry comments.

"The sheriff is a gringo. He cares little for our plight. We must take the law back," *don* Manuel Vargas grumbled.

"Manuel and I have also lost sons. The sheriff did nothing when our sons, Vicente and Alvaro, were murdered. How many more Spanish sons need to die. I say we take the fight to the Americanos!" *don* Luciano Gutierrez' voice escalated.

Angry comments circulated the room and the voices in the room reverberated as the *don's* anger peaked.

"It is the Santa Fe Ring, not the sheriff. They are intimidating the government officials and the sheriff knows they will fire him and find another if he crosses them," *don* Leonardo gruffed in the sheriff's defense.

The Santa Fe Ring of unscrupulous politicians and bankers knew exactly how to get rich. Much of New Mexico's mineral rich land was owned by the Spaniards. Stretched across miles and miles of unprotected acres and only marked by stone pillars, the land was ripe for the plucking. Most Spaniards spoke little English and could not defend themselves. The government made sure the fight was in the courts, which was foreign to the Spanish *dons*.

"How can we find any justice when the people elected to serve are the same ones who rob us of our heritage?" *don* Ramon interjected into the argument.

"I heard a rumor that the Attorney General, Stephen Elkins, is the leader of the Santa Fe Ring. He is sworn to uphold the laws here in New Mexico. Is it not his bank who generates mortgages on our repossessed Spanish land grants? He steals our land for nothing and then sells it to speculators," *don* Daniel explained.

"I think all the government officials are corrupt. Name one who has defended our rights. Even Spaniards in the government are not raising our cause. I've even heard rumors a few *caballeros* are part of the Santa Fe Ring working against us for a profit."

"Who would do such a thing? Where is their Spanish honor?" *don* Luciano protested.

"We must take matters into our own hands and fight, with swords if we must," *don* Daniel argued. As one of the silver-haired elders in the room, he stood and brandished his ornate sword.

Fighting and defending their rights ran in Spanish blood. Spaniards battled invading Moors for over seven hundred years and conquered the Aztec Empire. The ancestors of early Spanish colonists to New Mexico fought against the odds of survival to create their world here in Santa Fe. It was not long ago, these *dons* or their fathers defended themselves from raiding Apaches. Then the American Army under the leadership of General Kearny came to Santa Fe. He brought over 2,500 heavily armed soldiers and the *dons* gave up without a fight. Anything else would have been suicide.

"I agree we must fight, but we are ranchers. We have no authority. If we fight the government, they will only bring down the soldiers upon us like they did to *don* Luis Baca. They shot him inside his own house," *don* Pedro retorted.

Don Pedro reminded the *caballeros* of the killing of *don* Luis Maria Cabeza de Baca. All Spaniards knew of the travesty perpetrated upon *don* Luis de Baca. His was the first New Mexican Spanish land grant to be invalidated. The government wanted part of his land along the Gallinas River for the town which was now called Las Vegas. His dispute and distrust of the government led to *don* Luis' untimely death. Although the government finally relented and allowed the Baca heirs to retain much of the original land grant, the Town of Las Vegas prevailed and *don* Luis Maria Cabeza de Baca was dead.

"It is the way of the Americanos. They have no honor. They believe they have the right to this land because of something they call Manifest Destiny. They believe they are justified to spread across this country and kill anyone who gets in their way," *don* Ramon said.

"Yes, especially anyone with brown or red skin. They killed many of the Indians and sent the rest to reservations. Perhaps that is what they plan for us Spaniards," *don* Pedro groused.

"My son Benjamin says we must fight in the American courts, not with swords or guns. I've hired an attorney to represent my claim," *don* Ramon said.

"Your son Benjamin is a *culón*. Alvaro often told me he was, so I suppose he is just like his father," *don* Luciano called *don* Ramon and his son chickenshits.

"How dare you call me that!" *Don* Ramon stood and pulled his sword as he retorted in an angry huff.

"*Señores,* we must not fight each other," *don* Leonardo tried to restore peace.

In the old traditions, the Spaniards respected each other's property. An occasional duel was fought over a woman, but never over land. They were good neighbors and pulled together when things got tough. Being under attack from both squatters and the government was new to their psyche, especially because they struggled to understand English and the new laws.

"So how do we fight?" *don* Ramon asked lowering his sword.

"We must form an alliance to help each other and to show the Santa Fe Ring we cannot be dismissed so easy. If we stand together we will have more power and we can break the ring," *don* Leonardo asserted. Heads around the room nodded in agreement.

Chapter 40

Rusty Jennings, the cook at the Sutton bunkhouse had a bad feeling since Pete Carter and Jake McNab showed up several weeks ago. Pete stayed on and Rusty knew the ranch needed good men, but it was not long before Rusty heard snippets of conversations and several of the Texans and Pete were thick as thieves. Rusty distinctly heard the words rustle, herd, and Wyoming in bits and pieces of hushed conversations. He had no hard proof, of course, just a feeling. He wanted to tell Miss Cynthia, but shied from doing so. Accusing Pete of planning a cattle rustle might get him shot or fired.

Instead, Rusty talked to Armando Delgado. Armando was one of Miss Cynthia's trusted Mexican *vaqueros*. Armando and the other Mexican cowboys did not mix with the Texans and he was sure Armando would not be involved in any wicked plan. Rusty had learned quite a bit of Spanish since coming to New Mexico, so it was not hard to talk to him.

After telling Armando his suspicions, he learned most of the Mexican *vaqueros* were planning on going to Socorro for the Catholic festival, the *Fiesta de Santiago,* and would be gone Thursday night and not returning until sometime late on Saturday. Armando and Rusty agreed, if any plan was devised, Pete and the Texans would think Friday was the perfect opportunity. Still they were only guessing and maybe Rusty was imagining all of it. Maybe the Texans were just glad Pete was back at the ranch. He was a likeable enough cowpuncher and a hard worker.

Pete rode into Jed's camp guided by firelight Wednesday night. Everyone was sitting around the fire finishing a stew Pappy made with some of the beef from yesterday.

"Hey Pete. Good ta see yew," Jed said.

"Good ta see yew out of jail," Pete replied. Jed

introduced Pete to Crabclaw, Tom, and Rick and Pete greeted Jimbo, Pappy, and Breed.

"Hey that smells good."

"Hep yerself," Pappy said. Pete grabbed a plate and starting wolfing down the stew.

Pete took his time as he settled in next to Jake. "What the fuck, Pete. Dun ya be so fuckin smug," Jed admonished him. "What did ya learn about the cows at the ranch?"

Pete laughed. "It ain't gonna be no problum. The cows r fat and ready fer market. On Fridee, the Mescans are gonna be celebratin some greaser fiesta. One of the boys tole me the Mescans will be a leavin on Thursdee and celebratin all day on Fridee in Socorro. Anyway, with the greasers gone, it would be a good day to take the herd. I got four of the boys to hep us," Pete spilled the plan.

Jed was thrilled with the news about the Spanish celebration. Taking the herd just got a whole lot easier. "Pete, are all the Mescans working for the Sutton widder going to this festival?" Jed asked.

"Yeah and almost every Mescan in town. It be some big shindig at the church up there in Socorro."

"I tole yew boys this was goin to be as smooth as cream gravy," Jed smirked.

"Well now yew got one problem, the way I see it," Breed said. Breed seldom said anything, so everyone listened. "The Goodnight-Loving Trail is on the tother side of the Rio Grande. The cows are on this side. How ya gonna git em across?"

"Breed's right. I heerd one of the Mexes talkin about the same problem. He said there was a shallow spot just north of the town at the end of the main road. Otherwise ya gotta so south of Fort Craig or up the road to Socorro."

"So we cross em past the town," Jed said.

"Only way to reach that spot is by going through the center of town. That ain't so smart," Pete told him.

Jed pondered the dilemma for almost a minute. "Didn't yew say em greasers are all leavin on Thursdee and goin to Socorro for the festival? Sounds to me like the town will be empty."

"Yew gotta be pretty stupid to try and rustle a herd through the center of a town," Crabclaw spoke up after listening to the others. "Yew shud git em across the river south of the town."

"Yew cain't. The river gits deeper south of town and besides the Army fort is there," Pete said.

Crabclaw was getting more frustrated with this group of misfits with each passing day. The would-be gang of rustlers were just a group of stupid cowpokes. They never rustled anything before, let alone a large herd of cattle. Jed convinced him taking the herd was easy. Well taking it might be easy, getting it across the Rio Grande to the trail north was another.

Jed ignored the complaints. "Okay, we go thar afore sunup on Fridee. Em greasers will either be gone or asleep. Pete, yew git on back to the bunkhouse and tell the boys ta be ready. Listen up everybody, we only got one day to git ready. Tomorrow, Pappy yew git on up the trail. Head northeast till yew find a good spot fer a camp. Corky yew n Glenda foller Pappy with the remuda. We'll catch up ta yew. Just stay put thar an wait. Everyone else, git yer gear stowed and clean yer guns fer the fight we gonna have gittin that herd," Jed ordered.

Later everyone found their spot to sleep. Corky and Glenda chose a place near the river's edge on a patch of soft grass. After washing up, they crawled under a blanket, both were naked. "Glenda, this will be the last time we may git a chance to make love. We're gonna be on the run headed up the trail. Iffin all goes well, we'll be moving fast to Wyomin."

She responded with a passionate kiss and reached down and took his penis in her hand. It did not take much to get the young man hard. Even though she was not in love with Corky, she liked having him inside her. She liked his attention. He was a sweet boy. Honest and kind. Corky began to moan.

From a short distance away and behind a shrub, Crabclaw watched as the young couple stripped naked. Glenda's pale skin shone softly in the moon's light.

Unaware they were being watched, she turned fully toward the shrub where Crabclaw hid. Her firm breasts had large pink nipples. Between her legs was a mound of thick brown hair. Crabclaw breathed deeply wanting to shove Corky into the river and take his prize now.

The two naked lovers crawled under the blanket and Crabclaw stroked himself as he watched the blanket move up and down in the moonlit night. "She's yers fer now boy, but she will be mine soon enough," he mumbled to himself. When he was done, he snuck off into the night unnoticed.

On Thursday, Armando stopped by the bunkhouse after the breakfast meal.

"I've asked several of my men to stay in San Marcial instead of going to Socorro. They will be stationed near the river crossing and on the escarpment where they can see the herd. I will also stay in town close by and watch for the Texas cowboys to make a move," he told Rusty.

Rusty agreed it was a good plan. He wished he could be of more help. He was still pretty handy with a pistol, but after getting gored by a steer and almost losing his life, Rusty was not able to ride a horse any longer.

"Gracias amigo. I hope I am wrong and tell your men to say nothing."

CHAPTER 41

Friday morning the rustlers woke early before sunup. Jed insisted on a cold camp. Breakfast was biscuits, jam, and bacon Pappy cooked yesterday afternoon. Pappy, Corky, and Glenda left the previous day and were headed up the trail.

Jed led the group on a trot wanting to get to the ranch before sunup. Breed and Jimbo rode near him, while Jake, Crabclaw, and the two young cowboys, Rick and Tom trailed behind. Worry consumed Jed's thoughts. It had all seemed so easy when he was just talking, now he wondered what trouble they might encounter once they started the herd moving.

The plan was to move the cows up the main street of San Marcial to the river crossing. According to Pete, the greasers left yesterday for the big fiesta in Socorro, which was about fifty miles away. The town should be empty. Once they got the herd past the village and across the river, they could turn the herd east and get to the Goodnight-Loving Trail. The well used trail followed the Pecos River north through to Colorado and ended at Cheyenne, Wyoming.

All was dark and quiet when they rode near the bunkhouse and found Pete with four Texas cowboys waiting at the entrance to the ranch. Jed nodded a greeting to the four Texans who he knew from his time working here at the ranch. "Howdy boys. Glad yer joinin up with us. Are yew ready?" Jed asked.

"Shur nuff. Yesterdee we dun moved the herd to the north pasture whar we can git em goin fast through the village."

Jimbo and Breed pulled up their bandanas to hide their faces. Jed and Jake started to do the same.

"Pull them bandanas down," Crabclaw hissed. "Iffin yew takin this herd through that town, then yew need to act normal. We just Sutton cowboys movin the herd. Yew look like outlaws, someone will notice."

Jed bristled at Crabclaw's authority over the group. Last night he was giving orders at the camp. Unfortunately, the men listened knowing Crabclaw was a seasoned rustler. He cautioned the men to keep the herd calm. "Do not let them stampede," he told them several times.

"Yew heard him, now lets go git em cows," Jed said.

Jed and the rustlers followed the Sutton cowboys toward the north pasture. It was not yet daylight, so they rode slower than a gallop. They could smell and hear the herd before they saw the cows. Jed was glad Pete and the boys from the Sutton ranch thought to move the herd closer to San Marcial yesterday. It would make today's job easier.

The pasture was long and spread from the river to the escarpment of the nearby hills. Pete told them the herd was large, in the thousands. Jed thought Pete was probably exaggerating. Now that he had a look himself, a grin spread across his face.

The rustlers stopped near the quiet herd. "Now member, we dun need no stampede. Just go down thar and round em up and start movin em up toward town. Member, we just Sutton cowboys doin the job of movin em cows from one pasture to another. Stick to yer positions and don't worry nun about no strays," Crabclaw reminded them.

Crabclaw began acting as the leader yesterday and Jed disliked it. Unfortunately, the men followed him. Even Jimbo and Breed thought he was a more experienced leader and trusted his judgment.

"Yew heard im. Git down thar and turn the herd north to town," Jed ordered.

Crabclaw, Rick, and Tom got out to the lead. Jimbo, Breed and the four Sutton men took the left flank, away from the river. They rode as singles, ready to keep the herd from turning left. The river created the natural boundary and the cows would not go willingly into the river. Jake, Pete, and Jed headed for the rear.

Before dawn Friday morning only three Sutton

cowboys showed up for breakfast. These three were not cowboys who originally came from Texas with John B. Sutton. They were outsiders, drifters who joined the ranch this spring. Rusty wondered where the others were, as cowboys never missed a meal.

"Where's the rest?" Rusty asked them. "Dun know," Lefty replied. "They was all up and gone when we woke up this mornin."

"More fer me," Freddy said with a grin. He sat and piled bacon and biscuits on his plate.

Rusty wished he could go tell Armando what he surmised could come true. He only hoped Armando had men in place to stop it.

Pancho and Jose rode to the escarpment early Friday morning before dawn broke. Armando asked them to watch for unusual activity with the herd. It was still too dark to see the river across the valley, but the sky was beginning to lighten to the east.

Jose pulled out his pouch and made himself a cigarette. As he smoked, he saw dust rising from the valley floor.

"Jose, down there." Pancho nodded seeing the dust starting to rise into the air.

"*Vámonos,*" Jose threw away his cigarette and spurred his horse to a gallop. Pancho followed.

When they reached the valley floor, the cows were moving at a steady pace north coming toward them. Three cowboys were riding in the lead. It was impossible for Pancho and Jose to see how many cows or men followed.

"*¡Estop!*" Pancho yelled for the cowboys to stop. The Mexicans rode hard yelling and waving their hands at the rustlers. Jose hollered for the cowboys to turn the cattle around.

Seeing the two men in their *vaquero* hats Rick grumbled, "Shit, I thought all them greasers was gone."

Tom spurred his horse into a gallop. "Yehaa," he yelled.

Crabclaw did not like this plan from the beginning. Jed was an idiot and he wondered why he ever agreed to come along. Rick yelled to Crabclaw as the two *vaqueros* came within their range. Crabclaw turned and fired. The shot missed and the two Mexican cowboys kicked their horses. One of the *vaqueros* raised a pistol and fired. Crabclaw fired back.

This time the *vaquero* jerked on his horse, though did not fall. Suddenly Crabclaw heard the snorts of the lead cows. Hooves began to pound loudly. The mass of the herd, thousands of tons of beef on the hoof would follow the lead cows. He saw Tom ahead with the herd barreling toward him. He darted his horse right, then left. Suddenly Tom and his horse were caught in the middle of the herd, then disappeared down in the middle of the stampede.

Crabclaw wanted to kill the two *vaqueros,* but the herd was his immediate problem. Cattle were ornery and determined once a stampede started. Nothing could stop them now.

Cynthia Seeley woke when she heard the baby gurgling from the crib. Sunlight was creeping over the eastern mountains and it was not unusual for the baby to wake before sunup. Little Ed always woke hungry and had a big appetite like his father, Big Ed.

It was unusual to wake without Big Ed at her side. He decided to stay in town last night because most of the Hispanics left to go to the *Fiesta de Santiago* in Socorro. Even Tomás, Teresa, and their family headed to the celebration and Ed thought someone should stay in town. A tiny sleepy village, San Marcial had to contend with the Texas cowboys from the ranch. It was the ranch Cynthia inherited from her first husband, John B. Sutton.

She picked up Little Ed and cuddled him. Cynthia loved being a mother and loved being married to Big Ed. He was a kind and generous man, nothing like the hardened Texas cattleman, John B. Sutton. She had to thank John however for marrying her, a whore from Austin, and bringing her here to San Marcial. She was not happy he was dead, but she was very much in love with Ed Seeley. Little Ed burrowed on her chest finding one of her breasts and started to nurse.

Letting the baby nurse, Cynthia rocked him gently and hummed a tune. Suddenly she heard gunfire. It was not uncommon. Often in the early morning, the cowboys spotted some predator near the herd trying to pick off a calf for a tasty breakfast. Then she heard another volley. With Little Ed in her arms, she walked out the back door and stood on the veranda. The vast valley of the ranch spread out below her house. John B. had the house built with views from all directions. In the dim dawn light she could barely see a dust cloud from the north side of the veranda.

Consuelo, Cynthia's housekeeper drove her buggy up to the front of the ranchhouse. On her way from town, Consuelo evaded a large herd of cattle. Thousands of cows were headed down the main road toward San Marcial. When it was safe, she continued on her way to the ranchhouse. She drove with more speed than usual. Consuelo found Cynthia nursing Little Ed on the back veranda.

"*Señora*, the cows they run that way," she said pointing north.

"What do you mean?" Cynthia asked. Her initial thought was perhaps some strays got away from the herd and ran off.

"*Muchas vacas estan corriendo,*" she explained in Spanish that many cows were running away.

"Consuelo, take the baby inside. Big Ed is in town. I'll take your buggy and go find him." Someone or something had spooked the cattle. Ed had always warned her about a stampede and how dangerous they were. "Cattle are stupid. They will run until they fall down trampling everything in their way," he had told her. Luckily it had never happened on the ranch before.

With a scarf, she tied her long reddish auburn hair at the nape of her neck. Cynthia jumped up to the buggy seat and snapped the reins to get the old horse moving and headed the buggy down the road from the house. The town of San Marcial was about five miles away. More gunfire and the pounding sound of fast moving hooves filled the morning air, but she kept the old horse running at a fast pace toward town. As she reached the main road heading into San Marcial, it was already filled with running cattle. Dust and snorting filled the air. Through the dust cloud, she saw some men on horseback chasing the herd, at least she thought they were giving chase.

Cynthia pulled up and saw cattle running straight for the town. One of the cowboys riding alongside, shot into the air and yelled, "Get along, yehaa!"

Cynthia's brain swirled. The cowboy who she did not recognize did not seem to be trying to stop the cows, instead he was pushing them forward. Soon another cowboy rode with the herd, swinging his lasso and slapping it back and forth and yelling.

She snapped the reins and started the horse and buggy. The cowboy was intently yelling at the cattle as he rode nearby. She did not recognize him through the dust and dim morning light.

"What the hell are you doing?" she screamed over the sound of the fast moving herd.

The cowboy turned, saw the buggy, and heard someone holler at him. He looked to see, but could not see the driver of the buggy through the dust.

"Stop! Come back here!" he heard a voice scream at him.

Without thinking, he took aim at the horse's head and shot two bullets. With a thud the horse stumbled to its front knees and the harness gave way, causing the buggy to skid. The right wheel hit the dead horse tossing Cynthia clear of the crumpled mess and dead horse. The cowboy spurred his horse leaving the broken buggy and helpless driver behind.

CHAPTER 42

Ana Teresa stormed up to her room at her uncle's home after the confrontation with her father. The first thing she did was retrieve her wedding ring from its hiding place. She put it on her finger.

"I will never take you off again. Never, no matter what happens. I would rather die first," she said looking at her hand.

Quickly she opened the dresser drawers and began to pack. Bibiana did not need her help anymore and she was free to leave. She meant every word she said to her father and wished she said even more. She wished she had told him Rafael was everything he was not. Rafael was kind and generous. He was loving, loyal, and hard working. Most of all he treated everyone with respect – the foundry workers, the Summers' cook, the shop keepers in town, and even the *dons* who tried to hang him. Rafael held no anger or revenge in his heart.

A quiet tap broke into her thoughts. The door opened and it was her *tía* Agustina.

"You do not have to leave Ana Teresa. Your father is angry, hurt. He will see things differently tomorrow," she said.

"Hummph, you know that is not true. He is everything I said and more. He was raised to be such and will never change."

"What about your mother? She loves you."

"My mother loves dresses and parties. I doubt she even loves my father. She would never contradict his wishes. She is not like you, *tía*. I have seen you and Uncle Pedro. You have a loving marriage and Uncle Pedro respects you."

Agustina could not dispute what her niece said. Pedro was not sleeping at night with worry Bartolo was going to take this hacienda for his own regardless they had spent their life here. Marcella was dismissive and rude to everyone. Agustina wished they had stayed in Spain.

"It is all right *tía*. I have a home and a husband. If you and Uncle Pedro ever need anything, Rafael and I will help you. You will always be welcome under our roof. Now please go have Juan get the buggy ready. I am going home."

Monday morning Rafe and Carlos got an early start from El Paso headed up the Chihuahua Trail toward Santa Fe, thankful to be back in the United States. To their surprise, the *Fiesta de Santiago* celebration by the Spanish-speaking people had been in full swing over the weekend. Puppets, street food vendors, costumed dancers, and music filled the plaza until late into the night.

Santiago and Rayo nudged each other wanting to race, but the two tired riders were in no mood to let them play. The two nights at the Hotel Stratton had been less than peaceful.

"Hell of a weekend, eh Carlos. Even some of the cowboys joined in on the fiesta."

"The *Fiesta de Santiago* has always been one of my favorites. Santiago is the patron saint of Spain. When I was in Madrid, the celebration lasted days," Carlos said.

"Every time I started to fall asleep, gunshots woke me. You know how cowboys think shooting up in the air is fun. I hope no one got hurt," Rafe complained.

"Perhaps we should spend tonight at the inn in Las Cruces and hit the trail hard tomorrow," Carlos suggested.

"No we should push on. I miss Ana Teresa and her parents must be in Santa Fe by now."

"And I miss Bibiana and the baby, too. Perhaps I should not have left them," Carlos mused.

They kept a steady pace all day only resting the horses once and having a quick meal from their saddlebags. As night was falling, Carlos thought they should stop at the spot where the Rio Grande made a large U-shaped turn. After watering their horses, they tethered them in the cottonwood grove and built a small fire. Rafe cooked the last of the bacon and made coffee.

Dawn was only a slight glimmer in the sky when they

heard the sound of horses and six men on horseback rode into their camp. Rafe rolled out of his bedroll and stood up. The fire was burned to embers and the six men were only barely visible, although Rafe saw the shape of their hats and heard the jingle of their conchas. These were Mexican cowboys, *vaqueros*.

"*Buenos dias,*" Rafe said in a friendly voice.

"*¿Quién eres tú?*" the *vaquero* in the lead growled, "Who are you?"

Rafe was surprised by the Mexican cowboy's demeanor. He had traveled often along the Chihuahua Trail and never been bothered by *vaqueros*.

"I am Rafael Reyes de Estrada and this is Carlos Zuniga. We are traveling to Santa Fe."

"You are on the lands of *don* Juan Dionisio Anaya," the *vaquero* told them gruffly.

"Thank your *patrón* for his hospitality. Perhaps we can build up the fire and put on a pot of coffee. We have a little food to share," Rafe said.

Somewhat reluctantly, the *vaqueros* dismounted seeing the men were Hispanic and not Anglos. Carlos built up the fire and started the coffee. While the morning dawned, the *vaqueros* told them of squatters trying to settle near the Rio Grande. The *don* owned many acres here along the river and the land grant to the Anaya family was as old as New Mexico itself. The *patrón's* ancestors came from Mexico City with *don* Juan Oñate's first caravan in 1598.

When they finished the coffee, the *vaqueros* apologized to Rafe and Carlos. "Be careful. There is trouble brewing everywhere," they told them.

Hastily packing their gear, Rafe and Carlos pushed north. They kept a vigilant watch on both the trail ahead and behind them.

"Should we stop in San Marcial or keep on going?" Rafe asked Carlos.

"I think we should stop. It will be safer in town than camping on the trail."

CHAPTER 43

When Rafe and Carlos rode into the village of San Marcial, New Mexico, they saw damaged property, corners of stores were caved in and lower windows were broken. One section of the sidewalk roof was toppled in a heap. Several mules and dogs lay dead on the sides of the road, flies buzzing around the carcasses. Two small houses on the south side of the village were burned to ashes.

"This looks like a war zone. What the hell could have happened here?" Carlos spoke out first.

"Hurry, let's get to Tomás' house," Rafe said and spurred Rayo. When they passed Big Ed's Saloon, they saw the wooden pillars holding up the front wooden awning broken down on the ground. Other stores were also damaged, almost like a giant monster rushed up the main street brushing whatever got in its way along the street.

At Tomás house, they quickly dismounting and ran to the front door and knocked until Teresa opened it. "Is Tomás here?" Carlos asked without giving her the formal greeting.

"No, Tomás fue a Socorro," she said Tomás went to Socorro.

"¿Qué pasó en el pueblo?" Carlos asked her what happened at the village.

"No lo sé. Tomás dijo que eran vacas," she said Tomás told her it was cows.

"It does not make sense, Carlos. What does she mean it was cows?"

"Let's go find Ed Seeley, he'll know what happened," Carlos said.

They mounted up and rushed back to town. Big Ed's Saloon door was locked. Across the street Arturo was working on the front of his damaged mercantile.

"¿Qué pasó en el pueblo?" Carlos asked him what happened at the village.

"Alguien le robó el ganado a la Señora Seeley," Arturo said

someone stole Missus Seeley's cattle. He also told Carlos, the rustlers drove the herd right through the village early in the morning several days ago.

"*¿Dónde está Ed?*" Carlos asked where Ed was.

Arturo told them Ed was at the clinic at Fort Craig where they were caring for Missus Seeley, but they might be back at the ranch by now.

"She was hurt?"

"*Sí.* The cowboys they shoot her," Arturo said.

"Let's go see if they are back," Rafe said. They mounted up and rode the horses hard the five miles to the Seeley ranch. Neither of them spoke along the trip, fearful of what might have happened to Cynthia.

Rafe knocked on the door and Consuelo, the housekeeper, answered. He asked if Ed was in.

"*Sí, por favor entra,*" she asked them to come in and led them to the parlor. A few moments later, Big Ed came from the back of the house.

"Ed, what happened to Cynthia?" Rafe asked when Ed Seeley stepped into the parlor.

"She suffered a broken arm, bruised ribs, and facial cuts. Some shock, but she seems to be coming out of it now."

Rafe and Carlos were relieved hearing Cynthia was not shot as Arturo told them.

"How did it happen? We saw what happened at the village and Arturo told us someone drove your herd through main street," Carlos asked.

"Four mornings ago, rustlers stole the herd. Cynthia heard gunshots and took Consuelo's buggy and drove toward town to find me. When she reached the main road, one of the rustlers shot the horse causing it to drop and the harness came loose. The buggy crashed tossing Cynthia head over heels to the ground."

"I'm more mad now than hurt," Cynthia stepped into the parlor looking pale and walking gingerly.

"Cindy, you should not be out of bed," Ed admonished her.

"We were planning on driving the cattle north in a

couple weeks. We had a buyer, but now many are gone," she said. "It was my fault. I did not want Ed to take them north yet because of Little Ed."

"It is not your fault Cynthia. I keep telling you that," Ed said rather brusquely.

"Ed, do you know who did this?" Carlos asked.

"We think so. Rusty the bunkhouse cook said one of the Texans, named Pete who left when Sutton was killed, came back several weeks ago. He thinks he recruited some of the others to help. Thanks to Rusty, our foreman Armando and some loyal men were able to cut off some of the herd as they crossed the river. Pancho told me he saw seven or eight cowboys, maybe more, stealing the herd."

"They did it on Friday. Most of the town and many of our *vaqueros* went to Socorro for the fiesta to honor Santiago. The rustlers knew the herd and town would be unprotected," Cynthia added bitterly.

"How many head did you lose?"

"It is still hard to tell. Armando thinks over a thousand," Ed replied.

"What are you going to do now?" Rafe asked.

"Well, Tomás is in Socorro trying to get the sheriff to form a posse to go after the rustlers. He should be back today sometime. I'll tell you though, I have no faith the sheriff will do anything right away. Hell, the rustlers will be way up north by the time he gets off his ass to do something about it."

"We'll stay here until Tomás gets back and if the sheriff won't go after them, we can get our own posse and go after them ourselves," Rafe immediately spoke up.

"I was thinking the same thing, but I don't know how many of the men here in town would help me. You saw the town. The people are scared. Besides Cynthia getting hurt and all the damage, one *vaquero* was injured by the stampede."

"What about the Army? Fort Craig is close and has men," Carlos asked.

"The Army handles Indian attacks, but not local town issues. You know we don't have any real law here."

"Well, we'll wait for Tomás and see what he says," Rafe responded.

"Ed, do you think we could get the herd back?" Cynthia asked.

"I don't know. You need to quit worrying and get back to bed and rest."

"Here take these keys and get settled at the hotel. Help yourselves to the food and drink. Watch out for Tomás and come get me when he gets back," Ed offered and handed them the keys to the saloon.

After leaving Ed and Cynthia, Rafe and Carlos rode back to town. This was not the first time the town of San Marcial had trouble because of the Sutton cattle ranch cowboys. In the past however, it was due to the owner, John B. Sutton and his dislike of the local Spanish people. He allowed his cowboys to intimidate and steal from the local townspeople. Two of his men raped and killed a young Hispanic woman. Rafe knew this was different. The rustlers were after the cattle.

"We must help," Carlos agreed with Rafe as they talked about the situation on the ride back to town.

"I know. It isn't right, if the sheriff won't act. I'll stay and help. You go on to Santa Fe and tell my family what happened," Rafe said.

"No Rafe, I'll go with you," Carlos replied.

"Carlos you must go home to Bibiana and the baby. I've already kept you away too long and also put you in danger. If the sheriff does not help, I'll help Big Ed organize a posse. Otherwise, I'll come home right away."

"There you go again, trying to save the world. If you get involved you could be in grave danger going after cattle rustlers," Carlos warned him knowing it was in Rafe's nature to want to help Cynthia and Big Ed.

"Carlos, I owe Cynthia. I killed her husband. I know he was a bad man, but still I killed him. You must go home to Bibiana and tell Ana Teresa what happened here."

CHAPTER 44

On the afternoon of the second day across the river from San Marcial, the rustlers met up with Pappy, Corky, and Glenda. Pappy had a pot of beans summering on a fire and the rustlers ate a quick meal and changed horses before pushing the herd forward. Jed sent Crabclaw and Rick to keep an eye on their backtrail. So far as they could determine, no posse was on their tail.

That afternoon the wind started to blow across the New Mexico high desert and clouds began to gather in the distance. This time of year in New Mexico brought strong summer thunderstorms. An hour or so later, they could see lightning in the distance coming their way. Jimbo looked around seeing nothing but the relatively flat high desert of scrubby bush and dry grass.

"No place to hide frum that storm," he said to Jed. "Do yew think the critters will bolt iffin it starts crackin on us?"

Jimbo thought another stampede might kill the cows. With some luck the Rio Grande stopped the first stampede, so they were not exhausted as they might have been had it happened on open country like this. Cattle were hard to stop once they stampeded. Often fatigue was the only end to it.

"Hope they'r too tired to bolt. We gotta keep em movin," Jed replied.

Jimbo pulled away. Jed pulled up his bandana to cover his mouth and nose as the dust became choking. The storm was somewhat a blessing. The strong wind would erase their backtrail and create a natural dust cloud. It would make following them even harder.

Several bands of rain swept across them as they moved north. Huge drops pelted the rustlers, but it was a welcome relief from the choking dust. By the time they stopped for the night, they and their gear were covered in thin crusty dirt.

Jed noticed everyone including himself was dog-tired from lack of sleep and pushing the herd at a fast pace. Tonight Pappy's stew tasted like the tan dust which covered everything. Each man grumbled a thank you to Pappy and then made their way to a quiet spot. There was no laughing or gambling, only blessed sleep out of the wind.

Jed shook dust from his bedroll and placed his saddle on a fairly level spot. As he leaned back against the saddle, he thought about their situation. The rustle had not gone as Jed planned. Several miles south of the town, gunshots spooked the herd and they stampeded. The cows thundered down the main road of the town, ripping up everything in sight.

Several *vaqueros* had waited by the river crossing and started firing. The stampeding cows dove into the relatively shallow water, but it stopped their energy. Soon more cowboys from the ranch and a few local men showed up. In the chaos, one of the extra Texas cowboys enlisted by Pete was killed, a couple of the defending *vaqueros* were either killed or injured. Crabclaw and Rick reported Tom was trampled by the herd when the stampede started.

By the time Jed and the outlaws made it across the river, they took off with only a portion of the herd. Jed thought they made off with about one thousand head, which at thirty dollars each was still a sizable chunk of money. As his eyes closed and his brain drifted into sleep, Jed wished he was back in Round Rock with Bonnie Brunel.

For the next two days they pushed the herd northeast more or less twenty miles per day. Jed knew it was a risk and the cattle would lose plenty of weight in the process.

"A lot of em critters ain't gonna make it, iffin yew keep this pace up," Crabclaw warned Jed.

"Yeah, I know, but we ain't got no choice. We gotta make miles while we can. If I know Big Ed, he'll git some of his soldier friends from Fort Craig and cum after us."

"I hear yew, but like I said, we're gonna kill many of

em critters if we dun slow down," Crabclaw reminded him.

Jed knew it would take several days for Big Ed to get the sheriff in Socorro to mount a posse. The Socorro County sheriff and his deputies were the only lawmen in the county which stretched for hundreds of miles. Knowing how things worked, he was counting on the sheriff and a posse could not get started right away. Jed worried a bit however that Big Ed could get the Army to pursue them. The commandant at the fort might give Ed some soldiers.

The terrain in this part of New Mexico was flat and barren, with only small shrubs and dry wild grass. Breed spent his days scouting and found good watering holes each day where none looked possible. They watered their horses and let the cows get a quick drink before moving them on. Each night they ate and slept without any easy-going chatter or laughter.

When Rick and Jake grumbled at Jed over the dismal conditions, Jed ordered them to keep the herd moving northeast toward Lake Sumner. "We'll all take a break at the lake and let the cows fatten up there for a few days before heading up to the Raton Pass and into Colorady," Jed told them.

With no natural land breaks, Jed worried the herd would be easy to follow across the plain. Ed and a posse would know the only route north for the herd was the Goodnight-Loving Trail, which came up from Texas. The trail cut just east of Lake Sumner and Jed and the rustlers would finally catch it north of the lake.

On the fifth day several of the younger cows dropped dead. The dry, dusty miles of exertion were harder on the younger and older cows. Their back trail was now dotted with carcasses.

Crabclaw rode up to Jed. "Yew are one crazy fucker. Yew gotta let em cows rest," he demanded. "The buzzards will be signaling our position for miles around."

"We gotta get to Lake Sumner. We'll find grassy areas near water ponds and the lake to let em feed and rest. I'm sure Big Ed will come after us, so we gotta keep movin,"

Jed responded.

The following morning, Jed sent Rip to scout the back trail. Rip was one of the men Pete recruited from the Sutton ranch.

"Boss, ain't nobody follerin us. Looks like we plum got away." Rip reported after riding to the nearest hill to get a better view of the trail behind them.

"Tell the rest to slow the herd down at bit," Jed told him.

While the rustlers pushed the cattle, Glenda rode with Pappy in the wagon. They filled the days talking about the past and the future. Pappy told her all about the Mexican beaches. Glenda told him about her childhood in Mobile. Her father had been a minister. He wanted to come west because he heard there were lots of places without churches.

"He used to always say everyone needs God," Glenda told Pappy.

"Lots of people need God, some of em don't want im," Pappy explained.

The days grew long and boring. "How much farther to the lake?" Glenda asked Pappy so many times he was tired of thinking up answers.

After seven days, Glenda asked again, "How much farther?"

"Should outta be there by tomorrow missy," he told her.

"I can't wait to take a bath," she replied with a huge grin on her face.

Breed told Jed they were a day from the lake. It was a huge relief. From the looks of it, they had managed to get the good-sized herd to the Goodnight-Loving Trail without any posse dogging them. Only one thing bothered Jed now. It was Crabclaw. Jed saw him quietly talking with the men, one at a time. It did not seem natural. Jed asked Jimbo, but Jimbo said nothing which would lead Jed to believe the outlaw was up to something sinister. Then yesterday, Pete said something troubling.

"Jed, we need ta keep an eye on that jasper Crabclaw.

Pete tells me the man is up ta no good," Jake informed Jed.

"What da yew mean, up ta no good?"

"Cain't rightly say. Pete says it's bout some questions he is askin. I'll let yew know iffin I find out," Jake said and went on about his business.

At around noon on the ninth day from the start of the rustle, the herd waded into the shallow lake. There was pure joy in the gang, with a feeling of victory being voiced by several. Pappy setup a real camp and built a big fire. He roasted one of the young calves that got trampled along the trail. Glenda walked around the lake until she found a quiet inlet and took a long, sudsy bath. The men were less shy and dove in the lake in their long johns. Nothing but elation circulated around the camp, with the exception of Crabclaw.

Craig Moss, known to these men as Crabclaw because of his deformed hand, leaned his saddle against a gnarled tree trunk and sat back. He was slightly amused they had been able to pull off the rustle and get this far. It was not due to planning or precise execution of the plan, but rather dumb luck.

Unfortunately, his friend Tom Harren lost his life, trampled by the herd when they stampeded. Texas short horns were skittery beasts with a keen sense of hearing. One minute they could be calm and then any sudden sharp noise, such as a gunshot or crack of thunder, could turn them into thousands of pounds of running terror.

The rest of the gang were celebrating, thinking they had won a victory. Stupid cowboys. Craig knew they still had hundreds of treacherous miles ahead of them. Taking stock of the situation, Craig pondered his next move. He had talked to most of the men, one by one, over the last week, assessing their loyalty to Jed. Mostly the outlaws were in this for the money and only the money. Though they all liked Jed, he held no particular hold over any of them. Jake and Pete were Jed's friends and Craig knew they would back Jed's play. Corky and Pappy seemed more loyal to Jimbo and Craig had not approached Breed. The Indian owed Jed for his life over the incident in El Paso.

Now, the most pressing problem bothering Craig was the brand. At least two-thirds of the stock he saw had the Circle B brand on their rump. Even if the gang survived the harsh trail, the brand could get them hanged. No doubt a cable would be sent from the Socorro Sheriff's office to all the local law offices to be on the lookout for the rustled brand.

Chapter 45

Rafe spent a sleepless night at Ed Seeley's hotel. Dressing and walking downstairs he found Carlos in the kitchen cooking breakfast.

"The coffee is ready. I'll have these eggs done in a minute."

"You haven't changed your mind have you?" Rafe asked.

"No. I'll head to Santa Fe as soon as Tomás returns and we know what is happening. Hopefully we will be going together," Carlos replied. After hours of talking last night, Carlos finally agreed he needed to return to Santa Fe. If the sheriff in Socorro did not form a posse, Rafe planned on staying here in San Marcial to help Big Ed. Otherwise, Rafe would be going home too.

After breakfast, Rafe found a broom in the back room and began cleaning up broken glass near the front window. Luckily, only one pane was broken when a piece of wood from a splintered pillar struck it. Rafe unlocked the front doors and found more glass on the sidewalk outside.

The saloon's sign was hanging crazily to one side. The wooden support was broken like a toothpick, but the sign itself was intact. Across the street Arturo was hammering new wood around his front doors. Someone removed the dead animals which were on the street yesterday. Down the street, a man and his young son were sifting through the burned out ruin of their home or store.

Rafe and Carlos offered their services to Arturo and helped rebuild the pillars holding his store's awning. Arturo told them, that like most of the town, he had locked his store and was in Socorro at the fiesta when the herd was rustled. He crossed himself and said, *"Gracias a Dios,"* he thanked God.

Rafe knew if people had been in town that day, many would have been hurt or perhaps killed by the stampeding herd. Arturo told them one *vaquero* had been shot and one cowboy trampled, but no one knew the cowboy. He was not one of *Señora* Seeley's men.

It was late afternoon when Tomás Armijo rode down the main street on a tired horse soaked in a white lather. The horse breathed heavy and snorted through his nose fighting for his breath. Tomás had pushed the horse to exhaustion, leaving Socorro early this morning and galloping most of the way.

"Tomás!" Carlos called to him.

"Carlos, Rafael, what are you doing here? I thought you were in Mexico or on your way home."

"We were on our way north, but decided to stop and spend the night here when we found out about the cattle rustling. What did the sheriff in Socorro say?" Carlos asked.

Tomás jumped off and stroked the horse's face. He had ridden the horse hard, too hard, and the tired horse stood sweating and breathing hard. "Sorry Colorado, I needed to get home," Tomás spoke to the horse before answering Carlos.

"He will not do anything. He said his deputies are scattered all over the county and he cannot leave until most of them return. He is a *baboso.*" Tomás called the sheriff a drooling idiot with disgust in his voice. "I will form a posse here and Ed and I will go after the rustlers."

Rafe found he was disappointed at Tomás' words, but not surprised. Last night he fought with himself vacillating between feeling a loyalty to Big Ed's dilemma and then thinking it was not his problem. Tomás and Big Ed would understand if he went home with Carlos.

"We better get you home Tomás. Let me go get Rayo and you can ride him home. Carlos and I will trail Colorado back to your barn. Then we can talk more there."

By the time Carlos and Rafe rode the several miles to Tomás' hacienda along the river, a stableman was waiting to take Colorado to the stable for care.

"*Señor Armijo* is waiting for you inside," he told them as he took the reins for the red mare and Santiago.

Tomás greeted them at the front door. He had

cleaned up from the long ride, but looked haggard. He poured three brandies and they sat on the veranda. They talked about the rustle, reviewing what happened. Tomás was pleased to hear Cynthia was doing well.

"She could have easily been killed."

"Thankfully God spared her. We understand a cowboy was trampled and one of Ed's *vaqueros* was shot."

"Yes, and besides the damage in the town, I guess we were lucky," Tomás replied. "As soon as I get some of the men organized, we will go after the rustlers."

"It is a foolish idea, Tomás. The rustlers are probably killers and will put up a fight. You have no experience going up against men like that. Ed was in the Army, let him lead the posse. Maybe he can get some soldiers from Fort Craig to help," Carlos told him.

"Ed already tried and the commander of the fort told him his soldiers could not get involved. They are only allowed to protect the area from Apaches. We are on our own. The village is dependent on the cattle ranch. All the locals joined Cynthia, merging their small herds and sharing cowboy duties. If they lose the income by losing the herd, all the town will suffer. We have to try to recover the herd," Tomás explained the issues surrounding the situation.

"Carlos is going back to Santa Fe, but I will stay and join the posse," Rafe spoke up.

"Rafael, you must go home with Carlos. Ed and I will get a posse to go after the rustlers. This is not your fight," Tomás said.

"Do you have any idea who took the herd?" Rafe asked ignoring Tomás' comment.

"Rusty the cook believes it was some of the Texas cowboys who originally came with John B. Sutton. Remember, a number of the Texas cowboys did not stay when Cynthia took over and hired local *vaqueros*. Rusty told Ed a cowboy named Pete came back from Texas looking for work. Cynthia hired him back. Rusty noticed he was acting suspicious with some of the Texans, but he was not totally sure. We think maybe Pete was working with some other cowboys from Texas. Four of the original Sutton cowboys are gone, probably joined up with the rustlers. Thankfully Rusty talked to Armando, Cynthia's head *vaquero,* and they were watching the herd. They might have been able to stop the rustlers, but the herd stampeded," Tomás told them.

Several hours later, Tomás had the stableman saddle a brown mare and all three rode south to Ed and Cynthia's ranch. Ed was reclined on an upholstered chair asleep when Consuelo woke him up to announce the visitors.

"Huh . . . . oh Tomás. How'd it go with the sheriff?" he asked waking up.

"He'll send no help Ed, we have to do it ourselves. Three of my *vaqueros* will go. What about your men? Will they go with us?" Tomás asked.

Rafe stepped forward and added, "I'm going with you. Carlos is returning to Santa Fe."

Ed looked surprised. "I appreciate your offer Rafe, but this is not your fight. Go back to Santa Fe with Carlos. We will get these scallywags."

"No, I'm going," Rafe rejected any other option.

"All right. Four of the *vaqueros* have volunteered and two of the remaining Texas boys will go. One of them admitted to me he suspected something was amiss, and he feels guilty he did not say something," Ed stated.

"I reported to the sheriff in Socorro, one cowboy was killed and we have no idea who he was. I explained we buried him in the church cemetery without any marker. The sheriff said he would let us know if anyone comes looking for someone."

While the men were talking, Cynthia walked into the parlor holding Little Ed in her arms. The baby had shocking red hair and intense green eyes the color as hers. Even though only several months old, Little Ed filled Cynthia's arms.

"Carlos, Rafe, meet little Lee Edward Seeley. We just call him Little Ed," Cynthia said.

Carlos looked at the baby and suddenly missed Bibiana and his own baby, Benicío. He was thankful he would be going directly home.

"Congratulations. He . . . he . . " Carlos' sentence trailed off.

"He's big? Yes we know. We don't think he will be Little Ed for long," Cynthia said with a smile and a laugh.

"Tomás, get your men organized and be ready to go the day after tomorrow. I need one more day with Cynthia before we leave. Rafe, are you sure you want to do this?" Ed asked once more.

"Yes."

"Ed, Teresa told me to tell you, Cynthia and the baby are welcome to stay at our house until we get back or she gets well," Tomás said.

"I have Consuelo to help me, but if I need anything tell Teresa I will call upon her," Cynthia responded.

"Meet at the mercantile day after tomorrow at daybreak. I will have a couple of packhorses stocked with supplies and food," Ed said.

Long shadows off the San Mateo mountains stretched across the road as Tomás, Carlos, and Rafe rode back to town.

"Perhaps you boys should stay at the house until we leave. Teresa will be happy to have you both. Rafe, you and I need to discuss a plan," Tomás said.

Chapter 46

The early morning of Friday, August eighth, a group of men stood with their horses in front of the mercantile in San Marcial. Ed introduced the men to Rafe. He introduced Rafe as the man who shot John B. Sutton. A general murmur circulated. They had heard of the young Mexican *pistolero* who killed Butcherknife Bill and Ponyboy George and then beat John B. Sutton to the draw. Two heavily loaded packhorses stood quietly tied to the rail.

Carlos sat on Santiago nearby torn about his decision. However, Rafe was adamant he must go back to Santa Fe. Carlos tried to argue, but his cousin, Tomás, agreed with Rafe and convinced him to go home.

"Carlos, make sure you tell Ana Teresa why I am going with Ed. I know she will not be happy, but it is something I must do."

"I know Rafe. I'll tell her you can't help trying to save the world. Be careful my friend, this could be a dangerous venture." There was nothing else to say. Carlos wished Rafe good luck and asked God to go with them. He turned his horse west toward the Chihuahua Trail.

Sunlight was barely creeping over the eastern peeks as the posse of twelve men rode up the main street of San Marcial.

"We will head north and follow the tracks of the herd. Paco has scouted the tracks for the past three days and has a good idea where they are headed, so let's get going," Ed said and took the lead with Paco riding beside him.

Ed pulled two packhorses loaded with supplies. Each man was prepared for long days and nights on the trail. Bedrolls, rain slickers, and extra ammunition filled saddlebags anticipating a fight to retrieve the herd.

Ed's posse traveled hard for some sixty miles on the first day until they found a clear creek where they made camp for the night. They felt no need to move with stealth.

The rustlers were well ahead. Rico, one of the ranch hands, volunteered to do the cooking. Everyone tended their horses and made sure each was watered and fed. The horses were their lifeline.

Rico made a chile stew and warmed up cans of beans from supplies on the packhorses. He served them up with tortillas his wife made yesterday. Rafe knew to enjoy the meal, as the further they traveled the less food might be available. While they ate, Rafe sized up the ragtag group of men willing to help Ed find and fight the rustlers to take back his herd.

None of these men were killers, except Ed. He was a retired U.S. Army sergeant, who came to the New Mexico Territory to fight Apaches. Rafe worried about Tomás Armijo, a *criollo* Spaniard, a *hacienda* owner, the mayor of San Marcial, and a gentleman. Rafe met Tomás several years ago when Carlos brought Rafe to San Marcial for the first time. Tomás was Carlos' cousin. Rafe knew Tomás had not just joined this posse because he was the mayor. Ed was his friend and in a small village like San Marcial, friendship was akin to family.

Tomás enlisted three *vaqueros,* simple *mestizo* cowboys, who worked the Armijo land and tended to his cattle and horses. They were reliable, but untested in a gun battle with Texans.

Armando Delgado was one of Ed's trusted Mexican *vaqueros.* Pancho, Jose, and Armando were part of the reason the Texans had not totally succeeded. They were local Mexican cowboys who worked for Ed and Cynthia.

Two Texas cowboys, Lefty and Hank, volunteered. They were cowboys who did not come with the original Texans when John B. Sutton moved the herd to the ranch south of town. They came well heeled and looked tough and ready, but Rafe could not help but wonder where their allegiance might lie when the battle began. In his mind, Texans usually stood together. He decided to keep a close watch on them when the time came to confront the rustlers.

Two townsmen rode with the posse. Both were

storekeepers, unhardened men, but willing to help. Rafe was surprised one was Arturo, the owner of the mercantile. Knowing these two men brought no gun skills, Rafe feared most for their lives.

After evaluating the posse, Rafe could not help worrying. They were untested and untrained for such a fight. Perhaps Carlos was right that he should have just gone home and not made this his problem. However, the powerful words from his friend, Xihuitl the Aztec healer, came to him. "The Goddess who saved your life will call you. Do not ignore the urge to help those in need. You are under her protection."

The next day the posse rode off after a light breakfast of bacon wrapped in a tortilla and coffee. Paco rode ahead following the cattle tracks and leading the way. Rafe rode up beside Ed. "Ed, I'm worried about our posse. These are not trained gunmen, the men from town are shopkeepers. How will they react to a gunfight?" Rafe asked. Although it was not uncommon for townspeople to join a posse, usually a sheriff and his deputies were the leaders. This posse had no lawman nor anyone with the authority to take back the herd.

"Yes, I hear you Rafe. I'm worried too, but it's all we have. The rustled cows were owned by some of the ranchers of San Marcial, not just me. It was Cynthia's idea to intermingle the herds. It has been working well."

"What about the Texans working for you? Do you think they might switch sides?"

"When we get closer to the herd, I plan to have a talk with them. I'll excuse them if they don't want to kill other Texans, but I think I trust them or they would not have come."

They rode hard only stopping periodically to water and rest the horses and making camp before dark. Two days later the posse setup camp for the night near a small creek. To the west, a sparkling red sunlight exploded in what looked like a mini sunburst cast from the highest peaks. Rafe noticed large stone ruins jutting into the landscape just to the north and decided to go explore before the night meal. He thought a good walk after days in the saddle would be a good change.

There was still plenty of light as Rafe trekked his way to the ruin. The site looked abandoned at first, then he smelled fire and the smell of something cooking. On the far side several small huts with mud *hornos,* cone shaped mud ovens, were tended by Indian women. They appeared not to notice him, talking and tending the ovens.

He circled the area without disturbing the women and walked to the ruins. The tall structure resembled Catholic cathedrals constructed out of rough adobe brick. Only three walls still stood without a roof and the adobe brick windows were crumbling. Part of the walls showed where at one time they were covered in a whitewash. Entering the ruins, his eyes needed to adjust to the waning light. He heard something scurry off to his right. It was obvious where the altar used to be in an alcove in the front. He expected the ruin to be unoccupied, but saw a man kneeling near the front. Behind the altar an iron hook was all that was left where a large Crucifix would have been hung long ago.

Rafe quietly walked toward the altar not wanting to disturb the man who was obviously praying. As Rafe almost reached the man kneeling in prayer, the man stood up, twirled around, and drew his pistol. It pointed directly at Rafe's chest. Shocked, Rafe was not expecting the move and had no time to pull his gun. The man had him dead to rights.

CHAPTER 47

"You stalking me?" the man asked with an accent Rafe did not recognize. It was not southern or Texan or Hispanic. A smile on the man's face was bothersome, especially with the pistol pointed at his chest. Any wrong move on Rafe's part would probably mean death.

"Ah . . . ah, no sir. I did not want to disturb your prayer," Rafe stammered making sure his hands did not drop toward his pistols.

"Well, by the look of those two pistols hanging on your hips, you aren't much of a gunman letting a lowly preacher get the drop on you," the man said trying to hide a slight smile and a gleam in his eyes. The man was dressed in a plain black wool suit and black boots. His black shirt was topped with a white clerical collar.

"I meant you no harm. I don't use these guns unless threatened. I was just exploring this Catholic chapel ruin when I saw you kneeling at the altar. I thought you were praying not planning to pull on me mister," Rafe said.

The man took a long look at the young Hispanic. He was probably no more than twenty-five, tall and lean with tan skin. He wore a black Stetson and was not dressed as either a Mexican *vaquero* or a cowboy. The two guns around his waist however, belied his otherwise dapper appearance.

"You're Mexican?" he asked.

"I was born in Mexico on a large hacienda. Now I am an American. I breed horses in Santa Fe," Rafe replied.

"Where did you learn to speak English so well, and with a New England accent?" the curious man asked.

"I was adopted by a gunsmith in Santa Fe when I was a teenager. He was originally from Boston and he taught me English. Where are you from? You are not Texan or from the south," Rafe asked him.

The man chuckled. "I come from a town called Muncie. It's a small town northeast of Indianapolis, Indiana. Do you know where that is?"

"Yes. My adopted father and I traveled to Chicago. What are you doing way out here in the wilderness?" Rafe asked curious about the stranger.

"That is also my question. The Indian women talked about some cowboys and a large cattle herd moving nearby about a week ago. You don't look like a cowboy."

"Do you have to keep that pistol pointed at me?" Rafe asked.

"I guess you could have shot me in the back earlier, so I guess I can trust you, but don't give me any cause to get twitchy," he warned Rafe and holstered the pistol.

"I'm with a posse camped down by the creek. That herd of cattle was rustled from my friend's ranch near San Marcial."

The man nodded his head putting the pieces together. "I'm a newly ordained minister."

"Looks like you had a profession before you started preaching and it might have involved that gun," Rafe said with a slight grin.

"Yes, let's just say I was a bad man who found God and turned his life around. I came west because I heard they need the word of God here in the territories, and, well, there may be a warrant for my arrest in Illinois," the man said with a short chuckle.

"You got a job on your hands, mister. There are many pueblos, villages, and open range all over the New Mexico and Arizona territories. My name is Rafael Reyes de Estrada, but my friends call me Rafe." Rafe told him and stuck out his hand.

"Boy, that's a mouth full. I go by Pastor Dale, Dale Godley."

The name struck Rafe as quizzical. "Godley? Is that real or did you make it up?"

"Everyone asks me the same question. It's my family name. When I was an outlaw, people found the name even stranger, now I believe it is just another way God has worked in my life and shown me the error of my old ways."

"What is this old ruin?" Rafe asked him.

"I was told by a priest in Socorro about this place. He

called it Gran Quivira. There are several other ruins in this area. In the early 1600s, friars had the missions built in their effort to convert the Indians. I have seen them all and this one is the largest and best preserved."

Daylight was quickly turning the old ruin into darkness. Rafe could barely see Pastor Dale's face anymore. He hesitated, thinking, then said, "My friends are camped near the stream. Come with me, our cook will have food for us," Rafe offered.

"You sure? The women here have offered me bread and I have a bit of jerky," Dale replied.

"Yes. Like I said we are a posse going after rustlers. You will be welcomed and maybe you can say a prayer for our efforts," Rafe told him.

They carefully made their way out of the darkened ruin. After gathering Dale's horse, Dale followed Rafe down a path to the campsite. The fire was down to solid red coals where Rico was cooking a stew and warming tortillas. Ed looked up at Rafe and a stranger coming into camp. They were walking together and the stranger was stringing his horse.

"Hey Rafe, who's that with you?" Ed asked as they reached the camp fire illuminating them.

"Everybody, this is Pastor Dale Godly. Found him over at the ruined chapel. I asked him to share our meal."

A general murmur went around the men surrounding the campfire. "A preacher way out here. Don't that beat all," Hank said.

"Dale, this is Ed Seeley. It was mostly his herd that got rustled." Ed stood up to his full six foot four inch height and extended his hand.

In the glow of the fire, Ed looked at Dale Godley. Except for the clerical collar around his neck, Dale looked no part of a man of the cloth. He was about six inches shorter than Ed with a scruffy beard. He wore a black duster and leather gloves. His boots were dirty and well worn. The most odd thing about Dale was the butt end of a pistol worn backwards in his holster. It was a sign of a gunslinger.

"Bless you for sharing your meal." Dale took Ed's hand in a friendly and hearty handshake.

"Glad to meet you Pastor Dale. Welcome. Rico always cooks plenty. Perhaps you can give our food a blessing?" Ed asked.

"It will be my honor, Ed."

After the meal, Rafe, Dale, Tomás, and Ed sat around the fire talking before they turned in for the night. "So, Ed do you know who took your herd and do you know where they are taking it?" Dale asked.

"Not totally sure, but I think it was a cowhand who used to work at the ranch. The man quit and returned to Texas. I was told he returned looking for work and I think he had accomplices. No doubt, they scouted the herd and took it on the day of the *Fiesta de Santiago,"* Ed told him.

"Ah yes, the feast day for Saint James. I attended the celebration in Socorro just last week," Dale said.

"You are Catholic?" Tomás asked.

"I am not any particular faith and try to embrace all religions," Dale replied. It was a true statement. Although an ordained Presbyterian minister, Dale did not embrace any one particular religious dogma. He believed instead in the grace of God and thought all religions had good parts as well as bad.

"So, why are you all going after the rustlers and not the law?" Dale asked.

"The Socorro sheriff said his deputies were spread out all over the county and could not go until some of them returned. By then the herd would be long gone. Some of these men work for me and some are town's people helping. Tomás is our mayor and you met our friend Rafe here."

Dale turned to Rafe. "You said you were from Santa Fe. Did you come just to help?"

"He was on his way home to Santa Fe from Mexico and stopped for the night a few days after the stampede," Tomás explained.

"Stampede?" Dale asked confused.

"The herd got spooked and stampeded right down

the main street of San Marcial. It caused a lot of damage, but then in some ways it was a miracle. When the stampeding cows reached the river, it stopped them and the rustlers only got part of the herd."

"Did anybody get hurt?" Dale asked.

"My wife chased the rustlers and tried to find me in town. One of the outlaws shot the horse and she was thrown from the buggy. She broke her arm and got busted up a bit. Thankfully, she'll be all right, just mad as hell we lost the herd," Ed explained.

"So how many head do you think they got?"

"It has been difficult to estimate, maybe pushing a thousand," Ed replied. "Some are my brand, the Circle B, and others belonging to local families are unbranded."

"I guess out here in the territories you are pretty much on your own. Any of your group ever kill anybody? You are going after some bad men; are you ready for that?" Dale asked.

"I'm a retired Army sergeant. Rafe is a damn fine gunman. My cowhands are tough, but the rest . . . "

"Do you mind if I tag along?"

"You have no part in this fight. Why would you want to put yourself in danger?" Ed asked.

"You probably have heard and maybe don't believe God works in mysterious ways. There is a reason young Rafe here found me in the ruined chapel. I can use this gun," Dale said patting the butt end of the gun in the holster hanging to his side.

CHAPTER 48

The same day Rafe found Dale Godley at the ruin in the wilds of New Mexico, Carlos arrived back in Santa Fe. He rode directly to the de Soto hacienda expecting to find his wife and baby there.

The stable boy came from the barn and took the reins of Santiago when Carlos rode into the courtyard. "It is good you are home," the boy said.

Don Pedro met him at the door and instead of ushering him into the house pulled him down the veranda to the side of the house. "Carlos, I am so glad you are home," *don* Pedro said in a hushed tone to his son-in-law.

"Why are you whispering?"

"We must not let *don* Bartolo overhear us. So much has happened here."

"Where are Bibiana and the baby? What has happened?"

"I sent Bibiana and Benicío back to your home. One of the maids went with her to help with the baby."

"But, why?"

"After my brother Bartolo arrived, he claimed the hacienda as rightful eldest heir. When he went to the land office to validate the land grant for himself, the official said the controversy put the land grant in jeopardy. He was told since no heir was named by our father and I had already filed on the claim, this second claim put the entire grant into question."

Visions of what his family endured in Los Lunas filled Carlos' brain. Although he was not there at the time, American men came to the hacienda and when his father protested, they shot him on the steps to the house. It was the day his brother turned into a murderous outlaw.

"That's preposterous. They could easily choose one claimant over the other, either you because you claimed first or Bartolo because he is the eldest," Carlos said.

After several moments *don* Pedro continued, "Surely

that is true, however Bartolo threatened the clerk at the land office. He was furious. First he lost his ranch in California and now . . . he swears he will not give this up, not now, never."

Don Pedro put a hand on Carlos' shoulder. "I decided Bibiana and the baby are safer at your home."

"*Gracias.* I agree, but what about you and Agustina?" Carlos asked.

"For now we will stay. This is our home and if the authorities come, we will fight. You know I am bound by honor to support my older brother."

Again, *don* Pedro's words seared in Carlos' brain. He too had been bound by Spanish honor to defend and support his older brother Benicío. When Benicío became a murderous outlaw, what honor did he owe him then? Carlos decided Spanish honor had its limit the day Benicío killed Chiwiwi, which was the day Carlos shot and killed Benicío putting an end to his brother's madness.

"This is your home and not your brother's. I will help you to prove that," Carlos offered.

"Carlos you must go to your wife. She has been waiting for you to return. You must worry only about Bibiana and your son. Whatever happens here, will happen." *Don* Pedro took Carlos in a hearty *abrazo.* "Go now and keep Bibiana safe."

Carlos mounted his horse and rode from the courtyard. His father-in-law's situation was disheartening. It would not directly affect him, he had a home and a job teaching at the Catholic school, but it would greatly affect his wife.

"*Carlos, ¡gracias a Dios!*" Bibiana cried when she saw him. She was rocking and nursing the baby in the parlor. Carlos could not believe the change in her or the change in his young son. The baby looked twice as big as when he left just about a month ago.

"I have been frantic with worry. I should never have told you to go with Rafael. Promise me you will never leave us again," she demanded.

"I am here now and I promise to always protect

you," he replied.

She seemed satisfied by his reply, although he did not exactly promise what she asked. He had already decided to never go off with Rafe on any trip again. Rafe unnecessarily put them in danger in Mexico and though Carlos understood, he now had other priorities. Those priorities were here in Santa Fe, but if what *don* Pedro told him came to pass, danger was everywhere, even here.

"Where is Ana Teresa?" Carlos asked realizing she was not there.

"Oh, her father found out about her marriage to Rafael and she went home."

"Was he angry?"

"He was furious, called her a *puta,* and disowned her." Carlos was not surprised. *Don* Bartolo steeped in Spanish culture, believed in the Spanish caste system.

"Oh Carlos, my uncle Bartolo is a monster! He is claiming my father's hacienda and now has the government trying to take it all away," she cried out.

"I know. Your father told me. We will help in whatever way we can. On my ride here, I decided I will go talk to the lawyer. There must be something that can be done."

The baby finished nursing and happily started to gurgle on her shoulder. Carlos took the small bundle from her and cradled Benicío to his chest. Kissing his head, Carlos found the warmth and smell of his young son intoxicating.

"Gracias a Dios," he thanked God to be home.

The following day Carlos rode to the Summers' ranch and found Ana Teresa in the kitchen.

"Carlos! *Bienvenido,"* she welcomed him. "Where is Rafael? Is he not with you?"

"No he did not come back with me," he replied then Carlos told Ana Teresa the bad news about the cattle rustling in San Marcial. He tried to explain why Rafe joined Ed Seeley's posse to get the herd back. It was a message he dreaded giving his best friend's wife.

"I tried my best to talk him out of going, but you

know him. He will help anyone who is in trouble," he reminded her.

"Yes I know him. He thinks he can save the world from evil. It is what I love the most about him, but it also makes me afraid. I need him home now. When do you think he will come back?" she asked.

"I don't know. It depends on how far the rustlers have taken the herd," Carlos told her.

"What kind of danger is he in?" she asked wanting to know, but not sure she wanted to hear the answer.

"Don't worry. You know he is an expert with his pistols. Twelve or more men went with them and they might not even find the herd. I'm sure he'll be home soon."

CHAPTER 49

"Hey boss, spotted sum big cats over by the juniper groves near the water. We need ta go and scare em off," Pete told him.

"Ok, go git sum of the boys an git goin. No shootin. Dun wanna stampede the herd," Jed warned.

The gang and herd had stopped at Lake Sumner for a couple days of rest for both the cows and horses. Jed started the men rebranding as many cows as they could. Jimbo and Jed improvised the quick change from the Circle B brand to the Circle Bar 3 brand by using a branding rod to change the flat side of the B to a long bar that cut the circle. Jed, Jimbo, and Crabclaw agreed the change would be good enough.

Not all the cows had brands, and a few sported other brands. The men worked through the herd trying to separate the Circle B cows from the others. It was a tedious task and even working these several days by the lake, Jed thought only a small portion of the cows were rebranded.

Pete, Rick, and Breed spent the day tracking the big cats. They found paw prints near the water and the remains, mostly guts, of two young cows near a clump of juniper trees.

"They'r night hunters," Breed finally complained. "We ain't gonna catch em in the daytime." The others agreed and headed back to camp.

They started after nightfall with the help of a bright moon to look for the mountain lions. Rick spotted a pair of faintly illuminated eyes looking at them through the trees. He aimed his rifle and took a shot and got rewarded by a horrific howl.

"What the fuck, Rick. I tol yew no shootin! Yew mighta spooked the herd," Breed scolded the young cowboy.

"Ya, but I think I got the sumbitch," he replied. Cautiously the three rode to where Rick spotted the eyes.

"Thar, thar it is. The fucker is still alive." Rick jumped off the horse and ran toward the wounded cat on the ground.

"Careful Rick, they can get mighty mean when they're injured." Pete warned. Rick got near enough to club the large cat with the butt-end of his rifle. He hit it several times before the cat stopped moving.

"Let's go tell Jed we got one."

As they rode in Jed was standing near the evening fire. He had heard the shot and was pacing looking into the darkness.

"Yew dumbshits almost spooked the herd. Yew could hear that gunshot fer miles," Jed growled.

"Ya but I got the sumbitch," Rick bragged.

Just as the sun snuck over the eastern range, the rustlers got the herd moving again headed north. The contented herd moved slow at first, then about noon Jed ordered the men to move the cows faster. He knew they were rested and watered, even if the grasses around the lake were slim pickins for the large herd.

Breed knew the territory and the trail well. It was Breed who directed Jed on the best trail to the lake and knew the watering holes along the way. When Jed was languishing in the El Paso jail after saving Breed's life, he often pondered why he did it. Lost out in this barren part of New Mexico with a landscape giving few clues, he was mighty glad Breed was their scout. He knew where the water holes and creeks were located and watched for sign of Indians.

The nine drovers were doing their jobs keeping the herd together. On the long fast drive to the Lake Sumner, they lost some weaker stock, but with the rest and water, Jed hoped the worst was behind them.

Jed mostly worried about Big Ed. He was sure the retired sergeant would come after them. For now he relied on Rick to watch their back trail. Rick was to make sure no strays were left behind and rush forward if he saw anyone trailing them. So far, they traveled with no one following, but the herd was slow and it would not take long for a posse on horseback to catch up.

Several young weak calves died along the way and Pappy butchered them for meat. It was the way of a cattle drive. Their path needed to avoid any towns, however with the exception of a small town on the far side of Lake Sumner, nothing human broke the barren landscape of eastern New Mexico. Pappy had done a good job stocking the chuckwagon and Jed allowed him and Glenda to ride to the small lake village and refresh some supplies.

The next morning the rustlers continued pushing the herd following the lake north. They kept the cows moving, but at the top of the lake the herd swung right as if they knew it was their last water for a while. It took hours to get them moving north again.

Two days later Breed found a stream and Pappy setup camp. The tired cattle and horses were allowed to rest and get their fill of water. After the cowboys stripped their horses and turned them over to Corky, Crabclaw walked over to Jed.

"Say thar Jed, we gonna rebrand tonight?" Crabclaw asked.

Jed looked out over the large herd. It was already almost dark and the men were tired. "I dun think we gonna have time to do it. If I know Big Ed, he is on his way after us and we need to git movin in the mornin before sunup," Jed told him

"We ain't seen nobody in days. Yew need ta git these critters rebranded afor we git to Wyomin. Else how the hell we gonna sell these stolen cows? Yer putting ropes around our necks." Crabclaw was needling Jed on purpose talking loud enough for all the men to hear.

"I've been thinkin. We'll tell em the widder Sutton sent us to sell the herd. We kin just leave the brand alone. They won't know nuttin all the way up in Wyomin bout no rustled herd from New Mexico," Jed replied thinking he had come up with a good plan.

"That's not good," Crabclaw warned. "Whaddaya think fellers? I think Jed here is trying to git us strung up,"

Crabclaw was egging the discussion.

Finally Jimbo spoke up. "Ah give it a break Crabclaw. Jed's been doin all right so far. We ain't seen no posse after us and we got the herd." Several of the others nodded in agreement.

Crabclaw backed down. He knew his time would come to take over the outfit before they reached Wyoming. In the meantime, he needed to lay low and treat Jed as the leader.

They pushed the herd north for another two days. Even changing horses regularly with the remuda, their horses were showing signs of exhaustion. Jed could only hope the long drive would not wear them out totally. It was a miscalculation on his part, not having a larger remuda following the herd.

The herd was also fatigued. Breed found enough watering places, but the cattle had not grazed since they stopped at the lake. Today seven cows succumbed and they were not calves, but older otherwise healthy stock. Jed could tell every one of the rustlers was feeling the stress of keeping the stolen herd on the move and beginning to worry. They were still a long way from Wyoming.

None of them, except Crabclaw and Rick, had ever rustled cattle before. Jed and several others had been drovers for Texas outfits, but Jed had never been in charge. All he knew was driving herds at a pace not to hurt the cattle or themselves. On a normal drive, the herd would stop in towns along the way and the ramrod purchased hay and let the cattle feed in the pens for a couple days before heading out. It was something Jed underestimated for the rustled herd. They could not stop and even if they could, there were no towns along the way.

Before nightfall long shadows were overtaking them, and Corky rode up beside him. "Pappy says we need to stop. One of the wagon horses is almost lame and needs rest."

Jed signaled for the group to stop. Pappy and Glenda started to setup camp while Corky took the wagon horses to the remuda.

When the cows were herded and the men in camp, Jed told them how they needed a day's stop. He assigned nighttime guard duties.

Breed sat back listening. They were not in a good place to stop. Without water and any natural protection, like hills or canyons, they were ripe for the picking. He had ridden the Goodnight-Loving Trail many times and it was untamed, especially through Indian country in northern New Mexico. Apaches and Navajos attacked traveling herds early in the morning, driving off what they could before the camp woke up. Breed said nothing. He thought the Indians deserved to take what they could as payment for passing through their territory.

CHAPTER 50

Don Pedro left Ron Iverson's office still confused about the land grant. At Carlos' encouragement, they went to discuss the situation with the lawyer. With Carlos interpreting, *don* Pedro explained his older brother, Bartolo, left New Mexico many years ago relinquishing his claim here in Santa Fe to take an inheritance in California. The government in California took Bartolo's land and now his brother was trying to claim the de Soto family land grant here in New Mexico. Although Pedro had presented the documents to the land office, now the government claimed because there was no clear heir, the entire land grant was in jeopardy. The lawyer listened and nodded his head, but in the end could only say he would look into it.

Riding back to the hacienda, *don* Pedro grumbled. "Why is the American government so indecisive?" *don* Pedro asked Carlos.

"American law is judicial with courts, juries, and lawyers who argue both sides of an issue. They believe it is more fair."

"More fair? More fair than what?"

"More fair than a king or viceroy making all the decisions without having considered both sides. More fair than a tradition where the eldest heir gets everything by birthright and the younger siblings get nothing."

Don Pedro sputtered an unintelligible response. Carlos was right. His older brother needed to give up any claim to the land here in Santa Fe. It might be the old Spanish way, but it was not fair. His brother had done nothing to protect and preserve the Santa Fe hacienda. While he grew grapes and gave lavish parties in California, he and Agustina worked and went without many things during the hard times.

The situation made Pedro irate. Most of his life he thought the old Spanish ways were best. He was taught to feel superior to *mestizos* and Americans. He initially refused to let Ana Teresa marry as she wished. Sometimes he treated his servants and *vaqueros* with less respect. Well, now it was happening to him and he did not like it.

When they reached the courtyard, he jumped from his horse and strode into the house. "Bartolo!" he bellowed loudly. "Bartolo!"

He found his older brother sitting on the veranda reading the morning newspaper as if he had not heard Pedro calling him.

"You and Marcella must give up any idea to take this hacienda. If you continue, we all lose," Pedro huffed.

"I give it up? It is you little brother who needs to leave," *don* Bartolo almost sneered.

"You can go back to California, or Spain, or take the land in Las Cruces. This hacienda is mine and you know it. Agustina and I have worked this land and taken care of it since father died while you were growing grapes in Rancho Simi."

"You are forgetting I am the oldest."

"The Spanish traditions be damned. This is New Mexico, a territory of the United States, not Spain!" Pedro yelled.

Bartolo was surprised at Pedro's sudden gumption. It would not be allowed in the old days. Everything his younger brother said was true, but Bartolo knew his options were limited and he would be damned if he would leave.

"You should take the land in Las Cruces. I am being generous," Bartolo told Pedro trying to turn the tables on him.

"You know the land is barren. It will take time and money to build a house there and start fields. It is not near the Rio Grande and wells need to be dug."

"You're young little brother, you can make it work," Bartolo replied with a smirk.

"You told me you still have a little money in the bank in California. You could buy land here, but you will not have this property. My blood and sweat are in this hacienda, not yours!" Pedro shouted.

"Yes, I have some money at the bank in Los Angeles and I will borrow more using this land grant as collateral," Bartolo replied.

Just as Pedro was about to shout back, Agustina and Marcella walked onto the veranda. "What are you two shouting about?" Agustina asked.

"I was just telling Pedro how I will borrow against this hacienda after I prove my inheritance rights," Bartolo replied.

"We're staying in Santa Fe?" Marcella gasped. "I will not. This place is dusty and I cannot buy anything of value here. I want to go back to Spain as soon as we can."

Bartolo visibly bristled, though did not reprimand his wife. It was one thing to yell at his younger brother and another to upset Marcella. The money in the bank in California was hers from an inheritance. She was the only reason they had anything at all.

"Do not upset yourself, *querida*," Bartolo's tune changed as he addressed his wife.

"Oh Marcella, you must make up with Ana Teresa before you do anything rash. She is your only child," Agustina said.

"She is no longer our daughter. Where is this *mestizo* husband of hers. Why is he afraid to confront me?" Bartolo scoffed.

"Trust me Bartolo, he is not afraid of you. He is a good man. I used to believe as you do about *mestizos*. I was wrong. Rafael is a good husband and our friend," Pedro replied.

"Then you are the fool. No Spaniard would be friends with a *mestizo*."

"Perhaps you should return to Spain. Santa Fe is America and in America everyone is equal. It took me a long time to understand, but now I do."

CHAPTER 51

Ed Seeley's posse arrived at Lake Sumner at dusk where they found Paco sitting on a flat rock waiting for them. Paco had ridden ahead yesterday at Ed's request.

While waiting for the rest of the posse to arrive, Paco made inquires at the mercantile on the far side of the lake. The woman clerk remembered a man and young girl coming in for supplies about a week ago. She was surprised because no herd was moving through the town. The man told her they were camped on the far side of the lake. She also told Paco a small herd passed through the lake village three or four days ago.

"Definitely been cows through here. There are a couple of carcasses of the ones that did not make it. One had a Circle B brand. I cannot believe they are pushing the herd without rest and feeding. They will kill many, if they continue at this pace," Paco reported what he had learned.

"When were they through here?" Ed asked.

"Best I can determine the herd was here less than a week ago."

"Get rested. Tomorrow I want you to ride north. They can't be too far ahead. We will take time to rest the horses and ourselves," Ed told Paco.

Ed was weary and it came through in his voice. The closer they got to a confrontation with the rustlers, the more he worried about this group of men, not wanting any to get killed because of his cattle. Hearing the rustlers were probably almost week ahead of them made him ponder telling everyone they should just go home and forget the cows.

The posse stripped their horses and themselves. While the horses drank their fill, they dove and played in the shallow lake. Even Tomás and Arturo were in their longjohns and dripping wet. Laugher and playful bantering filled the air. Ed found it was the medicine he needed to think about going on.

After the camp was setup for the night, Rafe walked up to Dale, who was cleaning his pistol and rifle. He was curious about the gun-slinging preacher who seemed so strange. Rafe realized Dale was younger than he first thought, maybe not yet thirty with a slightly lopsided grin and hearty laugh. Sitting down nearby, Rafe began cleaning his own weapons.

"The fine silt here in New Mexico is hard on guns if you don't keep them clean. I appreciate a man who takes care of his weapons," Rafe said trying to think of something to start a conversation.

"Those are fine looking pistols you have there," Dale replied. "Ed called you a *pistolero*. Is that true?" Rafe cringed thinking the preacher thought of him as a killer.

"I'm not a gunhand, if that is what you mean. These pistols are double-action. My adopted father designs and makes them at his foundry in Santa Fe."

"Double-action? Can I have a look at one?"

"Sure," Rafe said, unloaded one, and handed it to Dale.

"Nice balance." Dale turned the pistol over several times and twirled it. "I've heard about them, never seen one though. Show me how it works," he said and handed it back to Rafe.

"The mechanism is all in the trigger. You just aim and squeeze. It's better than thumbing the hammer, and faster." Rafe aimed it up to the sky and squeezed the trigger twice. "You have to learn how to react to the kick to get the next shot to stay on target."

Rafe handed the pistol back to Dale. He looked it over again and squeezed tentatively on the trigger once, listening to the chamber pin hit. Then he did it twice in rapid succession. "Very smooth. Where can I get me a pair of these?" he asked.

"I make them in Santa Fe. Thought you gave up your bad ways and turned to God?"

Dale winked. "God told me I'm allowed to shoot snakes and varmints, even two legged ones. Those guns would come in mighty handy."

Rafe found Dale Godly full of contradictions. He was quiet and reserved, seemingly a man of the cloth who carried pistols and knew how to use them. He was well educated, but had a murky past. The Bible taught it was a mortal sin to kill, but Dale seemed to believe that commandment came with exceptions.

Rafe thought he understood however. He had similar faith, did not relish killing, avoided it, but when necessary would use his guns.

Later, Rafe was wide awake under his bedroll and Ana Teresa filled his thoughts. All along this dangerous venture he thought of her during quiet times, especially before sleep. At times he cursed himself for not going home to his bride. Carlos needled him for trying to save the world. Was that part of him or was it the Aztec Goddess Coatlicue demanding her due for his life. He did not know, but answered the call. At this moment, all he wanted to do was saddle Rayo and ride west. Ana Teresa's parents must be in Santa Fe by now and she needed him. Finally he drifted off to sleep.

Everyone was up early to the smell of bacon and eggs cooking. Arturo went to the mercantile in the village of Lake Sumner yesterday and bought fresh eggs, bacon and coffee. It was a feast for all this morning after a well needed rest. Paco took off to find the cattle trail as soon as he ate. Not long after, Ed was saddling his mare.

"Where you going Ed?" Rafe asked.

"Just for a short ride. Can't sit still."

"Your horse needs rest," Rafe reminded him. Even Rayo, who was the strongest and biggest of the horses showed signs of fatigue. Rafe was glad they were taking a break.

Ed pondered a moment and then pulled the saddle from his horse, dropping it on the ground. Fatigue and guilt swirled in his mind as he wondered if all this effort was in vain.

"I feel sorry for the cows. They are pushing them hard without food. We may be chasing a ghost herd," he said.

After leaving camp, Paco rode to the end of the large lake. Where the lake stopped, deep muddy tracks covered the area. A herd had tried to enter the water and the deep tracks showed they had been turned north. The tracks looked fresh, only several days old. The tracks were the only cattle tracks coming from the west side of the lake. He followed the mass of cow tracks north until they tangled with others approaching from the east side of the lake. The large lake was a well-known stopping spot for herds coming from Texas up the Goodnight-Loving Trail.

Yesterday, he scouted the east side of the lake. He spotted tracks headed north from town. He knew somewhere past the lake, the Goodnight-Loving Trail went straight to Colorado. It would be impossible to separate the tracks of various herds on the main trail. Paco turned his horse and headed back to camp.

When Paco returned to camp, Rico was cooking the evening meal. He was met by Ed and Tomás before he dismounted. "Found the tracks, but once north of the lake they merged onto the main trail. It will be easy to follow the trail from there, but I'm just not sure how to separate your herd from others."

"We'll be making better time than the herd. Hopefully we'll catch them in a couple of days. Better get that horse brushed down. Rico bought a sack of oats in town. Make sure he gets some," Ed said.

Ed turned to Tomás. He looked a bit ragged as he was not used to riding for days and sleeping on the open ground. In fact most of the work on Tomás' hacienda in San Marcial was done by *vaqueros* and stable hands. Tomás was a Spanish *don* by birth, educated in Santa Fe. His wealth was inherited and as the prominent person in San Marcial, he was elected mayor.

"You don't look well Thomas," Ed told him. "Perhaps you and Arturo should go home. This is not your fight. The *vaqueros* and cowboys will take care of this."

"No, Ed we will see this through together. We have seen worse from those Texas cowboys."

"I just don't want anyone to get killed, because of

some fucking cows, especially those of you who don't have a dog in this fight," Ed replied.

"The entire town is behind you and Cynthia, Ed. You have given the town hope and help against the Texans and every man here knows it. We will all fight."

"I know, I know. You Spanish drop your plows, close your schools and stores to go fight, just like your ancestors did against the Moors for hundreds of years. You've told me that story many times."

"Yes, it is in our blood," Tomás said.

"I guess that includes Rafe. He's part Spanish," Ed retorted.

"What about Dale?" Tomás asked.

"Dale sure is the strangest preacher I ever met," Ed said with a grin.

"Yes he certainly is. Nice fellow, though. We will ask him to bless this posse in the morning before we head out," Tomás agreed.

CHAPTER 52

"Boss, saw a big dust cloud behind us. There's another herd coming this way. Whaddaya want to do?" Pete asked Jed as he rode back into camp.

"Damn." Jed knew from his years of droving, herds gravitated to each other. Separating them later was difficult.

"Perhaps we just take em too," Crabclaw goaded Jed.

Crabclaw sat in the shade of the chuckwagon contemplating his options. First, he regretted getting mixed up with Jed and this crew. They were all a bunch of greenhorns, especially dumbshit Jed. He was naive thinking he could drive this large herd quickly up to Wyoming. Crabclaw could see the cows getting edgy as each long and hot day past without enough food. In the world of droving cattle to market, rustled or not, it was survival.

"There's a big box canyon over yonder off the trail some," Breed said.

"Which way?"

"Thatta way," Breed pointed to the west.

"Can it hold the herd?"

"Big enuff."

Jed threw his unfinished coffee over the fire and it hissed. "Git em cows movin. We gotta get em into the canyon before the other herd gets here."

"Pete, yew and Rick find yerseffs a good spot to keep a watch on that herd," Jed ordered.

By nightfall, the herd was tucked in the canyon and Pappy was cooking the evening meal. Jed pulled a bottle of whiskey out of his saddle bag and passed it around.

"How long yew thinkin we can keep these critters without water and food?" Crabclaw asked after taking a long swig of the whiskey. He purposefully needled Jed in front of the men whenever possible.

Crabclaw had made up his mind to wait until the herd was sold to take all the money and Glenda. He felt confident he could pull it off without any problems. Hell, these were just dumbshit cowboys, not real rustlers or killers. They would probably scatter in a heartbeat from fear of getting a bullet from him.

Jed tried hard to make the men think he was in charge. He knew Crabclaw was needling him and trying to make him look like a fool in front of the others. He knew this venture was now out of control. The herd was tired, hungry. Every day of delay meant more trouble.

He worried a showdown was coming, could be the sheriff from Socorro or could be Big Ed. The dream of buying the small ranch north of Austin, Texas, for him and Bonnie was beginning to fade out of his mind. Survival took over those thoughts.

Later that night as Jed stood near the chuckwagon and the men sat near the fire Pappy asked him, "Jed, what r our chances we can git the herd up ta Wyomin?"

"I dun know Pappy."

"Looks like it ain't workin out like yew planned. It takes time movin a herd this size. Like yew, all I cared bout was gittin that money. Now I kin see it was just a dream."

"It ain't over yet Pappy. Cud be we can git the herd up ta Wyomin." Jed handed Pappy his empty coffee cup and walked off.

About an hour before sundown, Paco rode back on the trail to meet up with the moving posse. He trailed a small herd moving north yesterday until he was sure it was not Ed's large rustled herd. The small herd went straight north, but a wide swath of tracks led off into the canyons to the west. Paco rode up beside Ed and filled him in on what he found.

"I think they saw the smaller herd coming and hid in a box canyon. They must be in trouble or they might have taken the smaller herd," Paco said.

"We've seen some of the dead ones along the way. Those cows must be starving," Ed replied. He was beginning to think this effort was futile. Even if they retrieved the herd, getting a thousand hungry cows under control would be difficult.

Ed called over to Lefty and Armando and told them

what Paco said. "You two ride ahead and see if you can find the herd in the canyons. Be careful. They might have lookouts if they are pinned down."

Lefty and Armando took off at a gallop. They found the spot in the trail where the large herd turned off. Checking their weapons, they headed for the south side of the canyon and carefully worked their way up a narrow trail. Finally they began to hear the bellowing from a large herd.

"Let's get back to camp," Lefty said.

"*Sí,*" Armando replied. "*Vámonos.*"

Pete rode back to the campsite in the canyon leaving Rick on the high wall of rock to keep watch. They watched as two men rode to where they could see the herd and then the men rode off.

"Boss, we saw two men on horseback scoutin the herd. Could be from that other herd and they follered the tracks we made when we turned the herd toward the canyon," Pete reported to Jed.

"Pete, git yerseff back up thar with Rick. Keep a watch out fer em jaspers. It could be men from that other herd or it could a posse. Iffin you see anyone comin again, one of yew git back here on the double and let me know," Jed ordered.

"Corky, git all the hosses saddled and ready. Take the team and the remuda over ta the far end of the canyon outta any direct fire."

"Jimbo, Breed, yew git to where yew kin keep the herd in the canyon. We cain't let em stampede outta here if any shootin starts. The rest of yew, check yer weapons and get a position to make a stand. Pappy douse that fire," Jed ordered.

"Looks like yew in a pickle," Crabclaw gruffed.

"Yew such a big rustler and gunhand, go do yer job," Jed groused back. Craig would have shot any other man dead on the spot, but now was not the time. If shooting started, Craig planned to escape with at least his life and maybe with the girl.

Armando and Lefty rejoined the posse. They reported what they saw and described the canyon.

"Reminds me of a battle we had with Apaches holed up in a canyon down on the Gila when I first reported to Fort Craig. We couldn't get them out and we lost two troopers when we tried to assault them directly. Only way we got them was with plenty of cannon fire. Too bad we ain't got no cannon," Ed mused.

"These aren't Apaches and they have to worry about the herd as well as themselves," Dale said. "It'll give us an advantage."

They discussed options. Armando did not think he and Lefty had been seen, so the posse should have surprise on their side. After talking over many options, Ed took control, using his military experience. "I want two volunteers to circle the canyon from the north and gain the high ground. You'll need to wait there until we attack the mouth of the canyon."

"I'll go." Rafe volunteered.

"I'll go with him," Dale spoke up.

Ed looked at them. Rafe was capable and resourceful, but he was not sure of Dale. After all he was a preacher. Would he be up to killing if he had too?

"Dale, are you sure you want to do this? You don't have to," Ed asked looking doubtful at the preacher.

"You can count on me Ed. I believe God set me on my course to do good, and getting your herd back is good," Dale told him.

"You'll have a little moon light, but it will be low on the horizon so its gonna be difficult finding your way in the dark. Be careful," Ed told them.

After Rafe and Dale rode out from the camp, Ed gathered the rest of the men. "If any of you do not want in this fight, tell me now. I'll not think bad of you," Ed said.

"Don't worry Ed, we're all with yew," Lefty assured him.

"Let's go get those cows back," Armando spoke out.

CHAPTER 53

The maid brought a letter delivered to the hacienda for *don* Pedro who was reading in the parlor. The letter addressed to *Señor* Pedro de Soto was from Ron Iverson, Esquire. Opening it, Pedro realized it was in English and he needed Carlos to translate.

"Have the stable boy saddle my horse," he barked at the maid.

Pedro put the letter on the desk and headed upstairs to change into a more suitable *traje* for a visit to the lawyer's office. When he returned downstairs, Bartolo was standing near the desk holding the opened letter.

"How dare you try to usurp my claim Pedro. I am the heir to this land," Bartolo screamed waving the letter in front of Pedro's face. Bartolo was partially fluent in English and could understand the letter enough to know Pedro visited a lawyer concerning the hacienda's ownership.

"I own this hacienda and intend to keep it," Pedro yelled back.

"You forget your place little brother. You are sworn by honor to support me. You have no rights to this hacienda or any other unless I allow it." Bartolo sneered.

"You have nothing but memories of this home. You and Marcella should go back to Spain. It is what she wants, not this," Pedro told him.

"No, you and Agustina will leave this house at once and never return," Bartolo growled back. This hacienda was all he had left and he would not give it up.

His brother's words were more than Pedro could take. Grabbing a sword from the rack, Pedro screamed, "Let's finish this now."

A slight smile curled on Bartolo's lips. "As you please brother." He dropped the letter on the desk and pulled a thin rapier from the rack putting his hand into the handle guard and whipping the slender blade back and forth.

Bartolo quickly thrust and Pedro parried, deflecting

Bartolo's blade. The tips of the blades clinked as the two lunged and then retreated. Growing up, the two brothers engaged in fencing matches. Bartolo, older by three years, usually bested Pedro. That was many years ago and Pedro had many years of practice and lessons.

A swipe of Bartolo's sword sliced the parlor drapery. Pedro backed into the entryway and stood his ground as Bartolo approached. They parried back and forth clashing blades as they fought.

A taller man, Bartolo drove his shorter brother out the front door backing him down the veranda steps into the courtyard. With more room, the two engaged in the mortal combat of old Spanish tradition.

Bartolo was surprised at Pedro's expertise. It was not something he remembered. He only remembered besting his smaller and weaker little brother. Bartolo pressed forward and pivoted striking his sword neck-high. Killing his brother was not inconceivable.

Pedro ducked the blow and returned a slicing blow which Bartolo was barely able to deflect. The edges of the blades clashed and the metallic sound reverberated in the courtyard. Bartolo made a quick empty fade and then more quickly pivoted and sliced his blade across Pedro's chest, just catching the sleeve of Pedro's suitcoat and cutting through the woolen jacket.

Bartolo backed a few steps and stood in a ready stance. "You are better than you used to be Pedro, but you are still no match for me," he sneered. "The next time, there will be blood."

"*¡Desgraciado!* Father was happy when you left for California. On his deathbed he admitted you were not of his loin, but of another's, his brother Silvio. You are a bastard, I am the rightful heir to this land and if you want this hacienda you will have to kill me for it."

Pedro had promised to keep the secret his father confessed on his deathbed. At the time it seemed easy. Now Pedro relished hurting Bartolo. If he was to die today, he wanted Bartolo to live the rest of his life in shame.

Pedro's words stung. Bartolo was taller and had a

hawkish nose with straight light brown hair. Pedro's face favored their mother with curlier brown hair and gray eyes. As a boy, Bartolo remembered whispered rumors by the de Soto's servants. Although his father treated him kindly, something always made Bartolo feel estranged. His *tío* Silvio in California welcomed him graciously and always made him feel loved.

Pedro took Bartolo's slight hesitation and clashed his rapier against Bartolo's sliding it up to the hilt. "You may kill me, but you will always be a bastard," Pedro growled into Bartolo's face.

"Lies! You lie like the slovenly dog you are. You lied to me about my daughter and now you lie to me about my birthright!" Bartolo screamed at Pedro.

Finally, the shouting brought their wives and servants out of the front door. Marcella screamed seeing the two clashing their swords and threw her hand up to her heart.

"Stop! Stop it!" Agustina yelled firmly as she brazenly strode down the steps and came close to the brothers. "Pedro, your life is worth a hundred haciendas to me. Stop this fighting. If Bartolo and Marcella want this hacienda, then so be it. We will leave."

The swords fell to their sides. Agustina put her hand over the knuckle guard of Pedro's sword.

Marcella followed her lead and walked down the steps. She walked up to her husband. "Bartolo, you know I do not want to live here in Santa Fe. You promised to take me back to Spain." Marcella stared directly at her husband's reddened face. She did not understand his obsession with besting Pedro for a hacienda she did not want.

Two hours later Carlos and *don* Pedro sat across a desk from Ron Iverson. Pedro had not changed his suit and Carlos asked him about the tear in the sleeve, but received no response. Pedro brought the letter, which Carlos translated into Spanish, but even Carlos had to admit it did not make sense. The two decided they needed to see the lawyer in person.

"Good afternoon, Mister Iverson," Carlos greeted

him. "We are sorry to trouble you, but the letter is confusing."

"Yes, I admit the land concepts and legal rules are probably not easily understood. Let me try to explain," he said. As Ron Iverson spoke, he paused frequently so Carlos could translate into Spanish for *don* Pedro.

"Spanish land grants, such as yours, were modeled after European methods of land distribution. Land was conveyed through commendation, royal decree, or as yours with an official document. However the boundaries of the land are vague, mostly noted by crude maps with landmarks and communities as boundaries. Most land grants here in New Mexico are marked simply by stone markers on the four corners. It has been an accepted method for many years."

After Carlos interpreted, *don* Pedro nodded his head in understanding and agreement.

"As you know, after the Mexican-American War in 1848, the Treaty of Guadalupe Hidalgo agreed to recognize land grants made by the Spanish and Mexican governments in New Mexico and five other western territories. However, land ownership patterns are very different in the United States. Our system views the earth's surface as an imaginary grid laid out on a piece of flat paper. Land is defined by this grid of ranges, townships and section numbers."

"So are you saying the Spanish land grants do not fit into this imaginary grid?" Carlos asked.

"Exactly. Also, land in the United States is owned by deed which can clearly identify it by the grid's definition and thus can be bought and sold."

His explanation made sense, but Carlos did not understand how that invalidated the Spanish land grants.

"But we believed the Treaty of Guadalupe protected the Spanish land owners. Is this not true?"

"Yes it is true, but complicated. The United States has a system to establish land ownership by using a method of survey. A Surveyor General was appointed here in New Mexico in 1854. It is his job to survey the territory and review all land claims. You can see gentlemen, it is difficult for the surveyors to accurately place the land grants into the grid method of surveyance. Further, the land grant documents are . . . well let us say less than accurate and quite frankly often open to interpretation."

"You mean they are written in Spanish," Carlos responded.

Ron Iverson only responded with a nod of his head. He knew *don* Pedro and the other *dons* he was representing had legitimate arguments. The American government and specifically the Santa Fe Ring here in Santa Fe were exploiting the language and cultural issues to rob the Spanish of their property rights. There were even rumors, some local *dons* were helping the Santa Fe Ring against their friends and neighbors.

"What about *don* Pedro's claim. Where does he stand?" Carlos asked.

"Carlos, tell you father-in-law, I am trying to make the land office understand his claim. It is in question because they do not understand the claim by his older brother. This type of birthright inheritance is not part of the United States system of inheritance. When there is a death with no provision, all children are entitled to equal shares of any property or wealth."

"You mean they would share the hacienda property here in Santa Fe as equal partners under the law?" Carlos asked.

"Yes."

CHAPTER 54

"Whatcha thinkin Pappy?" Jed asked.

"We got nuff firepower and that Crabclaw jasper is a killer. He's been through gunfights before. He'll hep us git through this, yew kin bet on that."

"I shur hope yer rat," Jed replied.

Corky was standing nearby with Glenda and heard the comments. "I'll be ready, Jed. I didn't cum all this way ta go home empty handed. Glenda and I have plans to go ta Californee and buy a little spread."

Glenda took Corky's arm and they wandered away to where Corky had the remuda settled.

"They be green Pappy. They dun know what they're in fer. When the fightin starts, dun know iffin I can watch out fer em. We may be fightin fer our lives," Jed said.

"I hear yew, but the boy's been practicin with his pistol and he ain't scart. That Glenda's purdy good with a pistol too," Pappy replied.

Hearing a horse in the darkness, Jed nervously whipped out his gun. Without a fire, only the slight part of a moon and stars gave the dark canyon any light. Rick rode up to where Pappy and Jed stood.

"Jed, I rode up round the canyon thinkin I could see who was scoutin us. I saw bout eight men camped out not far south of the canyon. I think it cud be a posse."

Rafe and Dale skirted the mouth of the canyon until they could approach the high cliff from the north side. They made their way northeast picking their way around boulders and scrub juniper using light from the setting moon. Rayo led the way like he knew where he was going. Dale's horse followed. They finally reached a spot where Rafe thought they could setup a perch. They tethered the horses and grabbed blankets before settling themselves against a boulder for the long wait.

"Say Rafe, where did you get that good looking

Appaloosa?" Dale asked in a quiet voice just to break the tension.

"I raised him since the day it was born."

"What kind of name is Rayo."

"It means thunderbolt in Spanish. It's mother was having trouble giving birth and the horse master reached his hand in and repositioned the foal. Just as a thunderbolt struck a tree outside the barn, the foal popped out. I named him Rayo after that tremendous thunderbolt."

"I've been watching him. Most intelligent horse I've been around and well trained. He responds to your slightest touch or sound."

"I trained him from a colt. He's saved my life more than once."

"Yes, you said you are a horse breeder in Santa Fe. I've been wanting to ask you how you got involved with the posse. Why are you here and not in Santa Fe?"

Rafe paused. It was an easy question with a long answer. Why was he here? Why was he not in Santa Fe with his wife? Would Dale understand Rafe's calling by an Aztec Goddess?

"Ed is my friend. I was on my way home from Mexico and stopped at San Marcial for the night. Tomás could not get the sheriff from Socorro to help so I volunteered, besides Ed's wife got hurt by the rustlers and I don't like it when innocent people get hurt. I'm obligated to help those in need and like I said, Ed is my friend." Rafe hoped his simple explanation would suffice.

"What do you mean you are obligated to help those in need? Obligated by what?" Dale asked, curious about the statement.

Rafe thought about it for a bit, then told Dale the story about how a silver star amulet he wore around his neck saved his life when a bullet struck it instead of piercing his chest. An Aztec healer cured him from the injury, but Rafe had a scar in the shape of a star on his chest. The Healer told him it was the symbol of the Aztec Goddess Coatlicue, the preserver of life. The Healer taught him the Goddess saved his life for a purpose and now he felt bound to help others, especially those in need.

"It is like I hear her calling to me. I feel it deep in my chest beneath the scar," Rafe said.

"That is a fantastic story. Many cultures have similar beliefs. Christianity believes the entity God or the Holy Spirit can call to people. Buddhists have a saint of compassion called Avalokiteshvara. Catholics have many saints and some people feel their presence," Dale replied.

"The Healer was an Aztec medicine man, a shaman. He studied the religion of the ancient peoples of Mexico, which has been passed down for generations by word of mouth. After he saved my life, we traveled from village to village and he taught me many mysteries, known only to the Aztecs."

Dale kept asking Rafe many questions. He was fascinated learning about the philosophy of the ancient people of the Americas. It fit with many of his own thoughts about the great religions of the world. Each had unique and yet similar beliefs.

"I wish I had the time to visit Mexico and learn about the Aztecs. Too bad they were wiped out by the conquistadors," Dale said.

"Well, not all Aztecs were wiped out. The Healer and I found a hidden village with direct descendents from the place they called Tenochtitlan, the same place where the Spanish built Mexico City."

"Fascinating, some day I would like to go there," Dale said.

They talked well into the night about religion until Rafe said, "Dale, I'll take the first watch, you get some sleep."

"Rafe, wake up," Dale whispered as daylight lightened the eastern sky and he shook Rafe's shoulder. Groggy and sore from sleeping on the rocky ground, it took Rafe a moment to realize where he was. He was dreaming he was home in bed with Ana Teresa's arms around him, when Dale shook him awake. Rafe rose up, but Dale stopped him. "Stay down."

Dale pointed down to the herd and a few rustlers

mingling around the chuckwagon. It was a sight they had not been able to see in the dark last night.

"What's going on down there?" Rafe asked.

"Not much. There are only a few men near that wagon and no fire. It makes me suspicious they know we're coming."

"So maybe they have guards posted near the mouth of the canyon already," Rafe replied.

"Probably. Keep a sharp eye out for any movement," Dale said.

As the sky lightened, the scene took on an eerie surreal color reflecting off the reddish canyon walls. Rafe and Dale discussed trying to warn the posse, but there was no time. They should be attacking soon.

"Hey, look near that wagon. It looks like a woman." Rafe pointed to one of the figures at the rustlers camp.

"A woman? We better be careful not to shoot her," Dale said.

Rafe was watching the canyon walls and studied their position. He spotted several well guarded positions along the cliff where he thought a man might be posted.

"Let's move around to where we have a better view of the mouth of the canyon. I think it's where they might take a position. Once we see the posse, their lookouts will have to show themselves. I will rapid fire this double-action rifle, and you fire your rifle as fast as you can. Hopefully, it will confuse them and make them think there are more guns up here," Rafe told Dale.

Working carefully, hiding behind a shelf of rock, they found a better location to have a clear view of the mouth of the canyon. Once in position, all they could do was wait and watch. Rafe grabbed several pieces of jerky from his saddlebag and all the extra ammunition and rechecked his weapons.

Dale chewed on the jerky. It had been several years since he killed a man. It was before he found God and took his vows. He thought about it a lot last night while Rafe was asleep. He volunteered to help this posse, yet now he faced his demons. Rafe's story about the Aztec Goddess gave him comfort. Perhaps God was working in a similar way through him. It was a question which nagged him greatly. God's word said, thou shalt not kill, yet the world was full of bad needing to be set right. Dale picked up his rifle and made sure a bullet was in the chamber.

Chapter 55

It was still dark when Ed wakened. Ed had hardly been able to sleep thinking how he might not get back to Cynthia and Little Ed. The thought tore at his heart. After spending most of his life in the Army, he never thought he would get married and certainly never thought he would have children. Now he had a beautiful wife and the first of several children, or so she told him often.

He wondered if the others were feeling the same. On top of regret he felt guilty. Most of the herd were his cows. He wished now he said to hell with them and just told everyone to forget about the herd. They could all be safely back in San Marcial right now.

It was not because he cared so much for the money the cows represented, but it was symbolic of the struggle between the Texans and the Hispanics of the town. Cynthia had talked many of the smaller ranches into combining the herds and sharing equally in the grazing land and effort to manage the herd. It was a boom to the town and many of the Hispanic ranches. For the smaller ranches, losing their cows could mean losing everything.

Later after breakfast and the sun rose, Ed gathered the posse. He described the plan.

"I'll ride out in front. Armando, Pancho, and Lefty will be positioned outside the mouth of the canyon in case the herd tries to stampede. Once Rafe and Dale see me, they will open fire. We will give them time to pin the rustlers down, then we ride in. Get any guards at the mouth first. It won't be as easy for them to hit targets on horseback. I just hope the herd doesn't panic and stampede. If that happens we are all in danger, so take cover and protect yourselves," he continued explaining the plan of attack.

Up on the vantage point along the south wall of the canyon, Pete and Rick had been hunkered down behind a boulder since last night. They knew no one would attack until daylight and although one of them was supposed to stay awake, they both fell fast asleep after the moon set.

Jimbo was on the south canyon floor behind two scrubby mesquite trees. It was not much shelter. Breed found a boulder with a view of the mouth of the canyon. He hid behind several small boulders in a pile where he was protected if he was laying flat along the ground. Pappy stuck close to the wagon loading his rifle and readying extra ammunition. Jed assigned the three Texas cowboys who joined up with them tasks to keep the herd calm.

Crabclaw dispersed with the others. Later in the dark, he snuck back closer to the camp. There was no way he was sticking out his neck for Jed.

Pappy made Glenda sleep in the wagon overnight. She knew Pappy was worried. He told her a posse was coming after them. She was scared and loaded her small pistol, hiding it in her skirt pocket. After using a gnarled tree to hide while she hiked her skirt, she wandered over to where Corky was rolling his bedroll near the remuda.

"Mornin Corky," she greeted him.

"Yew best git back into the wagon," he said. He had never spoken so gruffly to her before.

"But Corky . . . " she started to say.

"Git now. Yew stay in that wagon and keep yer head down when it starts."

Corky's stomach riled. He puked several times overnight thinking about today. He did not want to die and knew he was no match for any gunman. All of his bravado was gone and the only thing left was a scared nineteen-year-old boy.

Rafe and Dale waited in nervous anticipation until they spotted Big Ed on his horse. A bit of a distance behind him, the rest of the posse rode in twos. Rafe and Dale scanned the canyon walls and the few men mingling near the wagon. Below them the large herd was calm and only lowing quietly.

The rustler lookouts, Rick and Pete, spotted a horse

ridden by a big man pop into their vision. Pete recognized
Big Ed. Pete aimed at him, but just for a moment he
hesitated. Big Ed was the saloon owner in San Marcial. A
man who many times gave the cowboys drinks when they
were broke. He was a good man and these were his cattle.

Rafe saw a movement high on the south wall of the
canyon. Something glinted in the morning sun. He took
aim with his GSW rifle waiting to see the movement again.

Ed was riding slowly and his rifle was on his hip.
Rising slightly and looking down his rifle barrel, Pete had
Ed in his sight. He thumbed the hammer on the rifle.
Suddenly a report resounded in the canyon. It echoed off
the canyon walls and sounded all around Pete. It was
strange because Pete did not think he fired yet. He could
not remember pulling the trigger. The colors on the far
canyon wall became intense, then he was looking at the
blue of the morning sky and his chest hurt.

"Pete, Pete," Rick said seeing Pete falling back to the
ground. From somewhere in the distance Pete heard his
name being called. Then he heard nothing at all.

"What the fuck," was all Jed could say when bullets
started coming down on them from the cliffs. He was
standing well behind the wagon near a tree when the first
shots sounded. He grabbed his rifle and ran. The cattle
began to low and move in a circle at the sound of gunfire.

Rick saw a rifle flash come from the north ridgeline
and not from below. He fired several shots at the ridge
wondering how ambushers sneaked past them.

Rafe and Dale pulled back and heard bullets hit
below them after they let off a volley. Dale took a quick
peek and saw Ed and the posse at the mouth of the canyon.
Across the canyon a man rose up on the south canyon wall.
Dale aimed and fired.

Below them gunshots filled the air. They waited a
minute, waiting to see if Dale's shot hit a mark. No gunfire
flash was returned from the spot on the south wall.

The posse and Ed came barreling into the canyon
firing at anything that moved. Above them they heard
reports from high on the canyon wall and Ed hoped it was

Dale and Rafe protecting them.

Rafe saw the posse below riding hard into the canyon. The cows were bellowing loudly at the commotion and kicking up a curtain of dust. From the cliff wall, their vantage point was quickly diminishing.

"Come on. I think we took care of the lookouts. The posse is here now, let's go get our horses," Rafe said to Dale. They grabbed their ammunition and rushed down to where they tethered the horses, mounted up, and rode down a path to the mouth of the canyon.

Jed ran with his guns and took a position behind the wagon. It was the only real protection on the empty canyon floor. The cows were panicky. Their snorts and bellows filled the air along with gunshots. Jed looked toward the mouth of the canyon and could vaguely see figures on horseback, but the blazing sun and dust from the moving cows blurred the scene. He steadied his rifle on the wheel of the wagon.

When the shooting from the rim of the canyon started, Crabclaw ran to the remuda and grabbed his saddled horse. Shots reverberated all around the canyon. He saw Corky bent over near a rock puking. Jumping to the saddle he skirted the moving cattle nervous to the commotion. Reaching the wagon, he found Jed aiming his rifle down the canyon.

Jed did not hear Crabclaw ride up behind him. "Got us pinned down, yew dumbshit," Crabclaw growled at him. Jed whirled to see the deformed outlaw behind him.

"And what hep are yew? Yew plannin on savin yer own skin while the others are out there shootin. I shudda known yew was a coward," Jed spit out the word coward.

"I play the odds and yew just busted." Craig Moss raised his pistol and took aim at Jed. He had him dead to rights and there was nothing Jed could do. Craig thought the stupid cowboy deserved to die now. It would give Craig revenge, instead of letting him hang by a rope.

Just as Craig went to the pull the trigger, a large steer knocked his horse. The movement knocked Craig and the pistol fired. Jed went down in a heap.

More gunfire echoed around Craig and sounded closer by the second. In one motion, he jumped from his horse to the back of the wagon. Glenda cowered inside with Pappy. He shoved Pappy to the bed of the wagon and heard his head hit with a thump. Grabbing Glenda he pulled her out the back. She struggled some, but was no match for his strong grip.

"Git on that hoss!" Craig demanded.

Glenda struggled in his grip. "Let me go!" she screamed.

"Yew wanna die?" Craig asked her.

Outside the gunfire continued. Glenda knew she would be arrested or killed as a rustler. Rustling was a hanging offense. The deformed outlaw scared the shit out of her, but was maybe giving her a way out. Obeying his command, she straddled the horse. Craig jumped on in front of her and grabbed the reins.

CHAPTER 56

Rafe and Dale reached the entrance to the box canyon. The canyon was filled with dust as the cattle milled. The noise of the animals was almost deafening, then several gunshot reports from further inside the canyon echoed. Rafe could not tell riders from cows in the mayhem. They barely reached the mouth when about a hundred head of cattle stampeded toward them.

"Dale, move!" Rafe yelled. Rayo instinctively bolted to safety and Rafe was glad to see Dale's horse follow.

Outside the canyon, Armando saw cattle bolting. He, Pancho, and Lefty gave chase, trying to get in front of the running cattle. "Yeeha! Yeeha!" Lefty yelled swinging his lariat at the cattle trying to force them to turn right and mill. Pancho followed Lefty's lead.

Once clear of the stampeding cattle, Dale and Rafe sat on their mounts watching. Out of the dust, they spotted a man with a woman straddled behind him riding hard out of the fray. Rafe lifted his rifle, but Dale put up his hand to stop him. Kicking his horse, Dale rode off after the escaping pair.

The gunfire subsided. Armando, Pancho, and Lefty worked together to stop the cows from stampeding and the dust was settling on the canyon floor.

By the time Rafe rode into the canyon, Ed and Tomás were rounding up the outlaws. Arturo was holding a rifle on the small group. Four of them were wounded, one was an older man and one was bleeding from his shoulder. His blue shirt was stained with blood. They were sitting against the chuckwagon.

Seeing Rafe ride up, a great relief spread across Ed's face. All of the posse was accounted for and alive, except for the Dale."

"Everybody all right?" Rafe asked jumping off Rayo.

"All good here, Tomás and Paco got winged, nothing serious. Where's Dale?" Ed asked.

"He took off after a man and woman fleeing on a horse."

"What!" Corky stood and yelled, "Glenda, Glenda."

"Shutup Corky, she's gone," Pappy snapped at him.

"Did they get the stampede stopped?" Ed asked.

"I think so. Armando and Lefty seemed like they were getting them under control," Rafe replied. Cows milled around the canyon floor, but with the gunfire stopped, they were beginning to settle.

"Who's in charge here?" Big Ed asked.

"That'd be me," the man with the bloody shirt spoke up.

Ed finally looked at the man closely. The face was familiar. "Jed Clements? What the fuck were you thinking. First you bring that fucker, Luke Payton to San Marcial and I had to kill him, now this shit. Just couldn't stay in Texas, could you. I should just shoot your ass right now and be done with you," Ed's voice crested in anger as he yelled at Jed.

"I don't blame yew Big Ed. Do what yew have to. I deserve it," Jed responded. He was defeated. All his dreams of a little ranch outside of Austin and marrying Bonnie were now gone. Even Glenda was gone. Crabclaw waited for his chance and fled with her. All Jed could do now was wait for the bullet to kill him and why not, he had nothing to live for.

Tomás put a hand on Ed's arm to calm him. "Is this everyone?" Tomás asked.

Jed looked around. Pappy was holding his head, Corky sat looking stunned and scared. Rip had taken a bullet in his leg. Jake and Bill were standing near the wagon unharmed.

"Jimbo's missin and two men were up on the cliff. I dun know bout them," Jed said.

"Think we took care of the ones up on the cliff. At least they stopped shooting," Rafe told Ed.

"Lefty, you and Paco go see if you can find this Jimbo feller," Ed told them.

Breed hid behind a large boulder halfway up the

canyon. When the posse came, Breed found the best hiding place he could find and stayed hunkered down. This was not his fight. As the dust from the herd began to thin, he saw the posse had the outlaws sitting near the wagon. Rick, Jimbo, and Pete were missing from the group. Breed had watched Crabclaw pull Glenda onto his horse and gallop off.

Armando came riding up and said the stampede was stopped about a half mile away.

"Over here," Lefty shouted.

Ed and Rafe walked to where Lefty stood with Paco. Jimbo lay on the ground dead. Blood seeped from his chest onto his checkered shirt.

"Whaddaya want we should do?" Lefty asked.

"See if you can find a shovel in the wagon and bury him," Ed told them.

"What about the two up on the cliff?" Rafe asked.

"I guess the buzzards will get a good feast."

Big Ed's brain swirled with indecision. He should turn these rustlers into the sheriff in Las Vegas. Part of him wanted to kill the rustlers here in the canyon, especially Jed, but he just was not that kind of man.

He and the posse were exhausted and almost a thousand head of his cattle milled on the canyon floor. "I won't kill you Jed, but you and your crew will help me get the herd to Las Vegas. If you all behave, I'll put in a good word with the sheriff there and maybe you'll live," Ed said.

Jed was just as surprised by Ed's offer as the rest. He expected far worst for this fiasco.

"Ed, I will go as far as Las Vegas, then I need to go home," Rafe told him.

"Thank you, Rafe. You and Dale did a great job keeping them hunkered down while we rode in. They gave up pretty easy, not knowing how many of you were up on the ridge, but I'm worried about Dale."

Rafe looked over at Jed and asked, "Who rode out with the woman?"

"His name is Craig Moss, goes by Crabclaw cause he has a deformed hand. He's a killer. Fucker shot me in the shoulder. He's one crazy dangerous fucker. Iffin I were yew, I'd let him and the girl go."

"Dun say that Jed. He's got Glenda an she's innocent!" Corky yelled out.

CHAPTER 57

Before noon, Ed and the posse had the cattle organized and moved out the box canyon heading north. Pappy drove the chuckwagon and Corky resumed his duties with the remuda. Jed rode in the wagon unable to ride.

"Yew shur r lucky," Pappy told him as they rode.

"Yew mean cause Big Ed didn't shoot me dead fer stealin his cows?"

"Naw, cause that Crabclaw feller didn't. He had yew in his sight and then a steer knocked his horse and he only winged yew. I saw it from the wagon," Pappy told him.

"What happened to Breed. I never saw him after the fight. Ya think he got it?" Jed asked.

"He may be a half-breed, but he's full Injun when it comes to being sneaky. I'm countin on him being hid somewhere back in the canyon. Why didn't yew tell Ed bout him?"

"I dun know. Figgered he didn't deserve to be caught up in this mess. I only hired him cause he knew the trail. He weren't really a rustler." Jed shrugged and actually hoped Breed had escaped.

Ed did not push the cattle hard, letting them set a slow pace. He made Tomás, Armando, and Arturo return directly to San Marcial. With the help of Jed's rustlers, they had enough men to push the herd. When Tomás tried to stay, Ed convinced him Cynthia, Teresa, and all the townspeople would be distraught with worry. "Go home and tell them we are fine," Ed said.

A little while later Rafe rode up beside Ed. "I'm worried about Dale. If that Crabclaw is as mean and handy with a gun as Jed said, Dale may be in trouble. I'm going to go look for him," Rafe said.

"My men have the herd well in hand and the rustlers are unarmed. I don't think they will give us any trouble. After you look for Dale, head on back to Santa Fe. You've done enough," Ed told him.

"Thanks Ed. I'm sure Ana Teresa is worried." They stopped their horses and Ed stuck out his hand.

"Thank you again, Rafe. Stop and see us when you travel south again. I owe you," Big Ed told him.

"Good luck getting the cattle to Wyoming."

Rafe left Ed following the herd on the trail north. Riding hard back to the canyon, Rafe picked up several sets of fresh tracks headed east. He hoped one set belonged to Dale Godley. On the way Rafe worried he would find Dale dead, bushwhacked by the gunslinger named Crabclaw. It took most of the day to find him.

"Hey, what are you doing way out here," Dale called out. He and Glenda were sitting in the shade of a juniper tree near a creek feeding a small lake.

"Came looking for you. We all thought you might be dead. What happened?"

"I saw the man and this girl fly out with the stampede. Something told me to go after them. I was worried about the girl. They were riding double, so I caught up. The man shot at me, but I kept my distance and kept up with them. He ran out of bullets and could not reload. She told me he gave her the pistol to reload it, but she took it instead and tried to hit him. The gun flew out of her hand in the struggle. Soon the horse gave out and stopped. He took cover amongst a clump of juniper scrub and she ran the opposite way. I pulled my gun and circled around him. He must have had an extra pistol with him."

"No, he took the one I had in the pocket of my dress. I had pulled it out wanting to kill him," Glenda explained.

"When he saw me ride by, shots came at me but I kept riding and took my aim. He's over there dead. I want to bury him, but she told me to leave him to the coyotes. He was mean to her and everyone else in their gang. So I just left him there. She said his real name is Craig Moss, but everyone called him Crabclaw. I saw his right hand and it's deformed and looks like a claw."

"What about her?" Rafe asked.

"She's just a girl. She says they found her in the Texas

desert after Comanches killed her family. They were on their way to California."

"What are you going to do with her?"

"Well, been thinking. This isn't any kind of country for a young girl alone. For that matter, I've been rethinking God's plan for me. Glenda and I have been talking and we're going to head east back to Indiana. I can take over my father's church there."

"My pa was a minister too," Glenda piped up.

"You never told me your father was a preacher," Rafe said to Dale thinking it was another strange coincidence both of their father's were ministers.

"I guess with a name like Godly we are destined to follow the word. I thought God was telling me to come west, but seems as if I have to break too many commandments out here. I'd like to hang up these guns forever."

At noon two days later Rafe rode up to the horse barn at the Summers' ranch in Santa Fe. He wanted to ride directly to find Ana Teresa at the de Soto hacienda. However, the prospect of meeting her father in his filthy condition caused him to come home first. He had been in the saddle for almost two weeks without any creature comforts and most of all without a bath.

Esteban came out and greeted him, *"Bienvenido, Rafael."*

"Thank you Esteban, give Rayo a good rubdown. He's filthy. Scrub him and give him all the oats he can eat."

"Sí señor, I will take care of Rayo, but you are *muy* filthy yourself," Esteban told him and they both laughed.

Eagerly, Rafe walked to the house to announce his arrival home. First he looked in the kitchen, then bounded to the second floor. The house was unusually empty and quiet. Finally, he walked out the kitchen door having decided to find George in the foundry.

Kneeling in the garden, Ana Teresa wore a dirty white apron, gloves, and a large straw hat. Rafe was shocked to see her, then smiled broadly at her disheveled appearance.

"Oye peón, ¿dónde está la señora de la casa?" Rafe called to her. He called her a *peón*, and asked, where was the lady of the house.

Ana Teresa heard Rafe's voice and relief swept her body. She stood up with her hands on her hips and turned toward him.

"I am no *peón, señor.* What is a dirty *vagabundo* doing at my house?" she retorted calling him a vagabond.

"I am no vagrant *señora.* I live here with a beautiful woman. What have you done with her?"

Laughing, she ran to him and jumped wrapping her arms and knees around him. Tears rolled down her cheeks. He held on to her and took in the sweet aroma from her hair. Finally she let go and stood squarely in front of him removing her hat. The bright sun lit up her face. The tendrils of her brown hair framed her face and tears glistened on her cheeks.

"You, *señor,* are in trouble with me. Why did you not come home with Carlos? What could be more important than coming home to me?" Rafe thought she was teasing, though her voice sounded peeved and her expression angry.

"I am so sorry, Ana Teresa. Don't be mad. I have told you many times, there is something in me which wants to help those in need. Cynthia was hurt by some cattle rustlers and the sheriff in Socorro would not come to help Ed go after them. He needed my help."

"So, if you were killed you would have left a fatherless child and lonely wife behind," she said with her hands on her hips.

It took Rafe a minute to register what she just said.

"¡Santa María, madre de Dios!" was all he could say blessing Holy Mary, the mother of God, at her news.

"You better pray to the Holy Mother, if you dare go away from me again," she told him and then her face broke into a smile.

"Are you . . . are you sure?" he stammered.

Ana Teresa nodded in a response. A new light shined

over him, he was sure he saw it. It happened when he stared into her golden brown eyes. Speechless, he took her in his arms and held her never wanting to let go. Finally she broke his *abrazo.*

"*Señor,* I think it is best if you go and clean your *vagabundo* body. Even the unborn one is getting upset with your odor. Go now," she ordered him.

After a bath, Rafe walked to the dining room and Ana Teresa had a meal ready for them with a bottle of wine. She was dressed in the latest American style dress, stylish and practical. "You look beautiful, Ana Teresa," Rafe raised his glass of wine and took a sip, as she did too, with a slight blush on her cheeks.

He was so overwhelmed with the news, Rafe completely forgot about the other most important issue in their lives. Finally remembering Rafe asked. "You have not told me of your parents.

"They are staying at Uncle Pedro's hacienda. They found out about us and I came back home here to live."

"Well, are you going to tell me how they feel about me?"

"My father disowned me and ordered me out of Uncle's Pedro house. Now, he is trying to claim the hacienda."

"I must go and see your uncle and talk to your father."

"Rafael, it is not a good time for you to meet him."

Chapter 58

The following day Rafe sent a message to Carlos and Bibiana letting them know he arrived back to Santa Fe safely. He invited them for supper that evening at the Summers' home. George and the family were delighted with Rafe's safe return and Josefina ordered the cooks to prepare a special meal in celebration.

When Carlos, Bibiana, and the baby arrived in the early evening, the Summers girls immediately commandeered the baby from Bibiana's arms. The baby, almost three months old, was cooing and smiling at the girls to their delight.

"I can see he will be the delight of everyone!" Josefina exclaimed as Benicío grabbed for her necklace with his tiny fingers. "I'm sure your parents are overjoyed Bibiana."

"Yes, my father is smitten. He is already talking about buying a pony from Rafael for Benicío's second birthday." The women laughed and played with the baby until the maid called for dinner.

Standing around the large table, George said a special prayer giving thanks for Rafe's safe return and for the new life which the Lord blessed upon Carlos and Bibiana. At the end of the prayer Rafe added, "And Lord bless the unborn child who will join this family next spring."

For several moments the silence was deafening as the family digested his words.

"*¡Gracias a Dios!*" Josefina exclaimed.

Excited conversation filled the room with congratulations for Rafe and Ana Teresa's soon-to-be parenthood.

"Looks like our children will be playing together as we hoped," Carlos said.

"Yes and hopefully many more."

The meal of spicy pork roast, chili dusted potatoes, and baked squash was served. The happy conversations overlapped between babies, the trip to Boston, the wedding in Mexico, and the new twin foals who were now both strong and healthy. Reymundo kept a close eye on them, but allowed them to run with the mothers in the pasture.

When the men excused themselves to the parlor for a brandy, the women took the baby upstairs. George lit a cigar and puffed it until the tip glowed. Rafe stood by the large empty fireplace thinking of how many times plans and conversations were discussed here in this room. His hand ran along the smooth wood mantle. The wood shone from many coats of polish to protect it from the smoke of the fires.

"What do you think Big Ed will do about the rustlers?" George asked.

"He said if they helped him get the cows to market, he would put in a good word with the sheriff. Big Ed is not a vindictive man. I think in the end he was more worried about getting anyone hurt than he was about the cows."

"I had a wire from Tomás. He and Armando arrived back in San Marcial. They will try to restore the damage done in the village before Ed gets back," Carlos told them.

"Now that you are both going to be fathers, it is time to think about the future here in Santa Fe. Hopefully there will be no more dangerous ventures in your futures," George admonished.

"We didn't ask for this to be a dangerous venture. It was a simple trip to go to my mother's wedding." Rafe tried to dismiss George's warning.

"Yes, until you try to save the world and take on everyone's problems as your own," Carlos chided him.

"What do you mean?" George asked.

Carlos and Rafe related the story about the *peóns* plight in Mexico. Rafe explained how he freed the condemned *peóns* in Jiménez. Carlos told George how the *Federales* came to the hacienda after the wedding.

"I could not let it stand, *don* Jorge," Rafe told his adopted father. "I'm also worried about my family in Torreón, but there is nothing more I can do."

George puffed on his cigar listening to Rafe and

Carlos tell about the trip into Mexico. Nothing about the stories were a surprise. Politics harbored evil both in Mexico and here in Santa Fe. Daily, the newspaper was full of editorials and articles about the escalating violence over the Spanish land grants. Only several days ago, someone took a shot at the Surveyor General's crew as they were surveying a property.

Trying to change the subject, George asked, "Rafe, when will you meet Ana Teresa's parents?"

"She is against my doing so. Her father has disowned her and she says he will kill me."

"Surely he will change his mind when he learns he is to be a grandfather. Ana Teresa is his only child and yours will be his only grandchildren," Carlos interrupted.

"True, but they will be *mestizo*. She says he will never be able to accept them. Ana Teresa says he unconditionally believes in the Spanish traditions and believes our marriage a taint on the family name."

"He is a fool," George said bitterly.

"He is also exerting his birthright over *don* Pedro claiming the hacienda as his," Carlos told them. "They dueled in the courtyard just last week. Luckily the women stopped them before any mortal harm was done."

"With swords?"

"Yes. *Don* Pedro is not backing down to Bartolo's claim of birthright. We met with Ron Iverson several times to try to settle it at the land office."

They spent another hour talking about the trouble over the land grants and the trouble at the de Soto hacienda. The conversation finally ended when Bibiana brought the sleeping baby downstairs in her arms and she and Carlos bid the family goodnight.

CHAPTER 59

For several weeks, Rafe and Ana Teresa discussed the situation about her father. Rafe's heart ached for his wife's dilemma. She tried to hide it from him, but he could see and feel her pain when they discussed the situation.

"I must go and try to reason with him," Rafe said as they got ready for bed. "I do not want this hanging over our heads, especially yours now that you are pregnant."

"No. He will not change. If he tries to kill you, you will have to defend yourself. I do not want to lose either of you. Besides, Bibiana says he is distraught about the land grant and threatening to throw her parent's off the hacienda. Does this sound like a man who will compromise? If he would do that to my aunt and uncle, do you really think he would change his mind about you being a *mestizo?*"

"But I must try. Otherwise I will always look weak and afraid in his eyes."

"Please Rafael, give it some time. Perhaps after the baby is born and all these property issues are settled, we can approach him."

Rafe nodded not wanting to upset her more. She was strong, but how long could she endure being shunned by her parents? Rafe decided not to give up on her family, hoping to find a way to make her father reconcile.

Several days later, Carlos came to the foundry looking for Rafe. Benjamin Pacheco came with him.

"Rafe, the *dons* are meeting tomorrow at the Palacio Cantina to discuss the land issues. *Don* Leonardo has called a meeting to unite the Spanish land grant holders. They feel it the only way they can fight what is happening. *Dons* owning all the land grants surrounding Santa Fe have been invited," Carlos explained.

"My father asks for you to come. The *dons* want to discuss buying the guns and ammunition they need to defend their properties," Benjamin added.

"Me? Perhaps George should go," Rafe replied knowing the Spanish *dons* did not allow *mestizos* in the Palacio. Rafe and George were already filling several orders for pistols and rifles for Benjamin's father and several other *dons*.

"My father and *don* Pedro specifically asked for you to come," Benjamin told him and reluctantly Rafe agreed to go with them.

The following day as Rafe rode to downtown Santa Fe with Carlos and Benjamin, they discussed the situation and the upcoming meeting with the *dons*.

"Carlos, this war cannot end well for the *dons*. More and more people are coming west and they don't give a damn about land grants. All they care about is the bill of sale they hold, legal or illegal," Rafe told them just before they arrived at the Palacio Cantina.

"Of course I agree. My father was shot by government officials over our land in Los Lunas. I did not realize it at the time, but now believe it was the government officials helping a land grabber." Carlos reminded Rafe of the event in Los Lunas.

"There's the cantina. I can't believe I will be allowed to go inside. The last time I came looking for Diego, the Madame ran me out. Some of the old *dons* backed her up with their swords drawn against me."

Carlos chuckled. "Those old *caballeros* would have sliced you up with their swords. They may be old, but you better believe they can still wield a blade. But don't worry, you are invited today and they want your help. However, keep a low profile until they ask for you."

Rafe thought how things had changed over the past several years in Santa Fe. Several of the *dons* accepted him and now many others might be seeking his help. It was not that long ago they wanted to hang him.

Dismounting, a stableman took their horses to the small corral already filled. Rafe admired the ornate Spanish saddles. Distinguished by a large pommel and embossed leather foot guards on the stirrups, the saddle's silver studded bridles gleamed in the bright sunlight.

Carlos led the way to the door. Today, no music greeted them as he opened it. Only cigar smoke wafted out. *Caballeros,* the Spanish aristocrat *dons* of Santa Fe, stood around in groups conversing with each other. No one noticed them as they entered. Benjamin led them to where his father *don* Ramon was engaged in conversation with *don* Pedro.

Rafe absorbed the elaborately decorated Palacio. The cantina had proudly catered to *caballeros* from families of pure Spanish ancestry for years. The smooth stuccoed walls of the cantina were decorated with weapons and murals. Large paintings of *conquistadors* filled all the walls with the far wall covered in a grand painting of Juan de Oñate on horseback. He was the first governor of the Kingdom of New Mexico.

The floors of the Palacio were covered with thick European carpets. Elegant etched mirrors reflected the paintings. Crystal chandeliers, rich draperies, and imported furniture from Spain shone brightly in the lights from the many coats of polish.

"Thank you for coming, Rafael. We are waiting for a few more *dons* to arrive before we start. Stay close to me," *don* Pedro told him.

Two *dons* standing not far from them were in a heated exchange. He recognized one of the *dons* from his trial. He was not sure but thought it was Diego's father. The *dons* were dressed in their finest *trajes.* The short-waist suit jackets gleamed with silver buttons and elaborate embroidery designs. Underneath the jacket, colorful sashes were tied with the fringed ends hanging down. Most trousers were adorned with silver conchas down the sides ending in a ruffled bellbottom. They all wore the traditional flat-crowned hat, some with embroidery around the edges and most carried a sheathed sword dangling from their waist.

While they waited, Rafe looked up to the second floor railing and noticed a beautiful woman looking down scanning the room. It was Virginia Barceló Verdugo, the

Madame and owner of the Palacio Cantina. She was dressed in a black gown trimmed in red. On her head, a tall *peineta* held a long black lace *mantilla* covering her shoulders. Rafe had only seen the woman twice before today. Once when he came to the cantina looking for Diego de la Torre and then again when she testified at his trial for the murder of Diego. Surprisingly, her testimony helped him during the trial.

Rafe nudged Carlos and focused his eyes on Virginia. "I should go up and thank her for testifying on my behalf."

"No let it be. Believe me, you would not be allowed in here if it were not for *don* Pedro. Keep a low profile until you are asked for help," Carlos replied.

Rafe seemed mesmerized by Virginia and continued to steal glances to the balcony. While he watched, a *caballero* appeared from a room upstairs and went to stand behind Virginia. He whispered into her right ear. She acknowledged with a noticeable head nod, before he descended the stairs.

"Carlos, who is the man coming down the stairs?" Rafe asked.

Carlos took a glance and said. "It is Alvaro Gutierrez's father, *don* Luciano." Two young *caballeros* met him and escorted him to the far end of the room. Rafe noticed they were both carrying holstered pistols and walked beside *don* Luciano like bodyguards. *Don* Luciano wore a sword and his spurs clinked as he walked.

The front door opened and several *dons* entered making their way into the group. Apparently they were the last to arrive. A tall *don* strode to the front, stepping up to the small platform where the guitar player usually sat.

"*Caballeros, su atención, por favor,*" *don* Leonardo called the room to attention. "We are all here to discuss what to do about the land squatters and more importantly those who are selling our land illegally."

About an hour after Rafe, Carlos, and Benjamin left for the city, Ron Iverson rode to the Summers' ranch. Esteban came out to greet him.

Iverson wasted no time and asked. "Is Rafael Reyes or Carlos Zuniga here?"

"No señor, they went to the Palacio Cantina with Benjamin Pacheco."

"I was afraid of that." The lawyer pondered a moment. The Palacio was not a place he could intervene, even though several of the *dons* were his clients. Taking out a notebook from his coat pocket, he quickly wrote a note and tore out the sheet. He handed it to the stable man.

"Please, go to the cantina and give this note to Rafael and only Rafael. It is important. You must hurry."

"Sí señor."

Esteban pocketed the note and ran to the stable. By the time he rode out of the barn, the lawyer was gone.

Chapter 60

The atmosphere in the Palacio Cantina grew somber as each of the *dons* stood up and gave their opinions on what to do about the squatters. Some of them told of their encounters with the squatters, and several told of bloodshed and death. *Don* Eduardo repeated the story about his son's death by a squatter accusing his son of stealing cattle. The cattle were *don* Eduardo's and it happened on his own land near Tesuque.

"They were well armed and they killed my only son, Javier," *don* Eduardo told the group.

Many other complaints were heard and discussed. *Don* Leonardo purposely wanted them to vent their frustrations. Some of the local *dons* were less worried about their estates, because no land grabbing had happened here in the town of Santa Fe, although all had been required to produce their documents.

Don Pedro stood and spoke, "My son-in-law was stripped of his birthright and his father killed on the steps of their hacienda in Los Lunas. I tell you it could happen anywhere, including here in Santa Fe."

Don Pedro emphasized the point so the *dons* from Santa Fe would fully understand the seriousness of the problem. He did not discuss his own problems with his hacienda and the trouble with his brother. Unfortunately, Bartolo heard about this meeting and insisted on attending. He was sitting several tables away with *don* Daniel Archuleta.

"I will kill any squatters who come onto my land. My *vaqueros* are vigilant and ordered to kill them before they even setup a camp," *don* Armando bragged.

"Your hacienda is small and easy to defend, but the sheriff will arrest and hang your *vaqueros* for such an unprovoked action. Did you tell them that?" *don* Antonio Peralta asked.

"*Don* Armando is right. We need to defend ourselves.

Are you too old or too weak to fight? Are you not Spaniards?" one of the *dons* from the far side of the room yelled out.

Some of the *dons* did not know the speaker, but *don* Pedro recognized his brother Bartolo's voice.

"We need better weapons and more *vaqueros*. My hacienda is over six thousand acres. My *vaqueros* cannot be everywhere," *don* Sebastian de la Torre responded. Other murmurs circulated the room in agreement.

"*Señores, señores*, talking about fighting is all well and good, but we must talk about the group known as the Santa Fe Ring. They are the root of this problem. They are powerful and pushing the government to work against us. Even the sheriff is under their control." *Don* Leonardo tried to focus the conversation to what he thought was the heart of the problem.

"Who are they, this Santa Fe Ring? Give us names," a voice demanded.

"It is rumored our local banker, Stephen Elkins, is one. His bank took control of the Beaubien-Miranda land grant. Now he and the heirs to the Miranda grant call themselves the Maxwell Land Company and they have all the mineral rights to the land."

"Old Lucien Maxwell sold his grant when gold was found in Elizabethtown. He got rich, not killed," someone said.

"He was not killed because he is a gringo. What do you think would have happened if he was Spanish?" *don* Armando asked.

Chaos erupted in the room. The story about the Beaubien-Miranda land grant was well known all over New Mexico. Lucien Maxwell, originally from Illinois, made a fortune in New Mexico after he married Guadalupe Miranda's daughter, Luz. Stories were rampant about his mistreatment of Hispanic servants and workers. They sold out the mineral rights to her father's land grant for an enormous fortune when gold was found in the hills surrounding Taos.

"It is the Easterners. They do not want Spaniards

here and are trying to move us out!"

"Not all are Easterners, but they are connected to the government. Guadalupe Miranda, Luz's father, was assistant to Governor Armijo."

"This is exactly the problem. The Santa Fe Ring consists of powerful attorneys, bankers, and land speculators, even our politicians. The men elected or appointed to uphold the law are using it against us to get rich," *don* Leonardo told the group trying again to bring the discussion to the problem of the Santa Fe Ring.

Grumbling circulated the room.

"You need better weapons. Look at me. I have bodyguards. This is not 1783, this is 1873. You need guns and rifles to defend your land," *don* Luciano argued. Two well-armed *caballero* bodyguards sat by his side.

"My son-in-law works for *señor* Summers weapons company here in Santa Fe. I have made an order for new weapons to defend my property," *don* Pedro told them. "The first order will come next week. At that time you can all look at the guns and if you are satisfied you can order more."

When Esteban arrived at the Palacio Cantina, he quickly dismounted. Esteban knew he could not enter the aristocrat's bastion, so he ran to the back and excitedly knocked on the backdoor. He had a few friends who worked here and occasionally some of them snuck out a bottle of tequila and food. The door opened and Pánfilo, the dishwasher, stuck his head out.

"Esteban, ¿qué quieres?" What do you want he asked.

"Tengo un mensaje para mi patrón," Esteban told him he had a message for his boss.

Pánfilo opened the backdoor. They slipped through a tapestry from the kitchen to behind the bar in the main room. The *caballeros* were arguing, engaged in heated conversation and did not notice.

Esteban scanned the room and spotted Rafe and Carlos sitting with *don* Pedro de Soto. After several repeated attempts, Esteban attracted Rafe's attention.

Rafe saw Esteban standing next to the bartender waving at him. Concerned something had happened at home or at the foundry, Rafe quietly rose and walked to him.

"*¿Qué estás haciendo aquí? ¿Hay algún problema en casa?*" Rafe asked him what was he doing here and if there was a problem at home.

"No, I bring this note from *Señor* Iverson." After Esteban handed Rafe the note, Pánfilo pulled Esteban out of the room. Virginia would fire him for interrupting the *dons*.

Returning to his seat, Rafe opened the note and read it, then showed it to Carlos. They looked at each other, surprised at what they read. Reaching across the table, Carlos handed the note to *don* Pedro. After he read it, his eyes widened in disbelief.

CHAPTER 61

"Don Luciano, what can you tell us about the Santa Fe Ring? What can you tell us of the people in the government?" *don* Pedro stood up and asked. The room quieted at the hard cutting edge in *don* Pedro's voice.

Rafe had never met *don* Luciano Gutierrez. It was his son, Alvaro, who had several times accosted Rafe and threatened him. Benjamin told Rafe, it was Alvaro who ordered the dandies to burn Rafe's house, and it was Alvaro and his friend's who tried to lynch Rafe.

Don Luciano stood as if standing up to defend himself. "I know nothing of such things *don* Pedro. Why do you ask me?" *Don* Luciano's voice was cold and calculating.

"I have a note from my lawyer, naming you as the main Spanish speculator. You are helping them steal land grants from your own people." *Don* Pedro waved the note from Ron Iverson in the air as he spoke.

"How dare you accuse me of such treachery! You will pay for this, *señor!"* he warned.

"So tell us how you paid for the new equipment and increased your sheep herd?" *don* Antonio pressed him. Several *dons* had recently noticed *don* Luciano built a large barn and bragged about increasing his flock. *Don* Antonio knew it to be almost twice as big as before.

"Why do you need bodyguards here at the Palacio?" another voice called out.

Don Luciano looked around the room to see all eyes were staring at him. He backed away from his table and pulled his sword. At his move, the two young *caballeros* stood by his sides with their hands ready to pull their pistols. All three slowly backed away toward the bar.

"Es verdad. ¡Desgraciado!" *don* Antonio yelled as he realized the accusation was true. *Don* Pedro and *don* Ramon headed to block off *don* Luciano's retreat to the door behind the bar.

Chaos erupted in the room. *Don* Luciano glared at his

friends. *Don* Bartolo knew some of these *dons* when they were young men. Years ago, they were the young dandies of Santa Fe. Luciano Gutierrez was one the leaders. Somehow, the revelation Luciano was helping the Santa Fe Ring and getting rich from it did not surprise Bartolo. The young Luciano cheated at cards and told lies about his friends to gain favor and power. Bartolo stood and moved closer to the *dons* surrounding Luciano and pulled his sword.

Rafe had been keeping a low profile during the meeting. *Don* Pedro requested his presence here only to answer questions and take gun orders from the *dons*. A few knew who he was, but others had paid him little regard. The *dons* were only armed with swords, but the two bodyguards were well heeled. Sensing it might be a lopsided fight, Rafe rose and headed toward the bar. He squeezed past several *dons* to get closer.

Don Ramon Pacheco, Benjamin's father, pulled his sword and headed toward the three retreating cowards. One of the young bodyguards made a gesture to go for his gun. Rafe pushed his way past *don* Ramon and moved near the *caballero* bodyguard. "Do not pull that pistol, *señor*," he warned the man.

The young bodyguard hesitated. His *patrón* brought him here for protection. He was told it was for intimidation only. In front of him, twelve angry *dons* glared at him and his *patrón*. Some had their swords drawn, however only the young *pistolero* was armed with two guns.

A tall *don* was in the front of the group. Rafe did not know him. His ornate sword was in his hand and his *traje* was impeccable. The *don* glanced at him and Rafe was struck by some familiarity.

"¡Babosos!" *don* Luciano called the other *dons* drooling idiots as he drew his sword.

The tall man advanced toward *don* Luciano. "You always were a coward Luciano and a cheat," he sneered. "I am not surprised you would sell out your friends. You have not changed since you were a boy!"

As the tall *don* took a step closer, the young

bodyguard went for his pistol. Rafe saw the movement. His GSW pistol leveled at the bodyguard's chest in a blur of movement. Before the *caballero* had his thumb on the hammer, a bullet from Rafe's pistol struck him in the heart. The impact threw him backwards into the Palacio's bar. Rafe pointed his gun at the other bodyguard before he could respond.

"Drop it *señor.*" The man obeyed and dropped his pistol to the floor.

Don Bartolo looked at the young man next to him. He was not a *don.* He was dressed in a dark wool suit with a two-gun gunbelt wrapped around his waist and no sword. His tan face proved he was not a full-blooded Spaniard. Regardless, *don* Bartolo acknowledged his expert action with a nod of his head.

Don Luciano stood with his sword extended waiting to defend himself. There was no fear in his eyes. He was good with the sword, very good, and it was not long ago he won a duel up in the Village of Taos.

The man standing squarely in front of him was Bartolo de Soto. He and Bartolo had been friends long ago before Bartolo left and took an inheritance in California. They were the young dandies in Santa Fe many years ago and Luciano was the best. When they practiced their swordplay Luciano always bested Bartolo.

Bartolo controlled the adrenalin wanting to rush through him. The man holding the sword in front of him was Luciano Gutierrez. They had a history, but it was long ago. He was sure Luciano felt superior and it made a few drips of sweat slide from his temples. Many years ago, Luciano was his better, but Bartolo had honed his sword skills over the years.

There was a sly grin on Luciano's face. "So you have returned," Luciano sneered at Bartolo. He was egging his opponent into making the first move. Bartolo was trim, in good shape, not with a rotund belly like most of the older *caballeros,* but Luciano knew he was superior.

The other *dons* had retreated to safety after Rafe killed the bodyguard. Now seeing the two with swords drawn, several inched forward hoping for a good show. Virginia retreated to the stairs.

They touched swords and quickly began slashing, feinting and parrying, then slashing some more. Attacking and counterattacking the clash of the swords filled the room. Back and forth they thrust and retreated. Bartolo backed Luciano down the bar. Luciano was good, but Bartolo thought he had the upper hand.

The singing of rapier blades striking and swishing filled the room. Everyone was mesmerized by the battle. The older *dons* remembered their battles and wounds, the younger ones wished it was them in the fight.

Luciano twirled and jumped behind several tables out of Bartolo's reach. Two *dons* hurried behind Bartolo and shoved one of the heavy tables out of the way. Bartolo rounded another table and slashed at Luciano. He ducked and Bartolo's blade sliced a large hole into one of the tapestries on the wall.

In response, Luciano feinted and then thrust and missed by a large margin. "Not as good as you once were," Bartolo scoffed. Luciano's only reply was to yell to his bodyguard.

"Emilio, don't just stand there, shoot him," Luciano yelled.

The young man looked at his gun he had dropped on the floor. The young *pistolero* who shot his partner was still keeping his eye on him. Going for the pistol was certain death and he decided to ignore his *patrón's* request.

Amidst the chaos of the swords, the *dons* scurried from one side of the room to the other, wanting to see the fight and wanting to avoid the flying blades. As the swordsmen neared the stairs, Virginia fled to her room upstairs and shut the door.

Soon Bartolo forced Luciano up the stairs. The height of each step gave Luciano an edge however, his footing was uncertain. As he backed up, he slashed and parried, but kept backing up until he reached the second floor.

By now both the sword fighters knew each other's

moves. Luciano, now on level ground, forced Bartolo back down the stairs. This time it was Bartolo who had uncertain footing. Whirling, he jumped several steps until he was on the flat floor again. Taking a stance, he waited for Luciano to come down the stairs.

"Do you yield?" he asked Luciano.

"Never," was the reply.

They feinted and parried, attacking, and counterattacking. Bartolo felt his fatigue and tried to ignore it. He had not been in a sword fight for many years, though believed he was the better fighter.

Luciano noticed fatigue in Bartolo as his knee dipped when he feinted. Stepping back, Luciano faked and thrust. It was the opening he needed. When Bartolo counterattacked, Luciano's rapier was aimed at his heart. Bartolo went down to his knees.

"Desgraciado," *don* Pedro cried out. Others gasped at the outcome. Seeing Bartolo lying on the ground, five *dons* pulled their swords. *Don* Pedro pulled his sword and went after *don* Luciano with the others. He was bound by honor to avenge his brother and kill *don* Luciano. Everyone in the cantina wanted justice against the Judas, who betrayed his friends.

While the sword fight went on, Carlos and Rafe rushed to the wounded *don*. Blood seeped from the front of his shirt.

"Carlos," *don* Bartolo grabbed at Carlos' arm. "Help me."

"You know this man. Who is he?" Rafe asked.

"This is *don* Bartolo de Soto, your father-in-law."

"What?" Rafe asked incredulous with the news. Quickly he took off his coat and placed it under *don* Bartolo's head. The man's light golden brown eyes looked up at Rafe's.

"Don Bartolo, they have sent for a doctor. Stay with us, do not close your eyes," Rafe told him.

"Who are you? You were very brave shooting the man with the pistol," he said in a weak voice.

"Don Bartolo, this is Rafael, Ana Teresa's husband,"

Carlos told him.

"Rafael, you . . . you are . . . " *don* Bartolo grabbed his arm unable to finish his sentence.

"Señor, Ana Teresa loves you," Rafe told him.

"I . . . a . . . tell my daughter I am truly sorry." He then grabbed Rafe's arm tightly. "Take care of her."

A deadly cough came out of the wounded man and his eyes began to fill with tears. His grip fell from Rafe's arm.

"Stay with us *don* Bartolo. You are going to be a grandfather. You must live to see him."

Don Bartolo smiled and closed his eyes. A few moments later he expelled his last breath.

In another part of the room, a victorious yell erupted. *Don* Pedro came rushing to his brother's side, with the tip of his sword covered in blood. *Don* Bartolo lay on the floor, dead, his shirt stained in blood.

"Is he?"

Carlos nodded.

Don Pedro made the sign of the cross.

FIN

Please continue reading a preview of the next Young Pistolero Series adventure by Robert J. Alvarado, *Justified Vengeance* (Book 7) 2019 Sierra Press.

CHAPTER 1

"I tell yew, me n Clay Allison scart em greasers up in Cimarron," Kip Donohoe bragged to a group of cowboys at a saloon north of Santa Fe. A big talker, Kip loved to brag and tell embellished stories of his exploits. The cowboys listened intently, believing everything he said was the gospel truth and Kip loved an audience.

In the saloon, Jerome Westfield sipped a beer and listened to Kip's stories. He was on a trip from San Gabriel to Santa Fe to buy lumber and other building supplies and stopped at the saloon for a drink. Listening to Kip, Jerome thought he was just what the settlers needed to defend their land deeds from the Mexicans. Jerome waited until the cowboys drifted off and Kip was drinking alone at the bar, before he spoke to him.

"I was mighty impressed by your stories," Jerome walked near Kip and told him. "I think you are just the man we need up in San Gabriel."

"Who are yew?" Kip asked narrowing his eyes to slits.

"Name of Jerome Westfield. Me and a group of settlers came from Missouri with deeds to land here in New Mexico. When we got here, they tried to tell us the land was owned by some Mexican. They've been trying to get us to leave ever since and causing us a lot of trouble."

"I heerd of such things," Kip responded then turned and studied his whiskey glass.

"They've been harassing me and the other settlers, saying we bought our land illegally. They claim the land belongs to a greaser named *don* Lorenzo Salazar. They say it was a Royal Spanish Land Grant to his family many generations ago. Fuck the Royal Spanish! What they hell do they have to do with this land in the United States? We have legal deeds we bought in Missouri," Jerome explained trying to get the gunfighter interested in their plight.

"Why do yew think I cud hep?"

"We're just farmers looking for good land to plant and raise our families. We're not unwilling to fight, but we need someone handy with a gun."

"What kind of trouble they givin yew?"

"The greasers claimed I stole a prized bull from them. They came with guns, lassoed it and tried to take it. My friends and I shot it out with them. We killed one of the Mexicans, but the bull and two of my friends got shot and died."

"Did yew steal that thar bull?"

"Nah, it was just wandering as a stray," Jerome told him.

Kip Donohoe nodded his head knowing how the Mexicans did not fence in their livestock. Cows, sheep, and other stock often grazed on the large parcels of land the Mexicans claimed as land grants.

"Yew telling me, em greasers came and took yer bull and kilt two of yew? Whadda yew want me ta do? Kill the greaser?" Kip asked.

"We need protection. We'll pay you. Maybe if the Mexicans see a gunman around, they will stop harassing us."

For the past seven and a half months Rafe doted on Ana Teresa so much, she often demanded he stop treating her like she was going to break. However, it did not deter Rafe's anguish. He feared something dreadful could happen to her and the baby, if he was not vigilantly keeping a watchful eye on her.

"You are driving me crazy, hovering over me this way," she complained.

"I cannot help it *querida*. I promised I would protect you. Remember when Billy tried to kidnap you? And what about the time you were taken in the silver wagon and the man tried to have his way with you? Not to mention how we were run out of Los Angeles by vigilantes," Rafe reminded her of some of the past times she was in danger because of him.

They were on the veranda of their new house overlooking the pastures of his horse ranch. Rafe took a lunch break from the foundry and had come home to have lunch with her. It was his normal daily routine to check up on her.

"Yes I remember, but I am in no danger now. I am going to have your baby. It is the most natural thing a woman can do. Please stop worrying."

"Well, I am worried about us going to *don* Lorenzo's hacienda in San Gabriel for the wedding," Rafe expressed his concerns. A wedding for *doña* Agustina's niece, Bibiana's cousin, was scheduled for Saturday at *don* Lorenzo Salazar's hacienda. *Don* Lorenzo was Agustina's father and a well-known bull breeder in San Gabriel. It would be a big affair.

"Why are you worried? It will be a joyous day and they will have a grand fiesta. You will dance with me," she said and went to him. She attempted to embrace him in a close dance position, but her protruding belly would not allow her to get close. They both laughed and Rafe leaned over and kissed her.

"*Querida,* the hacienda is near San Gabriel where there has been trouble with squatters. It was printed in the newspaper several weeks ago. Squatters stole one of *don* Lorenzo's prize bulls. He sent his *vaqueros* to get it back and gunfire broke out. One of his *vaqueros* and a few squatters were killed, along with the bull. Since then, armed squatters have attacked *vaqueros* whenever they see them alone on the range. We should not go. Besides, it is a long trip and it might be hard on you in your condition."

"Don't be ridiculous. We are going Rafael. I want to dress up and be around music and my family. I want to dance with you one more time before we are parents. My mother is excited about going too. She wants to meet people from other haciendas."

After Ana Teresa's father was killed, *doña* Marcella, her mother, chose to stay in Santa Fe after she learned she was to be a grandmother. It surprised Ana Teresa how her mother fussed and doted on her and was joyously awaiting the new life. She was not so doting when Ana Teresa was growing up.

"I hope she meets a widowed *haciendero* someday and will not be dependent on us. She is still a young and beautiful woman," Rafe said and chuckled. He did not mind supporting his wife's mother, but wished they had more privacy.

Losing to his wife's demands, they left for the de Soto hacienda Friday morning. Just before noon, *don* Pedro, Carlos, and Rafe mounted up and led the way from the de Soto house. Behind them, a carriage with Agustina, Bibiana, Ana Teresa, and Marcella followed. Marcella held ten-month-old Benicío, Bibiana and Carlos' young son, on her lap. *Don* Lorenzo and *doña* Amalia expected them by this evening for the wedding, which would start Saturday morning.

Upon their arrival late in the afternoon, Bibiana retired to her room with the baby and Rafe made Ana Teresa lie down in their bedroom. Agustina and Marcella sat in the parlor with *doña* Amalia. *Don* Lorenzo escorted *don* Pedro and Carlos to the smoking room. A servant poured brandy and gave each a Cuban cigar.

"Tell us about the bull you lost, Lorenzo?" *don* Pedro asked politely.

"My bulls are free to wander the hacienda. One day several of my *vaqueros* were looking for strays and noticed the squatters had one of my bulls corralled in a pen. When they tried to reclaim it, the squatters opened fire. My *vaqueros* had no choice but to defend themselves and try to take the bull. They killed two of the squatters and a stray bullet killed the bull, or maybe the squatters killed it in spite."

"It is not fair or right these squatters think they own what is not theirs," Pedro griped.

"It is a big problem here, Pedro. Squatters are

moving here and settling, saying they bought their land legally. In a way, I cannot blame them. They were swindled. They bought the land unseen, believing it was open territory," he replied with a sigh. *Don* Lorenzo felt no particular malice toward the squatters, however would not allow them to stay.

"I and the other *haciENDeros* have tried to evict them, but the sheriff will do nothing. He says it is government business. Now the squatters are fighting back," *don* Lorenzo explained.

"It is happening more and more, mostly here in the northern part of the territory where the haciendas are larger. We have not had as much trouble in Santa Fe, although the *dons* are cautious and vigilant," Carlos interjected.

"Carlos, Pedro tells me you work for a gun maker? If it is true, my friends and I need guns. Will you see if we can buy them from the maker?"

"You can discuss it with Rafael this weekend. He works for George Summers at the foundry," Carlos replied.

"Enough of this unpleasant talk of guns and squatters, please enjoy your brandy and cigars. Tomorrow will be a grand wedding, joining two powerful families. Tonight we rest for the big fiesta planned after the ceremony," *don* Lorenzo said and raised his glass in a toast.

Ana Teresa had a restless night not able to get comfortable on the bed. It kept Rafe awake trying to comfort her. Her restlessness made her nervous thinking the baby might decide to come early. Finally she slept for a couple of hours after Rafe got up, dressed, and left her alone.

In the morning, she felt better and she and Bibiana fussed all morning making themselves beautiful for the wedding ceremony. Ana Teresa had a special dress made just for the occasion, which was supposed to minimize her bulging belly.

"You will still be the most beautiful woman at the fiesta," Bibiana commended her cousin. It was not jealousy by Bibiana, but it was just a fact.

By late afternoon the fiesta had been going on for several hours. The courtyard was decorated with strands of flower garlands and candles. Long tables of food were setup on the outside perimeter. Each table had vases of fresh wildflowers. The *dons* and *doñas* were dressed in their finest dresses and *trajes*. A number of younger *caballeros*, sons of the *dons*, stood and drank tequila watching the dancers.

She and Rafe danced the bolero and the fandango, as well as she could in her condition. Dancing with her in the decorated courtyard reminded Rafe of the first time he ever saw her. She wore a red and black gown and he fell in love with her and her golden brown eyes. Ana Teresa asked Rafe to take her to a shady spot where she could sit and rest.

"You should go to our room and lie down," he said.

"No, I would rather stay here and listen to the orchestra and watch the people. Go and talk to the men. I will be fine," she replied.

The music from the small orchestra kept everyone dancing. Even small children danced with each other, making Ana Teresa laugh at their behavior. She noticed a short *don* in a brown *traje* danced with her mother several times. While she sat resting, Rafe joined a small group of *caballeros* on the far side of the courtyard. They were in an animated conversation drinking shots of tequila.

Outside the main entrance to the courtyard, concealed by a high adobe wall, Kip Donohoe, along with five sons of the land settlers arrived at the Salazar hacienda. Inside the courtyard, an orchestra played festive music and they could hear laughter.

"Put on the hoods boys and git yer guns ready," Kip told the group in a whisper. After Jerome hired him, Kip decided they should take the fight directly to the head greaser who claimed he owned the land. Although the man seldom left his hacienda, Kip spent long hours on a hill not far away and knew the man's looks. Killing him should easily settle the dispute about the land Jerome and the other settlers bought in good faith and then Kip planned on collecting a handsome reward from the settlers and moving on.

Putting on the red hoods with only eyeholes diminished the raiders sight somewhat. Two had rifles and the other four had pistols ready.

"Now!" Kip gave the word. They rode into the courtyard with guns blazing. They shot at everyone – men, women, and even children, but Kip sought out *don* Lorenzo. At first, everyone in the courtyard stood stunned in disbelief as they heard the gunshots and saw the red-hooded raiders. Most of the *caballeros* were unarmed or had swords at their sides. Screaming and shouts filled the air as they did their best to protect themselves from the hooded raiders.

"Carlos, take Bibiana, the baby, and Ana Teresa to safety," Rafe yelled. He pulled his GSW pistols and fired back at the raiders. One went down and another dropped his pistol, as Rafe's bullet struck his arm. The few other armed *caballeros* also returned fire and two pulled their swords. The previously peaceful courtyard was pandemonium. Gunfire whistled in every direction.

Kip spotted the hacienda owner and took a shot, missing his chest and hitting him in the arm. Several of the Mexicans were armed and returning fire. One in particular had two pistols and was a good shot. One of the young men who came with him lay on the ground and another had his gun shot from his hand. Turning his horse, he yelled to the others to go. The raiders headed for the courtyard entrance to escape.

"Get to your horses," Rafe yelled out.

It took precious time getting to the hacienda's corral. Rafe jumped to Rayo's saddle and several of the young *caballeros* followed him. They mounted up and ran the horses hard trying to catch up with the raiders. Neither Rafe nor any of the visiting *caballeros* knew the location of the squatter's camp. They rode until it got dark without finding the gunmen.

"We need to return to our families," one of the young *caballeros* told Rafe. He agreed, worried about Ana

Teresa.

All was quiet at the main house when Rafe and the others returned. The people had gone home. A dim light shone from the front window of the house and Rafe went and knocked on the door. *Don* Lorenzo opened it. He looked tired, old, and miserable. His arm was bandaged and in a sling.

"*Señor,* we did not catch them," Rafe reported.

Don Lorenzo only nodded his head as he ushered Rafe into the house.

Where is my wife? Did she return to Santa Fe with *don* Pedro?" Rafe asked.

Don Lorenzo hesitated, lowered his head, and spoke softly. *"Lo siento Rafael, ellos mataron a tu esposa,"* he said, they killed your wife.

SPANISH GLOSSARY

   Italicized Spanish words used repeatedly throughout the series which do not have an English counterpart, such as important = *importante* or Mama = *Mamá*. Other infrequently used words, phrases, and sentences written in Spanish are immediately explained within the text itself.

abogado: a lawyer, attorney at law
abrazo: a hug
abuelo; abuela: grandfather; grandmother (m;f)
adios: goodbye
alcalde: the mayor of a town or city
amigo(s); amiga(s): friend (m;f)
anglo(s): a word to mean a white man, an American
ayúdame: help, asking for help
baboso(s): drooling idiot (a slang or curse word)
bandido(s): a bandit or outlaw
bueno: good
buenos días; tardes; noches: good day; evening; night
bienvenido(s): welcome
cabrón: asshole or bastard (a curse word)
caballo(s); caballero(s): horse; horseman or gentleman
cállate: shutup or be quiet
cálmate; cálmese: be calm or calm down
camisa: a blouse or top
casita; casa: small home, home
chaqueta(s): jacket or suit coat
chico(s); chica(s); chiquita: young boy or young girl (m;f)
chingado: shit or fuck (a curse word)
cojones: slang for a man's testicles
compañero(s): companion, friends
criollo(s): pure-blooded Spaniard born in the New World
ciudad: a town or city
culón: a chickenshit (a curse word)
desgraciado(s): a miserable wretch or terrible person
Dios: God
don; doña: title for nobleman/woman
gachupín(s); peninsulares: pure-blooded Spaniards born in Spain
garruncha: means sword, slang for penis
gracias; muchas gracias: thank you; many thanks
grandee: Spanish nobleman, aristocrat (i.e. dandy)

hermano; hermana: brother; sister (m;f)

hacienda: a large plantation or estate

haciendero(s): the nobleman owning the hacienda

hola: hello greeting

Indio(s); India(s): means Indian (m;f)

jacal(s): small ramshakle house of mud and sticks

jefe: the boss man

mañana: tomorrow or the sometime later

mestizo(s); person of mixed Spanish and Indian (m)

mestiza(s): person of mixed Spanish and Indian (f)

mierda: same as shit (a curse word)

mi hijito; hijo; mijo; hijita; hija; mija: my son; daughter

muchacho(s); muchacha(s): like saying 'the guys' (m;f)

nada: no or nothing

Nana; Tata: nickname for grandmother; grandfather

padre: head friar, monk, minister, priest

pantalones: pants

paseo: the road, boulevard; place to stroll or ride

patrón; patróna: formal for a boss; a mistress (m;f)

pendejo(s); pendeja(s): slang for asshole (a curse)

pene(s): slang for a penis

peón(s): a peasant

peso(s): Mexican money

picaro: a womanizer

pinche: fucking (a curse word)

plata: silver

primo(s); prima(s): cousin (m;f)

pulque; pulqueria: a poor man's drink in Mexico

puta(s): a whore (a slang or curse word)

que?: what or why

querido; querida: affectionate meaning my dear (m;f)

rayo: thunderbolt

sarape: cape, loose coat or blanket

señor(es); señora(s): like saying Mr. or Mrs.

señorita(s): like saying Miss (young woman or girl)

sí: yes

tío; tía: uncle; aunt (m;f)

traje(s): ornate Spanish aristocrat's style of suit

vaquero(s): livestock herder or cowboy

vámonos or vamos: let's go, get out of here

www.ingramcontent.com/pod-product-compliance
Lightning Source LLC
Chambersburg PA
CBHW061935170626
46813CB00006B/2414